Soldier's Return

Charlotte paused. The door to Ward #3 was open. She saw him sitting in a wheelchair. In profile, his face was gaunt.

She took a deep breath. "John, honey. It's me. Charlotte."

"Go away," he said. She could see the unshed tears in his blue eyes. "I don't want you to see me like this."

His pain touched her in a way his love never had. She had to find a way to help him. In her best "belle" voice she said, "Why John, I do believe you've forgotten your manners."

His eyes flickered over her face, then went to the gift in her hand. He hesitated, looking for the lie that wasn't there.

He took the cane, then grasped her hand and brought it tenderly to his lips.

"Thank you," he said hoarsely. "I hope you will forgive me for not standing in the presence of a lady."

**Captain Randolph
was home from the war.**

GONE FROM BREEZY HILL

Nora Ashby

BERKLEY BOOKS, NEW YORK

GONE FROM BREEZY HILL

A Berkley Book / published by arrangement with
the author

PRINTING HISTORY
Berkley edition / July 1985
For information address: The Berkley Publishing Group,
200 Madison Avenue, New York, New York 10016.

ISBN: 0-425-07672-5

A BERKLEY BOOK ® TM 757,375
The name "BERKLEY" and the stylized "B" with design
are trademarks belonging to Berkley Publishing Corporation.
PRINTED IN THE UNITED STATES OF AMERICA

Special and heartfelt thanks to Geri Thoma for finding Breezy a perfect home; to Meg Blackstone, for helping to build it, from foundation to hearth.

To the loving inspiration of
Catherine Burns Larmore;

To the proud memory of
Ashby M. Larmore;

And to all the fine family descendants of
Clarence and Nora Burns.

Contents

Prologue

IN EUROPE and in the Pacific, the clarion call of danger had been sounded. It was the 1940s and America was at war.

On foreign battlefields of land and sea and sky, soldiers fought and died. On the altar of their broken and bloodied bodies, America sacrificed her innocence, never to know again the pure certainty that her cause was true, her purpose right. On the home front, in kitchens, bedrooms and living rooms, those left behind waged a different kind of struggle, to preserve and protect all they held dear, to nurture the hope of an everlasting peace.

1

We Interrupt This Program
December 1941

BREEZY HILL was not the grandest of old Virginia mansions, but the stately white frame house was beautiful. Rising majestically from the rolling green hill for which it had been named, Breezy was surrounded by magnolia trees that sheltered it through the changes of season. Their strong black trunks were deeply rooted in the earth. Their blossoms perfumed the spring air, and the anticipation of their blooming brought hope to the last endless days of winter.

Now, as James Clifton Whittaker walked toward the tree-shaded lane, Breezy gave him comfort. The house was his historian, the silent chronicler of his life and the passage of time. The house had blessed his marriage and embraced his four children through seasons of joy and sorrow. It had witnessed his grief when his beloved Elizabeth had fallen ill and slipped away from him, into the merciful peace of death.

As he contemplated the events of the past few hours, the house—the welcoming hospitality of the porch, shaded by gracefully swaying trees—stood before him, beckoning, giving him strength. Times had changed, the quality of life was not as sure as it had been, but Breezy remained, as always, a sanctuary, a true home.

Early this morning, he had lost his best friend Leonard Gilmer. Shaken by the shock of the sudden and unexpected death, Clifton had walked down to West Grove to pay his respects to the newly widowed Elvira. Moments later, he had been approached by his old friends, Dr. Giles Chappell and Walter Burns, urging him in subdued tones to assume Leonard's post as head of the Russell County Draft Board. Clifton had demurred, falling back on his familiar and well-known position that America had no business involving itself in a European war.

"Dammit, J.C.," Giles had erupted, pounding a table in frustration. "How long are you going to hide your head in the sand? Your Jeffersonian isolationism is obsolete, man. Just look around you—the world is on fire!"

Though the discussion had been cut short by the arrival of Reverend Lowell, the argument had stayed with Clifton, gnawing at his composure, his unswerving adherence to principles he cherished. In one of their rare disagreements, Elizabeth had described him as prideful and unbending, and those words, plaintively delivered, came back to him now.

He took off his bowler hat and ran his fingers through his thinning silver hair. Shading his eyes against the December sun, he surveyed the winter landscape around him. He stood tall and erect in his black suit, bearing his three-score years with a patriarchal stateliness. His face was lightly tanned and gently lined, his deep blue eyes clear and bright, as they searched some distant horizon.

He shivered, though he was perspiring in the unseasonal warmth of the day. He took a white linen handkerchief from his pocket and ran it lightly over his brow, as if to wipe away troubling thoughts, recent reminders of mortality and the fragility of life.

He turned his face towards Breezy, grateful that all was secure there, even if elsewhere in the world the fires of destruction grew ever hungrier.

* * *

WITH considerable satisfaction, Bessie surveyed her spotless kitchen, enjoying the sunlight that poured through the white ruffled curtains and highlighted the shine on the freshly waxed floor.

She looked out the window over the sink, watching the birds swooping and pecking at the grain feeder and at Mr. Clifton, who seemed to be enjoying one of his "quiet times." A grin creased her broad black face, as she mused over how Mr. Clifton had stood there this morning, before that bad news phone call, talking about the "eminent domain" of the mockingbird and the robin. She didn't make much sense of what he said, but she surely did admire that man's fancy way of talking.

She reminded herself to get a move on, what with ten mouths to feed and her angel food cakes yet to bake. Bad news or not, the whole family was here for Mr. Clifton's 60th birthday, and she meant to lay out a feast for the occasion.

She beat up the egg whites, then put the bowl aside while she fiddled with the dial of the RCA radio. "Drat," she muttered, when she found nothing but war talk. Used to be she could always get some humming music, but all she heard now was bad news about that Hitler. Even Roland was talking war all the time. The other day he had dragged her into the back parlor to show her where that Germany place was on the globe.

As she went back to her cake, slowly folding the whites into the batter, she heard Roland approaching through the swinging door that connected with the dining room.

"Boy, am I hungry," he said, dipping his finger into the bowl and sampling the mixture. She smiled indulgently. Such a handsome child, Miss Elizabeth's baby, with his straw-colored hair and sky blue eyes.

"What else you got to eat?" he asked, opening the refrigerator to look for himself.

"Cornbread and milk. Thas' all, you hear?"

Helping himself to a man-size chunk of cornbread, Roland sat down at the table. "Wish I could go to the movies again this afternoon. Boy, you should've seen that picture,

Bessie. It was great. *A Yank in the RAF*. Betty Grable . . .
She kinda looks like Charlotte."

"Uh-huh," Bessie nodded agreeably, though she had never
seen a picture show. Colored folks weren't allowed into the
Roseland Theatre.

"Wish I was older," he said with a sudden ferocity. "Wish
I was eighteen so I could run away and fight with the British,
like the guy did in the movie."

"Hush yo' mouth, boy. You is jes' sixteen, and you ain't
goin' nowhere but up them stairs and get yo'self washed
up. Scoot! And don't you go botherin' Miz Charlotte none
either. She jes' got them little girls of hers to sleep, and
she is havin' herself a rest in the back bedroom."

Roland thumped up the stairs, ignoring the reference to
his older sister. Having done her duty according to Charlotte's instructions, Bessie shook her head, as she so often
did when she thought of Mister Clifton's second daughter.
That girl was always resting or prettying up her face, when
she wasn't making eyes at that good-looking husband of
hers.

"Pretty is as pretty does," she muttered her opinion of
the Whittaker family beauty, as she filled the cake pans and
put them into the old coal stove to bake. Hearing Miss Meg
practicing on her piano, she heaped some cookies on a
pressed glass plate. It was good to hear that child make
music again. The house had been mighty quiet since she
went "up North."

As she passed through the dining room, she paused to
admire the table she had set earlier, with the white lace
tablecloth, the blue-bordered Haviland china and the good
silver, polished and shining better than new. She could
almost hear Miss Elizabeth's soft ladylike voice saying:
"Why, Bessie, everything looks lovely, just lovely."

The room had always been Miss Elizabeth's pride and
joy. All the furnishings—the mahogany table and the twelve
Queen Anne chairs with tapestry cushions, the carved side-
board, the big gold-framed mirror, and even the crystal
chandelier—all had been part of Miss Elizabeth's dowry,
come all the way from Atlanta by special train. She crossed
the hall to the back parlor and set the cookies on the piano.

"Heah, honey chile," she offered, "yo' best put somethin' in yo' stummick. Don't know when yo' papa and sisters be comin'.'"

"Thanks, Bessie," Meg smiled sweetly, her green eyes lighting up her heart-shaped face. "My favorites," she said, taking two of the gingerbread cookies.

"Ain't nothin', nothin' at all," Bessie muttered, pleased to see the girl eating. The child was skinny as a rail. Come all the way from New York on the train last night, fluttering like a butterfly about the fancy music school and her life in the big city.

"I'm going to play 'The Moonlight Sonata' for Papa's birthday party. It's what Mama used to play for him all the time. Do you remember?"

"Yes, indeedy, chile. An' I remembers yo' mama sittin' right there, lookin' so pretty, jes' like you." Bessie beamed at the dark-haired young woman with the delicate features, so much like her mama's.

"I still miss her sometimes," Meg said quietly. She stared down at her long, slender fingers resting on the keys, lost for a moment in a private memory. Then she looked up and smiled brightly. "Do you want to see my party 'ensemble,' Bessie? I found it in the neatest old shop in Greenwich Village. Wait till Charlotte sees it—I'll bet she'll turn pea-green..."

Bessie chuckled indulgently. "Go on, chile, go fix yo'self in yo' pretties. Do yo' papa's heart good."

"Right," Meg agreed, and off she went, skipping up the stairs in a burst of excited energy.

HOWARD Emmett and his wife, Emily Whittaker Emmett, sat on one of the four wooden benches surrounding the pot-belly stove in the gray waiting room of the West Grove Station. Their son Alexander, a thin, serious five-year-old wearing wire-rimmed glasses, played with a small tin car, running it along the ledge of the ticket counter. On the bulletin board behind them was a poster of a bearded man in a top hat, pointing his finger, with the caption: "Uncle Sam Wants You."

Taking a Camel from a nearly empty package, Howard stood up, tall and slender in his khaki uniform, and began to pace. "I should have written your father when you wanted me to—when I first got my draft notice. I put it off, and then it slipped my mind. I never seem to handle things well with your father. I always feel like such a blundering Yankee," he said nervously, running his fingers through his wavy brown hair.

Emily laughed, drawing herself up to her full five feet ten inches. She looked into the soft brown eyes that could smolder almost black with passion and make her feel so needed and cherished. "You are a Yankee, darling," she said softly, "a pure, blue-blooded Boston Yankee—not at all blundering, though definitely the absent-minded professor—and I love you dearly. We can handle Papa together, like we did when your mother insisted we get married at the Congregational Church in Boston, instead of West Grove Methodist. Remember how the feathers flew over that?"

Howard smiled in spite of his tension; Emily always knew how to make him feel better. He held his wife at arm's length, taking in her strong, angular face, her soft gray eyes, the silky brown hair pulled back in a simple twist. "I remember," he said huskily, recalling the way she had looked right after the wedding ceremony, when she had lifted her veil and kissed him, her eyes bright with tears and love. Now, as they faced the patriarch of Breezy Hill and his staunch but silent opposition to the war, they would band together once again.

THE colors of sunset spilled across the mahogany table, which was laden with bountiful, celebratory dishes. The crystal and silver and lace glowed in the clear winter light.

Initially, Howard's uniform had caused quite a stir among the family, but the battle had proved far less substantial than they had imagined.

"Mr. Whittaker, sir," Howard had started his explanation. "My apologies for not giving you some advance notice about this uniform, but . . ."

Clifton had blinked, as if he had not noticed the offending

uniform before. "No apologies necessary," he had said gruffly. "I may not agree with those who support this war, but I respect a man who answers his country's call of duty."

"Thank you, Papa." Emily kissed her father as they all sat down to dinner, their faces glowing warmly in the rosy light.

Bessie had outdone herself with the birthday dinner, serving up all of Mr. Clifton's favorites—baked ham, moist and shiny with her special fruit glaze, rich and chewy candied sweet potatoes, crisp green beans dotted with pearly white onions, and her incomparable melt-in-your-mouth cornbread.

Roland, caught up in the excitement of having a military man at the table, was filled with questions. "What do you do after morning drill, Howard?" he asked through a mouthful of sweet potatoes. "Did you go on any maneuvers yet?"

"Roland," Clifton interrupted, "this is a family reunion. Do you suppose we might defer this discussion of military procedures in favor of some family news?"

"Yes, sir," Roland obeyed grudgingly, angry that his father was again reprimanding him in public.

"Thank goodness," Charlotte agreed. "I've just been dyin' to tell everybody about the new house John and I just bought in the East End...the exclusive part of Richmond, you know. It's English Tudor, and we're planning to move the end of January...Isn't it splendid?" She touched her lovely blond hair, ready to bask in the family's attention, but it was not to be.

"Speaking of houses," Meg interrupted, and Charlotte drew her perfectly painted lips into a pretty pout. "What are you going to do about yours, Em?" Meg had fond memories of her summer visits to the small, old brick house on Beacon Hill, and she felt a pang of sadness for her sister.

"I'm going to rent the house," Emily said quietly, without a trace of self-pity, "and I'm packing our things for storage. Alexander and I will join Howard as soon as we can."

"I remember the day I brought your mother to this house," Clifton said, off in his private reverie, his voice distant, his face uncharacteristically tender. "She asked me to stop the carriage down by the turn in the lane. She saw the silver maples swaying in the breeze, and she said: 'We'll call our house Breezy Hill. Every proper home needs a name,' she said . . .'" His voice trailed off in a wash of memories.

Emily and Meg exchanged a silent glance, not quite certain of how to respond, knowing instinctively that Clifton's mood had to do with his birthday and the Judge's death. More than once, Emily had expressed her concern for their father since Mama's death, especially since Meg had gone away, leaving him with Roland as his only companion.

Bessie filled the breach as she replenished the platter of cornbread. "Breezy Hill," she repeated. "Yes, suh. Time sho' do fly, don't it? Seem like yestuhday, you and Miss Elizabeth come ridin' up de hill. Her lookin' so pretty, all in blue, carryin' a white parasol an' lookin' like an angel."

"I had the gate sign made for our first anniversary," Clifton continued. "I had it copied from the one at Elizabeth's home, La Font Place. Those were the good times . . ." His voice trailed off again.

"These be good times, too," Bessie said decisively, ladling a helping of green beans onto his plate. "Don't yo' be forgettin' that today."

"Hey, Howard," Roland interjected. "Did you see *A Yank in the RAF*? Buddy and I went yesterday, and . . ." Then, seeing the familiar stern expression on his father's face, he stopped, not wanting to bring on another reprimand.

Ever the family peacemaker and diplomat, Emily turned to Meg. "Tell us about New York," she said brightly. "You haven't written since you arrived at Juilliard. How is your first semester going?"

"It's wonderful," Meg enthused. "I have the best teachers . . . It's as if I'm hearing pieces of music for the first time, Em. It's a whole beautiful new world. One of my teachers is Professor Claessen—he's from the Berlin Conservatory of Music, and he's a friend of Otto Klemperer, the famous Beethoven conductor. He's chosen me for private lessons. He only takes a few students each year, and it's such an honor . . ."

"And what about your social life, little Meg? Surely you don't play the piano all the time? Haven't any of those New

York boys noticed how pretty you are?" John, Charlotte's handsome husband, loved to tease.

Meg blushed and dropped her long-lashed eyes. Delighted with this opportunity to tease his sister, Roland asked: "How about it, sis? Do you have some sissy boyfriend who plays the violin?"

"Don't be silly," she snapped. "There are plenty of nice men who play the violin."

"So who is it?" Emily coaxed. "I can see there's someone..."

"There is—but he isn't a musician. He's in medical school."

"A physician?" Clifton asked, interested now. "What is the young man's name?"

"David. David Steinmetz," she answered quietly, wishing she had said nothing.

"What kind of name is that?" Charlotte asked, ever alert to "things that mattered." "Where is his family from?"

"Vienna," Meg answered, her voice even lower. "They're Austrian. They run a restaurant in Greenwich Village."

Before anyone could press for more information, Bessie put out the overhead light and made her grand entrance from the kitchen, the first of her angel cakes ablaze with candles. On cue, Charlotte's daughters, Nancy and Carrie began to sing: "Happy Birthday to you..."

LATER, they sat in the parlor, three generations of Whittakers. The grandchildren offered their handmade gifts first: Alexander, somber and grave, handing over a carefully lettered book cover; Nancy, giggly and flirtatious, as she held out a white snowflake cut from folded construction paper; Carrie, poised and confident in her selection—a bagful of chocolate kisses, her favorite confection. And when the little ceremony was over, the children were allowed to go out to the barn for a visit with the cow—Peaches and Cream— while the grownups peacefully enjoyed a second cup of coffee.

"Here, Papa," Charlotte said, perching herself on the arm of Clifton's chair. "Open ours," she insisted, thrusting a large, elaborately wrapped box at her father.

He took the package; then noticing Bessie standing in the doorway, clutching a shoebox tied with brightly colored cord, he asked: "Is that by any chance for me, Bessie?"

"Yes suh! Happy birthday, Mistuh Clifton—an' many happy returns."

Solemnly, Clifton undid the cord and took out a pair of homemade slippers made from dark blue blanket scraps and stitched together with green yarn, the front flaps neatly tacked down, to give a "store-bought" look. "These are very handsome, very handsome indeed," he said, removing his well-polished shoes and sliding his feet into the new slippers. "A perfect fit," he pronounced, "and warm, too."

"Here, Papa," Charlotte insisted impatiently, unwrapping her gift. Inside was a black morocco leather briefcase, engraved with Clifton's initials on the brass clasp.

"Why, thank you, Charlotte, John," he said. "This is very fine . . . very thoughtful."

Like his wife, John Tyler Randolph had a certain perfection of appearance and bearing. But unlike Charlotte, John had acquired his courtly gentility, his ease with the world about him, through generations of patrician breeding.

"It's from Finch's," Charlotte explained, drawing out her moment in the spotlight. "And it's just like the one Judge Randolph uses. Now you'll be able to get rid of that old thing that's falling to pieces."

Before Clifton could defend the briefcase he had received on his graduation from law school, the doorbell rang. Roland jumped up to answer it.

The unexpected caller was Miss Jewel McInnes, once his mother's seamstress. She was in her church finery—a pink wool coat with a squirrel collar and high heel pumps, dusty from the long walk up the hill. She carried a large parcel wrapped in brown paper.

"Afternoon, ma'am," Roland grinned a welcome, glad for the possibility of more excitement to liven up the party.

"Afternoon, Roland," she said shyly, somewhat ill-at-ease at entering Breezy through the front door. "I have something for your father. It came on the bus. I told Gus at the drugstore I didn't mind bringing it up." Hesitating a moment, she added: "I knew it was your father's birthday . . . I thought this might be another present."

"Come in, ma'am," he said, remembering his manners. "Pop!" he called out, but Clifton was already in the foyer.

"Why, Jewel . . . Miss Jewel . . ." Clifton seemed to be at a loss. "What a surprise."

Roland stared first at his father, then at Miss Jewel. His father, always so confident and controlled, now looked uncertain and a little embarrassed, almost the way one of his own friends would look if you caught him talking to a girl.

"I brought this package for you," she said, once again holding up the box to explain her uninvited presence.

Clifton hesitated a moment, before his own social graces took over. "Come in, Jewel, do come in. Roland, take Miss Jewel's coat."

Roland did as he was told, then rushed back to the parlor, so as not to miss his sisters' reactions to the seamstress's intrusion. Charlotte looked as if she smelled something bad, while Emily looked plain uncomfortable.

"Come sit down," Meg invited graciously.

"Let's see what's inside the package," Roland urged, anxious to speed things along.

"A fine idea," Clifton agreed gratefully, noticing the New Mexico postmark as he undid the wrapping. "It's from Rose Mary."

"Oh, good," Meg said enthusiastically. "Aunt Rose Mary always gives the best presents."

Inside was a handwritten note, which Clifton read aloud: "For the chief of the Whittaker clan—to celebrate this milestone. Love, Rose Mary." He held up what seemed to be a pile of white-tipped black feathers, a look of puzzlement on his face.

"It's a headdress!" Meg exclaimed. "Oh, that's perfect. Put it on, Papa, oh, please put it on."

Clifton adamantly refused, shaking his head. "Sister Rose Mary has always been an original thinker," he conceded, smiling, "though I do believe she has been out there with the Indians too long . . . Why, I remember on my sixth birthday, she gave me a dead frog in a shoebox. Our mother fainted, as I recall." He chuckled, enjoying the childhood memory.

"Oh, Papa," Emily interrupted, for she had heard the fuller version of this story many times before. "You know perfectly well the frog was alive when she wrapped it— she just didn't make enough air holes in the box."

He nodded, rightfully corrected by his eldest daughter. In the silence that followed, he glanced surreptitiously at Miss Jewel, who sat on the edge of one of Elizabeth's antique and not very comfortable chairs, her face set in a nervous, pinched smile.

Gallantly, John produced three dark green bottles wrapped with gold ribbons. "Here you are, sir," he said. "There are no frogs in these. I know you don't keep alcohol at Breezy, but these are from my family's private stock. French champagne." He held up one of the bottles. "I don't suppose we'll be seeing any more of these until after the war."

Elizabeth had always called alcohol the "devil's poison," a bitter reference to the fact that drink had killed both her beloved father and her ne'er-do-well brother. Clifton had honored her wishes when she was alive, and in the years since, he continued to do so out of habit. "Thank you, John," he said solemnly. "I do accept the 'spirit' in which your gift of spirits is made."

There was a small chuckle of appreciation for Clifton's pun, as well as a sigh of relief from Charlotte, who had fretted for days over how her husband's gift would be received.

As the corks were popped and Elizabeth's best Baccarat glasses filled, the family joined in a toast to Clifton's "continued health, prosperity and longevity."

"Happy birthday, Cliff," Jewel whispered softly, as she sipped the bubbly drink, her eyes misting with the sentiment.

How strange, Meg thought, hearing Jewel's whispered "Cliff." No one except Dr. Giles ever used a nickname in addressing her father.

"How about a little music?" Roland suggested, pleased that the family celebration was livelier than expected, and that he had been included in the sharing of the champagne.

"Yes, let's." Charlotte turned the dial of the old Stromberg-Carlson until she found some band music. She never missed an opportunity to dance with John. She knew they made a handsome couple, especially when he whirled her around a dance floor. He took her hand, leading her smoothly to the melody of "I Don't Want to Set the World on Fire."

Clifton started tapping his toe and humming. Jewel caught his eye and smiled shyly. He frowned thoughtfully for a moment and then, emboldened by the wine and the day's emotional turmoil, he got up and walked decisively to where she sat. He made a small bow. Without a word, she rose and stepped into his arms.

They moved together, self-consciously at first, then with an ease and fluidity that astonished the family. In all the years of their parents' marriage, no one had ever seen Clifton dance. Now, he not only was dancing, he seemed to be enjoying it. What's more, his poise and proficiency told them this was not the first time.

Charlotte watched with increasing distaste, losing interest in her own dancing. When Clifton executed a sweeping dip, she stopped in her tracks. "Really, Papa!" she huffed. "I don't know what's come over you, and the only reason I see for this common behavior is the company you're keeping." She stalked out of the room, leaving a wake of stunned, embarrassed silence.

"I'd best be going," Jewel said shakily, backing out of the room.

"Let me see you home," Clifton offered, taking her arm, embarrassed by his daughter's outburst and by his own confusion, not certain of whether to be angry with the sentiments Charlotte expressed, or only with the rude manner in which she expressed them.

His friendship with Jewel had developed, almost imperceptibly over the past several months, since shortly after Jewel's husband Ralph had died. As he often did for the less fortunate people of the town, Clifton had offered to handle the legal aspects of Ralph's death for a token fee. And when he had dropped in one evening, to inform Jewel that the work had been done, she had invited him to visit for a while.

"Life was so hard for him," she said compassionately of
the man who had been gassed in the last war, who had spent
most of his days drunk and intermittently employed by the
railroad. And Clifton had been touched by this uncomplain-
ing requiem.

Since Meg had left and the house had been so empty,
Clifton had been discreetly keeping company with Jewel,
but he had hardly admitted to himself how much time he
spent there until now. When he was alone with her, in the
little apartment above the drugstore, sipping bourbon and
unburdening himself of his daily trials, or listening to her
chatter, or dancing to music from her small radio, he felt
comfortable, relaxed, almost youthful. Yet outside, in the
presence of those who knew him as James Clifton Whittaker,
Esquire, pillar of the community and patriarch of an old,
respected family, he felt paralyzed by the weight of propriety, unable to acknowledge that Jewel McInnes, a "common woman" as his daughter Charlotte had put it, was a
"lady friend."

She's a fine woman, he said to himself, as he led her
silently out the front door and down the steps. She does not
deserve to be embarrassed in this way, he thought. I must
speak to Charlotte. Yet even as he made this resolution, he
knew he would say nothing—because he did not want to
answer the questions that Charlotte would raise if he chal-
lenged her.

As he and Jewel left Breezy, Roland trailed Charlotte
into the kitchen, where she was regaling Bessie with a report
on Clifton's "disgusting behavior."

Although Bessie rarely found herself allied with Charlotte
in family matters, she was shaking her head, muttering:
"Lawdy, lawdy . . . Miss 'Lizbeth be spinnin' in her grave
if she be seein' dese goin's on."

"It doesn't make any sense," Charlotte finished primly.
"It simply doesn't make any sense."

"Hey, Char," Roland asked shyly, "do you think Pops
and Miss Jewel . . . I mean, are they, you know . . ." he
faltered, tracings of pink appearing against the downy blond
of his cheek.

Charlotte stared at him, aghast that he was putting into words what she had been thinking. "I'm not going to discuss this with you, Roland," she snapped. "You're much too young." She stalked out of the kitchen leaving her brother feeling reduced once more to the family baby, as Bessie continued to mutter her disapproval over the dishpan.

WHEN Clifton returned home shortly before three, no one mentioned Miss Jewel. The men had moved to the enclosed back porch, to listen to a broadcast of the Redskins-Eagles game being played in Washington, D.C. The women had remained in the parlor, to enjoy the WNBC Sunday afternoon concert from Philharmonic Hall in New York.

"They're going to perform Schostakovich's First," Meg said excitedly. "Professor Claessen says it's one of the greatest symphonies of our times."

Charlotte kicked off her black pumps with a sigh of relief. Having only a marginal interest in classical music, her mind was wandering to other areas. "I wish I could take Bessie home with me," she said wistfully. "I just can't get that Eloise to make a decent roast."

Meg sat cross-legged on the oriental rug, casting some gray wool onto a pair of knitting needles. Beside her, Carrie and Nancy were busy crayoning dresses for their paper dolls.

"What's that you're making?" Charlotte asked.

"A scarf...it's for 'Bundles for Britain'," Meg explained, her face thoughtful and serious. "Lots of us at school knit."

"Oh." Charlotte lost interest at once.

"Good for you," Emily said warmly. She turned the radio dial, just as the voice of John Daly was opening the program. As she settled herself into her father's favorite wing chair, she looked sharply at her younger sister and asked suddenly, as if the thought had just surfaced: "This friend of yours, Meg—is he Jewish?"

"A Jew!" Charlotte exclaimed. "How could you imagine such a thing?"

"Because it's true," Meg said quietly.

"Oh, my God," Charlotte blanched, fanning herself nervously, as she often did when she was agitated.

"What's a choo, Mummy?" Carrie asked, intrigued by the sound of the new word.

As Howard set the kitchen radio on the table on the back porch, Clifton offered John the editorial page of the Richmond *Herald Dispatch*. "Take a look at this," he said. "The article on the Japanese peace mission. I think this will support what I said to you before. Their ambassador and a special envoy have been meeting with the President and the Secretary of State . . ."

"Sir," Howard said quietly, "I'm afraid I don't share your optimism. If this country does go to war, as an officer of the infantry, I'd be among the first to go . . ."

"Roosevelt will not let that happen," Clifton said decisively. "The country will not support such a venture."

"But if it should happen," Howard insisted, "I wondered if Emily and Alexander might come to Breezy and stay with you."

Shaken, Clifton folded the newspaper. "Emily and Alexander will always be welcome here," he cleared his throat, "but I'm certain that will not be necessary."

"I think you should know," John said, "that I've been thinking of signing up for the Navy."

"Wow," Roland reacted, looking up from the game of tic-tac-toe he'd been playing with Alexander.

A silent glare from his father stopped him. "What about Charlotte?" he asked his son-in-law. "How does she feel about this?"

"I've brought the subject up several times, but ever since I drew a low Selective Service number last fall, she refuses to discuss it."

"I'm sure she would not stand in your way," Clifton said briskly, in defense of his daughter.

"Wow!" Roland exclaimed. "We'll have somebody in the Army and the Navy. I'll have to join the Marines!"

"That's enough," Clifton said harshly. "That's enough.

I will not allow that kind of talk."

"Come on, Gramps." Alexander tugged at his grandfather's trousers, impatient for his attention. "Come watch. Daddy's going to teach me how to play football." Howard had drawn a football field on a piece of cardboard and studded it with Bessie's green and white mints, to represent players.

"How about it, John?" Howard invited, reaching for a playful mood. "Want to play the white Eagles against my green Redskins?"

"I believe I'll take that challenge," John laughed.

"Two to one, the Redskins win," Roland chimed in, eager to be part of the mock combat.

"There will be no wagering in this house," Clifton said, more sternly than he meant to, as he pulled the wicker rocker up to the card table.

The Redskins scored a touchdown early in the game. A heated first down was underway, when a stadium loudspeaker suddenly drowned out the sportscaster's voice.

"Did I hear right?" Howard looked up from his game. "Was somebody paging Edward Tam?"

"Who's that?" Roland asked.

"He's the assistant director of the FBI." Howard reached over and turned up the volume. The voice was now paging Admiral W. H. R. Blandy. "What's going on?"

Suddenly the sounds of the stadium faded completely. There was a crackle of static. Then a strange voice, urgent and disembodied, took over the air waves:

We interrupt this program to bring you a special bulletin. The Japanese have attacked Pearl Harbor, Hawaii, by air, President Roosevelt has just announced.

"They've done it," Howard said quietly, holding Alexander so tightly that the child began to squirm.

"We must go to the women." Clifton's voice was hoarse, his color ashen.

"We're in it!" Roland was fairly brimming with excitement. "I've got to call Buddy."

Clifton rose unsteadily from the rocker, his eyes glazed and unfocused. "May God help us," he said, his voice breaking.

IN the parlor, Meg huddled in her chair, looking very young and very frail. "They've really bombed us," she said softly to herself.

"What's a bomb?" Charlotte's oldest girl, Carrie, asked.

"A bomb kills people," Emily answered heavily, her face frozen as she stared into space. Clifton went to her, patting her shoulder clumsily, reaching into his mind for words of comfort. Finding none, he remained silent.

"This is simply awful," Charlotte said indignantly because the event seemed to warrant some comment. Taking her husband's hand, she added brightly: "Well, at least you'll be safe."

John shook his head. "Things have changed, Charlotte Lee. No one is safe now."

Howard held his wife in the shelter of his arms. "We'll have to leave immediately," he said softly.

"I know."

"I love you."

"I love you."

"What are you all talking about?" Carrie asked, alarmed by the gravity of the atmosphere.

"Mommy," Nancy began to cry. "I want to go home . . ."

Bessie herded the children onto the porch, with an idea of somehow keeping them occupied and untouched by what was happening.

The adults sat together in the parlor, listening to further details of the attack. The mechanical voice on the radio gave more details of the bombing of the islands of Oahu and Manila, of the surprise attack at 7:58 that morning on all naval and military installations at Fort William McKinley and Nicholas Air Force Base.

The sound of the radio dominated the room. Outside, the front porch swing creaked. The sound of Bessie's voice was heard, singing a familiar old mountain song:

The choo-choo train
Goes round the bend.
Goodbye my lover, goodbye
It's loaded down with railroad men
Goodbye my lover, goodbye.

His phone call to Buddy concluded, Roland stood in the doorway, listening to preliminary accounts of damage and estimated casualties. Then, face grimly set, he went to the hall closet and took out the American flag which the family flew on national holidays. Solemnly, he carried it out to the porch and hung it from the porch rail.

From the front window Clifton watched his son, as church bells began to toll ominously down in the valley town.

WITHIN an hour, only Clifton, Bessie and Roland were left on Breezy. With all leaves cancelled, Howard was obliged to return at once to Fort Dix. John had offered to drive the Emmetts back to Richmond, where better train connections could be made. Meg, impatient to get back to New York, squeezed into the already crowded car, so that she, too, might catch a train from Richmond.

Clifton and Roland sat silently in front of the fire, still listening to the radio. After Bessie served them cold meat and salad on trays, Clifton turned to his son: "I'm going to call Walter. I've decided to fill the Judge's place on the Draft Board. There are times when history dictates our choices."

"That's great, Pop!" Roland exclaimed. Then, trying to temper his exuberance with a semblance of maturity, he added: "You're the best man for the job, sir."

Clifton's conversation with Walter Burns was brief. He said simply that in these new circumstances, his responsibility as an American was clear.

When he returned to the parlor, the radio announcer was saying that the President would not hold his usual Sunday evening fireside chat, that Mrs. Roosevelt would speak to the nation on her husband's behalf.

"Bessie," Clifton summoned. "Come in here. I want us all to listen to this together.

"This is an historic moment," he said gravely, as he took a pencil and a small notebook from his vest pocket and prepared to write notes.

Not long after the moving broadcast came to a close, Clifton announced that he would go down to his office for a while. Roland and Bessie exchanged a look of surprise.

"I'll bet he's going to see Miss Jewel," Roland said knowingly after his father was out of earshot.

"Hush up, boy. Yo' daddy say he goin' to his office, yo' got no business to say he not," Bessie huffed. She thought that Roland might be right, but knew it wasn't his place to question Mr. Clifton's veracity.

It was after three o'clock in the morning. Unable to sleep after so much excitement, Roland wandered down into the kitchen to forage for leftovers. There, in the center of the round oak table, resting against the salt and pepper shakers was a large Whittaker & Son envelope, with his own name written neatly in the center. Inside was a carbon copy of a typewritten letter:

December 7, 1941

My Dear Children,

I write you from my office, late in the evening of this fateful day which will change all our lives. From my window I can see the statue of that great Confederate soldier, Robert E. Lee, presiding over the darkened town square. As I contemplate this monument to our Civil War, I find it difficult to comprehend that we have embarked on yet another war, the second in my lifetime.

Tonight, after each of you had gone from Breezy Hill, returning to your separate lives and households, Roland, Bessie and I tuned into the Sunday Evening Fireside Chat, expecting to hear a broadcast from our President. Instead, it was his fine wife, Eleanor Roosevelt, who spoke on the radio. I wrote down her words, which will give courage to us all:

> *"You cannot escape anxiety; you cannot escape the clutch of fear at your heart; and yet I hope that the certainty of what we have to meet will make you rise above these fears."*

Inspired by these words, I announce that this letter to you all is the first edition of a weekly communication, which I shall call The Breezy Hill Bulletin. *For as each of us assumes the duties that this year will dictate, we must be united as never before. We must draw strength and purpose from the love we share with one another.*

So from your various home fronts, send me your news, and I shall share it with all. Joined together, we shall overcome the enemy that threatens our lives, our freedom and everything we hold dear. I close with the prayer that God will be with us and that the horror which is war will be mercifully brief.

> *Your loving father,*
> *J. C. Whittaker*

2

Report to Duty
February 1942

My Dear Children,

Winter this year seems long and particularly hard. In our mountain valley, sleeting rains have forced us to move the bird feeder from its pedestal in the garden to a kinder location under the porch eaves. Would that there were such simple remedies for human suffering.

The last Russell County Draft Board file is in place. The offices of Whittaker and Son are now fully functional and open for this terrible business of war. How difficult it is to accept the lessons that are forced upon us daily, as we contemplate the fragility of life, the suddenness with which beloved landmarks of permanence are scattered in every direction.

Billy Gillespie, our West Grove Gazette *publisher visited my office with a quotation he had printed up specially in his shop. It was a toast given New Year's Day by that fine English Prime Minister, Winston Churchill, as he traveled*

*to his recent conference with our President Roosevelt. I
share it, knowing how many sacrifices we will all be asked
to make before this war is won.*

*"Here's to 1942, here's to a year of toil, a year
of struggle and peril, and a long step forward towards
victory. May we all come through safely and with
honor."*

SITTING in one of the cream-colored velvet chairs that flanked
the marble fireplace at 53 Ridgecrest Drive, Charlotte read
the latest *Breezy Hill Bulletin*. She sighed, wishing her father
wouldn't go on and on about the war. It was all so depressing.

She skimmed through the rest of the letter hastily, reading
that Emily had found an apartment over a restaurant near
Fort Benning, Georgia, where Howard was now training,
and that she had rented out her house in Boston. In his quiet,
restrained way, Clifton applauded Emily for her courage in
making this difficult move.

At the end of the neatly typed three-page letter, Charlotte
found a reference to John and herself. But the brevity of
the mention made it clear that her father did not consider
the event an important family news item.

*From Richmond comes the news that Charlotte and
John have moved into their new home. A Valentine's
Day housewarming party has been planned.*

Charlotte fumed as she read the short paragraph, resenting
Clifton's subtle suggestion that she did not deserve as much
attention for establishing a beautiful home, as Emily did for
leaving one.

She put the letter down on the fruitwood table beside her
chair and surveyed the new living room, which she had
decorated in elegant shadings of beige and rose, humming
as she did a few bars of "Chattanooga Choo-Choo" to pick
up her spirits. She was so proud of her new home, so eager
to display it to the seventy-five guests she had selectively
invited to their first important "open house."

"Miz Charlotte..." Eloise stood in the doorway, her face a shiny ebony mask above the immaculate starched white uniform that Charlotte insisted she don daily as soon as she arrived at the Randolph home. "The table be done ready."

As she followed the maid into the dining room, Charlotte noted with some irritation the condition of the woman's shoes. I must remind her to polish them, she thought. I know they're cracked, but she could keep them clean. And that hair of hers—I do wish she wouldn't wear it in those negra braids. I wish she would try one of those straighteners.

In the wedgewood blue dining room, she flicked a small thread off one of the eight needlepoint chairs, arranged along the wall, and studied her table arrangement. She had chosen a white lace cloth with a red linen liner and a long low centerpiece of red roses and baby's breath. Everything was in place: the crystal stemware, the linen napkins, her wedding silverware and the small handpainted china plates for the assorted hors d'oeuvres.

"It's perfect," she said, filled with satisfaction. "I've done it! I just know the party will be a smashin' success."

"Yes, ma'am," Eloise agreed without enthusiasm, as she stood to the side of the table, her hands folded in front of her apron.

Charlotte wondered, as she often did, whether Eloise was capable of enthusiasm, or any emotion for that matter. The woman had worked for the Randolph family for many years. After she and John had come back from their honeymoon, Eloise had turned up, with an accompanying letter from John's mother, describing her as "a jewel and a treasure." Charlotte had never been convinced, though she was grateful for the free full-time help, and aware that she could not manage without it.

"My guests will be arrivin' in an hour, Eloise," she said. "I want you to get the girls up from their naps. I've laid out their new dresses."

"Yes'm." Eloise nodded and left the room.

Now it's time to get myself ready, she thought. I do hope my hair won't fall when I bathe. She touched her golden curls as though they were a treasure.

* * *

CHARLOTTE hurried into the large gold-hued master bedroom that was dominated by the cherry-wood four-poster
bed, a Randolph family heirloom. I'm so glad I chose the
filigree wallpaper pattern instead of the floral print, she
thought. Lovingly she passed her hand over the white crocheted bedspread and regretted that there wouldn't be enough
time for a little nap. Mama had always said that the perfect
hostess refreshed herself with a little rest before she greeted
her guests. Dear Mama, she had been such a lady. She
would have appreciated every single perfect detail of this
lovely home.

She took a scarf from her dresser drawer, to drape over
her hair while she bathed. As she carefully bobby-pinned
the fabric into place, she wondered if John would remember
to come home early from the office. She had reminded him
at breakfast, and he had nodded absently. He had been
uncharacteristically distracted these past few days. Some
legal problem, no doubt. Nothing to concern herself about.

Life had certainly been lovely these first six weeks in
their new home. How fortunate it was that their lifestyle
wasn't defined by the income from John's law practice.
How lucky it was that the large inheritance from John's
grandfather had come along on his thirtieth birthday, and
just as the old Johnson house had been put up for sale. And
what a perfect setting the gracious English Tudor manor
made for the kind of future she'd planned.

She had tried to show her appreciation for these blessings
in the best way she knew, by generously offering to John
the pleasures of her body at every opportunity.

"If I'd known you'd be like this," he'd murmured drow-
sily one night, as they lay together, sated and exhausted
under the gold satin comforter, "I'd have found a way to
buy you a house like this before."

Dear John, she thought fondly, as she turned on the bath
water and waited for the tub to fill. He was such a lamb.
She sank into the velvet chaise and kicked her sensible blue
pumps onto the thick white carpet. From the magazine stand

on the marble top table, she picked up the latest *Harper's Bazaar* and began to leaf through the pages. She was annoyed at the number of war-related messages that cluttered the pages. She frowned as her eyes scanned a Coty advertisement, a picture of a handsome Army officer and an attractive brunette with the caption: "His to serve—Hers to inspire." She closed the magazine and replaced it on the table. For a moment, she considered cutting out the ad and sending it to her sister Emily. That kind of thinking was much more Emily's style than hers. Poor Emily, she reflected, as she headed for the bathroom, she had such a dreary tendency towards self-sacrifice.

As she lowered herself into the scented bathwater, she thought of how relieved she'd been when John had stopped talking about enlisting. After Pearl Harbor, he had worried her to death for a while.

She soaped her perfect body and listened to the sound of chattering from the girls' rooms. She imagined how they would look, brushed and combed and picture-pretty in their new pink dresses. Carrie was asking one of her eternal "why" questions, forcing Eloise into one of her "hush your mouth" responses.

"I hate ruffles," she heard Carrie complain. "They're stupid. And they scratch my knees."

Charlotte sighed as she toweled herself off. She took the new full-skirted, red taffeta dress from the closet and held it against her body, admiring her image in the vanity mirror. How fortunate she was to be blond and so beautiful. Neither of her sisters could carry off a dress like this.

"I'M home." John's voice traveled up the stairs, as the front door closed behind him. "Where are all my girls?"

"I'm upstairs, dressing," Charlotte called back, as she pulled up the long back zipper. She sat down at the vanity to apply her makeup, listening to the familiar little sounds that came from the front hall. John was removing his overshoes, to keep the February slush off the Chinese rug, and hanging his overcoat on the bentwood rack near the door.

She blotted her lipstick, dabbed some perfume behind her ears and hurried to wait for her husband at the top of the landing.

John bounded up the stairs, and Charlotte smiled indulgently. He was usually so measured in his movements. He kissed her soundly on the forehead—and she waited for the compliments that were sure to follow.

But John said nothing about her outfit. Instead, he pulled a piece of crumpled yellow paper from his jacket pocket and waved it in her face. "I made it, honey! I made it! I'm being sent to Anacosta for E-Base training!"

"You made what?" she asked sharply. "E-Base what?"

"The Navy! The Navy has accepted me for pilot training!" He reached for her, but she pulled away, gasping as if she had been struck.

"But you couldn't," she managed to say. "You didn't— I asked you not to. You promised me . . ."

"I did not promise," he said quietly, his manner subdued now. "I said I would consider your objections. I did. But there were higher considerations. I could not ignore my patriotic duty."

"It is not your patriotic duty!" she shrilled, forgetting for the moment that she considered such a loss of control to be coarse and unladylike. "Your duty is to me and our daughters. Tell them you've changed your mind."

"I can't do that, Charlotte," he said firmly. "And I won't. I'm in the Navy now." He tried to put a hand on her arm, but she shook him off. "I'll be leaving in ten days for six weeks of basic training. During that time, I'll expect you to rent the house and put the furniture in storage, so you and the girls can join me in New London. That is where I'll be stationed."

"I won't do it!" She stamped her foot, almost losing her balance. She grabbed the newel post for support. "And besides," she pouted, "Eloise can't do it either."

"What in heaven's name does Eloise have to do with this?"

"I can't possibly go anywhere without Eloise. If we go at all."

"Charlotte," he said, with the same kind of measured patience he used when he talked to the children, "we can't possibly take Eloise anywhere. This is war time. There's a housing shortage. We'll be lucky if we can find accommodations for the four of us."

"You have no right to do this to me, John Randolph! You have no right!" she shouted, her fists clenched. "I won't forgive you for this!" she hurled at him, as she turned and fled into her bedroom.

As soon as the last of the party guests had departed, Charlotte marched stiffly upstairs and locked herself in the guest room. When John came up a half hour later, he knocked on the door and called her name. She refused to answer, throwing herself on the bed and pounding out her frustrations on the chintz-covered mattress.

The following morning, he did not knock again. Before he left the office, he explained to the girls that Mummy wasn't feeling well and needed to rest for a while.

Charlotte listened, from her self-imposed confinement, until the house was quiet, until John was gone and Eloise had taken the children to the playground. When she was certain she was alone, she slipped downstairs and called her best friend, Mary Sue Conley.

"Charlotte, darling," Mary Sue cooed into the telephone. "That was a truly sumptuous and elegant party. But I've been so concerned about you. We all noticed that you and John weren't speaking. Whatever is goin' on between you two?"

"John's joined the Navy," Charlotte wailed. "Without even telling me, and..."

Mary Sue listened to Charlotte's misery, murmuring "Oh, no" or "You poor thing" at appropriate intervals. But when Charlotte was finished, Mary Sue's final reaction was dreadfully disappointing. "Oh, dear," she said, "I guess this means you won't be here to help with the Spring Cotillion. How ever will I manage without you?"

Hoping for more comfort, Charlotte called a few more friends. But although some commiserated with her for having to move north and live among strangers, and some promised to give luncheons and teas before she left, no one seemed to really comprehend the full extent of her tragedy.

As a last resort, she dialed John's parents at Fair Acres. Her call was answered by Hilary, John's older sister, who reported that her parents had gone to look at a new filly over in the next county. Though she and Hilary had never seen eye to eye on anything, Charlotte took a deep breath and presented her case as convincingly as she could.

When Hilary answered, her voice was cool, her manner remote. "The Randolphs have always been a military family, Charlotte, since the days of George the Fifth. I'm sure Father and Mother will be proud to learn that John is making a patriotic contribution to that heritage."

Feeling humiliated and more isolated than ever, Charlotte ended the conversation and retreated to the guest room. When John came home that evening, she ignored his knock and his conciliatory invitation to join him for dinner. That night she scarcely slept at all, as she formulated, then discarded, one scheme after another, trying to salvage some personal victory out of what seemed to be a certain defeat.

She was awakened the next morning by a fierce pounding on her door. "Wake up, Charlotte! Wake up. Oh, do open this door. I have the most awful news!" It was Mary Sue's voice.

Charlotte opened her eyes, yawned, stretched her long, shapely legs, then padded to the door to admit her friend.

"What is it, Mary Sue? What on earth are you talking about?"

"Oh, Charlotte," Mary Sue wailed. "It's Carole Lombard. She's dead. Killed in a plane crash. I just heard the news over the radio, and I just had to come over. Isn't it awful?"

"Lord, yes," Charlotte agreed, for the blond actress was one of her favorites. "Poor Clark Gable. Whatever will he do without her?"

"Mummy! Mummy!" Carrie and Nancy, hearing their

mother's voice, came bounding to her side. "You're all better," Carrie exclaimed. "Did Daddy tell you we were all going to another new house? He said we could go on a train. And we could..."

"Not now, Carrie," Charlotte cut her off. "Go downstairs and tell Eloise to give you breakfast. Not another word about houses and trains, you hear?"

When the girls had filed downstairs to the kitchen, she turned to her friend. "Oh, Mary Sue," she sighed, "I surely do envy Carole Lombard."

CHARLOTTE spent most of the following two weeks attending teas and luncheons in her honor, returning home with small farewell gifts, all of which she packed into the barrels that were earmarked for shipment up north. She was civil to John in front of the children, but she continued to sleep in the guest room at night. She realized that she had made a tactical error, but she did not know quite how to buy it back. Like it or not, she would have to swallow John's decision for she was alone in opposing it, and without a single ally.

She searched her mind for a way to improve the situation but the ten days passed without a solution. Now here it was the evening before John was scheduled to leave, and she was still uncertain about how to break the impasse.

She'd instructed Eloise to prepare John's favorite dishes for dinner. That was no more than right, since he was her husband, and he was going off to a military base for six weeks. She made pleasant dinner conversation, and then put the girls to bed, pretending that nothing was wrong. Afterwards, she retreated to the bathroom, to a soothing scented bath, to consider what she might say to her husband before he went away.

Suddenly she heard an authoritative rap on the door, and her husband's voice, brisk and uncompromising. "Charlotte. Charlotte Lee. I want you out of that bath and in our bedroom in five minutes. Do you hear me?"

"Yes, John," she answered, her voice meek and compliant, and incongruous with the satisfied smile that spread across her face, as she sank into the water for a last luxurious soak. John had solved the problem for her. When a man positively, absolutely asserted his manhood as he had just done, only a foolish woman would refuse to yield. And Charlotte was no fool.

Perfumed and powdered and dressed for bed in one of her flimsier nightgowns, she strolled with an air of nonchalance into the master bedroom. John's suitcase was opened across her chaise, filled with neat stacks of socks, underwear and other assorted haberdashery. The sight of her husband packing his things suddenly made his departure real for her.

She did love him. Even if he was wrong. And perfectly awfully mean to drag her off to God knows where. And being Charlotte, she told John exactly that.

He looked at her, his expression bemused, exasperated and altogether loving. "Charlotte Lee Randolph," he said softly, "there are times when you try my patience. There are times when I . . . when I . . ." He looked at his wife for a moment, then he closed the gap between them with three long strides. He pressed his face into her hair. "I have missed you so much. So very much." He kissed her face and her throat, as he moved her down onto the bed. His hands lifted her nightgown, stroked her body, in just that special way she liked so much. She moaned with pleasure, with anticipation of more.

He pulled away for a moment. Her eyes opened and she watched him undress, admiring his slim tall body, enjoying the knowledge that he belonged to her. She sighed contentedly when he slipped back into bed beside her, resuming his attentions, worshiping her own perfect body with his fingertips, his lips.

"So beautiful," he whispered, as he raised himself above her. "My beautiful Charlotte."

She smiled languidly, arching to meet him, shivering with delight as he pressed into her, moving greedily now to take the pleasure she had denied herself for two long weeks.

* * *

"BUT I'm certain there has been some mistake! There must be!" Charlotte insisted, as she stood at the ticket counter in the crowded Richmond Station. "My husband made the sleeper reservations for us weeks ago. You cannot expect me to travel for eighteen hours in the coach car. Certainly not with two small children."

"People do it all the time, ma'am." The man at the counter looked impatient and not very impressed with the seriousness of her situation. "Someone with a higher priority obviously needed your reservation. There's a war goin' on, you know."

Though she felt like crying with annoyance and frustration, Charlotte would not give the man, or any of the strangers who surrounded her, the satisfaction of seeing her lose her composure. She drew herself up and said, with as much hauteur as she could muster: "In that case, we will take the coach accommodations, sir."

When the transaction was completed, she led her daughters into the waiting room and arranged them, one on each side of her, on a golden oak bench.

"I'm hungry," Nancy complained, sliding off the seat.

"We will eat on the train," Charlotte said firmly, taking the child's arm before she could wander away.

"Look!" Carrie said, swinging her skinny legs as she pointed to a young woman who held a toddler on a strap and a crying baby on her lap. The girl was unbuttoning her flimsy rayon blouse, pulling down a dingy brassiere strap to let the baby nurse.

"Carrie," Charlotte said quickly, "I want you to turn around and look at Mama. Now get one of your books from your bag, and I will read you a story."

Suddenly an announcement came over the loudspeaker: the Pilgrim to Boston had been delayed, and no new arrival time was yet available.

"Oh, no," Charlotte muttered under her breath. "This is clearly not goin' to be one of my better days."

"Mummy, I'm hungry," Nancy whined again. "And I want to go home now."

The choo-choo train
Goes round the bend.
Goodbye my lover, goodbye...

CHARLOTTE stared out of the dirty train window and remembered the old railroad song Bessie had sung to them
when they were all children. This train is going much farther
than round the bend, she mused. And it's not loaded with
railroad men; it's filled with soldiers and sailors, all going
off to war.

IT was late afternoon of the following day when the dismal
ride ended. The train was six hours late. By the time she
and the children stepped onto the New London platform,
they were achingly weary. Charlotte had mentally compiled
a long list of complaints she intended to present to John: it
had taken hours to get to the train's dining car; Nancy had
thrown up a cold and unappetizing meal, all over Charlotte's
blue faille skirt and matching pumps; a sailor had taken
liberties with her as she pushed her way towards a restroom;
the heating system had broken down outside of New York;
and Carrie had developed an earache. And in spite of her
efforts to keep her makeup fresh, her hairdo in place, Charlotte felt rumpled and grimy, which only compounded her
physical misery.

"Daddy! Daddy!" The girls revived when they caught
sight of their father, crisp and fresh in his white uniform.

"Here you are," he laughed, folding them all into his
arms, not seeming to notice how tired and miserable they
all were. "I can't wait to take you home. Wait until you
see, Charlotte. We have the entire middle floor of a wonderful old Victorian house. It belonged to an old sea captain,
and it's only ten minutes from the base."

Charlotte nodded, without sharing John's enthusiasm.
During the short ride, she closed her eyes, half listening to
her husband's account of how he had spent the past six
weeks of training, and how hard he had looked to find

suitable accommodations for them.

When they arrived at 23 High Point Street, she stared in disbelief at the sprawling three-story frame house with the turret on top. Was John blind? Or completely mad? Houses in this condition were to be found only in the bad part of Richmond. Couldn't he see that? She stood on the sidewalk, shivering in the light snow that had started to fall, while John unloaded the luggage.

She bit back the acid comments that came to her lips, determined to keep her thoughts to herself, until she could assess the entire situation and decide what could be done.

"Come on, honey," John urged. "Let's get inside. You and the girls aren't really dressed for this weather. When you get rested, I want you to meet our new landlady, Hester Longstreth. She's a spinster lady, retired now, but she used to be the town librarian. Her father built this house. When she was a girl, she and her mother used to climb that turret, to look for the captain's ship when it sailed into port."

As Charlotte mounted the threadbare carpeted stairs to the second floor, she took in the faded wallpaper, the dark and dreary wood paneling. It was worse than she had imagined any home of hers might ever be. She decided not to look too carefully at her new surroundings, not until she'd had a bath and some rest. She needed all of her strength to cope with this depressing environment.

As if he finally sensed her weariness, John suggested: "Why don't you relax a while, honey. I'll scramble some eggs for the girls and put them to bed."

"Thank you, John," she said gratefully. "I do need some time to refresh myself." She unpacked the perfumed bath salts, a gift from Mary Sue, from her leather cosmetic case, and retired to a large, white wood-paneled bathroom. She filled the claw-footed tub with hot water, stripped off her clothes and sank quickly into the scented bubbles.

She felt disoriented and not quite herself. The past weeks had all seemed so unreal, part of someone else's life, having nothing to do with the gracious, well-ordered existence she'd laid out for herself and her family. Ever since this war business had come along, her life had been altered and not

for the better. A short time ago, she had been the mistress
of a fine home, a member, by marriage, of one of the South's
premier families, a moving force in the Junior League, a
proud member of the Daughters of the Confederacy.

Now she had been transported, body and soul, to this
alien environment. Expected to live, servantless and friend-
less, in conditions of deprivation and sacrifice. In a northern
setting that obviously knew nothing of manners and gentility
and social class.

She wondered why none of this seemed apparent to
John. It must be that his head was just so full of this war
fever. Still, from all she'd heard, the war couldn't last very
long. Perhaps she and John would be back in Richmond by
summer, in time to enjoy the new golf course at the
country club.

Stepping out of the tub, she dried herself quickly in the
drafty bathroom and slipped into a new pale blue long-
sleeved nightgown, a gift from the girls in the bridge club,
for "the cold nights up North."

Carrie and Nancy were already sleeping soundly, in one
of the tiniest, most cramped rooms she had ever seen. A
converted linen closet, she guessed. She tiptoed into the
more spacious master bedroom, expecting John to be sitting
up in bed, waiting for her, ready to appreciate how feminine
and lovely she looked. Instead he was already buried under
the covers, his light snoring telling her that he was fast
asleep.

She looked at his face for a moment. It was such a strong,
handsome face. She loved this exceptional husband of hers,
in spite of the dreadful inconvenience his strange patriotic
notions had inflicted upon her. And it had been a long time
since he had held her close and told her how much he loved
her.

She turned off the bedside lamp with the tattered shade
and slipped into bed beside him. She slid her hand under
his pajama top and began to stroke his chest. He blinked
awake with a start, smiled sleepily and took her hand. "I'm
awfully tired, honey," he whispered apologetically, his voice
slurred with fatigue. "Had all-night duty yesterday." He fell

back onto the pillow and was quickly asleep again.

If this doesn't beat all, she thought. Nothing was going right. Nothing at all.

IT was just past noon, a week later, and Charlotte sat on the scratchy wine-red velour couch in the living room, still dressed in her pink taffeta robe, sipping a cup of coffee. She wondered, for the hundredth time, why John continued to behave as if their apartment was such a marvelous find. He reminded her, often enough, how much better it was than the accommodations most of the other families had. But she found it hard to believe that anyone who wasn't dirt poor could live in conditions worse than this.

The apartment was cavernous and dreary, an atmosphere that was compounded by the dark wood paneling and the heavy brown velvet drapes. Charlotte frowned as she glanced at the trestle table, with its built-in benches, set in the small alcove leading to the kitchen. All the fine damask cloths she'd brought with her were far too large for such a tiny table, and there was no adequate seating at all for guests.

Not that there was any time for entertaining, she thought sourly as she took another sip of coffee. John was at the base until all hours, and she had met almost no one since her arrival. On top of everything else, the weather had been so cold and miserable that she'd been stuck indoors, day after day, trying to keep her children from getting bored and from getting on her nerves.

"Mummy, can we play in the backyard?" Carrie called from the kitchen.

"No." Charlotte roused herself from her gloomy reverie. "It's cold, and there's snow on the ground."

"But we want to build a snowman." Carrie stood stubbornly in the wide doorway connecting the living room and kitchen, swinging her left foot.

"Mummy has a headache," Charlotte sighed. "I just don't feel up to facing the cold. You know you can't play outside alone."

"Be we wouldn't be alone," Carrie argued. "Doreen is

building a snowman, and a soldier is helping her. Come
and look."

At the mention of her neighbor's name, Charlotte frowned.
Doreen Lasky had introduced herself to Charlotte and the
girls earlier in the week, after they had met on the stairway.
It had been a rather strained encounter for Charlotte. Although Doreen had been boisterously friendly, she had a
sailor on her arm and alcohol on her breath and was clearly
not of the class and breeding Charlotte would have hoped
for in an upstairs neighbor.

Reluctantly she left the couch and went into the kitchen.
Carrie was standing on the stool she had pulled in front of
the sink, looking down into the backyard.

Outside, Doreen and the soldier were laughing, as they
picked up handsful of snow, packing them onto a chubby
snowman wearing a top hat and carrying a tattered mop in
one round fist. Doreen's long red hair fell from her green
knit cap, onto the shoulders of her plaid parka, as she made
a snowball and threw it at the soldier.

She's so common, Charlotte thought, working shifts in
an airplane factory and entertaining men at all hours of the
day and night.

"That's enough," she said briskly, drawing the heavy
brown drapes. "Get down—and put the stool back where
you found it—hear?"

The cluttered kitchen was now dark and even gloomier
than before. The morning's breakfast plates were still on
the table, and an open loaf of white bread spilled out onto
the littered counter top. Oh Lord, she thought, I need Eloise
here. I simply cannot manage this place.

Feeling a little guilty about disappointing Carrie, she said
in a softer voice: "Why don't you get a banana, honey? Go
into your room and play tea party with Nancy until my
programs are over. Maybe I'll feel better and then we can
all go out later."

"Okay," Carrie agreed grudgingly. "But I still don't know
why we can't go out now." She left the kitchen, scuffing
her Buster Brown oxfords in a final protest.

Finding the one clean glass in the cabinet, Charlotte
pushed aside the pile of pots and pans in the sink and ran

a glass of water to wash down two aspirin tablets. Ever since she had arrived in Connecticut, she had had one headache after another.

Then she sank onto the kitchen stool that was mended with adhesive tape and listened absently to the sounds of her children amusing themselves. Nancy was playing "Mummy" to her dolls, while Carrie was jumping rope in the narrow hallway that was still lined with boxes and barrels, not yet unpacked because there was no place to store Charlotte's impressive collection of crystal, china and linen. If she had the energy, she would tell Carrie to stop her jumping and do something quieter. All that pounding might be knocking bits of plaster onto Miss Longstreth's head, and Charlotte was not up to a visit or a complaint from her landlady. She did not share John's good opinion of Miss Longstreth. The two women had exchanged only a few words in the past week, but Charlotte thought there was nothing remarkable about the dried-up old spinster.

Sighing, she rose from the stool and turned on the RCA radio that sat on the counter. A masculine voice was singing: "Any bonds today? Bonds for freedom, that's what we're selling." Irritated, she turned down the volume, waiting for "The Romance of Helen Trent" to begin. She reached under the sink for the round enamel dishpan. Cleaning up was easier when she could lose herself for a little while in the afternoon serials.

"OKAY, girls," she called when the programs had ended. "Y'all can come in for some lunch now. Maybe we'll go outside for a bit, too."

Nancy appeared promptly, every curl still in place, her face unsmudged by the banana she'd eaten earlier. Her blue dress with its appliqued white ducks was spotless. Mama's little doll, Charlotte thought fondly.

"Where's Carrie?" Charlotte asked.

"Gone," Nancy said pleasantly.

"We're not ready to play games yet, Nancy. Not until after lunch. Go tell your sister to come out from her hidey place and help Mummy get lunch."

"Carrie's gone," Nancy repeated, "and I'm hungry."

"Carrie!" Charlotte's voice took on a sharp edge. "The game's over. Come out! I mean this minute!"

There was no answer to her call. She knelt down and took Nancy's hand. "Now I want you to tell me where Carrie is."

"Don't know. I'm hungry."

Getting up, Charlotte began to search the apartment. "Come help me, Nancy. We're going to find your sister."

"Okay, Mummy," Nancy giggled, always delighted to play a new game.

Charlotte opened closet doors and looked inside. On her hands and knees she checked under the beds, under the sofa and the chairs. Together, she and Nancy look behind the barrels in the hall, behind the living room drapes and under the sink, until it was clear that Carrie was not in the apartment.

Remembering the sound of Carrie's jump rope in the hallway, Charlotte thought the child might be sitting on the stairs, waiting for an opportunity to go outside. She rushed to the apartment door, opened it and looked down the stairs, but there was no Carrie. Just the jump rope, its red handles hanging over the bannister.

She went back into the apartment and took her short mink coat and matching hat from the tiny closet, panic beginning to mount in her chest. Trying to appear calm, she said to Nancy: "I want you to stay in your room and play with your dolls until I find Carrie. Here, you can have another banana and some cookies while you wait."

Charlotte ran down the stairs, her fears spiraling almost to nausea. Carrie, her willful and precocious child, on the streets of this strange northern town, in the snow, without even a sweater, perhaps even now at the mercy of a child molester. And her mama had been too busy with the radio to notice she was gone. Oh, John would never forgive her for this.

She ran out the door and onto the sidewalk. She began stopping passersby and asking: "Have you seen a little dark-haired girl wearing a green jumper and a white blouse?"

But no one had seen Carrie, and no one seemed to care; the strangers simply shook their heads and walked on.

Finally two young women trailed by three small boys stopped. They listened sympathetically as Charlotte explained that her daughter had simply vanished, and that she didn't know where to look.

"I'm Mary Johnson," one of the women said, "and this is Karen Binder. We're both Navy wives. We live in that brown clapboard house across the street."

"I'm Charlotte Randolph. My daughters and I arrived here a week ago. To join my husband—First Lieutenant Randolph."

"Where's your other daughter?" Mary asked.

"Upstairs." Charlotte pointed to the house.

"Karen, why don't you take the kids up to Charlotte's place," Mary suggested. "Stay with her little one, while she and I get this search organized. Call a few more neighbors when you get there. Tell them we need some more help."

Two hours later, a careful door-to-door search had turned up no sign of Carrie. The sky was beginning to darken, and the snow had begun to fall again.

A young ensign returning home from duty met the group of searchers on the street. After a brief conversation with his wife, he spoke to Charlotte. "I don't want to frighten you," he said, "but I think it's time to call the police."

Mary Johnson took Charlotte's arm and guided her up the stairs and into her own apartment. They were met at the door by Karen Binder. Mary shook her head in response to the other woman's silent question. "Kids give you any trouble?" she asked brightly.

"Not a bit," Karen answered. "They're playing 'huckle-buckle beanstalk.' I promised to get them some prizes from the dime store tomorrow."

"Why don't I take Nancy to my house while you talk to the police," Mary suggested. "I'll keep her until they find Carrie. Do you want Karen to stay here with you?"

Charlotte shook her head. She sat on the sofa, numb with fright and cold, watching the two women stuff the children into their snowsuits. When they had left, when she was alone, she continued to sit, frozen with anxiety, willing herself to make the dreaded telephone call to the police. To report that her child was missing.

She glanced at the ship's clock and noticed that the hands had passed five. Suddenly she heard John's steps bounding up the stairs. Oh God, she thought, what will I say to him.

Moments later, the door opened and John came in—with Carrie perched on his shoulders. Charlotte gasped and sank back onto the couch, too stunned to speak.

"What's the matter, Mummy? Do you still have your headache?" Carrie asked, as John deposited her on the sofa beside her mother.

"Honey, did you know there's a child lost in our neighborhood?" John asked. Then, noticing Charlotte's pinched face, he added: "What's wrong?"

"Oh, John," she said raggedly, "it's our Carrie! Carrie was lost!" She pulled the child close, stroking her hair. "Caroline Randolph," she said, her relief now edged with anger. "Where were you? Where have you been? I've been worried out of my mind."

"I wasn't lost, Mummy. I knew where I was," she said matter-of-factly.

"She came out of Miss Longstreth's when she saw me coming up the walk," John explained, obviously confused. "I assumed she had been visiting."

"I was, Mummy. She has so many books!" The child was flushed with excitement. "She read to me, and then she made us cocoa to drink. I like her, Mummy. She's not cranky and mean. Not at all."

"Everything's fine now," John reassured the child, gently pulling Charlotte's coat from her shoulders. "Carrie, why don't you go to your room and read for a while longer while Mummy and I talk." He disappeared into the kitchen, returning with two glasses. Reaching behind the Navy manuals in the bookcase, he took out a bottle of bourbon.

"I've been saving this for a special occasion. It appears as though you need some right now." He broke the seal and poured two long shots.

As Charlotte sipped the bourbon, she could feel the strength returning to her body.

"Now," John said, "why don't you tell me about it."

Charlotte sat up straight, penitent and defiant at the same time. "It was my fault. Entirely my fault. But John," she started to cry, "nothing has been right for me since we got here. I just don't belong here. Can't you see that?"

He stared down into the amber liquid for a moment, then put the glass down and took his wife's hand. Fixing her eyes with his, he spoke. "Yes, Charlotte, darlin', I have seen it. But I have expected you to rise above your difficulties . . . Do you know what I thought to myself the first time I met you?"

"What?" she said coyly, forgetting the wretched afternoon she had endured, for she loved to hear John talk about how he was smitten completely that first moment he had seen her at a W & L spring dance.

"I said to myself, that young woman is a thoroughbred. And I made up my mind, then and there, that you would be my wife."

"Did you really?" she whispered, snuggling her head against his chest. "What if I had refused you?" she teased, enjoying the reminiscence of a time when Charlotte Whittaker was sought after by dozens of eligible young men.

"I would not have taken 'no' for an answer." He kissed her fingertips lightly. "Because no other woman could hold a candle to you."

She sighed, accepting the compliment as her due.

"And," he continued, "I have understood that a thoroughbred is a special kind of creature. Requirin' special care and surroundings. But Charlotte," he said softly, taking her face in his hands, "the most special thing of all about thoroughbreds is their spirit." He kissed first her lips, then her eyes. "They always rise to a challenge."

Filled with his adoration, she squared her shoulders and sat up straight. "I will, too, John," she said fiercely. "I hate this place, but I will rise above it."

SHE awoke before the alarm clock went off. I must get up, she thought. There is so much I want to do today. But she lingered for a few more moments of comfort on the warm, strong pillow of John's arm. Maybe I should make a list, she thought. The way I did for Eloise, so I won't forget anything.

First she would surprise John and the girls by fixing French toast. Tonight she would cook a special dinner—something from the Fannie Farmer cookbook, or perhaps Bessie's fried chicken. Silver candlesticks on the silly little table. She would have to buy candles when she went shopping.

The clock ticking away at John's side of the bed showed five minutes to seven. Snuggling her face into the valley of his neck, she planted a kiss and whispered into his ear: "Good morning."

John stirred slowly. He was always tired now, from his long hours of pilot training at the base, followed by evenings of studying manuals at home. "What time is it, honey?" he asked groggily.

"Barely seven. Time for a nice hot breakfast. Then I'll drive you to the base. I need the car today."

"Fine. Good." John raised his head from the pillow. "But no breakfast for me—I have to be on base by eight."

All right, she said to herself. The French toast could wait until tomorrow. She slipped into her creamy silk bra and panties and laid out a navy pleated skirt and white ruffled blouse.

As she started for the bathroom, she saw that John had closed his eyes again. Leaning over, she nibbled his ear. "Wake up, sleepyhead."

Suddenly his arm reached from under the covers and pulled her down onto the bed. She laughed as he rolled over and pinned her down with his body. Through her delicate underwear, she could feel him, hard and demanding against her. As always, his desire excited her, made her feel strong and powerful, soft and yielding at the same time. Her hand reached for him, then stopped.

"John, sweetheart, we can't. The children . . . and you'll be late if we don't hurry."

"Okay, okay." He released his grip and lifted his body from hers. "But you haven't heard the last of this, Miz Randolph. I have plans for you. Tonight."

"Why, Lieutenant Randolph—how very bold you are,"

she teased, swinging her hips provocatively as she went into the bathroom. "I'll look forward to our rendezvous."

BY four o'clock, Charlotte was exhausted. She had finished her shopping and made a short visit to Mary Johnson's with a thank-you gift, a cake from the town bakery. The beds were made, the floors vacuumed, the furniture surfaces shiny, thanks to liberal applications from a new bottle of lemon oil.

As she bent over a large barrel to get a pair of silver candlesticks, she faced the fact that most of the things she had brought to New London were useless. I should have asked Emily, she thought, as she looked down at a large silver tray she would never have reason to unpack.

Just then, a decorating idea she'd seen in a magazine flashed through her mind. She foraged in the packing straw and found two silver bud vases and six rose-colored sherry glasses with leafy stems. Carefully, she lined up these treasures along the ledge that divided the wall paneling. As she completed her arrangement, a narrow shaft of late-afternoon light shone through the window, raising a glow in the pale red glass. She smiled with pleasure at this crowning touch.

When the clock struck four-thirty, she hurried into the kitchen. Covering herself with the new flowered apron she'd bought, she measured some shortening into a skillet and lit the burner, turning it to full flame.

"Step one," she announced triumphantly, measuring a cup of flour into a paper bag and adding salt and a tablespoon of coarsely ground pepper. She dropped the pieces of chicken into the bag, shaking vigorously, as Bessie used to do.

The window panes over the stove had misted over, and the melting shortening gave the already warm room a slightly greasy smell. Charlotte set the bag of chicken on the counter and opened the window a few inches. The dusty brown drapes fluttered limply as a cold breeze swept through the kitchen.

Returning to her chicken, she opened the bag and frowned. The flour was not sticking very well. She remembered that Bessie had dipped her chicken in egg batter first and won-

dered if she should wash the pieces off and start again. She
was just as nervous as her Mama had been in the kitchen.
Mama had never done much cooking on her own, and neither had Charlotte, an omission she was deeply regretting
at this moment.

Suddenly she caught the smell of something burning.
She whirled, dropping the bag of chicken on the floor. The
shortening had ignited and the brown curtains were on fire,
the wind sending bits of charred fabric like little black snow-
flakes all over the room.

Charlotte grabbed the dishpan, filled it with water and
threw it towards the blazing skillet, badly missing her target.
"Oh, Lord," she gasped.

The wind rose, sending the flames licking greedily at the
curtains. Clouds of smoke rose to the ceiling, scorching the
window frame. Do something, Charlotte's brain signalled.
Do something. But her feet seemed glued to the floor, her
eyes locked by the orange and yellow flames.

"Help!" she screamed. "Somebody help me!"

Seconds later, Doreen Lasky burst into the kitchen. It
took her only a moment to push Charlotte out of the way,
grab the open flour canister, and dump the contents onto
the flaming skillet. Then she yanked the curtains from the
rod, threw them into the sink and turned on the water, full
blast. The emergency was over.

"Is the fire engine coming?"

Charlotte whirled around and saw Carrie standing in the
doorway, holding her sister's hand. The two little faces
registered fear and fascination.

"Nope," Doreen answered cheerfully, kneeling to talk to
the children. "We don't need it now. Like they say in the
army, everything's 'snafu'."

"What's 'snafu'?" Carrie asked, as Nancy repeated the
new word, giggling.

"Well, honey, it means . . . uh . . . situation normal, all
fu—all fouled up. Say, why don't you kids go to my place
for a while until we get this mess cleaned up."

"Oh, no," Charlotte said immediately.

"Why not?" Doreen asked.

"Well," Charlotte lied lamely, "they might break something."

"Nothin' up there they can hurt," Doreen argued, looking straight at Charlotte. "Don't you think it would be a good idea to get them out of this stink for a while?"

Charlotte nodded, defeated by the other woman's logic. The two girls clapped their hands, their fear quickly displaced by the anticipation of exploring a new place. Moments later they were gone, with only the sound of their scampering footsteps trailing their progress upstairs.

"Honey," Doreen began, as soon as the children were out of earshot, "don't ever pour water onto a grease fire. That was something I learned when I was a kid, doin' kitchen work for my Pa on the ranch."

Charlotte nodded politely, not knowing quite what to say to this woman who had rescued her, this woman with whom she had absolutely nothing in common.

"Sure smells and looks like hell in here, don't it?" Doreen said, looking around the kitchen. "But it ain't half as bad as it looks. Let's get at it, so you can fix supper before your husband gets home."

"I don't know if I'm up to it," Charlotte sighed.

"Aw, honey, you don't mean that." Doreen looked down at her hands. "But before I do anything else, I better rub something on these blisters. Got any butter?"

"Oh, your hands—they're burned!" Charlotte was appalled that she had failed to notice Doreen's injuries. "I'm so sorry. Here," she said, taking the butter plate from the refrigerator. "Is it bad?"

"I've been hurt worse. Lots of times," Doreen said, as she rubbed the butter over her burns.

"Sit down, and I'll fix you a cup of tea," Charlotte insisted, filling the copper tea kettle and setting it carefully on a burner. Trying to make some polite conversation, she asked: "Do you enjoy your work at the factory?"

"Keeps me busy." Doreen placed the remaining chunk of butter back on the plate. "That's all I ask for, ever since my Charlie was killed at Pearl."

"Oh, my God!" Charlotte almost dropped the tea pot she

was preparing. It was the first time that Charlotte had met anyone who had lost someone in the war. "I'm so sorry."

"Yeah. Me, too." Doreen nodded. "It was rotten luck." She stared into her empty tea cup.

"I don't know what I'd do if anything happened to John," Charlotte said slowly, pouring boiling water into the tea pot, as she considered the war might be something more than a terrible inconvenience, that John could be hurt or even killed before it was over. "I'd cry forever, I guess."

"Yeah. I cried a lot at first. Then one day the tears dried up, and I went back to work." Doreen stirred her tea and laid the spoon aside. "See, we only got married in November, just before he shipped out." Her fingers stroked the handle of the spoon. "He looked so sweet in his uniform. Especially those dress whites. I used to tease him," she smiled, "about how quick he could get all those little buttons undone when he was in a hurry. You know what I mean."

Charlotte sat down on the other side of the table, staring at her upstairs neighbor, seeing her for the first time. "You're very brave," she said. "Braver than I could be."

"I'm not so brave." Doreen drew an imaginary circle on the table with a red-lacquered finger. "I drink a lot. It makes things fuzzy. I forget for a while. I go out lots. With men in uniform." She stood up and walked over to the bare soot-lined window, and with her back turned, she finished her confession. "Sometimes I sleep with them. I close my eyes and pretend they're Charlie."

I could never do that, Charlotte thought. Uncomfortable with the direction the conversation was taking, she said politely: "Why don't you just go into the bathroom and freshen up a bit? That always makes me feel so much better."

Doreen shrugged, sensing that she was somehow being dismissed, and left the room. As soon as she was out of sight, Charlotte began cleaning up furiously, trying to erase all signs of the fire and the memory of their conversation. But the charred window frame would not go away, and neither would the echo of what she had just heard.

When the phone rang, her answer was terse, different from her usually melodious greeting. Hearing John's voice she felt a sudden rush of gratitude and relief.

"I'm sorry, honey," he began, "I'm on late duty again. I know I promised..."

"It's all right, John, really," she said, with new understanding. I'll wait up for you."

"You don't have to do that," he said, but she could tell that he was pleased by her offer.

"I want to, John. I do. I love you."

"Love you, too, darling. Bye."

As she replaced the telephone on its cradle, she was aware of Doreen, standing awkwardly in the doorway. "Boy," she said, trying to lighten the heaviness her confession had left behind, "aren't I something? Here I come down to give you a hand, and I end up telling you all my troubles."

"Don't be silly," Charlotte said briskly. "You saved me from setting the house on fire." She dropped her eyes to the sooty linoleum floor. "Would you join us for dinner tonight? I could make some sandwiches..."

3

Dearly Beloved
October 1942

October 28, 1942

My Dear Children,

You all, of course, remember Miss Maggie Muse. She is the daughter of Rev. Muse, once West Grove's Baptist preacher. She has worked in the Clerk's Office occupying the same chair, in the same vault, by the same window for twenty-seven years, all the time preserving faded county exhibits and traditions. I stumbled over to that corner occasionally in connection with my legal labors and, of course, speak to Miss Maggie. She always sees that I get the volume I am after and, then, has a word to say about the weather.

I have been encouraged this week by the news reports that the German forces driving into Russia are being crippled by winter conditions, and our Miss Maggie predicts "that the snow over there will keep on comin' and just plum do 'em all in . . ." Could it be that this mad-man and his Nazi army—so obsessed with evil conquest and racial prejudice might be stopped before year's end? I pray so, as I know you do. . . .

* * *

RESTING her elbows on the two lumpy pillows of her dormitory bed, Meg tried to concentrate on the latest edition of the Breezy Hill Bulletin which had arrived in the morning mail. But she had scarcely begun to read when another cramp attacked. Reflexively she doubled over to block the pain, sloshing the contents of her tea cup onto the brown coverlet. Blotting up the mess with a towel, she grimaced her impatience at her temperamental body's familiar response to stress.

Ever since she had been a child, her stomach would get upset whenever she was nervous or excited. The coming competition next Friday was probably responsible for this latest attack. She had allowed Professor Claessen to enter her in the New York State Student Festival, knowing she needed the experience if she was to become a concert pianist. Though she had cherished this dream of Mama's for so many years, she wondered if she could survive a lifetime of such grueling pressure.

Music had been an integral part of her life since childhood. She could not remember a time when it had not been there, in the beautiful melodies Mama coaxed from the keyboard, in the stories Mama told—almost like fairy tales— of the glorious life she might have had, had she not chosen to marry Papa and live at Breezy. Later, when the gift of music had blossomed and grown in her, it had been a special bond with Mama, a way she could take away Mama's disappointment and shape it into a hope.

That hope had taken her all the way to New York, to Juilliard, against Papa's strong objections. Here she had immersed herself in music—in history, in theory, in techniques that unlocked secrets she had only dreamed before. But every so often, there were treasonous moments of doubt, moments when she wondered if she had the courage and the strength to take the dream beyond the sheltering confines of the school, to embrace it fully as her own, to become one with it, no matter what the cost.

The clock on her bedside table read 10:10. Time to get herself to the practice studio. The Professor expected her to have the A Major Polonaise perfect by Saturday, and she was still having trouble with the second movement. She got up from the bed and put on her favorite white Mexican blouse and tiered skirt, in an effort to raise her sagging spirits.

"Phone call for Meg." The voice on the other end of the door belonged to Nola, the fat cellist who lived at the far end of the hall. "It's a man. Says he's your doctor."

"I'm coming," she called, rushing out of the narrow room, down the linoleum-lined hallway, to the wall phone at the top of the stairs.

"Hello," she answered breathlessly. "Is that you, David?"

"Any other doctor on your case these days?" came back the teasing response.

"No," she laughed. "But why aren't you asleep? Weren't you in Emergency all night?"

"Yep. But I had to drive for Uncle Max—he's on jury duty."

She started to say something about how he needed his sleep, how he shouldn't be driving while he was tired, but she stopped herself.

"I've got some business downtown," he continued, "around City Hall. Want to meet me for dinner on the ferry?"

The Staten Island Ferry was their special place, ever since the first night they met. She had been standing outside Carnegie Hall after a concert, getting drenched from a pouring rain when he picked her up in Uncle Max's cab. Once inside he had offered her some coffee from the thermos he carried on the front seat. The next thing she knew, they were driving around Central Park with the meter turned off, talking as if they had known one another for years.

She wasn't sure how they'd ended up at the ferry but she thought it was because she'd said she hadn't ever really thought of Manhattan being an island. The next thing she knew, the cab was whizzing downtown. The rain stopped, and soon they were on the ferry, holding hands and singing Cole Porter songs.

"Hey, Princess," he said, interrupting her, "how about it? Want to have dinner?"

"Love to, doctor," she laughed. "What time?"

"Six o'clock. Meet you at the usual spot by the gate. You'll know me by the red rose in my teeth."

She laughed again and said goodbye, then hurried back to her room to get ready for the long day ahead. As she brushed her long, thick black hair in front of the bureau mirror, she wondered what business David might have around City Hall. Maybe it had to do with his state medical license.

She paused for a moment and stared at her smiling reflection, then chanted out loud, "Mirror, mirror on the wall, aren't I the luckiest girl of all!"

As she stood shivering on the ferry pier, she hugged the sleeves of her thin yellow cardigan. The night air was chillier than she had expected, and she wished she had worn her raincoat. David was late, which wasn't like him at all, and she was beginning to worry that something might have happened.

Her back ached from the weight of the package she was carrying, so she shifted the paper shopping bag from her right hand to her left. She was tired but satisfied from her long day at the piano, relieved she had finally conquered the Chopin composition.

It was a particularly intoxicating triumph, for she felt that Chopin was the greatest master of the keyboard, the composer who best expressed her secret soul. When she played Chopin's music, she felt like a collaborator, and not just an instrument, for he seemed to invite her to pour out her heart, to give way to her private dreams and longings.

Finally she saw him, her David, moving through the crowd lining up for the ferry—her tall, handsome, dark-haired man, wearing his familiar black leather jacket, and waving a red rose. Moments later he was standing before her, bowing and offering the flower. "Did you recognize me, or was I just a face in the crowd?" he teased.

"Never a face in the crowd," she said emphatically. "Never." She took the rose, smelled it appreciatively, then smiled and presented him with the shopping bag. "Now here's a present for you."

"What's this?" He frowned, but she could tell from his voice that he was touched. "I told you—no more presents,

Remember?" David was fiercely proud about his limited financial means and very defensive about the many surprises she enjoyed showering on him.

"Take it," she insisted, pushing the parcel into his arms. "And come on—I don't want to miss my dinner." The ferry bell clanged a warning, and the crowd pushed towards the dock, sweeping them along before he could protest again.

Hand in hand they ran onto the ferry, racing for the hot dog stand in the center of the closed middle deck. Flopping down on a bench, she said: "Come on, come on, open your present."

He ripped open the brown-paper wrappings and stared, mystified, at the roll of red plaid material. "What is it?" he asked.

"It's a bedspread! I stitched it myself," she explained, helping him unfold the fabric so he could fully appreciate it. "Without a sewing machine."

"I thank you. And my bed thanks you." He hugged her close, nibbling her neck with kisses.

She pulled away a bit. It was so against her upbringing to engage in what her father would call "public displays of intimacy." But David was irresistible, and soon she relaxed and melted into his arms. "How about it, doctor?" she whispered against his chest after a few sweet moments. "Where's that dinner you promised me?"

"I always keep my promises," he said solemnly, as he got up and took a place in the line at the hot dog stand.

She watched him, enjoying as she always did the strong lines of his broad forehead, the Roman cast of his nose, the sensual fullness of his lips. After he ordered their dinner, he turned around, and she expected his eyes to meet hers, his mouth to lift in a smile. But instead he was staring blankly out over the water, and his face held an expression of sadness.

Maybe he had a bad night at the hospital, she thought. Maybe someone had been brought in horribly maimed. Maybe someone had died.

When he brought their food back to the bench, she looked up at him tenderly. "Just what we both need," she said brightly. "Nothing like a good, messy hot dog to fix whatever ails you. Right, doctor?"

Nodding absently, he took a large bite. "Right."

Silently they ate the hot dogs dripping with mustard and relish and looked out the open windows onto the water, as the Statue of Liberty floated into view.

"When my folks came to this country from Vienna," he said, "they both cried the first time they saw that lady. Mom told me that when I was six years old. On my first day of school. I guess she thought it would help me know how lucky I was."

She nodded seriously, aware once again of the vast differences in their backgrounds, aware that so much of what she'd taken for granted in her world was new and precious to David and his family. He had told her, during that first taxi-date, how his parents had emigrated to the States during World War I, as the Austro-Hungarian Empire was crumbling, leaving their beloved Austria in ruins.

"All they had was what they could carry with them," he reminisced now, swirling the coffee in his cup.

"They must have been so brave," she said softly.

"That statue meant freedom for them. And it does for me. It's reminding me that what happened today has to be, that I have to be willing to defend that freedom. To fight for it."

"Fight? What are you talking about?" she asked, puzzled and a little alarmed.

"I was called down to Whitehall Street today. For my Army physical."

"Oh, no," she whispered. "Not you, too!"

"We knew it was coming," he said gently. "We knew when I finished med school that . . ."

She could hear no more. Standing up suddenly, she felt as if she were about to suffocate and had a desperate need to fill her lungs with fresh air; to flee from what she had heard. So she ran as far as she could to the front of the boat, until a heavy iron chain stretched across the open rail stopped her. She inhaled deeply, willing herself not to cry or moan or scream—all of the things she was afraid she

would do if she allowed herself to think about what David
had just said. I am a modern woman, she reminded herself.
I'm not one of the spunsugar belles who get sick headaches
and have fainting spells. An image of her mother flashed
unbidden through her mind, and she banished it immediately, ashamed of her moment of disloyalty.

She must behave the way her father had taught her. She
must not succumb to this flood of emotion sweeping over
her. For David's sake she must not lose control, she resolved, even as two salty tears slid down her cheeks.

Suddenly, from behind, she felt David's arms circle her
waist. Holding her against the warm shelter of his body, he
rocked her gently, sharing with her the pain of the moment.

Then he turned her around so that she might face him.
"Princess," he said softly, "will you marry me before I
leave?"

"Marry?" she echoed, trembling with the cold and a
confusion of feelings. This wasn't the way she had imagined
it would be for them. She still had two years of school . . .
private personal decisions to make . . . and now there was
suddenly no more time.

"I'll be getting a small salary from the Army," he went
on, brushing her wind-tangled hair from her tear-stained
face. "It won't be much, but I'm sure we could work it out
somehow . . . if you want to . . ."

"Want to?" She clung to him tightly, as if her love could
somehow keep him there with her, always. "Oh, David, I
love you so much!"

"It would mean a lot to me," he said quietly, as if he
sensed her hesitation, "to know that you were here, waiting
for me. I know it isn't fair . . ."

"Isn't fair? What are you talking about." This was her
David, her love. She would not lose him now. Resolutely
she pushed aside a flickering thought of Mama, telling herself that her circumstances were quite different. She clasped
his hands tightly in hers. "I want to be your wife," she said
passionately. "The rest of it doesn't matter."

Before she knew quite what was happening, David
scooped her up, whirling her slender body in a graceful arc.

"We're getting married!" he shouted to the small group of strangers gathering to disembark from the ferry. "She said yes!"

David's joy was infectious; several of the passengers clapped. And Meg, too, laughed, putting aside the fears of a few moments before. Then her stomach lurched and she pleaded, "Put me down, David. Please."

"Okay, okay," he agreed, setting her upright on the deck and peppering her face with wet kisses. "But only if you promise not to change your mind."

"Never," she said vehemently, heaving a sigh of relief as she tried to steady herself. But though her stomach settled itself, the world continued to spin. And suddenly David's face blurred, and her knees buckled.

"Oh, my," she heard a woman say, as she sank to the ground. "The bride has fainted!"

DAVID diagnosed her "swoon," as he called it, as a case of pre-nuptial nerves, and soon they were in the cab speeding along the darkened city streets, towards the Greenwich Village restaurant of his parents.

"I hope they'll be happy for us when I tell them," he said thoughtfully. "They're a little old-fashioned, Princess. They might be a little disappointed that you aren't . . . you know . . . Jewish."

"What?" Meg was startled. She had met David's parents several times in the restaurant, and they had always been gracious. She had never dreamed they might have reservations about her relationship with David.

"I don't want you to worry about it," David said decisively. "We're going to be married, I've made up my mind. I just don't want you to feel hurt if they need a little time adjusting to the idea. Please understand, Princess. It isn't you . . . it's just that so many Jews are dying these days, and they feel so strongly about carrying on the old ways."

Meg nodded, though she didn't really understand.

"Another thing—don't say anything to them about the Army yet, okay? One big announcement at a time."

"I understand," she said quietly. Time enough for his

parents to feel what she was feeling now. Confused. Cheated. Robbed of the time she had believed they had. Time for her to finish school. Time for David to begin his career. For him to know her family, for her to know his.

The cab turned the corner of Bleecker and Thompson streets and stopped in front of the Vienna Cafe, where they often shared a meal or two on weekends. There were no lights in the curtained windows, and a "Closed" sign hung in the doorway.

"It's later than I thought," David said, as he looked down at his watch. "I guess they're upstairs."

As Meg got out of the cab, she paused by the garbage cans that lined the street and looked up at the shabby tenement buildings that had housed generations of immigrant families, as if seeing them for the first time.

"Not much like Breezy Hill, is it, Princess?" David said, taking her elbow.

Meg was touched. David had read her mind, had understood that she was unconsciously comparing the differences in the places they had called home. Not wanting him to misinterpret her thoughts, she said hastily, "So you're a city boy and I'm a country girl."

Together they walked inside 412 Thompson Street. For the first time, she walked up the two flights of stairs, through the dim, musty hallway to apartment 2C. Winking at her, David rang the doorbell.

From inside a woman's husky voice called out: "Coming, coming—just a minute."

The door was opened by Eva Steinmetz, an imposing full-breasted woman. Her navy blue dress was covered by a crisp white butcher's apron. Her thick dark hair was twisted into a heavy braid coiled at the top of her head, her smooth olive complexion flushed from the heat of her kitchen.

"Come in, come in," she invited, wiping her hands on a checkered dish towel. She kissed David warmly and smiled at Meg. "Is nice you come too."

"Where's Papa?" David asked.

"In the kitchen. We play dominoes." Eva motioned them inside. "Uncle Max, too."

Meg looked around the living room that was crammed

with overstuffed furniture upholstered in mohair and brocade and covered with crocheted antimacassars. A bowfront china closet displayed Mrs. Steinmetz's prize pieces: a porcelain demitasse service bordered in gold, a brass souvenir from the World's Fair, a miniature of the Statue of Liberty and two Dresden china cupids.

To Meg, it was an atmosphere that was very heavy and foreign, yet not unwelcoming. To her genteel eye, refined by generations of exposure to clean lines and good designs, the clutter was a little jarring. But her love for David warmed and softened her first impressions.

Turning from the room, she followed him and his mother down the long, narrow hallway to the back of the apartment. On the yellowed wallpapered walls hung photographs of countryscapes which she assumed were Austrian, and black and white souvenir pictures of places like Coney Island and Niagara Falls.

They passed two bedrooms and the bathroom, and finally, at the end of the corridor, there was the kitchen, brightly lit and beckoning with the sound of voices and a radio playing.

In the middle of the room, two bald, middle-aged men sat at a bright blue, rectangular table, playing dominoes and listening to Gabriel Heatter's evening broadcast. Mrs. Steinmetz clapped her hands and announced, "Max, Maurice, see who our David brings home."

David's father, a bear of a man with dark curly hair and flashing black eyes, stood up abruptly, jarring the game beyond retrieval. As he rushed around the table to greet her, she was struck by the striking resemblance between father and son. "Come in, Megan," he said, making the same courtly old-fashioned bow he had made the first time they had been introduced. "Please," he urged, pointing to a chair, "please sit and be comfortable."

Mrs. Steinmetz hurried to the refrigerator to find refreshments for David and his girlfriend. She began to heap some creampuffs and napoleons onto a heavy white china platter.

"So what's happening?" asked Uncle Max.

"What's happening is . . ." David began, his face serious

and composed. Then he took Meg's hand and squeezed it. "Meg's going to marry me . . . We're getting married."

Maurice sat upright in his chair, and Eva gasped, almost losing her grip on the plate of pastries. "It is so?" she asked softly. "It is so?" she repeated, her face a study in conflicted emotions.

In the silence that followed, Meg began to feel uneasy about what her prospective in-laws might be thinking but not saying. Struggling to stay calm, she concentrated on the news, on Gabriel Heatter's deep baritone voice, as it reported the German advance into France, but his words triggered a new kind of insecurity. Once David was in the Army, how long would it be before he was fighting over there?

"I think I say goodnight now." Uncle Max stood up. He picked up his jacket from the back of the chair and the cab keys from off the table. In the doorway, he clapped a hand onto David's shoulder and said heartily, "Good luck, boy. Good luck to you both."

"How about it?" David prodded his parents. "Don't you think it's great? I know this is kind of sudden. But I do have my M.D. and you've been trying to marry me off for years."

Meg suddenly felt light-headed and weak. She sank into the nearest chair, her eyes riveted on Eva's hands as they arranged and rearranged the platter of pastries.

"So you decide to marry without talking to your Mama and Papa," Mr. Steinmetz said heavily.

David cast a worried glance at Meg. "Maybe we should talk now," he said. "Inside." He stood up and shepherded his parents towards the living room. "Wait for me, Princess. Make yourself comfortable."

But it was difficult to be comfortable as she heard the rise and fall of voices arguing, as she caught phrases like "but she is not one of us" and "you will break your mother's heart." She covered her ears and tried not to listen. Then she noticed the telephone that sat on a small table under the window. Impulsively she decided to call her father, who would surely give her the support and encouragement she needed when she told him her news.

As she dialed the operator, she reminded herself that Clifton would be taken aback by the suddenness of her announcement. It was his way to plan far in advance. He might have some difficulty accepting the fact that she was no longer his little girl, especially since he had never met David. But he loved her, and he would want her to be happy. He would accept the hastiness of her marriage as another circumstance dictated by the war.

Impatiently she waited for the call to travel across the miles, down the Blue Ridge mountains to the southwest corner of Virginia. Finally she heard her father's sleepy voice answer and accept the collect call.

"Hello, Papa," she began nervously. "It's me, Meg. I'm sorry to wake you, but I have something really exciting to tell you." She took a deep breath. "It's about David. David Steinmetz. Remember my telling you about him?"

"Is he the young Jewish boy you've been seeing?" Her father was suddenly alert.

Meg flinched and when she answered, her voice had a defensive edge. "Yes . . . yes, David is Jewish." She paused and then rushed to let out her news. "Anyway, Papa, he asked me to marry him and I said yes."

It sounded all wrong when it came out. Too sudden. Suspicious almost. She knew it did. Apprehensively, she listened to the silence at the other end of the line. "Papa?" she asked, "are you still there?"

"I'm here," came the distant reply, cool and unsatisfying. She knew the tone of voice; it was the same one she had heard as a child, whenever her father was angry or disappointed.

"Did you hear what I said?" she asked, expectantly, impatient for him to respond. Bravely she started to explain again. "I'm going to get married."

"I see."

Her father was known to be a man of few words, especially at times of crisis, but this was too much. "Please," she begged, "say something."

Clifton cleared his throat. "You leave me nothing to say.

Your decision has obviously been made."

"We're in love, Papa!" She was about to burst into tears. "David is such a wonderful man. Doesn't that make it all right?"

"Love has nothing to do with it."

"Nothing to do with it?" she pleaded, her voice rising. "What do you mean?"

"The boy is not a Christian . . . I never thought I would see the day when one of my daughters would . . ." his voice cracked, "would involve herself with one of them."

Meg was stunned. Struck absolutely dumb. She could not believe what she had just heard. Her father, a man who had always prided himself on his liberal views, on his compassion and his humanity, had just damned David for being a Jew. There was nothing she could say now that would make any difference. Not even the fact that David had been drafted would matter. She hung up the telephone.

With tears streaming down her face, she ran down the hallway, through the living room, past David and his parents and out of the apartment.

David caught up with her on the street. She was leaning against a cafe window, sobbing and trying to catch her breath.

"What's wrong? What happened?" he asked.

"Everything's wrong," she choked out, unable to look him in the face.

"Let's talk about it," he said softly, circling an arm around her shoulders. "We'll go to the park."

Silently they walked the two short blocks to the northeast corner of Washington Square where a crippled newspaper vendor called to David as they passed. "Hey, doc—when you comin' back to the old neighborhood? Lots of sick folks waitin' here for you."

Without breaking pace, he waved and called back, "Another time, Buzz."

The park was crowded with people enjoying the mild autumn night. They walked in silence until they found an empty bench to the left of the massive arch that dominated the park.

"My father doesn't approve of our marriage," she blurted out, throwing up her arms in disgust. "Because you're Jewish."

"I guess we do have some problems," he said quietly.

"That's an understatement," she sighed heavily, slumping down on the bench.

"I should have spoken to him first," David said reflectively. "I should have asked his permission to marry you. Maybe if I call tomorrow and talk to him . . ."

She stood up and started to pace, fists clenched, tears streaming down her lovely face. "I can't believe it . . . I just can't . . . My father is a fraud . . . a narrow-minded, bigoted fraud. And your parents hate me!"

"Easy now, easy." David gathered her close and stroked her hair as she sobbed out her pain and disillusionment on his shoulder. "Nobody hates you, Princess. I told you— my parents just took it for granted that I would marry somebody Jewish. But they can't make that choice for me. They'll come around. And so will your father. I've been up against this kind of thing before, sweetheart. We can't let it throw us. Your father loves you. I'm sure he'll change his mind for your sake."

Meg wanted to believe what he was saying, but her mind was racing ahead. How would the rest of the family react? Emily hadn't made any negative remarks about David, but Charlotte would surely be a disaster. She felt as if she and David were all alone, isolated by their love from everyone they'd cared for. "No, David," she said fiercely. "It won't be over so easily. Don't pretend with me. It's just beginning."

THE next morning Meg stirred before the alarm went off, awakened by the all-too-familiar churning of her stomach. As she jumped out of bed and ran to the bathroom, she cursed the "delicate nature" that made her body so vulnerable.

She knelt over the porcelain toilet, retching, trying to take some comfort from the fact that the pressures of the concert would be over in just six days.

When she was able to stand, she turned the taps on full force and stepped under the shower. She closed her eyes and steadied her slender body against the force of the water, willing it to lighten her spirits, wishing it could wash away the problems that burdened her very soul.

She reached for thoughts of David, of the wedding they had planned last night. City Hall, next Saturday. She had always dreamed of white lace and red roses in a candlelit church, of her father, solemn and proud as he took her down the aisle . . .

No! she reminded herself sharply. There weren't going to be any childhood dreams come true, not with a civil ceremony in a city building in a two-year-old linen suit, the only white thing she owned. Her family would not be there to celebrate what should be the happiest day of her life.

She stepped out of the shower and wrapped herself in a towel. She looked at her reflection in the mirror. "Why?" she demanded vehemently. "Why?" She stared intently into her own green eyes, enormous and vivid in her pinched white face, but there were no answers. And Meg knew that her childhood had come to an end.

IN the high-ceilinged, ornately furnished music room facing Central Park, Meg waited nervously for her Saturday morning lesson with Professor Claessen to begin. As usual, the professor's wife had placed a pot of coffee and a plate of sweet buns on a small table in the corner.

Usually Meg enjoyed the second breakfasts at the Claessens, appreciating the opportunity to collect herself. This morning, she didn't dare eat or drink anything. Instead she shuffled the sheet music on the stand of the rosewood grand piano, then sat staring into space, reviewing again the traumatic events of the night before.

"Good morning, Liebchen."

Meg jumped. "Good morning, sir."

The professor bowed stiffly, then strode across the room. "How has Herr Chopin been treating you?"

"His sharp progressions are tricky," she answered succinctly, "but I think I've got them."

"Let's see, shall we?" the tall, aristocratic man said, taking his usual observation position in the curve of the piano. Handsomely dressed as always, he wore a black velvet jacket and a maroon silk cravat and carried the ivory baton that had been given to him by the Munich Symphony shortly before he and his wife had fled the Nazis.

He rapped the baton lightly against the piano and raised it gracefully. On cue, she placed her hands on the keys, as she had been taught. She closed her eyes and silently counted out three measures of the composition. She looked up, and on the downsweep of the baton, began to play.

The A Major Polonaise, opus 40, "Le Militaire," had been composed on Majorca when Chopin was living with George Sand. It was filled with the composer's yearning for the Poland of his childhood days, for the days before the Russian conquest. As Meg's fingers traveled across the keyboard, she raced back in memory to the mountain countryside of Russell County, to the innocent, carefree days before her Mama had died.

In the second movement, which represented the fall of Poland, the chords pounded at dissonants, and the tempo became restless, relentless. Gone were the sentimental pastoral themes. As Meg hammered out the musical representations of destruction, her control faltered, her fingers stumbled.

"Stop," the professor commanded, tapping the piano top. "You do not concentrate. We begin the second movement again."

He was right. She had not been concentrating. She took a deep breath and started again. But she was shaken by the reprimand, and though she tried to keep her mind on the music, her private feelings of despair and confusion took over. As the second movement became more complicated, her fingers felt frozen and unresponsive.

"Concentrate. Concentrate," the professor demanded, pacing behind the piano bench.

"I can't," she cried out. "I just can't!" She stared in frustration at her fingers, which seemed lumpish and heavy on the keyboard. "I'm sorry. I'm terribly sorry," she whispered, gathering up the sheet music.

The professor put a kindly hand on her shoulder and sat down beside her on the bench, his gray eyes filled with concern. "What is troubling you, Liebchen? Until I understand, you and Herr Chopin will not make beautiful music."

"David . . . You know David," she began, pausing to collect her thoughts, grateful that the Claessens knew and liked him. During the summer, she and David had spent several long, wonderful evenings in this apartment, enjoying the conversation and companionship of the older couple. "He asked me to marry him last night and I said yes . . . and everybody's being terrible because he's Jewish and I'm not!"

"So Liebchen," the professor nodded, taking the music gently from Meg's hands and putting it back on the stand. "Then we shall postpone Herr Chopin today and go into the drawing room."

Dutifully Meg followed him out of the music room, down the parquet-floored hallway to the double doors of the drawing room. He rapped twice. "Come in," Mrs. Claessen called out.

As the professor held the door for Meg, Mrs. Claessen rose from an armchair by the fireplace where she had been stitching on a large tapestry frame. "Do come in, child," the dark-haired, regal woman invited.

"Thank you," Meg said, walking slowly across the richly woven oriental rug, into the handsome book-lined room.

"Rebecca," the professor said to his wife, "my Meg has a problem."

It was the first time he had ever said 'my Meg' and the endearing familiarity of the words comforted her, as she took a seat on the pale blue velvet couch that faced the fireplace.

The professor walked over the hearth and placed his baton on the mantle. "You are aware that I am of German origin," he began. "I was born near Munich. My family line goes back, unbroken for many generations." He stared down at the logs burning in the fireplace. "Ironically, mine is the lineage which Herr Hitler reveres so much these dreadful days."

Only recently had Meg ever given any thought to the

professor's German ancestry, and that was only because she had heard a nasty rumor at school, to the effect that some of his relatives might be Nazis. Always before, she had thought of him simply, romantically, as a noble compatriot of Brahms, Beethoven and Mahler.

Meg had been listening so intently to the professor that she was scarcely aware that Mrs. Claessen left the room, until she returned, carrying a red lacquer Chinese tray, laden with a silver coffee pot and three dark-patterned cups and saucers. Placing the tray on the long low table in front of the couch, she finished her husband's narrative: "And I, my dear, am a Jew."

"Oh my..." was all Meg could say, feeling foolish because she had never stopped to consider why the professor had left his homeland so suddenly.

"So you see," Mrs. Claessen continued, as she poured the coffee, "we understand your situation very well." With silver tongs, she dropped two sugar cubes into a cup of black coffee and handed it to her husband. "We know it is difficult for families, for everyone, particularly in the beginning."

"It will always be difficult," the professor interrupted. "Let us not mislead the child." To Meg he said, "At this moment, my people are murdering hers, in our very homeland."

Rebecca Claessens' refined patrician face blanched at her husband's words. Putting down her cup, she touched his wrist. "We are not talking of war now, dear," she said quietly. "We are talking of marriage. The war does not belong in this conversation."

"Yes, it does," Meg protested. "David just got called for his Army physical. He'll probably be drafted any minute." Shakily, she put her coffee cup down. "That's why we're getting married so quickly. In a week actually."

"Then there is much to do," Rebecca said, taking Meg's hands in hers. "But first, and most important, you must understand what it means to be David's wife. You stand with him now, before anyone else. Remember that... always."

* * *

SUNDAY night at seven o'clock, David phoned her at the dorm. He had switched emergency-room duty with a friend, so that he could have a free evening. Could Meg come uptown? Even though she had an exam in Compositional Techniques the following morning, she didn't hesitate to say yes. She wanted every minute she could have with him, every precious moment, even if it meant doing poorly in what was already her worst subject.

When she arrived at Duke's, the favorite hangout of Columbia Presbyterian's young doctors, and their usual meeting place, David was already there, leaning against the brick wall by the entrance, studying a textbook under the light of a street lamp.

"Hey, Doctor," she called, "how about a recess with your favorite patient?"

"Princess!" he greeted her, shutting the book and taking her in his arms. "Let's skip Duke's and go to my place tonight. I have a surprise for you."

"Okay," she agreed easily, grateful that they now had a place they could be alone. Hand in hand they made their way down the tenement-lined streets, towards the apartment David had inherited from another med student at the end of the summer. The best thing about the apartment was that it was four blocks from Presbyterian Hospital. As a living space, it was small and dismal, furnished with a sagging bed, an erratic hot plate and a big, zinc bathtub next to the kitchen sink.

"We're home," David said, as he unlocked the peeling metal door. It was the first time he had referred to the place as theirs. "Wait here a minute," he instructed, leaving her in the hallway.

She wondered what he was doing and hoped he hadn't spent any of his meager taxi tips on anything extravagant. In a few minutes, she became aware of a soft glow radiating from the apartment through the partially open door.

"Come in, Princess," he invited.

All around the room, on every possible surface—the

broken-legged table by the window facing the alley, the leaky oversized refrigerator, the small bedside stand she had found at the Salvation Army store, even along the stained kitchen sink were white votive candles in small glass cups. Their flames made flickering shadows, little bits of magic and enchantment to soften the harsh edge of reality.

"Oh, David," she whispered, "it looks beautiful."

"Your sweater, madame," he said, as he gallantly lifted it from her shoulders. "Will you come this way, please?"

Smiling, she allowed him to escort her the next few steps inside. Spread across the table was a white cloth, a hospital sheet, and at its center sat a Columbia Presbyterian metal pail holding a bottle of champagne surrounded with chunks of ice. Two new tulip-shaped glasses stood in waiting, off to one side.

"Oh, David," she sighed, feeling very much like the 'princess' he always said she was. "This is wonderful! You're wonderful!"

Pleased with the success of his surprise, David began to work on opening the bottle, humming the wedding march as he did. "Make a wish!" he shouted as the cork flew across the room.

She closed her eyes and tried to imagine a pretty fairy-tale picture, of the kind that had once filled her head. But none would come, and she wondered if that meant she was truly grown up. She opened her eyes, and a trickle of tears rolled down her cheeks.

"Hey, hey, what's this?" He tilted her chin upward and kissed her nose. "As your doctor, I forbid this kind of thing. Here, I prescribe champagne for whatever makes you sad." He handed her a glass and lifted his own. "To you, Princess. To my one and only love."

"To you, David," she whispered. "Forever and ever."

"Now," he said, after they had finished the champagne, "may I have the pleasure of a dance with my beautiful bride?"

"But there isn't any music," she protested.

"Ah, but there is." He began to hum a Strauss waltz, as he spun her around the room.

Laughing in spite of herself, she joined in. They drank

more champagne and tried a two-step shuffle, giggling and bumping into furniture and then falling into bed.

"I thought about you all day," he whispered against her neck. "And I wanted you so much. Soon you'll be mine all the time. All mine."

"Yes, I will," she murmured contentedly, yielding to the warmth of his hands as he stroked her back, kneading away the day's tensions.

"Is it safe?" he whispered. "Could we?"

David had taught her how to calculate her fertile days, but Meg had lost count. Her pre-concert nerves had made her period late, so she really didn't know where she was in her menstrual cycle. It didn't seem important somehow, now that they were getting married in a week.

"Do you want to?" David asked softly as he tenderly brushed his hand through her hair. "It's all right if you don't. We can wait."

They had only made love once before, about a month ago, the first night David had gotten the keys to the apartment. They had found themselves alone in a place that was almost their own, and it had just happened. She remembered how there had been no sheets on the sagging bed then, and how rough the old mattress had felt against her back.

"I don't want to wait anymore," she answered, "I want you too. I'm not afraid." Putting aside her moral training of how young girls were supposed to behave, she reached up and began unbuttoning his white jacket.

When they were both naked, he leaned on one elbow and studied her body. With his long, strong fingers he slowly traced the contours of her limbs and torso.

She closed her eyes, feeling her love for him blossom tender and rich, filling her with wonder at the miracle that had brought them together in a world filled with so many people. She shifted her body, raising it over his, guiding him into her, feeling him swell inside her, hearing his breath catch as they rocked together, slowly at first, then more urgently, as they reached hungrily for a final shuddering wave of passion.

When they were quiet again, Meg reluctantly moved away from David's body and forced herself to look at the clock on the table. Forty-five minutes till curfew.

But David was fast asleep. She stroked his face with her fingers—then stopped. Suddenly she knew, with an absolute certainty, that she was carrying David's child. That was why she was sick every morning, just as Charlotte and Em had been. How stupid she had been not to think of it before!

She took David's hand and held it so tightly that he woke up. "What's wrong, sweetheart? What is it?"

She couldn't tell him, not just yet. "Nothing," she lied. "I just love you so much."

IN the days that followed, Meg forced herself to concentrate on her music and her school work. She would not give in to thoughts of her father, her possible pregnancy or her disapproving in-laws. David had assured her they would attend the wedding, but that was all he could say.

Finally it was Friday afternoon, the day of the concert. After a morning of classes and a final practice with Professor Claessen, Meg took a long walk through Central Park. As she strolled the windy paths, she wondered if she had made the right decision to keep the news of her marriage from her sisters and even Aunt Rose Mary. But after the blow of her father's reaction, she felt she simply could not risk any more disapproval, any more rejection.

She was still bewildered, for she had never seen any evidence of his prejudice before. But then there hadn't been any Jews in West Grove. As she searched her memory, all she could recall were her father's stories about Jewish carpetbaggers who had come south after the Civil War and cheated some of his relatives in the Appomattox area.

When she arrived back at the dorm, it was almost five. She was greeted by Miss Jean Barnes, the horsey-looking dean who was in charge of resident students. "Megan," she said crisply, "would you please step into my office for a moment?"

Meg followed, wondering if she was in for a tally of her late demerits. Miss Barnes went to her desk, which was decorated with ivory objects brought back from a sabbatical in India. She opened a drawer and took out an envelope marked "Special Delivery."

"I believe it's from your father," she said.

As Meg took the "Whittaker & Son" envelope, she saw that her name and address had been typed on her father's machine, which always hiccuped the letter "e." She winced.

"I hope it isn't bad news," Miss Barnes offered solicitiously.

Not wanting to share her problems with a stranger, Meg shook her head and hurried away, to the safety of her room. Sitting on the bed, she tore open the envelope and started to read. It was a short letter, blocked out in business form.

28 October 1942

Dear Megan Rose:

After considerable deliberation, I am forced to inform you that I will not be present at your wedding.

I cannot sanction your choice of a life partner. I believe you are making a rash and ill-considered decision you will regret.

I close urging that you reconsider your plans to marry and spare yourself and your family from future heartache.

Your father,
J. C. Whittaker

Two hours later, she stood in the wings of the Carnegie Hall stage, trying to concentrate on the deep breathing that would relax her. Onstage, a violinist, a music major from Columbia, was playing a Paganini rhapsody. His performance was conscientious but labored, and he had slurred the introduction of the allegro movement, a slip that would surely take him out of the running for the prize. He was the fifth contestant who had made a technical mistake, so she knew she still had a chance. A good chance, for none of the other contestants had been truly outstanding and she would be the last to perform.

"I've got to win," she whispered to herself, walking on

tiptoes towards the stage door, massaging her fingers as she did. She and David desperately needed the $500 prize money to set up housekeeping, for Papa's letter made it clear they could expect no future help from him. It was terribly unfair, she thought, since her sisters had received a generous dowry when they had married.

No doubt the small allowance her father sent each month would stop now, too. Certainly David's parents were in no position to help them financially even if they wanted to. She had to win.

Straightening her long black velvet skirt, Meg prayed to her Sunday School God, the God with the white beard and the Santa Claus face, who could, if He chose, allow her to play the Chopin sonata brilliantly. Thinking of God in His heaven made her think again of Mama, of how proud she would be if she could see her little Megan Rose today.

Mama had started her music lessons when Meg was five. Many times she had been told the story of how one spring morning she had been crouched under the piano bench, one of her favorite places, while Mama played. When Mama had returned to the kitchen for a cup of tea, Meg had crawled out, climbed up onto the bench, and with her right hand pecked out the Brahms theme which her mother had been playing. Her Mama had been so astounded and delighted that she had rushed out the door and driven straight down the hill, straight to the courthouse, insisting that Clifton be summoned at once to hear the news. It was a story most of the town knew, for Mama had been so excited that she had driven to town in her pink satin dressing gown.

The sound of applause broke her reverie. Crossing the fingers on both hands, she hurried back to the wings, to the appointed position of those waiting to go on. Her heart was pounding as she listened anxiously until the master of ceremonies called her name and announced that she would play Chopin's A Major Polonaise.

The concert hall seemed chillingly silent and ominously huge as she walked across the stage, yet suddenly she felt calm as she faced the grand piano. Once in front of the bench she made a low curtsy to the audience before she sat down. "You play for others," Mama had always said, "so be courteous and greet them before you begin."

She placed her fingers on the keys, closed her eyes and took the ritualistic three deep breaths and focused her mind totally on Herr Chopin and his composition. Then she lifted her head, flung back her long black hair and struck the first chord with all the power she possessed.

This was her piece of music now and she felt intoxicated with it, enveloped by its majesty. On and on she played with passion, savoring the melody in her head as it translated through her fingers and onto the keyboard. And as always happened when she was playing well, she forgot where she was, became possessed, as her imagination made her one with Herr Chopin's heartfelt singing of his love for his Polish homeland.

Finally the music built to its rousing, triumphant conclusion, and the last tinkling chords of the étude faded into the air. There was a breathless silence before the applause began and in that instant, she knew that she had won.

She stood as if in a daze, walked the few steps to the edge of the stage and made a low bow, "like a swan," as her Mama had rehearsed her so many years ago.

As she stood upright again, she saw David in the front row clapping wildly and shouting, "Bravo! Bravo!" at the top of his lungs. The sight of him brought tears of joy to her eyes. Without thinking, she blew him a kiss across the footlights. Then, embarrassed at making such an intimate gesture in public, she ran from the stage.

But the thundering applause called her back, and the rest of the evening was a brightly colored haze: the Philharmonic concert master complimenting her on a "dazzling" performance, Professor Claessen being summoned onstage, and finally, the coveted check being placed in her hand.

SLEEP was impossible that night. Her mind raced like a roller coaster, rising triumphantly with the memory of her victory, then plunging downward with the bitter recollection of her father's letter; the written statement of his bigotry and betrayal. She tossed restlessly, whiplashed by her own dark thoughts. Until finally from sheer exhaustion, shortly after the clock at St. Ignatius of Ninth Street struck five, she fell asleep.

It seemed only moments later that she was awakened by someone knocking at her door. "Go 'way," she pleaded groggily. "Let me sleep."

"Wake up, lazybones." The voice was a familiar one.

Then she heard the doorknob turn and the door open. Poking her head out from under the covers, she saw her older sister, standing in the doorway, carrying a suitcase and a large paper bag.

"Emily!" She blinked in disbelief. "Is that really you? What are you doing here?"

"Howard decided that someone from the family had to give you away. And since he wasn't available, he put me on the train." She paused to drop the suitcase at the closet door. "So here I am."

"I can't believe it!" Meg sat up and hugged her sister. "I just can't believe it . . . Oh, I was feeling so alone."

"You're not alone anymore." Emily kissed her sister's forehead affectionately, stroking her long black hair. Then she took off her brown gaberdine coat and hung it in the closet. "Look what I've brought you," she said, offering the paper bag. "I stopped at the store on the corner and picked up coffee and sweet rolls. So rise and shine, little bride."

"Thanks, Em," she said, though the idea of coffee brought a pang of queasiness to her stomach. She reached for the Japanese kimono that was draped over the bottom of her bed, hoping she wouldn't throw up.

"I called Papa yesterday and he told me," Emily reported, placing the bag on the cluttered desk top.

"So that's how you knew." Meg's voice quivered. "I got a letter from him . . ."

"He said he had written and explained his position. A point of view which Howard and I obviously do not share." Emily's tone was brisk and matter-of-fact. "Have some coffee. You look like you need it."

Meg took the cardboard container and sipped the bitter black coffee cautiously, grateful that her stomach was still under control, comforted that Emily had found out and come. Because of the seven years' difference in their ages, Emily had almost been a second mother, and her presence now made Meg feel that everything would be all right. Emily would make it right, just as she had when Meg had been a little girl.

"I didn't know how much I needed you until now . . . I was afraid to call," she confessed. "It means a lot to me that you're here."

"I know," Emily nodded. "That's why I came."

The two sisters looked at one another directly, acknowledging for an instant the bond of blood and affection between them.

"Can you believe it?" Meg asked, trying to make her voice light, as she looked away. "I'm getting married! Can you believe it, Em?"

"Just barely," Emily said wryly. "I can still remember changing your diapers, you know."

"Oh, no." Meg grinned. "Here we go again . . ."

Emily laughed and took a big swallow of coffee. "Now, speaking of clothing . . . Have you bought your dress? I hope not, because we want to give you your wedding outfit."

"Oh, Em. That would be wonderful. I want to look so beautiful for David, but I couldn't afford anything new." Meg hugged her knees with her arms. "Oh, Em, you're going to love him. I can't wait for you to meet him. He's so handsome and smart and funny . . ." She paused to get her breath, stabbed again by her father's rejection. "It's so awful that Papa won't give him a chance."

"I know," Emily soothed. "I know, Meg. Try not to think about it."

"I wish I could have taken David to Breezy. If Papa had met him, he couldn't act like this, I just know it. But there wasn't time . . ." She put her coffee cup down on the window sill and stared out at the busy street. "You see, David's been drafted."

"Does Papa know that?"

"How could he know anything? He wouldn't listen . . . He closed his ears and his heart to me."

"That won't last," Emily soothed, putting an arm around Meg's shoulders. "You're his baby girl, you know, and this was quite a shock for him..."

"A shock for him?" Meg retorted bitterly. "What about for me?"

EMILY and Meg spent the day shopping on Fifth Avenue. That evening David picked them up in Uncle Max's taxi and took them to the Horn & Hardart automat on 57th Street, for what he jokingly called "our pre-wedding feast." As Meg had predicted, David and Emily took to one another at once. No mention was made about the absence of Meg's father and David's parents, but the missing family members cast a heavy shadow on the celebration.

As she drifted off to sleep that night, Meg shared aloud what she was thinking. "I'll never forgive Papa, you know ...I'll never forgive him."

Saturday morning she was awakened by a body-wrenching wave of nausea that sent her racing for the bathroom. When she returned to her room, Emily was pacing, her face full of concern. "Are you all right?" she asked. "Do you think we should call a doctor?"

"I'm okay, really. This has been going on for a while, but it goes away in a couple of hours." As soon as the words were out of her mouth, she knew she had said too much. Not even with her favorite sister could she share her suspicion that she was pregnant. "It's nothing to worry about."

"You've been like this for a while?" Emily asked, her alarm growing. "And this happens every morning..."

"I'm sure I'm all right. Really. Don't you remember? I've always had a nervous stomach, and you must admit I've had a lot to be nervous about."

"Promise me you'll see a doctor anyway," Emily insisted.

"I will, I will," Meg laughed. "Don't forget, I'll be marrying one in just..." She looked at the clock. "Oh, no! Em! I forgot to set the alarm—it's 10:15."

Emily took over, calming and soothing her sister, helping Meg into the peach-colored Chinese silk dress they had found on the clearance rack at Saks. While Meg fixed her hair and makeup, Emily quickly slipped on her own dress.

As she pinned her hair into a twist, Emily caught a glimpse of herself, towering over Meg's elfin loveliness, in her green "professor's wife" crepe. For an uncharacteristic moment, she wished Howard were here, to make her feel less dowdy. Immediately she scolded herself for such vanity, especially on her sister's wedding day.

Within minutes the two sisters were racing from the dorm room, like Alice's rabbit, praying for a miracle that would get them to City Hall on time. When they reached the street, a fall shower had begun, evaporating all the free taxis from sight. For fifteen minutes they waited in vain. In desperation, Meg finally flagged down a Sunbeam bread truck and pleaded for a ride, so that she would not miss her own wedding.

"Hop aboard." The driver grinned. "And don't worry, lady, he'll wait for you." The driver barreled through the city streets in record time, but it was ten after eleven when he deposited Meg and Emily at City Hall.

They searched the huge lobby, but there was no sign of David. When they thought to ask at the Information Desk, the clerk informed them that the eleven o'clock Whittaker-Steinmetz wedding was taking place in room 217.

They ran up the marble staircase to the second floor. The hallway was crowded with couples waiting to be married. Most of the bridegrooms were in uniform. But it was the accompanying families Meg noticed: mothers sniffling into handkerchiefs, fathers proudly patting sons and fussing over daughters.

"No time for that now." Emily said kindly, understanding exactly what Meg was feeling. She pointed to the ladies' room. "Better get yourself prettied up in a hurry. I'll find 217 and make them wait."

"Right." Meg headed for the restroom, where she blotted her hair and stockings with paper towels. Fortunately her cape had protected her dress from the rain. Quickly she brushed her hair into the new upswept style Emily had helped her create last night. With her halo of baby's breath, she anchored the veil that covered her face. She was ready to be married.

Holding her orchid bouquet, a gift from the Claessens,

high above her head, she made her way through the crush
of people. Taking a deep breath, she opened the door and
whispered to herself: "Goodbye, Megan Rose Whittaker.
Hello, Mrs. David Steinmetz."

The small room was painted a drab institutional green.
Near a wooden lectern, a tall thin man in a gray suit paced
impatiently. "I simply cannot wait any longer," he said.
"We are twelve minutes late and others are waiting."

"I'm here," Meg called softly. Hearing her voice, the
small wedding party—David's parents, the Claessens, Emily and her beloved David—turned, murmuring appreciative
comments about her appearance. But it was only David she
saw, her wonderful, handsome David, looking like a fairy-
tale prince in his new dark suit and white tie.

"Hello, Princess." He smiled.

She blushed and dropped her head, suddenly feeling giddy
and almost faint. Professor Claessen hurried to a portable
phonograph, and moments later, Mendelssohn's Wedding
March filled the small anonymous space, transforming it
into a sacred place.

With slow pausing steps, Emily walked to her sister.
Solemnly, she offered her arm: "May I, Megan Rose, do
the honors?"

Caught up in the pomp and majesty of the music, Meg
took Emily's arm and glided across the bare wooden floor,
just as if she were in a red-carpeted cathedral. As the music
crescendoed into its final chorus, the civil servant, his voice
sharp and impatient, began: "We are gathered here today
to unite this couple in the bonds of holy matrimony . . ."

4

Shipping Out
November 1942

My Dear Children,

Reverend Lowell gave an unusually fine sermon this crisp November morning in our Methodist-Episcopal Church in the vale. His text was from the Old Testament, the book of Isaiah—which I will get to directly. It was a large flock gathered to hear the words of his ministry, though more of our menfolks are gone from the congregation than we are wont to count. After the services, there was a special organ recital by Miss Esther Quillen of Glade Springs, Virginia, honoring the Women's Missionary Society's ongoing crusade for war orphans across the world. . . .

So as we gather around our separate tables at this season of Thanksgiving, this American holiday which our forefathers sanctified as the day of giving thanks for the bounty of our great land, let us remember the words of the prophet Isaiah and trust that it will not be long until:

"They shall beat their swords into plowshares, and their spears into pruninghooks; and nation shall not

81

*lift up sword against nation; neither shall they learn
to war anymore."*

"Now, Roland," Clifton said sternly, as he unfolded his
napkin and prepared to begin the evening meal, "I don't
want you to give Emily and Howard any trouble. These are
hard times for them; do not add to their problems.

"Yes, sir." Roland nodded obediently. Lately he had
concluded that the best way to handle his father was to agree
with everything he said. He had no intention of adding to
his sister's problems, and he resented the fact that Clifton
thought it necessary to caution him.

He was thrilled and surprised at the chance to spend
Thanksgiving at Fort Bragg. When his father had decided
to go up to Lexington for a three-day Washington and Lee
Alumni Law Seminar, Emily had unexpectedly invited him
to visit them in North Carolina. None of the other West
Grove guys had ever been on an Army base, so he was
planning to take lots of pictures with his Kodak.

"Son," Clifton said, alerting Roland to pay total attention, for he only called him "son" when something serious
was at hand.

"Sir?" Roland responded, putting down his fork and wiping his mouth with his napkin.

"There's going to be a special meeting over at the Draft
Board tonight, and I want you to come along."

"Yes, sir." Roland nodded, trying to act nonchalant. He
had never been allowed at the Board office, except to unload
cartons or to move furniture. The place had been declared
off limits to him.

"There might be some trouble, so I want you to stand
watch."

"Stand watch?" Roland tried to contain his excitement.
"What kind of trouble, sir?"

"There's a young boy from Hyders Gap who's been
drafted. He doesn't want to serve."

"Doesn't want to serve?" Roland repeated incredulously.
"What kind of guy is he?"

"He seems to fit into the C-O classification," Clifton

answered matter-of-factly. "Men who have a conscientious objection to war."

"Conscientious objection to war." Roland snorted his disdain. "Jesus Christ!"

"I will not have you taking the Lord's name in vain!" Clifton said sharply. "How many times must I remind you?" He pushed his chair back from the table and stood up. "On second thought, perhaps it's not a wise idea for you to be there tonight."

"Please, sir," Roland pleaded, following his father out of the kitchen. "Let me come. You can depend on me."

Grudgingly, Clifton allowed his son to accompany him. Roland's task was to stand guard in the hallway outside the office, in case any angry townspeople attempted to interfere with the proceedings. A *Gazette* editorial had reported Zachary Mullin's position, with an explanation of the validity and merits of a pacifist's position. But the eloquent piece had failed in its intent and had aroused much anger and resentment. There was muttered talk around town that the boy should be taught a lesson about patriotism and manhood.

As summoned, all six Board members appeared for the special session that night, even Claude Peck and Joseph Newhard from Castlewood. The West Grove group consisted of Clifton, Nelbert Smithers, who taught English at the high school, Bernard Pyle of Pyle's Store, Jesse Combs who ran the Roseland Theatre, and Walter Burns. Somberly, all too aware of the difficult task before them, the men settled themselves around the table in the conference room.

The boy whose status was under question would be the last to arrive. Because his folks were poor—his father was a coal miner—the Board had provided him with bus fare for the twenty-two-mile trip across the county, and with a night's lodging at Miss Minnie's Boarding House.

Roland had been instructed to greet the boy courteously and to stay alert for any possible disturbance. At the first sign of trouble he was to ring the bell by the door three times and then run to the sheriff's office for help.

At 8:30, he heard footsteps on the stairs. Impatiently, he waited for the miserable coward who refused to fight for his country, expecting to see a skinny little sissy. Instead,

a tall, rugged-looking young man in shabby but clean overalls appeared. With him was a wizened old woman wearing
a yellow-flowered dress, made of the same feed sacks Bessie
used for her aprons.

When he saw Roland, Zachary Mullin took off his gray
felt hat and extended his right hand, introducing himself
and his grandmother, Mrs. Maggie Mullin. Roland ignored
the hand and pointed to the door. "They're waiting for you,"
he said brusquely.

When the Mullins were inside, Roland slipped into the
reception room, so that he might hear what was going on
while he kept an eye on the stairs.

Clifton opened the meeting by asking the boy some simple questions about his place of birth, his parents' names.
"Now, Zachary," he continued, "could you please explain
to the Board why you feel you cannot obey your country's
command."

"I don't believe in killing," came the simple answer.

"Most men don't believe in killing. Not unless they have
to," Jesse Combs said impatiently.

"It's war time, young man," said one of the men from
Castlewood. "Lots of young men have to do what they don't
want to do. Why can't you?"

"It's not God's way." The boy's voice was quiet but
strong. "The Bible says, 'Thou shalt not kill.'"

"It also says, 'An eye for an eye, and a tooth for a tooth,'
and those Nazis and Japs are murdering our boys. What
makes you think you're so high and mighty? Do you think
you're some kind of preacher?"

"Now, Bernard." Clifton's was the moderate voice. "Our
job is to question and record, not to judge, remember?"

"Ever since he was a young'un, he ain't never hurt
nothing'," the old woman spoke up. "Won't kill the hogs
his folks raise for eatin'. Ain't never raised his hand to no
one, even when they're askin' for a fight."

"Young man." It was Clifton again. "Are you aware you
could be sent to prison for refusing to serve?"

"Yessir, you told me last time. I'm not wanting to go to
prison, but if Mr. Thoreau and Mr. Gandhi did it, so can
I."

"Mr. Thoreau and Mr. Gandhi?" Clifton was startled by these references. "How in the world do you know about them?"

"My Granny taught me to read, and Mrs. Winchell, over at the library, she gives me books and newspapers."

"I for one don't give a damn what you're reading," said Nelbert Smithers. "Fact is, you're talking like a traitor, and that's that."

Suddenly Roland heard a commotion on the stairwell. Moving quickly he peered downstairs and saw a group of men armed with sticks and hoes.

"They're coming!" he shouted, slamming the door shut and locking it. Shouts rose in the hallway, demanding that the door be opened and the Mullin boy be handed over. Quickly he phoned Sheriff Boggs, and when he looked up he saw his father staring at the outer door. "Sounds bad out there," he said.

Clifton nodded gravely. "Our first responsibility, however, is to protect Mr. Mullin. He hasn't broken the law."

Roland was incredulous at this talk of law and responsibility in the face of an angry mob. "We'd better barricade the door," he urged.

Several of the Board members managed to brace Tillie's large oak desk and a file cabinet against the door, just as a hoe came through the glass pane.

Suddenly there were three gunshots. Sheriff Boggs' gravelly voice shouted: "Git! Next ones aren't goin' to miss, so git! Fast!"

Cries of "Don't shoot!" and "We're leaving" were heard, followed by a stampede of heavy footsteps down the stairs.

The Board members exhaled their relief, as they stood in the small reception area. Roland surveyed the wreckage in his father's office. Two of Clifton's prize hunting scenes had been knocked from the wall, and several chairs had been tipped over and broken. He turned to see Mullin standing alone, a look of pain and bewilderment on his face.

"Damn coward!" he shouted. "Look what you've done!" The boy bit his lip and said nothing. Infuriated, Roland lunged at Mullin, and before anyone could stop him, he slammed his clenched fist into the boy's face.

"Roland!" Clifton shouted, as Mullin staggered back, blood streaming from his nose. He grabbed his son's arm and slapped him twice. The room was suddenly quiet. "You are a disgrace," he ground out between clenched teeth. "Go home . . . now! I thought you were ready to be a man. I see I was mistaken."

Roland stared at his father's angry face for a moment, his eyes brimming with pain and bewilderment. Then he turned and left the room, his shoulders slumped in an attitude of defeat. The Board members followed, murmuring embarrassed "Good nights." Only Walter remained, gathering up his papers. "Well, J.C.," he began, intending to make a diplomatic statement that would ease the moment.

Suddenly the sound of clattering heels was heard on the stairs. Miss Jewel burst into the room. "Cliff . . . oh, Cliff," she sobbed. "Thank God you're all right!" She reached out to embrace him, then seeing Walter, she pulled back. "I heard those gunshots . . . all those people . . . I was so afraid that Cliff . . . that someone was hurt."

"I'm fine, just fine." He cleared his throat. "I do appreciate your concern . . . but there's no need to trouble yourself . . . it's all over now . . ." He took Jewel's arm gingerly and led her back towards the stairs.

"'Night, Cliff. 'Night, Mr. Burns." Reluctantly Jewel departed, leaving Clifton to face Walter's thoughtful gaze.

"It's none of my business," Walter began cautiously, "but as an old friend . . . well, I do wonder, J.C., about the . . . the suitableness of Miss Jewel . . . Don't misunderstand me now; she is a good and hard-working person, and my wife often mentions what a fine seamstress she is. But, J.C., for a man of your heritage, your standing in the community . . ."

"I appreciate your frankness," Clifton interrupted, anxious to bring the conversation to a close. "But it has been a long day, and I must get back to Breezy." He left quickly, unable to disagree with Walter's observations or to defend his relationship with Jewel.

* * *

STILL stinging from the public humiliation, Roland woke at dawn the next morning. He was eager to get on the bus to Fort Bragg, away from his father and out of town.

By the time Bessie arrived to fix breakfast, he had his bag packed and was waiting in the kitchen, pacing around the table. "Lawdy," she remarked, "you is like a wild dog dis mornin'. Whas' wrong with you, chile?"

While Bessie put on the coffee and mixed up the biscuit dough, he reported the events of the night before. "He was awful mad at me, Bessie," he concluded. "I don't know what's going to happen this morning.

"Sit, chile," she ordered, her cup of black coffee in hand. "You was wrong to hit that boy and you knows it."

Roland considered Bessie's reprimand for a moment. "So what do I do now?"

"You kin say you'se sorry, das what."

He thought again. "No, I can't. Maybe I was wrong to do what I did. But Papa shouldn't have hit me."

Bessie took in the set of his jaw, the determination in his voice. "Then you don't say nothin', chile, nothin' at all. Jes' give him time to cool down."

Promptly at 7:30, Clifton came through the swinging door, with a crisp "Good morning" that might or might not have included his son. Breakfast was a silent affair. Clifton unfolded the Richmond *Morning Herald* and remained behind the newspaper for the entire meal.

The silence continued during the ride to the bus stop. In front of the drugstore, Clifton handed him the basket that Bessie had fixed for Emily's Thanksgiving and said tersely: "I'm not sure you deserve this trip."

Roland winced, then boarded the bus, moving directly to a seat in the back. He did not look out the window or wave goodbye, so he did not see his father standing stiff and straight, staring down the road until the bus disappeared from sight. As soon as they were out of West Grove, he took out the Steve Canyon comic books he had borrowed from Buddy Pruner. He did not stop reading until the bus made its third stop in Wytheville, Virginia, where his Uncle Reginald, his mama's brother, used to live. After Elizabeth's death, Reginald had tried to persuade Clifton to send him to a military academy but his father had nixed the idea, saying that no son of his was going to be educated by military men.

Three passengers got on there, a fat woman carrying a potted plant and two boys in VPI Cadet uniforms. "Mind if we share the back regions?" the taller one asked, as he dropped his suitcase in the aisle and slid into the seat opposite Roland's.

"Can't have any fun in the front," the other boy agreed.

"Yeah, you're right," Roland said, slipping the comic books under his jacket, so he wouldn't be taken for a "kid."
"Where are you guys heading?" he asked.

"One of Uncle Sam's hotels," the taller one said, grinning and nudging his friend.

"What Jeb here means is that we're on our way to Fort Bragg. For basic training."

"Fort Bragg! Wow! Are you guys lucky!"

"Yeah," Jeb agreed, "that's what we think. Me and Hinton enlisted way back at graduation and Uncle Sam finally gave us the call."

"I'm going to enlist too," Roland said emphatically. "Only seven more months to go."

"How 'bout that," Hinton said. "This calls for a celebration." He fumbled through his duffel bag and produced a bottle in a brown bag.

"Great idea," Roland agreed, with as much sophistication as he could muster, though his drinking experience had been limited to stolen swigs of Wild Turkey from Buddy Pruner's father's liquor cabinet.

As Hinton's quart of scotch slowly disappeared, the boys became expansive, exchanging capsule histories of their lives and ambitions, forging a quick camaraderie that eased the long journey.

"I aim to get into Army Intelligence," Jeb said. "Undercover work is what I want."

"I'm not fussy," Hinton said, "I'll take whatever Uncle Sam dishes out. Just so I get to see plenty of action."

"I'm going to be a Marine myself," Roland announced,

his confidence buoyed by the alcohol. "Either land or sea is all right with me."

"How come?" Jeb asked. "How come the Marines and not the Army?"

"Marines look like real troubleshooters to me, and that's the kind of guy I am." Roland grinned and took another swig from the bottle, pleased with himself and the statement he'd just made.

"Here's to the Marines," Hinton toasted with a hearty gulp, then returned the scotch to Roland. "Finish it up, soldier."

It was late afternoon when the bus pulled into Southern Pines, the town near Fort Bragg. Roland smoothed his hair back with his hands, but as he stood up to tuck his shirt in, his head suddenly felt very fuzzy, his legs unsteady. "Holy cow," he muttered under his breath, "I'm in bad shape."

Squaring his shoulders, he tried his best to keep up with his new buddies, as the trio made their way down the aisle, singing a chorus of the "From the Halls of Montezuma."

The sidewalk in front of the bus station was dense with young men arriving for their basic training. Roland searched the crowd for a familiar face, and finally saw Howard, sitting on a bench, absorbed in a book. He was relieved that his uncle was alone—Emily surely would have known right away that he'd been drinking, but there was a chance Howard might not notice.

"Hey there, Howard," he called, unable to wave because he was carrying his suitcase and Bessie's food basket. He started to run toward his brother-in-law; then suddenly he tripped and sprawled face down on the sidewalk.

In a moment, Howard was at his side, helping him up, his face furrowed with concern. "Are you all right? What happened?"

"I'm okay," Roland muttered, embarrassed, as he struggled to his feet. "I'm okay," he repeated, and then he began to hiccup uncontrollably.

"Have you been drinking?" Howard asked, suspiciously.

"Yes, sir," Roland admitted, as he stared downward at the glass-flecked puddles of cranberry sauce, canned green beans and sweet potato batter which were spreading over the pavement.

"Good thing your sister didn't come along," Howard said.

"Yes, sir," Roland repeated, trying unsuccessfully to scoop the mess up into the basket.

"Hold on," Howard commanded. "You'll cut yourself. I'll get some help." He found a colored janitor in the station who promised to take care of the mess for a fifty-cent tip.

"We'll stop by the base and get you straightened out before I take you home," Howard said, as he turned the key of his black Studebaker.

"Yes, sir," Roland said again, wishing he could explain to his brother-in-law how good it had felt to be drinking scotch with those enlisted guys, how it felt to be on his own, away from his father's stern lectures and disapproving eyes.

But he said nothing, for in a short time, he was caught up in the excitement of arriving at Fort Bragg. Howard identified himself at the gate and drove down a long roadway lined with Quonset huts. "My regiment, the 60th Infantry, bunks at the far end," he explained. "It's quiet right now, the camp's out on maneuvers."

"Let's go," Howard said, as he stopped the car in front of his barracks. Inside, the lieutenant on guard leaned against the wall, leafing through a pinup magazine. When he saw his captain he snapped to attention.

"At ease, Bonelli," Howard commanded. "We need your help here. This is my brother-in-law, Roland Whittaker. He's had a little too much to drink. I thought I'd give him a 'Sunday Morning Special' before I take him home to his sister. So if you'll handle the towels and coffee, I'll take care of the water detail."

Roland followed his uncle down the narrow aisle bordered by bunk beds, crisply made up and covered with regulation olive-green blankets. He took in the metal footlockers, the family photos and pinups that covered the walls over the beds.

"Wow!" he exclaimed, as Howard led him into the bathroom, which ran the entire length of the barracks, and which had more shower stalls, latrines and sinks than he had ever seen in one place.

"Strip," Howard ordered.

Clumsily he managed to obey, until he leaned over to untie his shoelaces. A wave of nausea brought him to his knees, and he began to retch.

"Get under here," Howard instructed, helping his brother-in-law up and pointing to the nearest shower. "Get under and let it all come up."

The water was ice cold, and the shock of it made Roland double over and empty the contents of his stomach into the shower drain.

"How's it going, captain?" The lieutenant appeared with a towel and a tin cup filled with steaming black coffee.

"Definite progress. It looks like we're going to make it."

"Better hurry, captain. The guys will be coming back any minute."

"Right. Out you go," he called to Roland.

As Roland stepped out of the stall, the lieutenant began snapping the towel against the boy's naked body. "Jump!" he commanded, as Roland recoiled from the stings and then jumped.

"That's enough," Howard commanded, holding out the cup. And when Roland had downed the coffee, he said: "Now get dressed, fast. I want to be out of here before my company gets back."

"Yes, sir." Roland saluted automatically, and although he was still a little light-headed, he felt proud to have experienced the Sunday Morning Special. "Watch this," he boasted, as he put on his clothes in record time.

"Maybe we should recruit this boy to speed up the shower detail," the lieutenant joked.

"Not so fast," Howard laughed. "First he has to finish high school."

APARTMENT B at 59 Prospect Street was the clumsily converted back half of an old frame house. The makeshift walls were paper thin and often failed to keep out the daily noises of the Army families crowded into apartments A and C.

The furniture was secondhand, but Emily had worked hard to make the place as homey and comfortable as possible, knowing it would be the last place they would share together before her husband went away.

By the time Roland and Howard arrived, it was well after dark, and Emily's face was clouded with worry. "Thank goodness you're here," she said, embracing her brother and then her husband. "What happened to you?"

"The bus was late, and I had to make a stop at the base," Howard replied. "Sorry." He kissed Emily's forehead. "Anything for two hungry men to eat?"

"Dinner's overcooked," Emily warned as she set the meal out. Everyone was hungry and no one seemed to notice that the roast beef and the potatoes were a little dry, the brussels sprouts soggy.

"Boy did you get big, Alex," Roland observed. "Keep that up, and you'll be a basketball star."

"And you know what else, Uncle Ro?"

"What?"

"I can write now, not just print, really write."

"Boy, that's great, Alex. You're smarter than I was at your age, that's for sure."

"How's Papa?" Emily asked.

"That Draft Board is making him crazy," Roland muttered, forking a chunk of meat into his mouth. He chewed quickly, swallowed, then added curtly: "And that's not the half of it."

After dinner, two of Howard's fellow officers and their wives dropped by for dessert and coffee. Roland sat with the men, in the kitchen, on a stool, off to one corner, listening intently as the men discussed the range of the K-F rifle, and speculated about whether or not they would be a part of the Allied invasion of North Africa that had begun a few weeks before.

In the living room, the three women, separating themselves as usual from the war talk, finalized the arrangements for the 60th Infantry's Thanksgiving Dinner at the Grange Hall the next day.

Shortly before ten, the gathering broke up. The men had

to be up at 5:30 for morning drills and the women had to begin cooking for the sixty-eight people who would be celebrating the holiday together.

Afterwards, Emily finished washing the dishes and made up a bed for her brother on the sagging, three-cushioned sofa. "It's hard, Ro, waiting for Howard's orders to come," she admitted. "I don't know if you can understand that."

"I don't think so," he answered truthfully, speculating about how elated he would be when it was his turn to get battle orders.

"Anyway," Emily said, "we're glad you're here with us for Thanksgiving."

"Me too. Thanks for asking me," he said shyly.

"'Night, Ro."

"'Night, sis."

Roland was just settling himself under one of Bessie's colorful quilts when Howard came into the room. "Thought I'd have a last cigarette in here."

Roland didn't say anything, and Howard went on. "About today . . . I think that should be between us. Man to man."

Roland was relieved and surprised. Howard had always been an all-right guy. Even when he had been a college professor, he had never talked down to him or tried to make him feel dumb. But he had been sure that his uncle would report the incident to his father. And that Clifton would come down on him, but good. "Gee, thanks, Howard. Thanks a lot."

"Sure." Howard nodded as he paused by the back window overlooking the grove of pine trees and finished off his cigarette.

ROLAND was awakened the next morning by a tickling sensation on his chin. He shook his head and made a swatting motion. There was the sound of giggling. Opening his eyes he saw Alexander, in blue flannel pajamas, clutching a handful of pigeon feathers.

"Morning, Uncle Ro."

"Uh," Roland grunted.

"Did you know that I'm going to be the turkey in the play?" Alex asked, his dark eyes serious behind his wire-rimmed glasses.

"The turkey, huh? Well, he's an important guy on Thanksgiving, right?"

"Right. I'm going to have a special costume, with feathers. Mom said you would help me make the tail. Will you, Uncle Ro? Please?" Determinedly, the child sat down on the floor, crossed his legs Indian-style, and waited for his uncle to get up.

Roland yawned and threw back the covers. "A tail? Sure, Alex, just give me a couple of minutes to get dressed." In the cramped bathroom, he put on the brown pegged pants and the green crewneck sweater that Charlotte had sent for his birthday. Leaning close to the mirror, he examined his face for signs of stubble. He'd shaved yesterday, and he was eagerly watching for the time when he'd have to shave every day, instead of just once or twice a week.

Emily stood over the stove, wrapped in a blue plaid bathrobe, watching the coffee bubble in the glass-topped percolator. "Don't you look nice this morning."

"Thanks, sis."

"Can we start now, Uncle Ro?" Alexander waved a bag of feathers at his uncle. "Please?"

"Slow down, Alexander." Emily smoothed the cowlick on her son's head. "You know nothing happens in this house until we have our coffee."

"Uncle Ro doesn't drink coffee," the child argued. "So why can't he start now?"

"How about it?" Emily asked her brother. "Are you ready to take on the Whittaker habit? I was sixteen when I started."

Roland flashed back to the night before, to the strong black coffee he had drunk in the barracks' bathroom, remembering how manly he had felt. "I believe I will," he said, unconsciously imitating his father's phrasing and tone of voice.

"How do you want it?"

"Black," he decided, liking the strong, clean sound of that.

"That's how Howard likes it," Emily said, carrying two

mugs to the table. "Poor thing, he had to leave so early this morning. He didn't even wake me up in time to make him breakfast."

"He's already at the base?" Roland asked, wondering if any plans had been made for him to spend time at Fort Bragg.

"Yes. This is the last week of basic for another batch of recruits, so it's pretty busy for him." Her hand shook a little as she lifted the mug to her lips. "This is the part I hate most, watching them all ship out."

"But they're soldiers, Em," Roland argued. "They're supposed to fight. They want to." He took a sip of the black coffee, held the bitter liquid in his mouth for a moment, trying to get used to the taste. "I'm going, too, Em, as soon as I can."

"Oh, Ro!" Emily stared at her baby brother. The ten years' age difference made her still see him as a child. Safe from the fright that had suddenly colored all their lives. "Not you," she whispered, shaking her head. "Not you, too."

THE Grange Hall was buzzing with activity as Emily, Roland and Alexander came in. About a dozen Army wives were setting up makeshift tables with planks and saw horses. Children of all ages laughed and shouted as they ran around, playing games or trying to help their mothers.

It was early afternoon, and the Thanksgiving party was scheduled for 6:30, an hour after maneuvers would be over. For weeks the wives had run bake sales and canvassed local shopkeepers to get turkeys and "fixings" donated for the event.

"Emily!" one of the women called out. "You've brought us a man! And just in time. We need someone strong to fix this light fixture and the curtain on the stage."

Flattered at being called a man, Roland enthusiastically went to work, enjoying the compliments on his strength and on his cleverness with the hammer. It was quite a change from being told he was a boy who got in everyone's way.

For several hours the women and children worked, decorating the stage with black and white crepe paper streamers, cutting out pilgrim hats and making big rocks with bunched up newspapers and gray paint. About 4:30, the gathering broke up, so that everyone might go home and dress for the big dinner. Though he wouldn't admit it, Roland was exhausted, and for the first time he wondered if Marine boot camp might be harder for him than he'd imagined.

That night Howard was unusually quiet as he drove the family to the Grange Hall. Emily tried to fill the gap and launch the Thanksgiving season by leading them all in two choruses of "Over the river and through the woods..."

"But there's no river and no snow, Mommy," Alex observed when they had finished. "Not like when we go to Grandma Emmett's house."

"No, there isn't," Emily responded. "But a lot of things are different this year." She reached over to touch her husband's arm, trying to bridge the distance she sensed.

"So how'd it go today?" Roland asked, eager to find out more about the daily business of soldiering. "Anything exciting happen?"

Howard lit a cigarette. "Yes," he answered, taking a long drag. "A boy got shot."

"Holy cow!"

Emily gasped. "How did it happen?"

"Albertalli...you remember...the boy from Huntington...he panicked in the barbed-wire obstacle and accidentally shot himself in the leg."

"Boy, that sounds dumb," Roland muttered.

"Oh, Howard, I'm sorry one of your boys got hurt," Emily said sadly.

When they arrived at the Hall, clusters of soldiers and their wives were streaming into the white frame building, to the recorded sounds of Glenn Miller's "In the Mood."

Inside, the tables were already covered with food, including eight huge turkeys donated by local merchants. Aproned women continued bearing heaping platters from the back.

After the crowd settled in, an Army chaplain invoked a blessing on the dinner, finishing with "And may the Son of God bless all His children in their days and hours of trial..."

The meal was consumed in a mood of subdued camaraderie, but Roland was unaware of the underlying sadness,
the unspoken fears. He took in only the easy bantering and
the Army jokes, making a conscious effort to memorize
these, so he might share them with the boys in West Grove.

The highlight of the evening was the children's pageant,
a reenactment of the historic landing on Plymouth Rock.
Little Pilgrims and Indians delivered their lines enthusiastically, their faces serious with concentration. But when
Alexander, a mass of bobbing feathers, gobbled his way
towards center stage, there was a burst of laughter from the
audience.

"Hey, turkey," a soldier called out, "you'd better run for
cover or you're in big trouble." There was more laughter,
and Alexander stood frozen in a moment of indecision.
Then, hands on hips, he marched forward. "Be quiet!" he
called out and resumed his position, to the accompaniment
of loud applause.

"We're all turkeys, you know," a sergeant said, nudging
Roland. "Fattened up for slaughter."

"Not now, sergeant," Howard commanded sharply. "Not
here."

"WAKE up. Roland. Wake up." It was Howard's voice. As
he opened his eyes, Roland saw his brother-in-law, dressed
in his fatigues, standing in the darkness of the room.

"What time is it?"

"About six. Wake up, son. We have to talk."

Roland sat up in his makeshift bed. "What's happening?"

"I'm shipping out. Ten-thirty this morning, from the train
station."

"Gosh." There was something in Howard's somber de-
meanor that kept Roland from registering any enthusiasm,
though in fact he would have given anything to be in his
brother-in-law's place.

Howard sat down on the edge of the sofa and took a few
puffs on his cigarette. "I want you to take Emily and Alexander back to Breezy. Today."

"Today," Roland repeated.

"Emily doesn't know I'm leaving yet." Howard's voice broke slightly. "The orders came the day before yesterday. I didn't see any sense in spoiling the holiday."

"Gosh . . . what do you want me to do?" Once again Roland was feeling more grown-up than he ever had before.

"Emily will be getting up soon. I want you to take care of Alexander and give us some time alone."

"Sure . . . I mean yes, sir."

"There's a diner, Moon's Diner, about three blocks from here, on the corner of Prospect and Reed. It opens at seven. Alexander loves their pancakes. We . . . we usually go there for Sunday breakfast."

Roland nodded, waiting for more instructions.

"Come back around nine. Then Emily and I can tell Alexander together."

"Yes, sir." Roland was touched that his brother-in-law was confiding in him, talking to him, man to man. "I know I mess up sometimes, but you can count on me."

"I know I can." Howard smiled and squeezed Roland's shoulder. "While you're at the diner, call your father and tell him when you'll be arriving. Explain why I couldn't call . . ."

"What in the world are you two talking about so early in the morning?" Emily asked, tying her bathrobe sash as she walked into the living room. "How about some coffee?"

WHILE time was painfully short for Howard and Emily, it dragged along slowly for Roland as he tried to keep his nephew amused for two and a half hours. After they had stuffed themselves with wheat cakes soaked with maple syrup and played almost every song on the jukebox, Roland took Alex to the nearby newspaper store and told him to pick out any twenty-five-cent toy he wanted.

But as they stood in the hallway of 59 Prospect Street, Roland hesitated a moment before knocking. "Come on, Uncle Ro," Alexander urged, tugging at Roland's jacket. "I want my mom to see my airplane."

"Restrain yourself, Alex," Roland cautioned, startled at hearing himself use one of his father's phrases.

It was Howard who opened the door, bending down to scoop his son up for a fierce hug and kiss. Roland could see his sister standing in the bedroom doorway, still in her bathrobe, her eyes red from crying.

"Hey, sis," Roland waved awkwardly, not knowing what to say or do. "How are you?"

"Fine," she lied bravely. "How were the pancakes?" she asked brightly, walking towards her brother. "We don't have much time, do we?" she said quietly.

He looked at his sister and saw how pinched her face was. Impulsively, he hugged her clumsily, trying to give whatever comfort he could.

"I'll be all right," she said, pulling away. To show that she was in control, she added, "Howard's bag is packed, it's in the bedroom. Why don't you get it?"

"Right." Roland was relieved for the chance to do something practical. As he left the room, he heard Alexander ask his mother if she was sick. Poor kid, he thought, he couldn't understand why his mom was still in her bathrobe, why she looked so sad.

Inside the cramped bedroom that had been converted from a screened-in porch, Howard's duffel bag leaned against an old pine bureau. The bedcovers were twisted, the pillows crushed, the bottom sheet damp. Roland stared at the bed, fascinated and repelled by the images that came into his head, of Emily and Howard making love while he had been having breakfast with Alexander.

Roland's own sexual urges had been getting stronger and more persistent. He had dreams of "doing it" with Betty Lou Harris, who let him French kiss her whenever they went to the movies. But he never associated those feelings he had with anyone in his family. When he had found out about his father's dates with Miss Jewel, he had for a brief moment, and very much against his will, a vivid picture of the two of them locked in a lusty embrace. He had banished it immediately because it had embarrassed and unsettled him, just the way this bedroom did right now.

Hastily he picked up the duffel bag and returned to the living room. Emily and Howard were seated on the sofa, holding their son between them. "Will you bring me back a surprise?" Alexander was asking.

"That's a promise," Howard replied. "And I'll write you lots of letters. Will you write back?"

"Yep," the boy nodded. "With lots of words." Seeing his uncle, he announced: "My daddy's going to war, Uncle Ro, but he's gonna come back as soon as he can."

"What do you know about that?" Roland reacted smoothly. "So how about it? Are you and your mom coming to stay with Grandpop and me at Breezy until your dad comes home?"

"Yep," the boy replied, jumping off the sofa. "I'm going to pack, just like my dad." Playfully, he kicked the duffel bag. Just then there was a knock on the door.

"That must be Ralph," Howard said as he got up.

"So soon," Emily whispered, squaring her shoulders and standing up. "Come on, Alexander," she said, "it's time for Daddy to leave."

Hand in hand, Emily and Howard walked down the short dark hallway, followed by Roland and Alex, who was chattering animatedly. "I have to be a brave boy," he repeated. "Very brave and good to my mommy."

"That's right," Roland agreed absently, watching his sister and brother-in-law, sensing rather than understanding the powerful connection between them.

The front stoop was shallow and crooked, sheltered by a shingled overhang. It was there that the final goodbyes were said, while Captain Ralph Redken started the engine of the jeep that was parked out front.

Howard drew Emily to him, closed his eyes and held her tightly, as if he could take something of her with him. Then, pulling away, he grasped her shoulders and looked into her eyes. "Never forget how much I love you," he said huskily. "And keep busy, Em. It will help the time go faster."

Emily nodded, unable to speak, her eyes brimming with tears. Tenderly, she brushed a hand against her husband's cheek and let it linger a moment, feeling the touch of his skin against hers as if it were the first time. He kissed the palm of her hand and knelt down beside his son.

"Now, young man, give your daddy a hug." Alexander

wrapped his arms around his father's neck and clung to him desperately, as if he sensed at this last moment that there was something frightening in this farewell.

"It's all right, son," Howard said reassuringly, his voice thick with emotion. "It's all right," he repeated. Gently, he disentangled himself and patted his son's bottom in an attempt to lighten the moment. "I'll be back before you know it." As he stood up, he added: "Just don't grow too fast while I'm away. Okay?"

"Okay," the child promised, reaching for his mother's hand.

"Roland . . . how about walking to the car with me?" Howard asked.

"Yes, sir." Roland flung the duffel bag over his shoulder and followed his brother-in-law to the waiting jeep. After the bag had been stowed in the back, Howard extended his hand. "I'm glad you're here, Roland. Makes it easier for Emily."

"Me, too." He fumbled in his pants pocket and took out the worn rabbit's foot he carried for luck when he played basketball. "Here," he said, "take this."

"Thanks." Howard shook Roland's hand, turned and jumped into the jeep.

The vehicle drove off immediately, honking its horn three times as it went down Prospect Street, made a right turn and disappeared around the corner. Roland turned and hurried back up the walk, to his sister and nephew, who were still waving, the smiles on their faces slowly fading.

"Let's get this show on the road," he urged, adopting the tone the coach used to rev up the team. "Come on— we have to get packed and moving before it gets late."

Alexander raced down the hallway, back into the apartment, but Emily moved slowly, unsteadily. "I have to scrub the floor," she said resolutely when they were inside.

"Scrub the floor?" Roland repeated. He started to ask why in the world she would want to do that, but something in her face stopped him. He would humor Em, do whatever he could to make this day easier for her.

"Howard said to stay busy," she said, in a funny voice.

"Fine," Roland agreed, though he knew they'd have to get on the road soon, if they were to make it to back to Breezy in one stretch.

While Emily scrubbed ferociously at the worn linoleum floor, Roland helped Alex pack up his toys. When she was finished, she stood for a moment in the doorway, not knowing what to do next. "Come on, Em," Roland said, "get your things together. We're going home."

After their belongings were packed into suitcases and boxes, Emily insisted on calling the Army wives who had been her friends to say goodbye. She couldn't bear to see them, she said. It would be too hard. So it was not until afternoon when the black Studebaker finally headed across the mountains.

Emily had always been an excellent driver, but now she was tense and jumpy. Though she stared intently at the road and gripped the steering wheel tightly, her mind seemed to be elsewhere. Twice she started to pass another car, then jammed on the brakes suddenly. Roland tried to lighten the heavy mood by playing word games with his nephew, but Emily scarcely seemed to notice.

As they approached Route 22, which cut across the southern tip of the Blue Ridge range and bypassed some forty miles of the main route, a light snow began to fall. Roland suggested they take a shortcut, so that they might reach West Grove faster, before the storm got any worse.

It soon became apparent that the turn off the highway had been a mistake. High winds and the heavy snowfall made navigation of the narrow, winding road treacherous. Emily's driving became increasingly erratic.

"Careful, sis," Roland urged. "Pump the brakes nice and easy when the tires slide. Don't turn the steering wheel too fast."

She seemed to be paying attention, but a few moments later, as the car skidded around a sharp bend, she panicked and turned the wheel in the wrong direction. She gasped as the Studebaker spun around and slid into a ditch against the granite mountainside. Alexander started to cry, but Emily just sat behind the wheel, immobilized.

"It's okay, Alex," Roland said soothingly, lifting his

nephew over to the back seat. "Everything's okay. Time to be brave now, remember?" When Alexander was quiet, Roland took a flashlight out of the glove compartment and checked the damage. The car was still drivable, but help would be needed to pull it out of the narrow gulley.

He dug a couple of blankets out of the trunk and bundled Emily with Alex into the back seat. Together they all waited as the snow continued to fall, scanning the road for other vehicles. Almost an hour passed before headlights came slowly around the bend. Roland leapt from the car and flagged down the vehicle.

A beat-up old Ford pickup came to a stop, and the driver, a mountain man smoking a corncob pipe, got out. "You folks got trouble?" he asked.

"We skidded off the road," Roland explained. "The car's okay, but we can't get out of the ditch."

"See what we kin do."

"Thanks a lot, Mr. . . . ."

"Jeb Hoopes."

"Roland Whittaker, sir. My sister Emily and her son Alex are in the car."

The mountain man surveyed the situation silently, then returned to his truck. From under the front seat he pulled out an earthenware crock of corn liquor. "Have a taste," he offered Roland. "Warm you up a mite before we git started."

Roland accepted the jug, but remembering his experience on the bus, took only a small sip of the home brew. Fortified, the two men unloaded the baggage from the car and moved Emily and Alexander into the pickup. Then they took a plank from the truck and levered the car back onto the roadbed.

"Thanks a lot, Mr. Hoopes," Roland said. "We would've been stuck here forever if you hadn't come along."

"Bad night to be drivin' these roads," Hoopes observed. "Best follow me across the mountain."

"Thank you, sir." Roland looked over at his sister, who still seemed only vaguely aware of what was happening around her. "Maybe I should drive," he thought out loud. "My sister's upset. Her husband just went off to war."

"I see," the mountain man nodded. "Mighty sad."

"I don't have a license," Roland confessed. "I'm only seventeen."

"Don't worry me none," the man chuckled. "I been on these here roads since I was fourteen. Still don't have no license."

Emily made no protest when Roland said he would drive. She seemed relieved when he slid into the driver's seat. Everyone in the family knew that Roland spent most of his free time practice-driving Buddy Pruner's old jalopy around the back pasture.

The ride home was long and difficult, but Roland felt calm and confident and strong. He liked taking care of Em and Alex, protecting them, keeping his promise to Howard. He didn't act like a dumb kid, not when someone gave him a chance to show his stuff. Maybe Clifton would finally see that when he delivered Em and Alex safely at Breezy.

It was almost three a.m. when the trio approached Breezy. Every light in the house was on, creating a beacon that beamed them up the lane through the snow. As the car pulled in behind the house, Clifton and Bessie rushed outside. While Bessie bundled Emily and her sleeping son into the house, Roland started to explain to his father why they were so late, and why he had been driving Howard's car.

Standing there in his bathrobe and slippers, Clifton gave way to the tension and fatigue of the long night. "In the future, see that you don't operate an automobile without a license," he said brusquely, then turned on his heel and went into the house.

"Yes, sir." Roland ground the words out between clenched teeth, his hands knotted into fists as two warm tears slid down the icy coolness of his cheeks.

5

We Regret to Inform You
May 1943

4 May 1943

My Dear Children,

   Last Wednesday afternoon, as I paused to contemplate the passing scenes on "the Rialto," Miss Verna Tate stopped to inform me that Alexander had received the highest score for his grade level in the annual reading comprehension test (said test being given throughout the country, mind you). With her customary ebullience, Miss Verna went on to forecast greatness for our Alexander (and I, of course, could not resist a reference to her student as "Alexander the Great") and declared that teaching him was an experience which kept her "on her toes."

   Speaking of my grandson, he is the official second-in-command (his mother being the commander-in-chief) of our first Victory Garden. This very day in May, Emily has been inspired to begin tilling the soil behind the row of peonies by the barn and has put in six tomato plants....

* * *

"WHY don't you mention that I also have two brand new blisters?" Emily suggested, as she read the first draft of the current Bulletin over her father's shoulder. "That clumsy old hoe is awfully rough on the hands."

Collapsing into a striped canvas folding chair, she examined the blisters forming on her thumb and forefinger. Putting out a garden was harder work than she expected, and her father was no help at all. For years he had depended on John Henry to care for his yard, and war or no war, he wasn't about to change his ways. With John Henry gone to Chicago to work in a factory, Clifton still sat and supervised while Emily did all the work.

She did have Alexander's eager assistance. She smiled as she watched his small hands patting the mounds of earth around the infant tomato plants. Howard would be proud of their little farmer, she thought. Howard had less of a green thumb than she did, but she was sure he would be out there, on his hands and knees, alongside his son, talking as he worked, perhaps explaining to the child how the Egyptians developed irrigation so their crops would thrive when there was no rain.

Howard was always with her, in her heart and in her thoughts. Although she tried to keep busy, as he had asked her to, she missed him terribly, missed the easy conversations, the familiar rhythms of their shared camaraderie. Each night, before she fell asleep, she held his picture close and talked to him, reporting her day's activities, as she had when they'd been together. Then she kissed the photograph goodnight and replaced it on her bureau, taking some small comfort from this private ritual, from the sense that Howard was somewhere across the ocean, thinking of her too.

"Daydreaming again, Emily?" Clifton asked, looking up from his yellow legal pad.

"Caught me," she admitted, dropping her head to study her muddy tennis shoes. "I was just thinking that Howard would get a kick out of seeing me wrestle with a garden."

"I thought we might take some pictures of the garden for him," he said reaching for the black box frame beside his chair.

Emily nodded, touched by her father's thoughtfulness.

He tried so hard to be considerate these days. It wasn't easy on either of them, living together again in the old family home, but they were managing pretty well, all things considered. She was so much her father's daughter in many ways. A born organizer, so accustomed to doing things her way, it was inevitable they often bumped up against one another. Then there was Miss Jewel, who seemed to be casting an ever-growing shadow on life at Breezy.

"Refreshments, you'all!" Bessie pushed the screen door open with a tray of cold drinks and lumbered down the steps.

"Why, Bessie," Clifton said, eyeing the pitcher of iced tea with some amusement. "Aren't we rushing summer a bit?"

"When you's hot, you wants somethin' cold to drink, summer or not," Bessie provided.

"You tell him," Emily laughed. "Keep him in his place. These lawyers get awfully bossy if you don't watch them."

"Me too! Hey . . . me, too!" Alexander left his plants and ran pell mell towards the refreshments.

"Easy, there, easy," Emily cautioned. Haste and near-sightedness made skinned knees an everyday condition for Alexander.

Breathless but unbruised, he took a large gulp of his drink and announced: "I'm planting tomatoes, all by myself."

"Now, ain't that fine, Mr. Alex." Bessie clapped her hands and grinned fondly. "Ain't that growed up of you."

Emily was grateful that Bessie was part of her son's life now. His shyness, his unusual intelligence often kept him apart from children his own age. With his father away, he needed the loving support of adults more than ever.

"Time for some pictures," Clifton said, raising the camera and framing a picture of mother and son.

"Wait, Papa. Wait till I fix my hair." Emily searched for a comb in the pocket of her new overalls. She pulled out the crumpled letter she had received from Howard the day before. "Silly, isn't it," she said. "I always carry his letters with me."

"It isn't silly at all," Clifton said gruffly.

"Take my picture, Granddaddy," Alexander pleaded, dragging a tomato pole from the garden. "I want my daddy to see how strong I am." Waving aside offers of help, he struggled to prop the pole up, trying to recreate a picture he had seen in his favorite book, the story of King Arthur.

"Ready now, son?" Clifton asked, winking at Emily.

Twisting her hair into a knot, Emily took her place by Alexander's side. She grinned tenderly at her pint-sized knight, as the camera clicked twice, and the Breezy Hill gardeners went on record for Howard.

"Okay, Papa, let's have a picture of you, writing the Bulletin," Emily suggested, as Clifton wound the film. "I'll bet Howard would like to see his father-in-law hard at work."

Cooperating, Clifton sat back down, taking up his pad and pencil. Striking a scholarly pose, he began to write, reading aloud as he did:

We took several garden photos for our Howard, who is still in North Africa. Emily received a letter yesterday, dated April 22nd, informing us that the Allied troops continue their drive across the Sahara Desert. We are fortunate that Howard is not on the front lines. As a member of the Corps of Engineers and because of his facility with languages, he is presently assigned the task of reconnoitering the Arab villages and preparing for the installation of the troops.

As he paused to recheck his information, Clifton looked up and Emily snapped the picture.

The sound of the courthouse clock striking two caught them all by surprise. "Oh, my," Clifton said, replacing his pencil in his shirt pocket and tucking the pad under his arm. "The parade starts in half an hour."

"Will the band come, Mom?" Alexander asked, dropping the hickory stick to the ground and running to Emily.

"Yes, indeed," she said, as she knelt to wipe the dirt from her son's knees. "Now inside with you. Find Bessie and tell her that you need a bath."

"Aw, Mom," Alexander's face wrinkled in disgust. "Do I have to?"

"Yes, you do. No bath, no parade," she said firmly. It amazed Emily how much better she had become at disciplining her strong-willed child. Before Howard had gone, she had left all the "no" situations to him. Now these, like so many other responsibilities, had settled on her shoulders.

"But I took one this morning," her son continued to protest, as he walked slowly to the house, dragging the pole behind him.

Ignoring his last token complaint, Emily said to her father: "I'll put the tools away when we get back. I'd better get cleaned up myself now."

"No need to worry. The tools won't run away while we're gone. You go on inside. I'll be along in a minute." Clifton patted his perspiring forehead with a white handkerchief. "I'll just put old Peaches out to pasture."

Emily nodded. She knew that Peaches didn't need to go out to pasture. The old guernsey was perfectly content, staked in the yard, munching on the rich green grass. She knew that Clifton sometimes talked to the cow, thinking out loud the problems that had no easy solutions. And today's Send-Off ceremony was more difficult for him, more painful than he dared admit.

The barn needs a fresh coat of paint, she thought, as she watched her father walk toward the old building. Maybe I could make that another summer project. Maybe another color, the brown was so dull, and maybe a contrasting color for the gingerbread trim. She remembered hearing that when Grandfather Elkaniah had built it in the late 1800s, to house his carriage horses, the barn had been painted red. She wondered if Clifton would approve of a red barn.

Things change so quickly, she mused, as she picked up the tray and headed for the house. That old barn was once her grandfather's pride and joy. Now it was rundown, housing an old Packard and one tired cow. How things changed. It seemed only yesterday that its hayloft provided a special hideout for Roland; now it was a secret place for Alexander.

I wonder if Howard ever had a special hiding place, she

mused, as she opened the screen door. She would ask him
in her next letter.

As always in warm weather, Emily enjoyed the long walk
down the gravel lane into town. Bordered by wild flowers
and tall trees, the roadway was a protected country corridor,
until the lane met the main highway which passed through
town. She half-listened to Bessie telling Alexander how her
new lace-up shoes pinched her feet. And she wondered how
many more Send-Off parades she would have to endure
until the war was over, until Howard returned.

As the little group approached the ornate grillwork gate
that marked the end of the lane, they heard the high school
band striking up a John Philip Sousa march. "We should
hurry," Emily urged her father. "We want to get you on
that platform on time."

Clifton nodded and stepped up the pace. "Looks like
there's a big turnout today," he observed, as the town square
came into view.

They walked quickly past the shoe repair and Miss Minnie's Boarding House, towards the town square. Emily ached
for the people of Russell County. Today they would be
sending a third group of men and boys off to war. How
many will come back, she wondered, and then she immediately banished the sad and frightening thought from her
mind.

On the porch of Pyle's Store, Alexander spied a stack
of new metal hoes leaning against the bin of onions. "Look,
Mom," he pointed excitedly, "for the garden!" He bolted
up the stairs and grabbed a red-handled hoe, almost knocking the display over. "Can we have it? Can we? I'll carry
it home."

"Not with all these people around, you won't," she said
firmly, taking the hoe from his hands and replacing it with
the others. "We'll come back on Monday for it."

Bessie hobbled up onto the porch, her feet obviously
pained by the new shoes. "Look, chile," she said, "see that
there big ribbon..." She pointed to a huge banner draped

across the pillars of the brick town hall. "What that say?"

"Good Luck, Boys!" Alexander read proudly, as Mayor Ferguson, Sheriff Boggs and Reverend Lowell mounted the steep steps, towards a semicircle of fold-up chairs arranged on the recently erected wooden platform on the portico.

The high school band, outfitted in maroon and gold uniforms, was marching around the square, and Alexander strained to get a better look at the drum and bugle corps as they approached the courthouse.

"Can you take Alexander closer to the band, Bessie?" Emily asked. "I know he'd like that."

"Jeepers Creepers! Let's go!" The boy tugged excitedly at Bessie's skirt, and the two took off as quickly as her tight shoes would allow.

"Emily, oh, Emily," Clifton called from the sidewalk, waving a sheaf of papers in his right hand. Miss Jewel had appeared from nowhere, it seemed, and was standing by her father's side. It was the first time Emily had seen the two together in public. As usual, the buxom woman was overdressed, this time in an organza polka-dot print and a large picture hat. "Emily, I forgot to bring a copy of the recruitment list for the Mayor," Clifton said.

"Don't worry," Emily said, nodding politely to Miss Jewel. "You stay right there, and I'll run over to the office for the carbon."

THE once sedate legal library of her father's office was now cluttered with piles of government documents. War posters were tacked to bookshelves; like wallpaper they covered Clifton's legal volumes. Emily knew just where to find the needed carbon, for she had typed it the afternoon before. She hurried to her desk by the window overlooking the "Rialto," her father's whimsical name for the town square.

She had worked as a volunteer clerk for the past four months, ever since Ida Walters had left to have her first baby. The job strained her emotionally. Being part of the machinery that sent the county's men to war was difficult, but she felt it was important for her to make a real contri-

bution, on a daily basis, especially now that Alexander was
in kindergarten most of the day.

She picked up the three-page list from the wooden file
box by her typewriter. She was just leaving the office, when
she heard a timid knock on the door. "Come in," she called
out.

Mrs. Jake Jenks—Vandella, to the townspeople—a
country woman who came down regularly from Honaker to
sell honey, stood on the threshold, dressed in a homemade
calico dress and a small straw hat. "Please, ma'am," she
said nervously, clutching the worn handles on her purse,
"please, ma'am, could you tear up my boy's signin' up
papers? He's the last of my younguns to go. His pa, my
mister, he can't run the farm without him, not with his
sciatica and all."

"Come in, Vandella," Emily said kindly. "Come in and
sit down while I check the records."

Emily knew that it was too late to tear up the enlistment
papers, too late to change anything. She tried to borrow a
few moments' time, as she searched for the file on Homer
T. Jenks. She tried to think of what comfort she might offer
to the poor, worn-out woman. File in hand, she sat down
next to her and began to read the document aloud: "Homer
T. Jenks of Honaker, Virginia, enlisted in the Armed Forces
of the United States on March 27, 1943. He was examined
and found to be physically and mentally fit for service and
classified 1-A."

She looked up into the older woman's heavily lined face,
drawn tightly now with grief. "He did not list any special
circumstances, such as being the only son left on the farm,
or his father's poor health."

"We're proud folks," Vandella said quietly, her shoulders
slumped forward in an attitude of stoic defeat. "He wouldn't
have said nothin'."

Emily closed the file and shook her head. "I'm sorry,
but your son received his classification three weeks ago.
His government orders are to report to duty today."

The woman sat perfectly still for a moment. Then she
pulled her sinewy body straight up in the chair. Tears tric-

kled down her weathered face as she stared vacantly at the American flag hanging over the front window.

"I'm sorry, Vandella," Emily said softly. "I'm so very sorry, but Homer will have to go with the rest. There's nothing I can do..."

"It ain't fair," the woman said, almost to herself. "It ain't fair. He's my baby, Homer is. They could've left me my baby."

"I know," Emily said, reaching for Vandella's roughened hand. "It's hard, no matter how old they are. They took my husband last November."

"I didn't know, ma'am," Vandella said, looking directly into Emily's face for the first time. "You're Mr. Clifton's oldest, ain't you?"

"Yes." Emily reached into her purse and handed the woman a handkerchief. "But don't apologize. It's the same for all of us." She watched Vandella wipe her eyes and try to regain her composure. "Isn't your Homer the boy with the red hair and the beagle?"

"Yep. That there dog of his had pups and ain't et nothin' for days. Poor thing knows something's wrong. Ain't nursin', just sits and howls."

"You know, I've been thinking of getting my son Alexander a dog. He's almost six. Do you think he's old enough?"

"Ain't nothin' like a dog for a youngun," Vandella said, handing Emily back the handkerchief and adjusting the limp straw hat with its cluster of cherries on the brim.

"I suppose I keep putting it off, hoping his father will be home soon to take care of it. I think it would be nice if he gave Alexander his first dog."

"You've been mighty kind, ma'am." Vandella stood up and offered a bony hand. "I best be goin'. My men folks is waitin'."

Emily took the thin hand in hers. "I've got to run, too. My father is down there waiting for this list."

CLIFTON was pacing anxiously on the sidewalk when Emily returned. Miss Jewel was chattering brightly, trying to divert his attention. Before Emily could explain the reason for her delay, the band struck up the national anthem. Clifton took the list and hurried off to the reviewing stand. Miss Jewel followed close behind, making a place for herself along the courthouse steps.

Everywhere Emily looked, there were people clinging to their last moments together. Mothers tenderly handing over small packages of food or extra clothing. Fathers stumbling over words of advice, slipping a few extra bills into a back pocket. Wives and sweethearts fighting back tears, searching for the courage to smile. And suddenly Emily was no longer watching the parade or hearing the music. She was lost in the memory of last November and the day Howard had left.

She had thought it odd when Howard had roused Roland from his makeshift bed on the living room couch and sent him off with Alexander to the Moon Cafe for breakfast. Later, when she and Howard were alone, drinking their second cup of coffee on the back stoop, under the pine trees in the backyard, he had told her he would be leaving that day. He hadn't said anything earlier, he explained, because he had wanted to spare her the pain of counting off their last hours together. He had had his embarkation orders for three days: Departure time, 10:45, from the train station. Destination, unknown.

She had sat stone still, trying to absorb the news. For months she had tried to prepare herself, but when the moment had come, she had felt all the strength and resolve drain out of her. She had clenched her fists until the knuckles were white. Her throat had constricted, and she felt she could not speak. Struggling with her rising panic, she had reminded herself that her husband believed in the war, that she must too. She prayed that the belief would make her brave.

"Please come back to me," she had finally whispered.

"Of course I will," Howard had answered, taking her icy hands in his, trying to warm them. "Who else would put up with such an absent-minded professor?"

It was one of their favorite private jokes, and she had

taken some comfort in it. They had often laughed together because Howard could remember the most complicated mathematical formulas, but not his own phone number or their wedding anniversary. Each night, when Howard was teaching, Emily would sift through his pockets and try to decipher the scribblings he made on the scraps of paper, so he wouldn't forget anything important. She had enjoyed this wifely chore. Reading the fragments of ideas and thoughts that Howard jotted down made him feel closer to her.

"Emily," he had said, smoothing back her hair, as she laid her head against his chest, listening to the beating of his heart. "Emily, I couldn't live without you."

"And I wouldn't want to live without you," she had said, her voice nearly breaking. Then, with more strength than she had believed she possessed, she had stood and asked, "Shall I help you pack?"

He had nodded, his eyes filled with gratitude and love. Hand in hand, they had walked to their cramped bedroom. Following the Army regulation list, they had filled his duffel bag. While Howard was in the bathroom, gathering up his toilet articles, she had searched her belongings for something personal to give him. But all she could think of was the book she was reading, Irving Stone's *They Also Ran*. She had slipped it into the bag, among his socks.

Then suddenly he had been behind her, kissing her neck, his arms wrapped across her breasts. He had pushed her gently onto the bed. She had felt the rough weave of the bedspread against her cheek, as she turned to watch him unbuckle his belt and let his trousers fall to the floor.

"I'm going to miss you so much," he'd said, his voice choked with something more than desire, as he freed himself from his clothes and reached under her skirt, urgently seeking the warmth of her body.

She had wished that she could feel what he was feeling. She yearned for an immediate passion that could match his.

His body tightened and she heard him moan, "Oh, yes, Emily, yes." She had lain beneath him, taking her pleasure from his closeness, from knowing how much he needed her.

A few minutes later, the ship's clock in the living room,

a wedding present from her college roommate, had struck ten. She had counted the bell-like strokes, one by one, knowing it was time. She shook her husband gently. "Wake up, Howard. It's time to go."

But it wasn't until she put Alexander down for his afternoon nap, until she started packing for the trip to Breezy and saw the empty spaces where all his things had been, that she really understood that Howard was gone. Truly gone. She had dropped to her knees and prayed, feeling more frightened and alone than she had ever felt before.

"CAREFUL, miss," a stranger's voice warned, jarring her back to the present, as an arm reached out, and prevented her from stumbling forward into the gutter.

"Oh, dear," Emily said to the farmer in overalls who had his hand on her elbow. "I must have lost my balance."

Get hold of yourself, she reminded herself. Howard has been gone for six months, and you are here, in West Grove, at a Send-Off parade. Pay attention and stop dwelling in the past.

Thanking the farmer for helping her, she moved closer to the courthouse steps for a better view of the review stand. She watched Reverend Lowell lifting his arms over the gathered crowd and opening the program with a passage from the Book of Ruth. "Whither thou goest, I will go," he quoted, reassuring the recruits that the spirit of God and the prayers of their families would be with them in all the far corners of the world.

Mayor Ferguson, looking stouter than usual in his three-piece black suit, gave a rambling oration on Virginia's fighting heritage. For Emily, he redeemed himself somewhat by concluding with part of Roosevelt's speech to Congress the day war had been declared:

With confidence in our Armed Forces, with the unbounded determination of our people, we will gain the inevitable triumph, so help us God.

Enthusiastic applause rose from the crowd as the mayor left the podium, bowing like an oversized penguin, all the way back to his seat. The band burst into "God Bless America." Then, solemn drumrolls signalled the reading of the recruit list, and silence spread like a blanket over the assembled crowd. Proudly, Emily watched her father rise and walk, ramrod-straight and with quiet dignity, to the center of the platform.

One by one, each of the one hundred and twenty-seven recruits mounted the courthouse steps and lined up in front of the podium as her father, his face impassive, read the names. As Emily watched them, these fresh-faced boys, these familiar young men, scrubbed and combed and dressed in their best suits, smiling down bravely on the people who loved them, she felt a fresh rush of anguish.

After the final name was called, the band struck up "The Star-Spangled Banner." Led by Army and Navy officers from the Abington Induction Center, the recruits filed down the steps and lined up on the sidewalks, ready for the march to the train station. There, the 3:35 afternoon Zephyr would take them on the first leg of their journey to war.

"I don't want to go to the station," Emily told her father, as he joined her on the sidewalk. She felt weak, almost faint after watching the ceremony. "If you don't mind, I'd like to go home now."

"Then that's what we'll do," Clifton said, expressing his understanding and concern with a gentle pat on her shoulder. "Let me tell Miss Jewel we're leaving. You wait right here till I get back. Bessie and Alexander will be along shortly. I gave them money for ice cream cones."

As they rounded the curve in the lane, as the house came clearly into view, Emily noticed a military car in the side driveway. Thinking it might be an official from Abington, she turned to her father. "Were you expecting anyone?"

"No." Clifton shook his head and quickened his pace.

She hurried along beside him. "I don't see anyone, do you?"

"It's my daddy! It's my daddy!" Alexander broke away from Bessie and ran up the steep knoll of the front yard.

As Emily ran after him, she saw an Army officer get up from the porch swing. But it wasn't Howard. It was a stranger, a tall stranger in dress uniform. Catching up with Alexander at the top of the porch stairs, she apologized breathlessly: "My husband is in the Army, too, so my son thought . . . well, you know . . ."

The officer nodded as Alexander picked up the narrative: "My daddy is in Af'ca and has a jeep named Alex for me."

Bessie hobbled and huffed up the steep porch stairs. She took the child's arm firmly. "It's nap time, chile. Say good-bye to the man."

When the front door was closed behind Bessie and her son, Emily turned to the stranger. Before she could ask who he was and what he wanted, he stepped forward.

"Are you Mrs. Howard C. Emmett?"

There was something in his voice she didn't like, but she answered politely: "Yes, I am."

The officer removed his cap and lowered his eyes. Staring at the porch floor, he recited: "We regret to inform you that your husband, Major Howard C. Emmett, was killed at the Battle of Bizerte in Tunisia, on May 7th, 1943. His personal effects . . ."

"No!" she screamed. "No!" She pressed her hands over her ears and ran to her father who was standing at the top of the stairs, his face ashen, his hands clutching the rail. "Make him stop, Papa! Make him go away!"

But Clifton could not seem to move. He held the rail for support, his body bent over, as if he had been struck on his chest, his breath coming in short, irregular gasps.

Dazed and confused, Emily ran inside the house, slamming the screen door behind her. Racing through the front foyer and up the stairs, she stopped on the landing where a National Geographic map hung. There, with red-ribboned pins, she had marked the movements of Howard's company. With one swift movement she tore the map from the wall, then ran into her bedroom and locked the door.

* * *

SHE was safe behind the door. Safe from the tall officer with the gray hair. Safe from those awful, awful words. From the monstrous, unthinkable idea that her Howard, her own precious Howard, would not be coming home. He had promised her he would come back to her, and Howard never broke a promise. She shook her head rhythmically in a silent "no," as if she could shake away the cold official-sounding words that would bring her life crashing around her if she allowed them to take hold of her. With icy fingers she reached for the multi-colored afghan that lay neatly folded on her bed. She wrapped it around her, to ward off the winter chill that had fallen over the warm spring afternoon.

It was all a horrible mistake. It had to be. She still had Howard's crumpled letter, there in the pocket of the denim overalls she had flung hastily on the floor, in her rush to get to the parade on time. He was fine, he had told her so. Soon the Army would send someone else . . . perhaps another officer was on his way right now, to tell her that they were so very sorry for this dreadful mistake. Perhaps he was already here.

She opened her door a crack and listened, but all she heard was the sound of her father's voice, speaking on the telephone. She strained to hear what he was saying, and when she caught the words "Howard" and "killed in action," she wanted to run back downstairs, to stop him from spreading the awful lie. But she could not make her body respond.

She locked her door again and sank into Granny Sarah Belle's rocking chair by the north window, the blanket still draped over her shoulders. As a young girl, she had loved to sit in this chair, to look out on the bowl-shaped mountains peppered with scraggly pines and dream about the man she would marry. That dream had taken shape when she was eleven years old, on the day she had finished reading *Little Women*. She had decided that she was like Jo March, that one day she would go out into the world and find her own Professor Baer. And by some wonderful miracle, she had done exactly that.

As she rocked back and forth, she remembered how she had met Howard. She had been a junior at Randolph Macon and he was a graduate student at MIT. She had gone to

Boston for Easter weekend with her roommate, Eleanor
Curtis-Price. Eleanor's father was a physics professor at
MIT and he had invited several of his favorite graduate
students for tea, in honor of his daughter. Howard had been
one of them. Later, he had invited her to take a walk across
the Commons, and under the sheltering spring trees, she
knew she had found her professor. Less than fifteen months
later, shortly after her graduation, he had taken his first
teaching position at Boston University and they had been
quietly married.

On June 12th, they would celebrate their seventh anniversary, she thought. Suddenly she heard footsteps on the
stairs. She let the afghan fall to the floor, her body tensed,
wary. She heard her father's voice. "Emily. Please unlock
this door. Please don't try to carry this alone."

She had no answer for him. She wished he would go
away.

"Let me try, Brother." It was the unmistakable voice of
Reverend Lowell, booming through the door. "Emily, I've
come here to be with you in this hour of tribulation. Call
upon the Lord, and He will give you comfort."

Angrily Emily pounded the rocker with her fists. How
dare he talk about comfort! Or a Lord who would allow
such awful things to happen.

"Emily, baby." It was Bessie's voice, soft and low. "You
hear me?" She knocked on the door, to make certain that
Emily was paying attention. "I done sent Alexander over
to the Puseys for the night. Don't be worryin' none over
him. He don't know nothin', 'ceptin' yo' feelin' poorly.

"Honey-chile," she continued, "yo' sister's comin'."

"If only she would say something," she heard her father
say, as he paced up and down the hall.

Emily tried again to speak. Her lips moved, but her voice
would not come. She closed her eyes and willed them to
leave her alone.

"Leave the chile be," Bessie scolded. "She's a-grievin'
now."

Emily listened to the sound of footsteps fading down the
stairs. Alone, in the bedroom of her childhood, she stared
at the pale blue flowers of the wallpaper, until the afternoon

sun disappeared behind the mountains. As darkness crept into the room, she felt achingly, desperately alone. She opened the closet door and filled her arms with Howard's corduroy suits. Collapsing with them on the bed, she inhaled the last traces of her husband's presence.

With her face buried in the rough, thick fabric, she closed her eyes and was pulled downward, into a deep, dark spiral of sleep. As she lost consciousness, she moved her lips in a silent prayer, an urgent plea that the bad dream might be over, that Howard would soon be with her again.

WHEN she awoke, the room was dark. She heard a flurry of activity downstairs, the front door opening and closing. It had begun. The callers were arriving, to pay their respects. She would have to make an appearance. It was expected of her. She would have to leave the sanctuary of her room. Rising from the crumpled pile of Howard's clothes, she leaned over and picked up a package of his Camel cigarettes, which had fallen from one of his pockets onto the floor.

She took a cigarette from the pack and lit it, in a gesture that felt familiar and natural. Sometimes, late at night, she and Howard had shared a smoke, but it had never been something she did on her own. Inhaling deeply, she felt some strange satisfaction, some comfort in the ritual, in the sharp bitter taste of the tobacco.

In the mirror over the bureau, she saw a pinched white face which she scarcely recognized as her own. She had never thought of herself as a pretty woman. Handsome, at best, but like Jo, her favorite fictional character, more pleasing in her mind than in her appearance. Howard had always told her she was lovely, but now there was nothing lovely in the ghostly image that stared back from the mirror.

From the photograph on the bureau, Howard smiled at her, looking so handsome, so vital and alive in his uniform, standing in front of the stately bank of trees in their back yard at Southern Pines. She shook her head in silent disbelief. How could he look so happy when he was dead? She lit another cigarette.

Picking up the photograph, she quietly unlocked the door

and tiptoed down the hallway to the top of the stairs. Downstairs, in the foyer, Miss Minnie Yardley, her childhood Sunday School teacher, was talking.

"Mildred Sparks and I were in the drugstore when the man from the Army stopped in for a cup of coffee. He told us about Howard, so I thought I'd come by this evening."

Emily knew she would have brought a shepherd's pie as her gesture of condolence. Miss Minnie prided herself on the recipe, which she swore had been brought by her ancestors when they had come over from England with Governor Winthrop in the 1700s. Miss Minnie had brought a pie when Emily's mother had died.

"Where is Emily?" the birdlike voice asked.

"She's resting upstairs," her father answered. "This has been a terrible shock for her."

It was strange to hear them talking about her. She sank down on the top step, her knees weak from the prospect of going downstairs to face all those people, and took another drag from the cigarette.

A heavy-footed man joined the group in the hall. "When my George was killed on that tractor," he said, "my Sharon Lee didn't eat for nine days. I hope you won't have that trouble with Emily." She recognized the wheezing voice of Bernard Pyle, proprietor of the general store.

"It's only been a few hours," her father said quietly. "Thank you for the ham, Bernard. Bessie will appreciate it."

Then there was the click of high heels, coming from the back hall. "Here, Clifton, hand me those plates." It was Annie Burns. "Somebody really should go up and get Emily, you know. All these people want to pay their respects."

Emily almost choked on the cigarette smoke. Annie was right. She should be downstairs. She mashed out the cigarette butt in a plant saucer by the stairs and lit a fresh one before she started down. In her left arm, she clutched the photograph of her husband.

No one heard her footsteps. The callers had settled into the front parlor, listening to her father speak. "The officer told me that Howard died a hero, trying to save his company at Bizerte."

"That battle took place over two weeks ago." It was Billy Gillespie, editor of the *Gazette* and the town's unofficial historian. "According to all accounts," his gravelly voice continued, "Bizerte was the turning point in the North African campaign. It was there that the Allies finally pushed the Germans out."

"I suppose it's comfort knowing he died a hero," an unidentified voice commented.

"Hero or not, he was too young to die." It was Annie who spoke up sharply.

She was right, Emily thought. He was too young to die. He loved his life, his family. There was so much he wanted to do. It wasn't fair, she said to herself, echoing the words Vandella Jenks had used a few short hours—a lifetime— ago.

Emily had wandered into the middle of the foyer when Billy saw her. "It's Mrs. Emmett," he said to Annie. "I think she needs some help."

She froze, staring vacantly at Billy, as if she were trying to identify the husky blond man with the horn-rimmed glasses and the kind face. Annie rushed to her side. "Goodness, child, you don't have any shoes on."

Emily looked down at her long, narrow feet, which were covered only with stockings. There was a small run, beginning over the right big toe.

"Em! Em!" Roland ran up the back hallway, still in the baseball uniform he had worn in the big afternoon game over in Bristol. Clenching his fists, he stood in front of her. "Damn those Nazis," he choked out. "Damn them for killing Howard."

The Nazis, she repeated to herself. It was their fault that Howard was dead. They were the monsters who had taken her husband's life. But why hadn't they killed someone else? Howard wasn't a bad man. His grandfather had even been born in Germany.

"Look, Roland," she said to her brother, as she handed him the photograph. "Look, I took this photograph at Fort Bragg, just before he went away. Remember?"

Roland took the picture without looking at it. "I'll take care of it, sis," he said.

Clifton appeared, putting his arm around his daughter's shoulder and saying: "It's all right, Emily. Everything will be all right."

She shook her head, thinking: What a stupid thing to say. "No, it isn't, Papa. Yesterday the mailman came and brought me Howard's letter. He said he got the razor blades and the lifesavers. He said he wasn't near the fighting."

"Everything will be all right."

"Stop talking, Cliff," Annie urged, pulling at his sleeve. "Do something. Can't you see the child's in shock?"

"Where's Dr. Giles?" Billy asked.

"I'm right here," Giles called as he took out his worn black bag from the hall closet.

"Honey-chile," Bessie called, her arms outstretched, as she rounded the corner from the kitchen. "Come to Bessie, chile. You jest come here to Bessie."

Gratefully Emily rushed into the sanctuary of the black woman's bosom, moaning, "Oh, Bessie, he's gone. My Howard is gone."

"Hush, now, chile," Bessie crooned. "Jest come upstairs with Bessie. You needs rest. Up we go now, chile. Just hang on to Bessie."

Emily clung to Bessie's hand as they mounted the stairs together. At the landing she stopped, still dazed and confused. "My baby," she whispered. "Where's Alexander?"

"Your baby's just fine. He's gone visitin', remember?" Calling down the stairs, she ordered: "Dr. Giles, git on up here."

EMILY struggled awake from a drugged and restless sleep. For two long nights, she had dreamed the same dream. She was searching for Howard across an endless desert. Miles and miles she trudged, across mountainous dunes, through blinding sandstorms, as an unrelenting sun beat down on her. She awoke feeling parched and exhausted. As her eyes opened, it came, the desperate certainty that the nightmare wasn't over yet. It had just begun. Howard was lost to her forever. She was all alone.

How could she tell her son that his father was never coming back? How could Alexander possibly understand what the words meant? What would Howard want her to do?

She closed her eyes and answered her own question. He would want me to live, for myself and for our child. And so I must. I will keep busy. I will get out of bed and work in the garden, the way I always do before breakfast.

Forcing her numbed and heavy body out of bed, she slipped out of her nightgown and into the soiled shirt and overalls she had worn the day before. Without washing her face or combing her hair, she tiptoed downstairs out to the garden.

The grass was still wet with dew. The hoe was lying near the border of peonies, just where it had been left the afternoon before. Picking it up, she walked towards the garden she and Alexander had just planted. Then it struck her. The horrible irony of a Victory Garden. There would never be a victory now, not for Emily or her son. They had already been defeated. Finished. There was nothing to hope for, to pray for any more. The numbness that had taken her over gave way to a hot, blinding anger.

She swung the hoe, wildly, as if it were a weapon, hacking the pink blossoms from the peony bushes that bordered the yard.

Breathless and shaking, she plunged past the decapitated flowers, stomping the baby tomato plants to a pulp with her shoes. Finally exhausted, she fell to her knees and pounded the freshly tilled earth with her fists. "Howard, oh, Howard," she cried. "Why did it have to be you?"

"Emily! Emily!" She turned pain-glazed eyes towards the house and saw her father running across the yard, his brown bathrobe flapping in the morning breeze.

She surveyed the destruction around her, the broken blossoms, the mangled tomatoes, with an air of bewilderment. "The garden," she said blankly. "It's all ruined."

"It's all right," Clifton reassured his daughter, as he wrapped his arm around her shoulder. "It's all right, Emily. We can plant again. Come inside, now."

*   *   *

SHE sat at the round oak table in the kitchen, a willowware china cup clutched in her hand. She stared at the platters of food crowded onto the metal table next to the refrigerator. Bessie won't have to cook for days, she thought.

"Emily," her father began, as he poured coffee for himself. "Do you remember how we sat here together after your mother died?"

She nodded, remembering. Only three short years ago— at the end of summer. It had been the night before the funeral and she had crept down to the kitchen, unable to sleep. Her father had come into the room, his eyes red with weeping.

None of the children had realized how ill their mother was, though she had, for several years, spent more and more time "resting" on the rose velvet settee, with the brocade curtains of her bedroom drawn. But they had not suspected, even when Dr. Giles began to appear every day, that she was suffering from anything more serious than her sick headaches. Then, suddenly, she was dead.

"You made me some coffee," he said. "Do you remember? You made me drink it. Now you take a sip for me, won't you?"

Emily's hand shook, as she lifted the cup to her mouth and took a sip. The hot liquid tasted bitter, but she forced herself to swallow.

Clifton spoke quietly. "I know you can't believe it now, but your life isn't over. Time will make a difference. Your child, Alexander, he will make a difference. He will bring you back, little by little."

Carefully she replaced the cup on its saucer, staring into the dark coffee. "Is it enough?" she asked, almost to herself. "Is it enough to live for a child?"

"You four were enough for me," Clifton said. Just as he was about to say something more, Alexander pushed open the kitchen door. "Hi, Mom," he greeted. "I'm back."

Emily held out her arms to him. As her son skipped across the linoleum floor, she was reminded how much he looked like his father, and the thought gave her pain, rather

than comfort. She hugged him tightly, wanting never to let
him go.

"Hey, Mom," he protested. "I can't breathe."

Releasing him, she asked in a voice she tried to keep
even: "Did you have a good time?"

"Yep. We played with the trains," Alexander reported,
as he headed for the cookie tin on the metal table next to
the refrigerator.

"Honey," Emily beckoned her son, knowing she would
have to say something to him before someone else did.

Sensing that something serious was in the air, the child
asked a question of his own. "Is my daddy in 'departed'?"

"In 'departed'?" she repeated, not understanding what
he was saying. "Where did you hear that?"

"That's what Joey's mom said," he answered, reaching
for the plate of biscuits on the table. "She said Daddy was
departed."

"Oh, no," Emily whispered, as she clutched the table for
support.

"Come here, boy," Clifton said, rising from the table.
"What do you say about pancakes this morning?" He took
the child's hand and led him into the pantry, where all the
"fixings" were kept. "You can mix, and I'll flip. How does
that sound?"

"H'rray," the boy agreed excitedly. "I get to make pancakes, Mom!"

Emily smiled weakly until Clifton and Alexander were
out of sight. Then she buried her head in her arms, feeling
the cool surface of the wood table against her cheek, as she
wondered how she would tell her son that "departed" was
not a place on the map.

AFTER the pancake breakfast, which Emily only pretended
to eat, she decided she would have to get out of the house,
to go somewhere she could be alone with her son. The
phone had not stopped ringing since nine o'clock. Soon her
sisters would be arriving. Tonight another wave of towns-

folk would be calling on her. She wasn't ready to face them all, not just yet.

As if he sensed what she was feeling, Roland suggested she take Alexander to Cedar Creek, on the outskirts of town, for a little fishing. "A fine idea," Clifton agreed. "We'll take care of everything here."

So while Emily helped Bessie pack a basket lunch, Roland and Alexander rounded up the fishing gear and dug up a can of worms.

Just before they were ready to leave, Emily ran up to her bedroom. She took all of Howard's letters, which she'd kept tied with a blue ribbon, out of her top dresser and tucked them into her purse. She wanted something of Howard with her. She wanted to reread them and feel him close to her again.

But the letters were never touched, for as soon as they got down to the creek, Alexander demanded all her attention. He was awkward holding the fishing pole, unable to thread the worms on the hook without her help. As she stood watching her son in the green river valley, with the sun filtering through a canopy of spring tree limbs feathered against the blue sky, she tried to rehearse the words she would use. Empty sounding phrases marched through her mind: "I have some sad news to tell you . . . Your daddy has gone away . . ."

"Mom! Mom!" Alexander's high-pitched voice interrupted her thoughts. "A fish! A fish!"

"Hold on. I'll be right there," she called, as she slid down a boulder to the river's edge. She steadied the rod as it bent and quivered, but the fish eluded them, eating the bait and then swimming away.

Disappointed, they climbed the rocks once more. Undaunted, Alexander foraged through the worm can, ready to begin again. Sitting by his side, she took the cigarette from her shirt pocket and lit it, observing as she did how natural it seemed to be smoking now, just as Howard had done.

The child looked up from the squirming tangle of worms and said: "Uncle Ro said Daddy was staying in Af'ca forever and ever, but it was okay."

"I see," she said, searching her child's face for some sign of distress. "How do you feel about that?"

"I want to go to Af'ca when I'm growed up. I want to see the jeep named Alex." Wiping his muddy hands on his overalls, he reached in the basket for a chicken leg. When he was finished, he held up the remains, suggesting: "Maybe the fish like bones?"

"No, honey, they don't," she said, relieved that Roland had talked to her son and that he had done it so well. "We better head back to Breezy now. Carrie and Nancy are coming to visit."

"Jeepers creepers!" Alexander explained, using the expression he'd picked up from a song he'd heard on Bessie's radio.

When they drove up the lane and around the house, she saw that two unfamiliar cars had arrived: a green Studebaker and a yellow Checker cab with a New York license plate. Parking next to the Studebaker, Emily read "Unity Florists, Abington" printed on the driver's side. Flowers were being delivered. "Oh, God," she whispered as she turned off the motor. "Spare me any purple-ribboned wreaths."

Alexander was excited by the sight of the taxi, which looked just like a picture in one of his books. He jumped up and down on the car seat, pleading: "Please, Mom, can I stay out here? Please?"

The back door slammed, and Roland came down the walk. "Catch any fish?" he asked.

"Nope," Alexander answered cheerfully, happily distracted now by the yellow cab.

"Ro," Emily said. "Could you stay out here a while with Alexander? It might be easier..."

"Sure."

"And Ro—thank you for talking to him. I...I just..."

"Forget it, sis." He cut her off and squared his shoulders in a gesture she had never seen before. "Howard told me to take care of you, remember?"

Slowly she made her way up the back steps. Carefully she opened the creaky screen door, quietly crossing the linoleum-covered back porch, hoping to creep through the kitchen and up to her bedroom before anyone saw her.

The hope was short-lived. As she approached the kitchen she heard voices. Accented voices. Meg's in-laws. She tucked herself to the side of the jelly cabinet and slid the picnic basket onto the top shelf. She heard Mr. Steinmetz speaking.

"In our religion," he said, "we sit shivah when a loved one dies. So that is what we have come to do."

"I see," her father said, clearly having no idea what the other man meant. She knew about the ritual. Once she and Howard had gone to pay their respects when the father of a Jewish instructor at the university had died.

"It was very kind of you to come, Mr. Steinmetz," Clifton went on, "and to bring our Meg."

"Maurice. Call me, Maurice," the deep voice insisted. "We are all family, no?"

Then she heard the sound of paper bags rustling. Peeking around the door frame, she saw that the large man with the yarmulke on his head was stacking the contents of several bags on the kitchen table. Not wanting to be seen, she drew back against the wall, as Mrs. Steinmetz's musical voice identified the food: "I bring some apfelstrudel, a nice Sacher torte, some Mozartkugeln . . ."

"In the pantry," Bessie mumbled, clearly unsettled by having her kitchen invaded with strange visitors and strange food. "You can take dese folks to Mistah Roland's room. I'll git to de beds soon's I can."

"We do not want to make trouble in this hard time," Mr. Steinmetz apologized.

"No trouble at all," Clifton reassured his unexpected guests, trying to cover Bessie's lack of enthusiasm for the Steinmetzes and their offerings. "I'm sure Emily will be most appreciative."

Emily silently disagreed. She wasn't appreciative. These were just more people to be suffered and endured. Why couldn't anyone understand that she didn't want to be surrounded by people? Even well-meaning people. Why couldn't they understand that she just wanted to be left alone?

"So young to be a widow. So young," Mrs. Steinmetz was saying. "Such a shame."

EMILY crept up the back hall, past the back parlor door and the dining room, without being noticed. She was about to climb the stairs, when Charlotte came clicking out of the front parlor on a pair of high-heeled black pumps, dressed for the occasion in a black taffeta suit with a ruffled collar.

"Oh, my, it's you, Emily," she exclaimed, looking as if she had seen a ghost. She fumbled with the pen and the box of stationery she was carrying, not knowing what to say to the sister whose life had been so disarranged by this unexpected death.

"Hello, Charlotte," Emily heard herself say, as she stuck her hands into her pants pockets.

Carrie and Nancy peeked around the parlor double door, still dressed in their wrinkled sailor suits. "We slept on the train, Aunt Emily," Carrie boasted to her aunt.

"Thank goodness John was able to get us a compartment. I don't know what we would have done if we'd had to sit up all night with all those noisy soldiers." Charlotte was talking even faster than usual, Emily noted. "It was a troop train, of course," she added.

"Me and Mummy sleep on the bottom," plump, curly-headed Nancy said, grinning.

"It was a nerve-racking trip. They're much too young to travel well, you know." Charlotte patted nervously at her already perfect pageboy.

"Where's Alexander?" Carrie asked, restlessly shuffling a Mary Jane pump on the floor.

"Outside, in the back lane," Emily pointed the way, and the girls raced down the hallway.

"I do wish John could be here with me, but he's on a special reconnaisance, and he couldn't get leave. He sends his sympathy." Charlotte readjusted the ruffle at her throat. "Oh, Em," she wailed, "I don't know what to say, I'm saying all the wrong things." She started across the foyer, moving to embrace her sister, but Emily turned to avoid her.

Starting up the stairs, she heard herself saying: "It's all right, Charlotte."

"I'll just stay down here and get things organized." She took a tablet from a box and displayed a long list. "You know what I mean—death notices for the paper, notes to the people who came to call..."

"That's fine." Emily nodded, marveling at Charlotte's ability to make everything manageable by reducing it to a social ritual. "I'll go change my clothes."

"Oh, yes," Charlotte agreed, following her to the foot of the stairs. "A nice black dress..."

EMILY had scarcely closed the bedroom door, when she heard a timid knock. "The door's open," she called out, as she sat down on the bed and slipped off her pumps.

"Em, it's me." Meg came in, her swollen body covered loosely with an embroidered Mexican dress. "Oh, Em, I'm so sorry. So horribly sorry," she started to cry.

This was what Emily had dreaded most. The tears. The awful pitying looks. Rising abruptly, she went over to the window. "I'd rather not talk about it."

"I'm sorry," Meg apologized, swallowing her tears. "I didn't mean to upset you."

"It's all right." She heard herself repeating her father's empty phrase as she stared down at the cement birdbath in the side yard.

"Maurice and Eva drove me down in Uncle Max's cab. You remember, the one David used to drive. They didn't want me to come alone on the train. Not in this condition."

"I see," Emily responded mechanically, wondering how long Meg was going to stay in her room. She longed to stretch out on her bed for a moment. To be left alone.

"I've been thinking." Meg's voice quivered. "I've been thinking, I'm not going to tell David about Howard. I'm afraid it would upset him. I'm..."

"Please. Please leave me alone."

"Oh, Em." Meg looked as if she would cry again. "I'm so sorry," she said, backing out of the room. "I guess I'll go downstairs. Unless there's something I can do for you."

"No," Emily said flatly. "Nothing."

IT was several hours later when Emily awoke. She lay in her bed, staring at the ceiling, tracing with her eyes the familiar cracks in the plaster. She would have to get up and dress. They would all be waiting for her downstairs.

In slow motion, she got up from the bed and went to the closet. She pulled out the red dress with the padded shoulders and pleated skirt, the one Howard had bought her just before he left. "Red Badge of Courage," she said aloud, ruefully. Howard would understand her choice. The others would probably think the dress was an outrage, but she didn't care.

As she came out of her room, she heard the children playing in Roland's room across the hall. Looking in, she saw Alexander and his cousins sprawled on the floor, drawing pictures on a long roll of brown butcher's paper. Roland stood above them, directing their efforts. "Now how about some things growing in the garden," he said.

She stepped unnoticed into the room and watched her son. He was drawing a tall tomato plant, while Carrie carefully outlined a huge flower with red petals. Nancy was humming, as she scribbled some worms along the paper's edge.

Kneeling down, she examined the rest of the mural, which they had titled "Our Day." She saw a train puffing along a track bordered by some orange-dotted trees and a garden filled with oversized tomato plants.

"Thought the kids and I would tackle the Victory Garden tomorrow," Roland volunteered, as he shifted his weight from one foot to the other, not wanting to make any direct reference to the morning's destruction.

"That would be nice," she replied, wishing she knew how to explain what she had done.

Alexander tugged at his mother's sleeve, eager to show off his artwork, which was separated from his cousin's by a vertical black line. "This is a desert," he explained, pointing to a thick brown heap. "And that's a tank. And this is Daddy going to heaven."

Emily stared at the stick figure of a man with wings. She managed to say: "That's very nice, honey."

"Is my daddy a hero?" the child asked, his glasses askew, his eyes scrunched up in serious concentration.

Emily assumed he'd been talking to Roland again. She straightened his glasses as she answered. "Yes, Alexander, your daddy was a hero."

"My daddy is a pilot," Carrie boasted. "When he comes home, he tickles me and throws me in the air!"

"Okay, Chatterbox, that's enough," Roland intervened smoothly as she reached down to help Emily to her feet. "Hey, Em, Charlotte's been up here a hundred times, wanting to wake you up. I kept her out, but Mrs. Emmett has arrived."

Facing Howard's straitlaced mother was an ordeal Emily particularly dreaded. This was the first time Harriet Emmet had ever deigned to set foot in the Whittaker home, for she considered the Whittakers to be commoners, and the Emmetts, despite the loss of all the family money during the Crash, to be one of America's bluest bloodlines. She had never altered her original position, that Howard had wedded beneath him. Between the two women, a civil truce had been struck for Howard's sake, but now with Howard gone, Emily didn't know what to expect.

As she came down the stairs, Charlotte was placing a bouquet of white carnations on the hall table. Sighting the red dress, she gave Emily a look of alarm. "Are you sure you want to wear that?" she asked cautiously.

"Absolutely," Emily answered firmly, almost defiantly. Shoulders squared, she crossed the vestibule to the front parlor, the full skirt of the dress swaying as she walked. Near the doorway, holding court from one of the Queen Anne chairs, Mother Emmet sat, tightly corsetted in a black faille suit, holding her ebony cane in front of her and talking to Clifton.

"Emily," her father said gently, rising and walking towards her. "Would you like to sit down?"

"No, thanks, I'll stand." Politely, she presented her hand to Howard's mother.

The offered hand was acknowledged with a nod, rather than a touch. "Emily, your father tells me you will probably wish Howard's headstone placed in the West Grove Cemetery, next to your mother's grave. I will not have it." The cane was tapped sharply for emphasis. "My son's grave will be in the Beacon Hill Cemetery, where the Emmetts have been buried for generations."

Emily stared, fascinated and repelled by her mother-in-law. She's like a bald eagle, she thought, swooping down to collect the remains of the son she had always tried to possess. "How can you talk about headstones," she asked the granite face, "when we don't even know if there's a body left?"

"Emily, dear," her father interrupted, "there is no need for us to settle the question of a headstone now. However, there are certain . . . details that must be discussed. The memorial service, so Reverend Lowell can make the arrangements . . ."

Emily stared at her father, mute with reproach and disappointment. Not you, too, she thought. Surely you should understand . . .

"Memorial service?" she repeated. "Who said there would be a memorial service?"

The Steinmetzes sat on the sofa, looking a little uncomfortable and out of place. Mrs. Steinmetz stood up and rearranged the fringed black shawl that draped her shoulders. She offered the box of candy that had been balanced on her plump lap. "We came to sit shivah. To share your sorrow. A piece of candy to help you feel better?"

"Candy?" Emily echoed, feeling as if she were trapped in a roomful of strangers who were saying the most extraordinarily strange things to her.

"Em, dear," Charlotte interrupted. "The Bristol paper is on the telephone. They need some facts for the obituary. Was Howard professor of electrical or mechanical engineering? I can't seem to remember."

Emily looked at her sister in amazement. "Charlotte, Howard was my husband for almost seven years. Didn't you ever care enough to know what he taught?"

The sound of the doorbell brought the tense exchange to an end. Emily walked leadenly to the door, grateful for the opportunity to leave the room.

There, standing on the porch, was Vandella Jenks, dressed in her parade outfit, holding an Ivory Snow carton in her arms. She set the box on the floor. Carefully, she lifted out a small beagle pup and offered it to Emily. "When I heard tell of your husband's passin', I says to my mister, I says, 'There's a mighty lot of comfort in a pup,' so I brung this for your youngun."

A rush of tears came to Emily's eyes, for the first time since she had heard the news. She reached for the soft, long-eared puppy. "Thank you," she said, her voice cracking. "Thank you for both of us."

"Ain't much, considerin' your heartache," the country-woman said, as she walked on down the front steps and disappeared into the night shadows.

Emily hugged the small furry bundle close to her, feeling the life pulsing through its tiny body. And suddenly, it was as if a wall started to crumble, the wall she'd built between herself and her own feelings, between herself and all the people who loved her. She began to sob, huge racking sobs that shook her body, hot salty tears that ran freely down her face, staining the bright red dress. She stood on the porch for a long time, cradling the puppy, rocking it in her arms, almost on the very spot where her whole life had changed a little over forty-eight hours before.

Later that night, after the rest of the household was fast asleep, Emily heard her father drive down the lane towards town. He had said he was headed for the office. She wondered if he would write The Breezy Hill Bulletin or visit with Miss Jewel.

It wasn't until a week or so later, when she forced herself to go back to her job at the draft board, that Emily came across a carbon of the Bulletin her father had written that night. It was addressed only to Clifton's sons-in-law.

19 May 1943

My Dear Soldiers,

It is in grief and sorrow that I write you, for a tragedy has struck our family. Forty-eight hours ago, an officer from the Army delivered the news that your brother-in-law, Major Howard C. Emmett, had lost his life at the Battle of Bizerte.

Your wives and families are gathered here with us on Breezy and we are comforting Emily and one another, as best we can. As you would expect, Emily is bravely adjusting to her loss. Young Alexander, however, does not yet comprehend his father's passing or the finality of death.

We together on the hill cannot question God's will, just as you cannot question your duty in the field of battle. We must all persevere in this dreadful war, which has now added to its toll the name of Howard Charles Emmett and in the memory of his great sacrifice, reconsecrate our lives to its conclusion.

Now on to victory, my sons. May God bless and keep you and send you speedily home to us.

> Your devoted father-in-law,
> J.C. Whittaker

6

A Child is Born
June 1943

My Dear Children,

Rose Mary writes from her Indian Reservation out in New Mexico that her eleventh school year with the Hopi tribe is drawing to a close and that she is packing up for her annual summer visit. On stationery decorated with water colors of arrows and pots she says,

> *"I plan to leave Taos in my faithful old Polly Packard on the 6th and drive my way leisurely towards our valley corner of the Blue Ridge, hoping to arrive in time for the Flag Day parade. In case my meandering or Polly's mechanical temperament alters my schedule, be sure to save some firecrackers for me."*

So this week on Breezy, preparations began for our reunion. Alexander, aided by Roland, is setting up a teepee by the barn in honor of his Great-Aunt's arrival and Bessie is cooking up a storm. I decided, with Peaches and Cream's help, to trim the front meadow at the foot of the hill, and one evening on my return from the office staked out my "critter" (as Bessie refers to her) down there. Unfortunately, Peaches rejected the tall grass and "meandered" her way loose, choosing instead to feed on our prize hollyhocks!

As Bessie had predicted, Rose Mary did not arrive in time for the Flag Day festivities. But when she did honk her way up the long lane shortly before midnight, the entire family, with the exception of Alexander, who had fallen asleep on the sofa, was up and waiting.

After hugs in the driveway, the clan moved into the kitchen, where Emily had set out the remains of the picnic food—cold fried chicken, potato salad and deviled eggs.

In between bites, Rose Mary fired questions around the table, carefully avoiding any reference to Howard's death. What was the latest news from David? How was Charlotte managing in Florida? Did Alexander receive the drums she had sent? And was Roland ready for a vigorous summer of tutoring?

When she finally declared she simply could not eat another mouthful, Rose Mary stood up. "I'm exhausted," she admitted. "See you all in the morning." She looked over fondly at the baby brother she had loved and protected so fiercely when they were children, the man who still seemed vulnerable, in spite of the air of total composure he projected to the rest of the world.

"I'm glad you're here, sister," Clifton said quietly, as he took her arm and escorted her out of the kitchen. "We need you."

"I'm glad to be here," she said, ruffling his silver hair, "I've missed you all."

As she had done every morning for years, Rose Mary woke at dawn. She splashed cold water on her face and went downstairs, to begin her day with a few moments of meditation. She sat cross-legged on the front porch, eyes closed, feeling the incipient warmth of the rising sun against her eyelids. In the remembered familiarity of Breezy, she gave herself up to the quiet, focusing her entire being on the breath of life that flowed into her mouth and out through her nostrils. She did not hear Bessie walking slowly up the lane.

Bessie stopped and for a moment she thought of shaking Rose Mary's shoulder and asking if everything was all right, but as she had learned to do through the years, she kept her mouth shut, walking softly around the back way to begin her own morning routine.

She was taking the cornbread out of the oven when Rose Mary came through the swinging kitchen door. "Morning, Bessie," she called out cheerfully, squeezing the other woman's shoulders in a hearty embrace. "It's good to see you again."

"Mornin', Miss Rose Mary. Mighty glad to have you home. Mighty glad. There be a powerful sadness in dis house. I says to myself: 'Maybe Miss Rose Mary kin make it better.'"

"I certainly mean to try, Bessie. Sit down and have some coffee with me before everyone wakes up."

"Yes, ma'am." The black woman set out two cups and saucers and poured the coffee.

"Don't start 'ma'aming' me again, Bessie. We've known each other too long for that. Tell me about Emily . . . She seems a little quiet . . ."

"Too quiet, if you ask me. The heart done gone from that chile. She get up every mornin', she do what she spose to do. But her eyes be someplace else. The Reverend, he done come heah, but she always send him away. Shut herself up in her room, ever since po' Mistuh Howard die. 'Tain't hardly natural."

"It's eminently natural, Bessie," Rose Mary said, thumping the table with emphasis. "A great grief is like a great love, Bessie . . . it doesn't pass so quickly. She needs time . . . and help."

Bessie nodded vigorously when she heard the word "help."

"She not the only one who need help. Miss Meg be nervous as a cat. Scared her man goin' to get hisself kilt, too. Scared 'bout the chile she carryin'. Jus' like her mama was. She don' say nothin', but I kin see it . . . 'specially when she sit there at Miss 'Lisbeth's piano, makin' music like she don' dare stop."

Rose Mary reached across the table and patted the other woman's hand. "We're blessed to have you, Bessie. You're right, of course. Meg is frightened. She should be. We all should be. Terrible things are happening in this world of ours."

IT was Emily that Rose Mary tackled first, by inviting herself in to the inner sanctum of her niece's bedroom. Clifton had gone off to his office, and Meg had retreated to her piano. Roland, trailed by Alexander, had begun his weekly collection of tin cans for West Grove's Scrap Drive.

On her desk was a pile of handwritten pages, an open notebook and, to the right, where Emily could see and touch it while she wrote, a photograph of Howard in uniform. It was a little out of focus, but it was so much Howard . . . the serious eyes, the loving smile, the half-wave, half-salute he'd made just before she snapped the picture.

"What are you writing?" Rose Mary asked. "Something about Howard?"

"Yes . . ." Emily's response was tentative, guarded. "How did you know?"

"Seems natural to me," Rose Mary answered, stretching the truth a bit. "You're the literary Whittaker, aren't you?"

"I . . . I thought I'd do it for Alexander," Emily said, "for when he's older. I don't want him to forget his father."

"That's a beautiful thought." Rose Mary noticed how tightly Emily's hands were clenched. "Does it help you?"

"I think so." Emily stared at the photograph. "But it's still hard for me to believe that he's not coming back. I know I should be able to by now. But I can't . . ."

"That's natural, too, Emily. My Indians mourn their dead for a very long time. Many moons must go by before the

Great Spirit takes the dead into the sky. Until then, the dead are said to hover around the earth. Maybe this is still hovering time for you and Howard. Can you accept that and live with it?"

Emily took a deep breath. "I'm trying." She shared her daily litany: "I have to be strong, for Alexander. I have to be strong because Howard would expect me to be."

"You are strong, child. I'm proud of you. But that doesn't take away the pain, does it?"

Emily choked back a sob. "Oh, Aunt Rose Mary, it hurts so much, and I don't know what to do."

"Of course you do." Rose Mary held out her arms and held her niece close, stroking her forehead as she spoke. "You feel the pain, just as you're doing now. And then, child, you let go of all that foolish talk of 'must' and 'should.' Life comes back after the pain, Emily. Life. All you have to do is let it back into your heart."

Emily had stopped crying. She pulled away and looked at her aunt, hope mingled with the questions in her eyes.

Rose Mary went on, her voice strong and confident. "You have survived Howard's death. But survival is not enough. You are going to live again. The pain will soften. It won't ever go away completely . . . I won't lie to you about that. But it will get easier. Now you have to do your part and get on with the business of life."

"Howard said something like that, just before he left."

"He was right. We're going to find you something to do . . . something that wonderful mind of yours can take hold of and run with. Now wash your face and come downstairs. I'm going to have Bessie warm up some coffee and cornbread for us. Hurry up, now, scoot!"

Emily did as she was told. The cold water on her face felt good. As she started down the hallway, a poem tugged at her memory. Returning to her room, she went to her leatherbound Emily Dickinson collection and thumbed through the well-worn pages, until she came to number CLVIII, which began, "After great pain a formal feeling comes."

She read on through the spare, piercing verse to the last stanza, the lines that spoke for her broken heart.

This is the hour of lead
Remembered if outlived,
As freezing persons recollect the snow—
First chill, then stupor, then the letting go.

Her eyes filled with tears again, but she wiped them with the back of her hand and walked resolutely downstairs.

MEG could tell by the slant of light across the piano top that it was almost time for the mailman. Ever since the girls had come back to Breezy, Niles Hedley had walked up the long lane to hand deliver the mail every morning. He usually arrived around 11:30, just when the summer sun rounded the east side of the house and shone throught the parlor window.

Meg made herself sit down at the piano every day at nine, determined to maintain the same four-hour practice schedule she had had at Juilliard. Each week, Professor Claessen sent her a new set of assignments. This week, it was more Bach cantatas and Chopin's haunting B-flat Minor Nocturne. Technically, she had mastered them, but the music sounded as dull and uninspired as she felt. Her entire life seemed to center on the mail, she reflected, as her fingers moved in measured, even movements through Bach.

Being home on Breezy was not the same. She and Papa were on speaking terms only, like polite strangers. The memory of his initial cruel rejection of David still hung between them, though her pregnancy had softened his attitude towards her marriage. But her father's concern for her health, even for her husband's safety, did not move Meg. She reflected bitterly that her father's readiness to do the right and honorable thing now did not exonerate him from all those months of silent condemnation.

In fact, there seemed to be a frozen separateness to all their lives. Even Emily and Papa didn't talk much. Still mourning, her sister spent most of her time alone, locked in her bedroom. The only joy, the only pulsing energy came from the boys. From Alexander, who seemed to be growing and thriving in spite of his mother's perpetual air of sadness. And from Roland, who seemed to be coming into his own. She welcomed the boisterous camaraderie that had sprung up between her brother and her nephew, grateful that they seemed immune to the grayness that overlaid her days.

It had been three weeks now since she'd had a letter from David. Twenty-one hellishly long days. The second longest interval between letters since he'd gone away. When her long vigil began, Meg had made a compact with her own fears; she would not allow them free rein until ten letterless days had passed. Then she would redouble her prayers to her God and David's, especially during those anxious morning hours, before that heart-stopping moment when the mail arrived. And if there was nothing for her, no lifeline from David, she would take her fears to the piano and pound them out in a superstitious ritual of thunderous chords and anguished crescendoes, until she was too spent to think.

She promised herself that if no letter came today, she would go directly to her room and write to David, as if by thinking of him, by seeing him in her mind's eye, she could somehow guarantee his life. She would not express the awful thought that her letter might never reach its destination, might find its way into strange hands, official hands, because David, her David, would no longer be there to read it.

She tried always to fill her letters with images of life, of the life she was carrying in her body. She tried to make her pregnancy sound wondrous and miraculous. David would expect that. He didn't need to know that this child she was carrying felt foreign, alien, that her body felt bloated and ugly and not at all beautiful. That lately her sleep had been haunted by the same frightening dream: David in an Army uniform, a surgical mask over his face, standing in the middle of New York's Pennsylvania Station, where they had said goodbye. His arms would be outstretched, and she would hand him a baby wrapped in the striped Indian blanket Aunt Rose Mary had sent for Christmas. Looking down at the infant, he would ask: "Why is the baby like this?" And then, as he unwrapped the blanket, the child would come apart, limb by limb, and she would wake up, shaking with terror.

Dr. Giles, Emily, everyone in fact, assured her regularly that there was nothing to worry about, but she found it hard to believe them. Those first few months in New York when her body was racked with morning sickness, when she had nearly miscarried, had made her certain that something had gone wrong. Something she would see only when the child was born. The secret fear grew inside her, making sleep increasingly difficult.

As far as she knew, David was still somewhere south of London, caring for the legions of allied wounded who were being shipped in from the European theaters of war. She had pored over an issue of *Life* magazine, which contained a feature article on English battlefield hospitals. As she studied the grainy black-and-white photographs, seeing the primitive conditions, the awful crowding, she imagined David, her David, moving among the wounded, shoulder to shoulder with death and suffering.

The sound of the doorbell interrupted her thoughts. Jumping up from the piano bench, she bumped her distended stomach against the keyboard. "The mail!" she called out, as she ran to meet Mr. Hedley, murmuring a last rosary of private prayers.

There was a letter from David. Limp with relief, she sat in the wicker rocker on the front porch and slowly opened the envelope, careful not to damage the fragile pages in her haste. The last letter had been so mutilated by the censors that it had resembled a paper doily, but this one had scarcely been touched. When she had wailed her disappointment to Emily, her sister had explained how she and Howard had worked out a code in advance, so that his letters could escape the censors' scissors. But David tried to share his daily experiences in detail with Meg, forgetting that official eyes would be cutting out descriptions of military locations and troop activity.

She began to read this newest chapter in the life he was living without her, a life that would not, she prayed, kill

him or change him from the man with whom she had fallen
in love.

Dearest Princess,

*It's raining here. Again. Not like the rain we used
to love in New York. It's cold and gray and it mildews
the bandages in the camp hospital. We lost our gen-
erator during the last German air buzz, and we've
had to get by with a few weak batteries and some
candles we scrounged from the nearest village. Last
night a truckload of wounded came in and we lost
most of them on the table. Can't blame it on the bad
light—the heavy mortar shelling had done the job
already. But it's such a bad feeling not to be able to
see what you're doing, even if it's only to watch the
last rites with a scalpel in your hands.*

"Oh, David," she paused, wiping the tears that were
clouding her eyes.

Just then the screen door opened and Emily came outside.
"Thought you might like a cup of coffee," she offered.

"Thanks, Em. I have a letter from David. And there's
one from Charlotte. Here, you read it while I finish mine."

Emily took the pink envelope postmarked Pensacola,
Florida, and sat down on the wicker swing facing her sister.
Pumping slowly, she stared down at the valley town, remembering how it had been, short weeks ago, when she
still waited for Howard's letters, sat here with them, trea-
suring each word, reading and re-reading, before she would
share bits and pieces with her family, keeping the good
parts, the expressions of love and tenderness, for herself.

Meg went back to her letter, her face filled with worry
and concern. She continued to read:

*Guess I won't win any prizes for keeping a stiff
upper lip. Sorry about that, but talking to you like
this, telling you how I really feel—it keeps me from
going crazy. This isn't the kind of doctoring I planned*

*to do, piecing together human bodies that have been
blown apart, trying to fix what I know can't be fixed
and being sick about it.*

*I want so much to be with you, to take care of you
through these last months. I keep wondering how you
and the baby are doing. Better, I hope. I hate knowing
that you were so sick with this pregnancy, and I wish
I could be there to spoil you, to make it better. Let
me promise you that when this kid is born, when I'm
back, he's going to hear a thing or two from his old
man for giving his Mom so much trouble.*

"Oh, Em," Meg sighed, when she had finished. "I love
him so much. I'm so lucky to have him. So lucky."

"Yes," Emily said quietly, fighting the hot rush of yearning that threatened her composure. "Let's see what our
Charlotte has been up to," she said with false lightness. She
ripped open the envelope, and two newspaper clippings
slipped out. One featured a photograph, a trio of Navy wives
with Charlotte in the center. The other was a column titled
"Summer Season on Base."

"Look at this," she said, her voice edged with bitter
amusement. "Our Charlotte is still the belle of the ball.
She's giving parties, for heaven's sake. Parties!"

"Let's see," Meg said, reaching for the clippings. As she
scanned the news of Charlotte's latest social triumphs, she
thought how hard it was to love her older sister at times.
Times like this. When they were both younger, Charlotte
had often seemed like a glamorous and exotic creature,
sprinkled with fairy dust, beautiful, unreachable and unreal.
As she grew up, she had been alternately enchanted, amused,
bemused and sometimes exasperated with Charlotte's antics,
even wondering on occasions if they were really and truly
sisters. Now it was hard to be amused by Charlotte's preening and posturing. Her self-centered private world didn't
seem so pretty anymore. Not with David's pain and misery
freshly etched in her heart. Not while she gazed at Em's
dear face before her, now shadowed with grief and bereavement.

* * *

"So what do you say, Miss Megan Rose? How would you like to go for a drive?" Lunch had been eaten, and Rose Mary saw the opportunity for a quiet visit, alone with her youngest niece, her almost namesake.

"Thanks, Aunt Rose Mary, but I thought I'd go upstairs and write to David..."

"You can do that later. Look at you. You're as pale as a catfish belly. Some sunshine and fresh air will do you good. David would agree, I'm sure," she finished in her no-nonsense, no-disagreement-allowed tone.

Unenthusiastically Meg settled herself into "Polly Packard," as Rose Mary threw the car into gear, whistling "Carry Me Back to Old Virginny." Five miles down Route 4, at the Becker's Bridge crossing, she turned left onto a dirt road. "The old swinging bridge is still down there, isn't it?"

"Oh, yes!" Meg clapped her hands, her delicate features lighting up with memories of childhood. "I'd forgotten all about it! Oh, do you remember all those 'secret expeditions' we used to have out here on summer vacations?"

"Indeed I do. Here, take my hand and watch your step. Your father would send me to the gallows if I brought you back in less than A-1 condition. I'm sure he'd be happier if you spent the day reclining on a sofa, with a glass of lemonade in one hand and smelling salts in the other."

Meg giggled at Rose Mary's gentle poke at Clifton's notions of propriety. Hand in hand, the two women walked, deep into the woods, their footsteps gentled by the carpet of pine needles and cushions of moss. The cool stillness soothed and wrapped Meg in a feeling of peace. "David would love this place," she murmured.

"Then bring him here when he comes home," Rose Mary said briskly. Meg felt comforted by the certainty in that remark. Rose Mary had never dispensed pink sugar pills of false cheer, not even when they were children.

"It should be around this bend," Rose Mary said, "unless that desert sun has wiped my memory clean."

Sure enough, the path twisted and the swinging bridge came into view. As always, it seemed to Meg that this plank and rope construction would have been more at home in a

Tarzan movie than in Russell County. And yet it did belong here, hidden in the woody glade, a monument to love, built by a mountain man twenty years ago, to secretly visit his lady love by bridging the property lines disputed by their feuding families.

"Can we sit on the bridge and swing our legs?" Meg asked. "I mean, do you think it's all right for me to do it?"

"Certainly you can. You're pregnant, not crippled, for God's sake. Just don't do something stupid like catch your legs in the webbing."

Tentatively Meg lowered her awkward body. Most of the time she did feel like a cripple, for it felt as if all her natural grace had disappeared with the addition of all the extra pounds and inches.

Rose Mary's laughter boomed in the open air, as if she felt her niece's clumsiness. "Think you're heavy, do you dear? Watch this!" She thunked her chunky body down with an impact that rippled the bridge and coaxed another laugh from her niece.

"Sometimes I feel like I'm carrying around the Rock of Gibraltar. And my back aches so much."

"Some women are built better than others for carrying children." Rose Mary took off her beaded moccasins and white socks and wiggled her toes. "But you'll do. It's not much longer now, is it?"

"About three more months," Meg lied. "That doesn't sound like much, but it feels awfully long."

"You do want this child, don't you?" Rose Mary looked straight into her niece's eyes.

Meg flushed and broke the connection. "I love David."

"That's not what I asked you."

"It's just that everything happened so quickly. We were married, and I was pregnant..." She paused, guilty in the knowledge that she had conceived before her wedding, tempted to confess her sin and have it known, once and for all. "Then David had to go away, and I stayed in school and finished the semester. Then Howard was killed, so I came here ... to be with Em ... and because I had nowhere else to go..."

"And?"

"It's not that I don't want the baby. It's just that when David and I were together, everything felt right. Now he's gone and I'm going to be a mother, and everything's different. My life isn't anything like I imagined it would be."

"This war won't last forever. Before you know it, the baby will be born. David will come home, and the three of you will be back in New York."

"Do you really think so? Really?"

"Of course. I know it. And you'll have your music, too, just as you always wanted. A child doesn't mean the end of what you want." She said this with particular emphasis, understanding the fragile dream of a musical career that had been passed from Elizabeth to her favorite child.

"That's true, isn't it?" Meg said eagerly. "The professor said I could still perform after the baby was born, if I really wanted to. It's just . . . it's just so hard for me to believe that. New York seems so far away . . . sometimes I'm afraid I'll never get back there."

Rose Mary was silent for a moment. "Let's do something about it," she said. "Let's take a trip to New York. I haven't been there in years."

"Oh, do you think we could? Really? Oh, that would be so wonderful!" Meg sighed. "Professor Claessen's playing at Carnegie Hall next weekend! I've been longing to be there . . . but Papa would never let me go."

"Just leave your Papa to me." Rose Mary patted her niece's hand. "He's not such an ogre," she said tenderly. "Remember the fuss he made when you wanted to go to Juilliard? As I recall, he called me a meddling busybody when I encouraged you to apply for a scholarship. But in the end, he was proud of you, remember? He can be narrow-minded. That's his weakness. But he loves you. Never doubt that, no matter how many mistakes he makes."

"But you don't know," Meg protested. "You don't know how awful he was. The things he said to me, about David, and he didn't even know him. I can't forget that . . ."

"Then don't. Remember it. And use it as a lesson in what happens when being right is more important than being human. And forgive your father for being weak when you needed him to be strong."

"Funny . . . I never thought of Papa as weak. He always seemed so strong, so sure . . ."

"Meg, dear, my brother is a good man. But he is imperfect, like all God's creatures. If Clifton were as strong as you believed him to be, he'd be able to tell you he was sorry now . . . instead of trying to show you, without admitting that he was wrong. Accept that, little one. Accept it and make peace with your father. God knows we've all seen what happens when people aren't able to do that."

THAT night Rose Mary retired early. She brushed her short wavy hair vigorously and then stretched out on her bed, eyes closed, still wide awake, still thinking about her nieces. She needed Clifton's help, or at least his cooperation, to shake the girls loose of the melancholia that hung over them like a heavy shadow.

He would have to be convinced that time was not the only healer. After Elizabeth's death he had immersed himself in his daily routine, allowing time and comforting familiarities to soften his grief. But for Emily and Meg, there was little strength or solace in sliding backwards into the quiet rhythm of life at Breezy. They needed a solid anchor in the present, the hope of a bright, shining stake in the future.

THE following morning Rose Mary arranged to breakfast with Clifton downtown, in Stoots' Pharmacy, right next to the courthouse. Over the years she had found it easier to talk to her brother outside his home. Away from Breezy, Clifton seemed to unbend just a little, to relax away from his role as head of the household.

But as the waitress delivered two steaming plates of eggs and hush puppies, Clifton fidgeted against the red leather upholstery of their booth, his eyes darting from the front door to the counter. Later that morning she would learn from Bessie that Miss Jewel often ate breakfast in the drugstore. But for the moment, Rose Mary put Clifton's apparent unease to some urgent case that awaited him in the court-house.

"Clifton," she began boldly in an attempt to focus his attention, "Meg and Emily are in terrible states."

Her brother almost choked on a forkful of corn meal. "Don't you think you're overstating the case a bit, sister?"

Rose Mary recognized the rational, reasonable tone of voice. It was the same one that their lawyer father had also used when someone in the family was behaving in an excessively emotional fashion. "No," she said emphatically, taking a loud bite of toast. "You are underestimating the situation." She presented her case as briefly and effectively as she could. And knowing that her brother would only take her seriously if she had a solution to offer, she finished with her recommendations. "So as I see it," she said, "Emily needs a job. Badly. And Meg needs to get away from here for a while. To New York, I think. It will do her a world of good."

"A trip to New York? Are you mad, sister? In her condition?" Clifton looked at Rose Mary as if she had indeed lost her senses. "And a job for Emily? What in the world can she do here? There aren't even any selling jobs in the shops. The only open position in the entire town is at the *Gazette*. Stanley Walmsley just got called up. And Emily certainly can't be a reporter."

"Well, my goodness, that would be perfect!" Rose Mary was so excited that she sloshed the contents of her coffee cup all over the red table top. "Emily's always been good with words. She's certainly had a better education than poor Stanley ever did."

"Rose Mary, you can't be serious," Clifton sputtered, as he pulled paper napkins from the dispenser and mopped up the mess his sister had made. "Emily knows nothing at all about working on a newspaper."

"That's exactly what she needs," Rose Mary said triumphantly, as if Clifton had proved her point. "A challenge. Something that will demand her best efforts." She signalled the waitress to bring the check. "I'm on my way, Clifton," she said. "I've never met Mr. William Gillespie, but I do believe I will call on him right now." Before her brother could register an effective protest, she was out the door.

A FEW brisk strides brought her to the newspaper office which had been the courthouse livery stable when she was growing up. Billy Gillespie was eating a cheese sandwich and reading a printout of Saturday's *Gazette* when she arrived.

"Dammit," he muttered, slamming a fist onto his battered oak desk. The impact knocked his horn-rimmed glasses down to the tip of his nose. "Dammit," he repeated, "the whole damn line is off."

"Problems?" Rose Mary asked cheerfully, as she stood in the doorway.

"Who are you?" he snapped, embarrassed and annoyed at being interrupted and observed by a total stranger.

"I'm Rose Mary Whittaker, Clifton's sister," she answered, ignoring the newspaper editor's lapse of manners. She walked into the sparsely furnished room, noting the stacks of newspapers, the piles of books, and the fact that the place was in need of a general sweep-out. Without waiting for an invitation, she sat down in the chair facing the desk. "I'm the eccentric Whittaker. The one who lives out west with the Indians."

Billy laughed, his mood shifting abruptly. "I've heard of you," he admitted. "Maybe you've heard of me. I'm the Irishman from Chicago. The man with strange ideas. Like bringing big city journalism to this corner of the Blue Ridge."

"That's just what I've come to see you about."

"Oh?" Still smiling, Billy tipped his chair back, ready to enjoy this conversation with "the eccentric Whittaker."

"I understand that Stanley Walmsley has been drafted," she said briskly. "I have just the person to replace him."

"Really? Brought me one of your Indians?" he teased. "Because if you have, he'll have to type, cover all the social news, and..."

"It's not one of my Indians," she interrupted. "It's my niece, Emily."

Before the man could say anything, Rose Mary was out

of her chair, on her feet, a school teacher lecturing an uninformed student. "Emily graduated magna cum laude from Randolph Macon—where she majored in English Literature. She types very well. And," she leaned over the desk and looked straight into Mr. Gillespie's watery blue eyes, "she desperately needs a job. She lost her husband in North Africa, you know."

"I know," he said, his voice low and sympathetic. "It was a damn rotten break for her and the boy."

"She needs to work," Rose Mary was pleading now. "She needs something to do. Something to think about. Hire her."

"I don't suppose she has anything like newspaper experience," he asked, leaning forward in his chair.

"No," Rose Mary said, picking up her straw bag and getting ready to leave. "But she learns quickly. She's a lot smarter than Stanley, and she doesn't drink a drop. Think about it. Good day, Mr. Gillespie."

ALTHOUGH she was a firm believer in the power of positive thinking, Rose Mary was surprised to get a call from Billy Gillespie that very evening, shortly after dinner. He came straight to the point. "I'll give it a try," he said. "Tell your niece to come in tomorrow morning. I don't know where I'll find the time to teach her what's what around here," he grumbled. "The damn linotype machine just broke down."

"Thank you, Mr. Gillespie," Rose Mary said. "You won't regret it."

There was a moment of embarrassed silence. Then: "Tell Mrs. Emmett I look forward to having her aboard."

As she put the telephone down, Rose Mary suddenly knew exactly how she would put her plan into operation. First she would alert Clifton that the job was offered. Then she would talk to Emily, alone. She would appeal to her niece's patriotism, her sense of civic duty. She would describe Billy Gillespie's "plight" and persuade her niece to "fill in," at least until some other replacement for Stanley Walmsley could be found.

After registering a mild protest that she didn't know anything about working on a newspaper, Emily proved remarkably receptive to the idea of a job on the *Gazette*. Rose Mary caught a glimpse of something—gratitude, relief, in her eyes as they spoke. She realized that her niece had passed through the first numbing stages of grief and reached the point where she was asking the questions: What will become of me? What am I going to do with the rest of my life?

Pleased with her success, Rose Mary cornered Clifton in the front parlor, where he was poring over his Charles and Mary Lamb Shakespeare, the volume he called his "retreat." "Well," she said cheerfully, perching herself on the armchair opposite his, "our Emily starts to work tomorrow. Naturally, she's a little nervous..."

"Naturally," Clifton said drily, closing the volume on his lap. "Now I suppose you're going to bring up that ridiculous idea of a trip to New York again."

"That's exactly right," she laughed. "It's not a ridiculous idea. And if you love Meg as much as I think you do, you're going to let me change your mind."

THE dawning of June 13th was particularly lovely, Rose Mary thought, as she took her usual position on the front porch. An auspicious beginning for the trip to New York. She had just closed her eyes and started the controlled breathing that accompanied her meditation when she heard the screen door open. It was Meg fully dressed and flushed with excitement.

"I can't believe we're actually going," she said, as she gave her aunt a big hug.

"Well, it's true," Rose Mary said, patting her niece affectionately. "But you'd better quiet down before your father has second thoughts. He has been known to change his mind, you know."

"I know, I know. I'll be calm. Really. I'll be calm and quiet—at least until we get on the train."

"That's a good girl. Now go back upstairs and lie down. We don't want you exhausted before it's time to go to the station. And I need a few minutes to collect myself."

Rose Mary smiled as she watched Meg retreat into the house. As convinced as she was of the value of this trip,

she did feel a heavy measure of responsibility for Meg.
Even after she had managed to get Pullman berths on the
Silver Comet and convinced Giles that Meg badly needed
the tonic of a holiday, she had felt the full weight of Clifton's
reluctance. "I know I'm old-fashioned," he kept repeating,
"but I'm uneasy about this journey." Ultimately he had given
in, knowing he had no right to dictate to his daughter, and
feeling more than a little guilty about the strain of the past
that had tarnished their relationship. But with his permission
had come a stern disclaimer. "Understand that I still consider
this entire project to be ill-advised."

MEG genuinely liked the Steinmetz family. She admired
and respected the way they had made a life and a business
out of sheer hard work and determination. She appreciated
how much they loved David, how much they had sacrificed
so that he might have a good education, a fine and noble
profession. But when she was with them, Meg felt awkward.
There was a distance compounded by all the elements that
made them "different"—different from her, different from
the people she had grown up with. There were moments
when she was charmed and touched by their warmth and
spontaneity. But all too often their blunt way of speaking,
their frank emotionalism, the vividness of their manner and
expression, seemed overwhelming.

Before David went into the army, they had visited the
cafe often and spent many long evenings with the Steinmetzes and their little community of Eastern European immigrants. But after David had gone into training, their visits
became fewer. Without her husband to serve as a bridge, a
translator between her world and theirs, communication became difficult and Meg all but gave it up—until Howard
had been killed, when she had called them in desperation.

She felt guilty, now, that she'd only written once in the
past six weeks, shortly after they'd returned her to Breezy.
"I'm nervous," she said to Rose Mary, as the cab pulled
up in front of 412 Thompson.

"Meg, darling," Eva called out from the doorway of the
restaurant. Pulling her husband by the hand, she ran to open

the door of the taxi. "Come, come inside," she urged, raining heartfelt kisses on her daughter-in-law's cheeks. "Everyone has been waiting for you. Everyone wants to see David's wife."

Their "regular" table, hers and David's, was set and waiting, a bunch of fresh violets, Meg's favorite flowers, a welcoming touch beside her plate. Meg warmed to the gesture at once, feeling ashamed of her own reserve, her measured, careful responses to these kind and loving people. She took in the shiny faces, flushed with excitement and pleasure, the carefully pressed "best" clothes, and she resolved to try a little harder.

"So tell us," Eva insisted, "it is good with you and the baby? You are eating enough? And drinking milk every day? In the old country..."

"Everything is perfect," Rose Mary intervened. "Our Meg is in excellent health. And so is the baby. Otherwise, we wouldn't be here." She turned to Maurice. "How are your family and friends faring in Vienna?" she asked, genuinely concerned. The articles she had read detailed the plight of Austrian Jews following Hitler's bloodless Anschluss had filled her with horror and anger.

"It is hard," Maurice answered, his eyes growing blacker with grief. "Very hard. We have lost many to the mad man."

Eva reached across the table and wrapped her ring-covered fingers over those of her husband. She looked at Meg, her face set, her crimson mouth trembling. "David's uncle... Maurice's brother, Jacob. He is dead... in the camp at Dachau."

"Oh, no," Meg whispered, remembering the stories David had told her about his favorite uncle. A carpenter by trade. A talented painter who had illustrated his letters to young David with little drawings. She closed her eyes and remembered the gift Jacob had sent David when he had graduated from college—a small oil of a Biblical David slaying the lion. Her chest tightened with the pain she knew her husband would be feeling if he were here. "Have you written David?" she choked out.

"We have not," Maurice said quietly.

"Perhaps it would be easier after the baby is born," Rose

Mary suggested, ever practical.

"Have you names for the child?" Eva asked, grasping the opportunity to put grief aside and to think about life.

"Not really," Megan said slowly. "David and I talked about naming the baby Elizabeth after my mother if it's a girl, but we haven't chosen other names. I suppose we'd better do it soon..."

"Tell me, Mr. Steinmetz," Rose Mary interjected, "is it true there's a Jewish custom of naming children after relatives who have passed away?"

"It's true," Maurice said, running his blunt fingers absently through his wavy dark hair. Catching his wife's eye, he nodded, almost imperceptibly. "Eva," he said, a little nervously, "where are the pastries and the coffee?"

"They come now from the kitchen," she waved to a white-jacketed waiter, who brought a heaping tray of Viennese delicacies, a rich Sacher torte as well as a silver pot brimming with aromatic coffee.

"For you, Meg, Eva bakes these herself, early this morning," Maurice said, filling Meg's place with samplings of everything on the tray. "But first," he said, gripping Meg's hands so tightly that she winced, "we must talk of something important. Eva and I, we want...it would mean much to us, to David, too, we believe...if you would become one of us. So that our son's child may be born a Jew."

Meg sat very still, unable to speak for a moment, stunned by her father-in-law's request. "But I..." she stammered, "but David...he never...I don't know what to say," she finished lamely, wondering if it would matter to David now whether his child would be raised a Methodist or a Jew.

"Please think of this, Meg, dear," Eva said urgently. "We have lost so many in this war. In our religion, it is the mother who makes the child a Jew. It is you, Meg, who can give us a new life. To take the place of one that has been lost."

Meg shook her head, unable to agree, unable to say "no" to her in-laws' entreaties. She understood how they felt. She could even see a certain poetic righteousness in their request. But the thought of venturing into the dark mysteries of an alien religion seemed frightening and even a little repellent. "I'll write to David," she said, groping for a way to end the unsettling discussion. "I'll write to David to-morrow."

SITTING on a park bench outside the Metropolitan Museum, Meg conjured up an image of a beached whale, as she massaged her swollen ankles and wondered how it was possible to feel so fat and clumsy without exploding. Aunt Rose Mary had insisted on visiting the exhibit on ancient Chinese art, but after a few minutes, Meg had decided to sacrifice culture for rest.

Watching the crowds passing by, she was struck by the determined briskness of the city's people, in contrast with the leisurely, ambling pace of Main Street. She was glad she had come to New York, revived by the sense that she might still reach out and take what she wanted, even with this baby growing inside her. But being here made her miss David even more. Somehow she kept expecting him to rush around a corner and take her in his arms, to come screeching down the street in Uncle Max's cab and wave her inside.

"Hey, lady," a lanky young Marine called out. "Mind if I sit down? My bus stops here."

Meg hesitated. At home a pregnant woman was always treated with respect, but here, now . . . several tipsy soldiers had already gotten "fresh" with her as she walked through the hotel lobby.

"My wife's going to have a baby," the Marine said, taking off his hat respectfully. "She's back in Kansas."

"Sit down," Meg invited, reassured by his boyish face and neighborly manner. "Is this your first baby?"

"Nah—it's our second," he said proudly. "We have a boy, fourteen months old. Named Arnold, for my father, but we call him Buzz," he laughed.

"Your wife is so lucky," Megan said wistfully. "This is our first baby, and my husband's overseas. He's in the army." She smoothed the full red skirt over her knees. "He's a doctor."

"You must be proud of him," the boy said. "Don't worry about the baby, ma'am," he said kindly. "My wife said there was nothing to it. She said it wasn't much worse than going to the dentist."

"Really?" Meg didn't feel much reassured by the comparison. "Will you be home when the baby is born?"

"Nope." The Marine looked down at his highly polished black boots. "I'll be shipping out soon."

"I'm sorry," she said, comforted that there was at least one other woman out there somewhere who was feeling what she was feeling, praying the same prayers and sharing the same fears.

A city bus clattered to a stop in front of the bench, and the Marine stood up, hat in hand. "Got to be going now, ma'am."

"It was nice talking with you," she said. "Good luck to you with the baby—and everything."

"Good luck to you, too," he called back as he boarded the bus. "Hope it's a boy."

Meg waved as the door folded shut and the bus pulled noisily away, heading down Fifth Avenue in a cloud of black exhaust.

"Somebody else rooting for a boy, huh?"

Meg jumped at the sound of Rose Mary's voice. She turned to see her aunt holding two dripping ice cream cones. "What have you got there?" she teased. "A souvenir from the Chinese exhibit?"

"You can see perfectly well what I have. A good idea gone bad with the heat." She thrust the vanilla cone at Meg, keeping the chocolate for herself. "Eat up, girl, and then we'll head back to the hotel, so you can take a nap before the concert." She paused to take a large lick. "I might have a sleep myself. Feels like I've walked to China and back."

THAT evening they asked the taxi driver to drop them at the corner of 57th and Fifth. "I want to walk a little," Meg insisted. "I'm so excited!" She squeezed her aunt's hand. "Thank you for bringing me here. I couldn't have done it without you."

"Nonsense," Rose Mary said gruffly. "All I did was run a little interference for you. I'm sure you'll be doing the same thing before you know it, for that little one you're carrying." She patted Meg's swollen belly.

As they approached Carnegie Hall, they saw a dense crowd milling around the entrance. And as they moved closer, they saw placards waving and two policemen standing in the street, trying to contain the angry mob.

"Keep the Nazi out!" the pickets shouted. And then there was an answering shout: "No Krauts in Carnegie!"

Meg grabbed her aunt's arm. "Look! Oh, look what's happening! They're demonstrating against the professor . . . just because he's German. They can't do this to him, they just can't!"

"Now don't upset yourself." Rose Mary gripped Meg's elbow and held her until she saw a clear path from the street to the lobby. Then she took her hand and moved Meg quickly past the demonstrators and into the hall.

In spite of the ugly crowd out front, the hall was filling to capacity and Meg felt a rush of pride in her professor. As they settled into the excellent front-row seats that had been delivered with the professor's compliments, Meg immediately opened her program, eager to see what he had chosen to perform. She was pleased to find a program dominated by Chopin, with some Liszt and Debussy, and she was thrilled to find two selections that she had been studying during the past year. She wondered if she would ever perform them in a concert hall like this one.

As the lights of the great overhead chandelier dimmed, the green velvet curtains parted and a hush fell on the crowd. Onstage, a massive grand piano was lit by a single spotlight. After a few quiet moments, the conductor of the New York Philharmonic, Igor Minsky, walked to center stage and bowed to the applauding audience.

Holding up his arm to command silence, he made his introduction: "Ladies and gentlemen, it is an honor to present to you Mister Heinrich Claessen, one of Europe's most distinguished pianists. Tonight we have the privilege of hearing this artist in his first performance on an American stage. Let us give him a warm welcome."

The applause that followed was thunderous, and a few in the audience even stood in tribute as the professor strode across the stage with that formal grace that Meg so admired. When he reached the piano, he bowed and sat down on the bench, flipping the tails of his formal jacket in one quick precise movement.

Exactly as he had taught her, he rested his hands on the keys for a moment and closed his eyes. Then raising his hands, he brought them down, conjuring the first chords of the throbbing Liszt Concerto in E Flat. Chord by chord, he built a magnificent tension, crescendoed into the haunting coda theme and moved with exquisite timing into the crashing, powerful climax. As the last notes echoed through the hall, Meg felt the wetness of tears on her cheeks, a surge of pure joy in her chest.

The professor rose and bowed, in acknowledgment of the deafening applause, the shouts of "Bravo." With Rose Mary's assistance, Meg got to her feet, clapping as loud and hard as she could.

Then suddenly, before she could see exactly what was happening, a man had jumped onto the stage, shouting "Nazi! Nazi!" and rushed towards the professor. He pushed him to the floor and began to pummel him. Two musicians rushed onto the stage and tried to grab the man, but he shook them off. Racing for safety, he jumped off the stage, landing in the front row, and losing his balance fell hard against Meg. She screamed with shock and pain as she was pressed back into the seat. Hands grabbed at the man, pulling him off her, but it was too late. She had slipped into unconsciousness.

SHE opened her eyes, and then blinked against the harsh light. Where was she? Carnegie Hall, she remembered, as she tried to focus on her surroundings.

"She's awake, doctor," a voice said, and as Meg turned toward the sound, she saw a young woman in a nurse's uniform.

A hospital. She was in a hospital. Trying to clear the fuzziness in her head, she whispered her fear: "My baby? . . . My baby?"

It had happened, just the way it had been in her dream.

Something was wrong and now her baby was dying. She touched her empty belly. "No!" she cried out. "No . . . no!"

"Megan Rose." It was Rose Mary's voice. With difficulty, Meg turned her head to see her aunt standing beside her bed.

"My baby's dying," she whimpered, searching Rose Mary's face for the truth.

"No. He's fighting, Meg." Rose Mary stroked Meg's forehead and leaned closer. "And you know the Whittakers when they make up their minds to fight. Stubborn as plow mules and just as tough."

"I want to see him. Please, can I see him?"

"Your baby's in an incubator," the white-coated doctor said, preparing a hypodermic. "You can see him as soon as you're stronger. We had to do a caesarean section, and you need to rest for a while."

As the needle pierced her skin, she closed her eyes, her lips forming her familiar childhood prayer: "Now I lay me down to sleep . . . I pray the Lord . . . I pray the Lord . . . Oh, please let my baby live . . ."

SEVERAL hours later, she opened her eyes again. The hospital room was dark, except for the narrow lines of street light filtering through the drawn venetian blinds.

"Nurse!" she called out, desperately wanting news of her baby. "Nurse!"

"Hush, hush, Meg. You must be still." It was a man's voice. Her father-in-law.

"My baby?" she asked.

"The baby is good," he said tenderly, his face lined with pride and weariness. "He is very little, but he will grow. Do not worry yourself."

"Thank God! Oh, thank God!" she sobbed. As she tried to move, she felt a sharp pain in her midsection, and she moaned reflexively.

"Not to cry," Maurice said urgently. "It is not good for you to cry."

She closed her eyes, trying to brace herself against the pain, wanting David so much that she could almost see his face. It wasn't fair that he couldn't be here with her now.

"What's all this about?" Rose Mary demanded, hurrying into the room, followed by a nurse and David's mother.

"Is the baby really all right?"

"Not only is he all right, he's been screaming his head off. We might even have an opera singer in the family."

"You'll have to calm down," the nurse insisted. "I'll give you something for the pain now, and then I'll bring the baby. But you must keep still. You don't want to strain your incision."

"The boy is beautiful," Eva said. "So beautiful. And so much dark hair."

"I want to call him Jacob," Meg said, looking at her in-laws. "I think David would like that."

Maurice gripped the rail of the bed. "A good name," he said, his voice unsteady. "Thank you, Megan. Thank you for that."

"And James," Megan looked to her aunt, "for Papa... Jacob James Steinmetz."

"For all of us," Rose Mary said, smiling at her niece. "A new life... a new beginning."

"Here you are, little mother," the nurse said, as she placed the tiny bundle in Meg's arms. "Just for a minute now."

"Mother..." Meg whispered as she stared down at the little pink face, the unruly thatch of soft black hair, the eyes shut tight in sleep. A strange wonder filled her as she touched the baby's hand, as the tiny fingers curled around her finger. He knows, she thought. He knows that I'm his mother. And she felt a love more fierce, more protective than anything she had ever felt before. A new life, she thought, as the nurse gently took the baby from her. A new dream, she said to herself, as she slipped into sleep.

7

Good Will Toward Men
December 1943

20 December 1943

My Dear Children,

It is growing so dark now, by reason of the lowering clouds, that I can scarcely see the type. From the front of my office I looked to the north, and the hill in the back of the courthouse could not be seen at all. Instead there are white streaks of snow, drifts towering above the courthouse like great white arms reaching up into the heavens.

It is not exactly night and not quite light, but it is evidently "just before Christmas, since all through the Whittaker house, every creature has been stirring and every last mouse." Even Roland has been in holiday labor helping Old Santa with Alexander's order for an electric train, while Bessie is breaking all previous records for cookie production this year.

Did you know that Billy Gillespie sends copies of his West Grove Gazette to all our Russell County boys in military service? In yesterday's holiday edition, he reprinted this greeting received from Harlan and Aurora Wilson's boy, Ollie, who is with the Allied forces in Europe:

*"Merry Christmas from Holland and the battle-
fronts and me to everyone in Southwest Virginia! Over
here we give thanks to God for this season of gladness
in a world of sadness, for its light of brightness, its
reviving breath of cheer. . . ."*

EMILY clutched the newel post at the top of the stairs and
resisted the urge to yell "keep quiet" at her sister. Downstairs, Meg had been practicing the same passages from
Handel's Messiah over and over, for what seemed like hours.
But though her nerves were sandpapered thin, Emily felt
she couldn't complain since the music was for the Christmas
Eve program at the church.

To calm herself, she took a pack of Camels from her
pants pocket and lit one. Inhaling slowly, she leaned her
head against the hall window and looked down at the town
in the valley. She had smoked a lot of cigarettes since the
day word had come of Howard's death. Clifton objected,
of course. He said smoking was unladylike, but then so
much of what she did or said these days seemed to disturb
her father, for one reason or another.

Their latest discussion had occurred a few weeks ago,
when she'd started wearing trousers to her job at the *Gazette*.
Though she had tried to explain how warm and practical
they were, Clifton had ignored the logic, insinuating that
her new way of dressing would somehow tarnish the family's reputation. After all, he had pointed out, none of the
other townswomen wore trousers in public.

In vain she had tried to persuade him with a fashion
article from *Life* magazine, picturing women throughout
America in pants, and describing them as the latest thing.
But he had curtly dismissed the trend as one appropriate
only for city folks.

According to him and the unwritten West Grove rules,
no one, and especially no one from the fine, upstanding
Whittaker family, was supposed to deviate from the norm.
If she were back in Boston, it wouldn't matter how she
dressed. But she wasn't.

Maybe when the war is over—she began the thought as she put out her cigarette in the saucer of a violet plant. But there her speculation stopped for she didn't know what she would do when that time came. Lately it seemed as if the war would go on forever, though now that Howard was gone, it didn't seem to matter much how long it lasted. Nothing really seemed to matter much—except for Alexander.

She ached as she remembered how different things had been this time last year. Right after Howard had shipped out, she had made up a Christmas parcel for him—of books, cigarettes, warm socks and vest, pictures drawn by Alexander and a fruitcake baked by Bessie. She had wrapped each item separately and accompanied them with poems.

She could still recite some of the lines, for she had labored hard for the words, for the thoughts which would amuse Howard and make him smile as he unwrapped the objects. Stop, she reprimanded herself as she lit another cigarette, this is exactly what I mustn't do. I must not dwell on a Christmastime when Howard was still alive. I must not allow the memory to burden this first holiday without him.

"Miss Emily, Miss Emily..." Bessie shouted up the stairs. "Telephone fo' you. They sez it long distance..."

Stubbing out the cigarette, Emily hurried down the stairs, wondering who it could be. Selfishly, she hoped it wasn't Charlotte announcing that John had gotten a leave and that they would be descending on Breezy for Christmas.

The voice on the other end of the wire identified itself as a Washington, D.C. operator and asked for the wife of Major Howard Emmett. It had been months since she had thought of herself as a wife, and her voice quivered as she answered: "This is she..."

"Go ahead, sir," the operator instructed. "We have your party on the line."

"This is Sergeant Clyde Anderson, ma'am. I was in your husband's battalion."

"Oh," she managed to say, vaguely remembering references to a Sergeant Anderson in Howard's letters, a bright young man with whom he sometimes enjoyed playing chess.

"I have a Christmas present for you. Major Emmett bought it before . . . before . . . I brought it back when I got shipped stateside. I'd like to deliver it, if that's all right?"

"A present from Howard?" It was over eight months since he'd been killed. A stranger wanted to bring her a Christmas gift from him. She was confused.

"Ma'am, if you'd rather I didn't come, I could ship the present . . ."

"Please forgive me," she urged. "We'd be pleased for you to come and visit. We have plenty of room."

There was a significant pause before Sergeant Anderson answered. "Thank you, ma'am, but I'll just be delivering the present and moving on. I thought I'd come the day after tomorrow, if that's all right?"

"Of course. Whenever you'd like," she said graciously, though it seemed odd that the man wouldn't, at least, spend the night.

It was almost a day's train ride from Washington to West Grove, a long way, but perhaps the man was hurrying home to his family for the holidays.

When she hung up, she did not know how she felt. She had been trying not to think about Howard, and now a friend of his was coming and bringing her something from him. It was almost more than she could bear.

KNOWING Sergeant Anderson was coming, Emily's feeling about Christmas changed; the dull heaviness gave way to an uneasy sense of holiday spirit. In preparation, she resurrected the carton of tree decorations that she and Howard had accumulated over the years—one of the few things she had taken with them to the Army bases. She selected out the tin angels from Austria that he had given her their first Christmas and set them out on the mantle. Though Howard's friend would have no way of knowing they were special, it gave her pleasure to make the gesture.

The day Sergeant Anderson was due to arrive, Emily went to work at the *Gazette* as usual. That morning she had the tedious task of setting type for the holiday store sales.

She was so nervous and distracted by the approaching visit she made a mess of it.

"What's the matter, kid?" Billy asked, his voice kind in spite of his offhand manner.

She looked up and saw concern, and perhaps something more, in his watery blue-gray eyes. "Nothing," she said, "nothing, really."

"Holiday jitters?" he persisted, adjusting his glasses, and she was taken aback, as she often was, by how perceptive he was, under his blunt style. She liked that about him. It was easy to talk to him, to be with him. He didn't treat her like a breakable child, the way so many local men treated women and the way her family so often treated her.

His manners were crude at times, and sometimes he even yelled at her when she made mistakes, as if he expected her to do the job as well as a man could. That pleased her, rather than upset her. He was one of the few men she'd known, other than Howard, who gave her credit for the intelligence she had.

Unlike Clifton, he watched the personal changes in her and was impressed by them. He complimented her on the sleek, short haircut, winked and whispered a "hubba hubba" when she first wore trousers. And he made no comment at all about the number of cigarettes she smoked during working hours.

Sometimes, when she was at the *Gazette,* she felt a new kind of excitement in herself, in what she was doing. Outside of Aunt Rose Mary (and that was different because everyone thought she was eccentric), none of the women in the family had ever had a career. Sometimes she felt like a pioneer. She enjoyed writing, especially when Billy let her venture from social news into what he called "features." She felt good when he paid her one of his throwaway compliments.

"I suppose that must be it," she finally answered. "An Army friend of Howard's is coming today, and I suppose I'm a bit on edge..."

"Sure you are. But you'll be okay. You're a trouper. Listen," he said, "why don't you just pack it in and take the rest of the day off? You must have a million things to do."

"Oh, Billy," she said gratefully. "That would be wonderful, but what about all this work? It'll take you hours to finish up alone."

"So what?" he growled unconvincingly. "So it'll take hours. Holidays are for kids and families, and I don't have either."

She stopped what she was doing and looked straight at him. She had heard her share of gossip about Billy: a wild past, a drinking problem, a ruined career in Chicago. But this scarlet past had somehow left Billy without much of a present. Suddenly she regretted her selfishness in taking so much of his help without ever seeing that he might need a little kindness, too.

"Then come on over and share ours," she said firmly. "I won't take no for an answer, even if you are my boss."

His craggy face softened and he grinned shyly. "Thanks, Em." He squeezed her shoulder. "I think I'll take you up on that." Was it tenderness that she had seen in his blue eyes?

EMILY returned home and headed straight for the kitchen, counting on a cup of Bessie's strong coffee to give her a quick pickup.

"Here comes Simon Legree," Meg teased, as she warmed a baby bottle in a pan. "Look how hard Bessie's working. She hasn't stopped all day."

Bessie chuckled. At Emily's request, she was stuffing pork chops, once Howard's favorite. She had bought the chops with the last of the December meat rations.

"Oh, Bessie," Emily said apologetically. "Are you mad at me?"

"No, I ain't. Ain't promisin' nothin' either," she fussed. "You wants folks to do somethin' special, you s'pose to give 'em 'nough time."

"I'm sure dinner will be perfect," Emily said reassuringly, as she sat down with her coffee. Meg was seated next to her, feeding young Jake his afternoon bottle.

"Papa called while you were out," Meg said, wiping the baby's mouth with a kitchen towel.

"What did he say? Not another late night?" Since the recent call for more troops, Clifton had worked at the Draft Board almost every night. The pressures of the position were showing, and Emily was concerned. Recently, Dr. Giles had confided that their father had high blood pressure.

"No," Meg answered. "He said he was taking Miss Jewel to the Royale in Abington for holiday tea, so he might be late for supper." She smiled indulgently, as if she were discussing some new antic of Jake's. "Papa's getting daring, isn't he?"

But Emily wasn't in the mood to endorse Clifton's first public date or his absence. "He's going to be late? Tonight? I was counting on him!"

"Call him and remind him. He obviously just forgot."

Emily considered her sister's suggestion, but her sense of fair play cancelled it. "No," she said. "I can't do that. Papa's entitled to his own social life. I'll manage."

"Hey, Mom!" Alexander rushed into the room, his wire glasses askew, as usual. "It's snowing! *Now* Santa can come with his reindeers, right?"

IT was almost eight o'clock when Sam, the station master, called to say the Silver Clipper was finally in. Three hours and twenty minutes late, due to track problems around Richmond.

"Sam's going to bring Sergeant Anderson up on his way home," Emily announced. "Oh, I'm so nervous. I wish Papa was home."

"Take it easy, Em," Meg said, as she picked out chords for a new choir arrangement of "O Little Town of Bethlehem." "You'll be fine."

"When do we eat?" Roland asked, looking up from his old model train set, which he was fixing up for Alexander. "I'm starved."

"Dinner's been ready for hours," Emily said. "I'll just freshen up a bit."

"Try some rouge," Meg suggested. "You look pale."

Upstairs, Emily peeked into her son's room. The boy had fallen asleep holding his favorite book, *Now We Are Six*. In repose, he reminded her so much of Howard—the same quizzical expression, the same sharp, angular planes of his face.

After dropping a kiss on his forehead, she tiptoed down the hallway into her own bedroom. For a moment, she stood in the dark and spoke to Howard's picture, as she often did. "I miss you," she said longingly. "I still miss you so."

Car headlights then shone in the room as they came up the dark, snow-covered lane. "Oh, Howard," she whispered. "How I wish you were the one coming home tonight."

"Hey, sis," Roland called up loudly, "you'd better get down here quick."

Emily hurried down the foyer stairs vowing she would speak to her brother about his annoying habit of sounding cryptic alarms. "What is it?" she snapped. "What's going on?"

He grinned, knowing he did have a genuine bombshell to deliver. "It's Sergeant Anderson," he said. "The guy's a Negro!"

"A Negro?" Emily almost dropped the pack of Camels she was carrying. "Well," she said, mustering an air of calm and authority she did not feel, "I'm sure we can all manage to conduct ourselves in a civilized and proper manner." Then, realizing how stuffy, imperious, and like her father she sounded, she added: "You and Meg see to supper, and I'll greet our guest."

In spite of her words, Emily was far from confident about how she would handle this visit from a colored man. Back in Boston, she and Howard had occasionally entertained people who were foreign, an Indian engineer from Bombay, a Chinese mathematician. But never had they entertained any Negroes.

As far as the Whittaker family was concerned, as was true of any proper Southern family, no person of color ever came into the home except to work. Still, she told herself, what she had to do was remember that these circumstances were different—this man had been a buddy of Howard's.

He was sitting in one of the big wicker porch chairs on

the back porch, eyes closed, his head leaning against the back of the chair. His skin was very dark, as dark as Bessie's. He looked very tired, and she felt a twinge of guilt that the man had traveled such a distance to deliver Howard's gift, knowing full well in advance that it would be awkward for him to spend the night.

As she brought a welcoming smile to her lips, she thought of something Howard had once said, that for better or worse, war brings changes that have nothing to do with battles or changing borders.

"Sergeant Anderson," she said, extending her hand. "I'm Emily Emmett."

The man got up clumsily from the chair, swaying a bit before he steadied himself. She wondered if he had been drinking, and then scolded herself for the thought. Just because the man was colored . . .

"Mrs. Emmett," he extended his hand tentatively and she took it, thinking that this was the first time in her life that she had shaken a colored man's hand. Sergeant Anderson was a big man, probably in his early twenties. His uniform was wrinkled from the journey, and it hung loosely from his rather gaunt frame.

He caught her eyes, and she shifted her gaze to a spot just over his shoulder. "My," she said brightly, "it certainly is coming down tonight."

"Yes, ma'am," he said, "it's snowing hard."

"Well," she said, "we'd best get on inside . . . It can be quite chilly on this back porch."

The man hesitated for a moment, as if he wanted to say something. Then he shook his head and followed Emily, dragging his duffel bag and a large, thin bundle wrapped in burlap.

She paused a second in the hallway and considered taking the sergeant into the kitchen—to sit down at the round oak table, decided against it and led the way into the front parlor. "Please sit down," she invited, wondering if her tone was normally polite or artificial. "Supper will be ready soon."

"Thank you, ma'am." He twirled his military cap in his big hands, his eyes not meeting hers. "The major talked about you and Alexander all the time," he said softly, as if he weren't sure he should be reminding her. "He showed all the guys your pictures."

"Yes," she said, remembering all the snapshots she'd sent. The Army hadn't returned them with Howard's things, and she had wondered what might have happened to them.

The sergeant touched the package which he had propped against the sofa. "This is your present. Would you like me to open it for you?"

She stared at the misshapen object. How exactly like Howard, she thought. Even in the middle of a war, he had thought of her, had taken the time to buy her a gift, just as he had done regularly from the first days of their marriage. Suddenly she missed all their things, which were now in storage in a Boston warehouse, and everything about their marriage.

The sergeant took a penknife from his pocket and quickly cut the rough cord that bound the package. "I was with the major when he picked this out—in a souk in Marrakech."

She nodded, remembering Howard's detailed descriptions of North Africa, his growing fascination with the Arab culture that was so different from anything either of them had known. He had even expressed the hope that one day, under kinder circumstances, he might show her Morocco and some of the wonders he had seen.

As Sergeant Anderson peeled away the burlap, a layer of straw spilled onto the rug. "Sorry, ma'am," he apologized, kneeling down to collect the mess. He lost his balance and lurched forward.

"Are you all right?" she asked, concerned now. The man was behaving in a very peculiar manner.

He took a deep breath, and she saw a flicker of pain across his face. "Yes, ma'am," he said heavily. "Caught some shrapnel in Bizerte. It still kicks up once in a while, especially if I move too quickly."

"Bizerte," she repeated the name of the place where her husband had lost his life. Then she remembered her manners. "Can I get you something? An aspirin, or a cup of tea?"

"No, thanks. Here you are, ma'am." He finished removing the wrapping and handed her a heavy octagonal brass tray, intricately engraved with Arabic letters intertwined with geometric shapes.

"It's beautiful," she whispered. As her fingers touched her gift, she felt a shock. Howard had touched this tray, stroked its shiny surface, admired the elaborate workmanship. And he had thought of her. As her fingers moved against the cool metal, she could almost feel him here with her.

"Ma'am?" The man rose to his feet clumsily, pulling up his duffel bag, as if to leave, and then pitched forward in a dead faint.

"His vital signs are stable," Dr. Giles said, as he got up from the floor, where the colored man still lay unconscious. "We should get him to bed. Roland, give me a hand."

"We can put him in your room, Papa. It's the nearest," Emily said to her father, who had just arrived in the parlor doorway and was still wearing his snow-covered overcoat.

"My room?" he asked. "Who is this man? Will someone kindly tell me what's going on here?"

"Papa, it's Sergeant Anderson, Howard's friend. He passed out."

"The medical records found in this man's bag indicate that he was just released from Walter Reed Hospital in Bethesda," Giles supplied. "There's shrapnel in his gut and left leg. He's had intensive stomach surgery and obviously he's weak as hell."

"He's a hero, Pop," Roland chimed in excitedly. "There are all kinds of medals in his stuff—a Purple Heart and a lot of striped ribbons."

"He was injured at Bizerte," Emily added.

"I see," Clifton responded cautiously, frowning as thoughtfully as he did in court, when he was assembling bits of evidence.

"Young man," Giles briskly patted the soldier's cheek. "Sergeant Anderson, I'm a doctor. Are you in pain?"

"A little," the sergeant replied hoarsely. "In my stomach." He tried to raise his head, but couldn't. "I guess I'm not as strong as I thought I was..."

"I certainly must agree with you there," Giles drawled, replacing his stethoscope in the worn black leather bag he'd carried for more than thirty years. "Nothing too serious, however...nothing a few days in bed won't cure."

"But, sir," the man protested, "I have a ticket on the midnight train back to Washington."

"Out of the question," Giles said briskly. "You were foolhardy to attempt the journey in the first place. But now that you're here, you must stay put." He turned to Clifton. "Come on, J.C.," he said, "let's get this man to bed."

Emily watched her father compose himself as he walked the short distance to Sergeant Anderson's prone body, knowing how hard this was for him and worrying about how he would manage it. "Sergeant Anderson," he cleared his throat. "I'm Clifton Whittaker, Emily's father. I insist that you be our guest until you are well enough to travel. It's the least we civilians can do for one of our soldiers."

Dear Papa, Emily thought. She had known he would not behave badly, but she knew, too, how heavily history and tradition weighed against sheltering a person of color in his home, in his very bed.

The sergeant seemed to understand the effort that Clifton was making, and he attempted to respond in kind. "Thank you," he said. "Thank you, sir."

"Well," Giles said impatiently. "Now that we've concluded the amenities, shall we get this man off the floor?"

IT was two o'clock the following afternoon. Sergeant Anderson had been asleep for sixteen hours. Emily sat in the chair beside the window, staring at the black man lying so still against the white linen of her father's bed. The sight of him was still strangely unsettling, though she had been in and out of the room all night, keeping a close watch on the patient, as Dr. Giles had ordered.

The afternoon sun was beginning to melt some of last night's snowfall. It warmed her back as she settled into the

chair and tried to read *Between Two Worlds,* the latest
Upton Sinclair novel she'd borrowed from the library.

Sergeant Anderson was quiet now, but twice during the
night he had cried out in his sleep. The terror in his voice
had stabbed her with pain, made her think, as she did so
often, of how it might have been while Howard was dying.
Of the moments, perhaps hours he had suffered while the
life was leaving his body. Had he known he was dying, she
wondered. Had he been in great pain? Was he afraid?

She prayed that it had been easy, and if not easy, quick.
She prayed that death might have caught him unaware, had
taken him before he could know that he would never see
her or their son again, never...

"Where am I?" The sergeant was awake, his expression
confused and uncertain as he took in the unfamiliar surroundings.

"You're in Papa's bed," she explained. "You collapsed
last night, and you've been sleeping ever since."

"I remember now." He shifted in the bed, exposing his
upper body. She stared, almost against her will, at the muscular arms, the broad shoulders under the regulation Army-
issue olive drab tee shirt, and she could feel herself begin
to flush.

To cover her discomfort, she began to chatter. "Papa
moved down here after Mama died. This used to be her
sewing room. You can see that it's really too small for all
this furniture..." She gestured at Elizabeth's heavy mahogany bedroom set. And then she felt foolish, prattling
away about family history to a total stranger. "Did you sleep
well?" she asked.

He smiled. "I slept great...It's the first real bed I've
slept in for a long time."

Once again she thought of Howard, of what he must have
endured all those months away from home. "Are you hungry?" she asked.

"I'm starved," he admitted, embarrassed at imposing in
his helplessness. "There was nothing to eat on the train."

"Let me get you some soup," she said. "It's turkey noo-
dle—we always have it for the holidays...I..." She wanted

to explain how she had felt about the gift, but before she could, Alexander burst into the room, dressed in his snow-suit and frosted with snow.

"Hey, Mom, I went down the hill all by myself." He grinned proudly.

"On the sled? You went all the way down by yourself—without Roland? Oh, honey . . ."

"You must be Alexander," the sergeant laughed. "Con-gratulations on taking your first hill."

"Thank you," the boy said solemnly, saluting with his left hand. "Are you the sergeant?"

"Yeah," Anderson smiled, returning the salute. "But you can call me Clyde, like your dad did."

The boy approached the bed and stopped, scuffing his shoes against the carpet. "You know my dad?"

"Yes, sir. I'm the guy who painted your name on his jeep."

"Jeepers, creepers." Alexander ran to his mother and tugged on her slacks. "Did you hear that, Mom? Did you?"

"Yes, honey, I did." Emily stroked the cowlick on her son's head, remembering his favorite photograph, framed on his bureau, the one of Howard sitting in the jeep, with "Alex" painted in white across the panel under the wind-shield. The picture had arrived one dreary gray day last February. Alexander had been recovering from the mumps, and he had insisted on sleeping with it under his pillow for weeks.

"I'd better get the soup," she said, finally snapping back into the present. "And I should call Dr. Giles—he wanted to be told when you woke up. As for you," she turned to Alex, "you'd better let me help you out of that snowsuit. And stop bothering Sergeant Anderson."

"He's not bothering me. I'll bet he can get out of that snowsuit all by himself, can't you, soldier? Your dad always said you could do just about anything you put your mind to."

"He did?" Alexander brightened again. Eagerly, he tugged at the zipper on his jacket. "What else did he tell you about me?"

"Well," Sergeant Anderson began, and Emily hurried out of the room. She didn't want to hear any more about Howard. This visit had stirred up too many memories that she'd tried to put away. Perhaps there would come a day when her memories of Howard would be like photographs in an album, scenes she could look at from time to time and feel warmed by a pleasant nostalgia. But that time wasn't here yet.

THE next day, while the rest of the family attended Christmas morning services at church, Emily had volunteered to stay home, to watch the turkey and to keep an eye on Sergeant Anderson. The day before Clifton had abruptly given Bessie a "vacation," after deciding it was awkward for her to have one of her "kind" as a guest in their home and to have to wait on him.

After she set the dining room table she poured herself another cup of coffee. This day was hard, harder than she imagined it would be. Her first Christmas as a widow. She hated the sound of the word. It was ugly and final. Nothing of joy in it, nothing of hope for the future.

During the opening of Santa's gifts, the morning ritual of cinnamon buns and coffee around the tree, she had almost broken down. Her eyes kept drifting to the brass tray, which Clifton had placed on the mantel, and she didn't know whether she was missing Howard or feeling sorry for herself. There were so many changes upon her, all at one time.

Clifton had boldly invited Miss Jewel for dinner, and Billy was coming, too. And Bessie wasn't going to be with them today. Nothing was the same, and there was no choice but to move forward into a future that seemed full of changes and unknowns.

She checked the turkey, which was browning nicely. Of all the Whittaker girls, she was the only one who'd learned any kitchen skills. Since she was the oldest, and since Mama had spent so much time in her bedroom with her migraines, Emily had been raised to take charge. She'd done her share of grumbling then, but later she had been grateful, especially when she saw how handicapped Charlotte and Meg were, how difficult it was for them to assemble a meal.

She filled the sink with soapy water and started to scrub up the pots and pans she'd used. She had done these things hundreds of time before, yet she felt different, dislocated and out of place in this kitchen of her childhood. Where did she belong now? Would she ever feel at home anywhere again without Howard? she wondered.

"Oh, Bessie," she yearned aloud for the woman who had been a constant presence throughout her childhood, the woman who was so often her anchor these days. "I wish you were here. I wish I hadn't allowed Papa to send you away."

Suddenly she remembered one of Rose Mary's old sayings: "Whatever the day's doom, our hands have their everyday duties to do." Resolving to try a little harder for Alexander's sake, she switched the small kitchen radio on and tuned it to some Christmas music. There, that was better.

Alexander had loved the new red tricycle. From the moment he'd found it under the tree, he'd ridden it nonstop on the back porch. Months before, Howard had written, saying that his son should have a tricycle. "Seven is a fine year for new wheels," he said. Emily had tied a big bow on the handlebars and printed a card saying: "With love from your mom and dad."

She had meant to give her child a sense that his father's love was still with him, but the message had confused Alexander. Once again he had begun asking for his father. It was so hard to know what was right.

She thrust her hands into the soapy dishwater, to renew her assault on the pots and pans. As she reached for what she thought was a saucepan handle, she screamed with pain. She had grabbed the blade of a butcher knife by mistake. Even before she pulled her hand from the sink, she could feel that the cut was a deep one. Her blood was quickly coloring the dishwater red.

Somehow, she managed to wrap a dish towel around her

palm. She sat down to steady herself, knowing she should do something quickly, for the towel was turning a deep crimson. She started to sob softly. She was terrified and immobilized by her own fear.

"What's wrong?" It was Sergeant Anderson, barefoot and pajama-clad, his face creased with concern. "I heard you scream..."

She held out her hand mutely. He opened the towel, examined her palm and rewrapped it quickly. "That's a bad cut," he said. "Do you have a first-aid kit?"

She nodded and pointed in the direction of the pantry, where Bessie kept emergency fixings for the children's cuts and scrapes. He returned quickly with the white tin box.

First he swabbed the wound with peroxide. "Easy now," he said soothingly, as she gasped with the fresh pain. He applied butterfly strips of tape, to close the wound, and then he wrapped clean white gauze around the hand.

She watched silently as he worked, appreciating the gentleness of his touch, the sureness with which he applied the dressings, and suddenly, just as with Bessie, she felt no distance because of his blackness. And she was ashamed she ever had.

"That's it," he said, as he applied the last bit of bandage. "That should hold it together."

"Thank you," she said gratefully. "Thank you very much, sergeant."

"Clyde," he smiled. "You've been looking after me, and now it's my turn. Can I make you a cup of tea? You look a little shaky."

"Oh, yes, that would be nice..." She looked over at the clock. "But there's not time. I have to finish dinner."

"No, you don't," he said. "Tell me what to do. I know my way around a kitchen." Proving his point, he plucked Bessie's spare apron from the hook by the sink and tied it over his pajamas. "Sergeant Clyde Anderson reporting for duty," he saluted.

The sight of the big man standing there with a flowered apron over Clifton's striped pajamas was so comical that she started to laugh.

"That's what the major said you were like," he said softly. "Just the way you are now."

The mention of Howard's name sobered her quickly and suddenly the tears came again and she couldn't understand why they were falling. She started to cover her face, to hide her embarrassment. Emily had never cried when anyone else was present, not even when she was a little girl, not even when Howard died.

"Let it go," the man urged quietly. "Just let it out...I cried like a baby when the major went..."

"How...how did it happen?" She blurted the question out before her courage left her. She sat up at attention, fascinated and frightened at the same time, not knowing if what she was about to hear would make her feel better or infinitely worse. Yet she didn't say the words that would make Sergeant Anderson stop talking.

"We knew from the beginning we didn't have a prayer," he said. "We couldn't do a reconnaisance, and we didn't know how strong the German position was. Our position was on a hilltop, and we had to cross a ravine—Bizerte was a sprawling city, on rugged terrain...Two companies had already been lost.

"The major asked for three volunteers to stay with him on the hill as decoys. He sent the rest of the company around the back of the hill, to knock out the German arsenal. He told us we probably wouldn't make it, but he said the other guys might. His plan worked, ma'am, and it turned the battle around. The arsenal they blew was a main supply depot."

She closed her eyes, etching forever in her mind a picture of the battle. Then she looked directly at the sergeant and asked the question she'd been afraid to form. "Did he...I mean, how did he..."

"He died in my arms, ma'am."

She sat there quietly for a while, feeling as if a burden had been lifted from her. It was so like Howard. Brave, intelligent, logical. He cared about his boys, as he called them, and so he had found a way to save as many as he could. He had died nobly, and he hadn't died alone. "Thank you," she whispered.

"He was the best person I ever knew."

That was exactly how she felt. Meeting Howard and marrying him was the finest thing that had ever happened to her. Their marriage had made her feel whole. Maybe that was why she felt so horribly dislocated and forlorn now.

"I'm going to college after the war," the sergeant said. "I promised the major I would."

"I wish I knew what Howard would have wanted me to do," Emily admitted.

"Just what you're doing," the sergeant answered promptly. "Doing the best you can, being the best you can."

She smiled. That sounded exactly like something Howard had said. Or was it Howard? No, actually it was Billy Gillespie who had said, "Emily, you have talent and skills yet untried. Do the best you can with them or you'll never forgive yourself." How strange . . .

Suddenly she heard the horn of Clifton's Packard announcing his arrival in the driveway. "Oh, my," she said, "here they come . . ."

She ran upstairs to wash her tear-stained face. A bandaged hand would be enough to explain. As she passed her bedroom, she paused for a moment and went inside. She looked at Howard's picture and ran her fingers lovingly over the silver frame.

"All right," she said softly. "All right; Howard. I understand. I forgive you for leaving us."

She reached into her pocket with her good hand and pulled out a cigarette. Clumsily she lit it, inhaled deeply and walked over to the window. She stared out at the snow-covered mountains—and remembered how her husband had always teased her, saying they weren't mountains at all, only overgrown hills. "You Virginians," he would say, "you have such exaggerated notions about the splendor of your state."

Taking a deep drag from the cigarette, she felt peace at last. On May 17, 1943, in Bizerte, Tunisia, Howard had given his life, for his country and for his men. It was now eight months later, 1943 was ending, and Howard's friend, this man who had held him in his arms as he died, was downstairs.

"Hey, Mom." She heard the clatter of her son's feet in the hallway. "Hurry," his reedy voice urged as he opened the door. "It's time for turkey."

"Coming," she said, smiling as she took his hand and walked downstairs.

As they approached the dining room, she heard Sergeant Anderson explaining: ". . . and I'm sorry I'm not dressed for dinner, but after Mrs. Emmett's accident . . ."

"Emily, are you all right?" Clifton asked when he saw her.

"I'm fine, Papa. Sergeant Anderson . . . I mean Clyde . . . did a fine job on my hand—even Dr. Giles would be impressed."

She stopped when she saw that her usual place at the table, to Clifton's right, was already occupied by Miss Jewel, who was resplendent in a green chiffon dress printed with red poinsettias. The bright colors vividly contrasted with her freshly hennaed hair, and Emily wondered, not for the first time, how on earth Papa could find her appealing, after Mama's classic, refined elegance.

"Hey, sport," Roland called to his nephew. "Got your seat ready." He patted the volume of *Shakespeare's Collected Works* that he'd set on the chair next to his.

"Okay." Alexander ran to his beloved Uncle Ro, who was king of the day after his gift of the electric trains.

"Here you go." Roland lifted the boy up and settled him comfortably. "Best place I can think of for Shakespeare," he said under his breath.

"That's enough." Clifton reacted sternly to this heresy against his favorite author. Turning to Emily, he asked: "When is Billy arriving? I believe we are almost ready to begin."

"I'm sure he'll be along any minute, Papa," she said defensively.

"I think it's just lovely that you're having a gentleman guest," Miss Jewel intervened. "Such a nice man, too."

Emily was irritated by Jewel's description of Billy's status—and was relieved that the doorbell rang then, before she said something rude.

Emily had never seen Billy in a suit and tie and vest

before. His white shirt was neatly pressed and his hair was slicked down with tonic. He was freshly shaven, and there was about him the distinctive aroma of bay rum. Emily had never seen her employer so well groomed, so well turned out. Why, he's good looking, in a rugged kind of way, she thought as she beckoned him inside.

"Merry Christmas, Em," he said shyly, not at all his usual brash self. "I hope I'm not late . . . I just couldn't seem to get this darn thing done up." He thrust a small package, wrapped in Christmas paper and a lopsided bow, at her.

"Why, thank you, Billy—you shouldn't have . . ."

"Open it," he commanded, and then he watched anxiously as she undid the ribbon and paper.

"A Parker pen," she exclaimed. "What a lovely and thoughtful gift."

"I had your initials put on," he pointed out.

"I see . . ."

"I figure if you're going to be a serious writer, you'd better have a good pen."

"Hey, Em . . ." Roland called out. "Get in here, so we can eat. I'm starving."

Smiling, Emily slipped the pen into the side pocket of her dress, and they hurried inside.

As holiday greetings were exchanged and Billy was introduced to Sergeant Anderson, Jewel gave Clifton a meaningful nudge. Meg came in from the kitchen with a basketful of rolls. "We can start now," she said, triumphant at having gotten the meal on the table. "That is, if my son will stay asleep long enough for us to enjoy this meal."

"Now don't you worry, dearie," Miss Jewel said smoothingly. "If that little darling cries, I'll look after him. Why I was just saying to Cliff the other day, it's been years since I held a baby."

Emily bit her lip. She knew it was unreasonable and unfair, but she resented the woman's friendliness, the way she was insinuating herself into the family. "Someone should say grace," she said, more sharply than she meant to, "before the food gets cold."

"Very well," Clifton responded. Clearing his throat, he bowed his head and prayed: "Bless this food to our use and our lives to thy service." Before he finished with the usual "amen," he added: "We are thankful, Father, for the gift of Miss Jewel McInnes . . . and Sergeant Clyde Anderson and William Gillespie at our table."

As Emily murmured a grudging "Amen," she wondered what her father was thinking of when he thanked God for Miss Jewel. There was a time when she believed he was totally predictable, but now he was changing, too. Just when she had adjusted to one set of changes, there were more. Why hadn't anyone told them, when they were all little girls, that this was what being grown-up was all about? She caught Billy's eye, and he winked at her, as if he knew exactly what she was thinking.

"Miss Jewel said I could have the wishbone," Alexander announced from atop his literary pedestal. "And she likes to play checkers!"

"That's fine," Emily said mechanically. "Just fine."

"Hey, sergeant." Roland leaned forward eagerly. "How're you feeling? Some of my buddies want to come up to see you this afternoon if it's okay."

"Roland." Clifton looked up from his carving and glared at his son. "I have told you that the sergeant is recuperating from serious wounds. He is not here for your entertainment."

"It's all right, sir," the sergeant smiled good-naturedly. "I'm feeling much better. I'd be glad to visit with Roland's friends."

After the meal was over, fruitcake topped with cream was served in the parlor, in front of the fireplace. Afterwards, Miss Jewel announced with a giggle that Cliff's Christmas gift was hiding behind his chair.

As he opened the big gold box tied with green ribbon, she said: "Oh, I do hope it fits—it makes me so nervous to make something without a fitting."

When he held up the brown velvet smoking jacket trimmed with gold braid, she urged: "Oh, do put it on."

Despite his embarrassment, Clifton dutifully tried the jacket on, mumbling, "You really shouldn't have gone to so much trouble, Jewel. This is so . . . elaborate."

"Don't be silly," she chided, smoothing the lapels. "This

is exactly what you need. A fine gentleman like you deserves something special, doesn't he, girls?"

Meg agreed, laughing, but Emily bristled at Jewel's proprietary manner.

"Do you know what your sweet father gave me?" Jewel asked rhetorically. "The nicest bottle of perfume. All the way from Paris, France. Channel Number Five."

"Chanel," Emily corrected, before she could stop herself.

There was a moment of embarrassed silence. Billy stared at Emily, a look of puzzlement on his face.

"My, my," Miss Jewel laughed nervously, "I'm not surprised I can't say it right—I've never had anything that nice before."

"You deserve it," Clifton said vehemently, surprising himself. Jewel's gaffe had made him uncomfortable, as did many of her social mistakes. Yet he knew he was wrong to be so narrow in his ways. Jewel McInnes was a simple and loving woman, and when they were alone, she made him happy. It was not her fault that she was a little rough around the edges, or that she was accustomed to a different kind of society from the one he and Elizabeth had enjoyed.

"I guess I'd best be going," Billy said, getting up to leave. "Big day at the *Gazette* tomorrow. I do thank you all for having me today. This is the nicest Christmas I've had in years."

As Emily walked him to the door, he said quietly: "Merry Christmas, Em. I hope 1944 is going to be a happier year for you."

"Thank you, Billy." She looked into his eyes and saw something that made her blush and look away.

"And, Em," he went on, patting her shoulder, "don't be too hard on your father. He has as much right to a new life as you do."

She hung her head and said nothing, feeling shamed by her own small-mindedness, her lack of Christian fellowship on this sacred holiday. She waved to Billy as he walked away.

As she closed the door, she twisted her hand the wrong

way and winced. I can't seem to do anything right today, she thought. She started to walk back to the parlor and stopped. The holiday festivity was suddenly too much.

"I'm going out for a bit," she called out. "I'll be back in a while." Before anyone could protest or ask where she was going, Emily had on her coat and was out the door.

As soon as she got into the Packard, she could see that driving was going to be difficult with her bandaged hand. Awkwardly and with some pain, she started the motor. Holding the wheel carefully, she made her way down the lane.

At the highway, she hesitated, not knowing which way to go. She considered driving to the *Gazette* and working on her new column—but then she remembered there would be no heat in the building today. She turned right, in the direction of Hyders Gap. As she traveled east on 19, she saw the familiar turnoff to Slab Town, the colored folks part of town. Impulsively she turned onto the dirt road, towards the clusters of lean-tos near the railroad yards.

Approaching the frame shack that had been Bessie's home as long as she could remember, she was surprised to see a light in the front windows. The shack was unpainted and small, the roof sagged and the scraggly trees on either side of the porch seemed to hover to protect the pathetic little home. She stopped the car and got out. Hesitantly she made her way up the rickety stairs. For years the family had simply honked the car horn to let Bessie know they were there. It was another unwritten West Grove rule that white people did not go into the colored homes.

As she stood on the narrow porch, deciding whether or not to knock, she heard the sound of Christmas music on the radio. Suddenly the door swung open, and there was Bessie in the doorway.

"Come in, chile," she invited, as if Emily's presence on the porch were an everyday happening. "Come in. You catch yo' death out heah."

Emily looked around the single room. It was square and crowded with furniture, mostly old cast-offs from Breezy. The walls were covered with funny papers. A fire burned in the black pot-bellied stove, illuminating the drab room with a friendly light. In one corner was a single bed covered with Meg's old yellow chenille spread.

"Take off yo' coat and set," Bessie invited, offering a straight-back chair padded with a pillow.

"Papa told us your sister was coming from Castlewood to spend Christmas with you." Emily sat down and carefully covered her bandaged hand so Bessie wouldn't be alarmed.

"Charlene done gone to Atlanta. Her Ruby is feelin' po'ly, and they'se three younguns needs carin' fo'."

"You mean you've been here all alone these two days?" Emily was stricken with guilt.

Bessie nodded, taking up the patchwork that lay on her chair. "Been workin' on another quilt for the church," she explained.

"Oh, Bessie. It's awful that you've been spending Christmas all by yourself. We didn't mean for that to happen. It's just that with Howard's friend being colored, Papa thought it would be hard for you . . ."

"Lawd have mercy." Bessie shook her head. "So thas' what's on Mistuh Clifton's mind. Ain't that foolish."

Once again Emily felt that she had failed to live up to the holiday season, that she had failed to be "the best" she could be, because she had been too worried for herself to care about anyone else. "I should have made sure you were all right," she said penitently. "Papa meant well, but I knew he was wrong. Everything I've done this Christmas has been wrong. Everything." She clenched her fists. "It makes me think that Alexander and I just don't belong on Breezy any more."

"What you sayin', chile?" Bessie looked up from her sewing, a look of puzzlement on her face. "'Course you belongs. You belongs on Breezy, and you belongs with yo' family. What else you got in dis heah world?"

What else indeed, she asked herself. Everything that mattered was here now. If she didn't quite fit, if things had changed, then she would have to change, too, until the pieces of her life did fit together again. "You're right," she said. "And you belong there, too. You're family, too, Bessie. Come back with me now, and we'll finish Christmas together." She stood up quickly. Now, she had a purpose.

The black woman chuckled as she rose from her chair. "'Bout time you knowed what was what, Miss Emily. You the smart one in dis heah family." And arm in arm, the two women closed up the little shack and walked to the car.

8

Promising to Be Faithful
June 1944

June 11, 1944

My Dear Children,

A letter arrived at my office this week from my son-in-law, David Steinmetz, stationed in England where he cares for American Army wounded transported across the channel from European battlefields. The letter traveled across the Atlantic with amazing swiftness (only six days en route) and somehow missed the eagle eyes and scissors of the military censors.

David wrote on a prescription pad, saying he was fine and enclosing "something historical for the Bulletin Chronicles." It was a copy of General Eisenhower's message to our soldiers before the heroic June 5th D-Day invasion of the beaches of Normandy. (Unlike Shakespeare's Henry V, he was not able to address all his troops directly.) The message began:

"You are about to embark upon the Great Crusade, toward which we have striven these many months.

*The eyes of the world are upon you. The hopes and
prayers of liberty-loving people everywhere march
with you."*

*We as a family, joined and in our individual endeavors,
must also remember we are on a crusade as we march
through our everydays and hold high the light of our unwavering faith that our war time sacrifices and separations
will soon end. . . .*

"But Mary Sue, honey." Charlotte pouted impatiently into
the telephone. "You just don't understand. I'm stayin' here
because it's my patriotic duty. I'd love to be back in Richmond with you all, sugar, but it's simply not possible."

At the other end of the line, Mary Sue was going on and
on about how difficult it was to organize the Country Club's
Spring Promenade without Charlotte's help. "What are we
goin' to do," Mary Sue wailed, "with all the young men
gone? All the decent ones anyway. And how on earth are
we goin' to present the debutantes properly when hardly
any of them are goin' to have escorts?"

Charlotte sat down in the wicker chair by the double
window and stared out absently at the distant view of the
harbor, cradling the phone against her shoulder and tapping
her pink satin mule in irritation. It was late Thursday evening, and both her girls had been tucked in for the night.
Surveying the small living room of the rented stucco cottage,
Charlotte wrinkled her nose, as she did every time she
thought of the tacky way she was being forced to live. Good
thing Mary Sue can't see this place, she thought. She'd
never understand why I'm living here until John comes back.

All the furniture, such as it was, was made of wicker or
wrought iron. Back home in Richmond, they would have
called it porch furniture, but here in Pensacola, where the
climate never seemed to change, people painted the stuff
black or white and actually used it indoors.

"We have the opposite problem here," she said, reaching
for the bottle of fire-engine-red nail polish on the table and
securing the receiver in the crook of her neck. "Too many

men. Why, for last week's dance, we had to bus some girls all the way from Gerde Springs, and that's sixty miles away."

Charlotte finished the first two fingers of her right hand, as she listened to Mary Sue describe the gazebo that the Promenade Committee was constructing as a presentation stage for the debutantes. A slight sound caught her attention, and she turned to see a pajama-clad Carrie, tiptoeing into the room, a book tucked under her arm.

"Mary Sue," Charlotte interrupted, glad of an excuse to end her friend's monologue about a social event that she would not be present to share. "I really must hang up now. Carrie is awake."

Putting down the telephone, she capped the nail polish carefully. There were already two bright red spots on the woven grass rug, remnants of spills the children had made during their "dress-up-and-play-Mommy" games. Charlotte dreaded having to explain them to the landlord.

"Well, young lady," she said, annoyed by her daughter's appearance at a time when she expected peace and quiet. "What do you think you're doing up so late?" She stood up and adjusted the v-neck of her peach dressing gown.

"I had a dream about Daddy," the child said pensively, as she crawled up onto the wicker sofa. "He was reading to me."

Charlotte felt a small pang of guilt for her daughter's sadness. John had always made time to read the children to sleep after he came home from the base. "I'm sorry, darling," she said, erasing the impatience from her voice. "I've just been so busy."

"So busy," the child repeated somberly, reminding Charlotte, as she often did, of Judge Randolph, John's father.

"Only one chapter, hear now?" Charlotte warned, willing to go only so far to expiate her guilt. "Then back to bed." She opened *The Five Little Peppers and How They Grew,* a birthday gift from Emily to Carrie, and wondered as she did why on earth her daughter enjoyed such books. "Really, Carrie," she said, "I just don't understand why you want to hear about such a poor family. Why, they're not like us at all."

Carrie ignored her mother's remark and pointed to Chapter Four, "Trouble for the Little Brown House."

Charlotte was halfway through the chapter in which Miss Jerushy, the town busybody, paid a threatening visit to the fatherless Pepper household, when the telephone rang.

"Excuse me, darling," she said, hoping it would be Isabel Houston, who was married to John's chief bomber and a registered member of the DAR in Atlanta. They were supposed to discuss the theme of Saturday's cotillion. The other wives described the weekly socials as canteens but Charlotte liked to think of them as cotillions. It was just one of the ways in which she tried to make the best of this very dreary life.

The child nodded her acceptance at losing Charlotte's attention, an expression of resignation settling on her face. Slowly, with a beginning reader's fierce determination, she pressed on, trying to translate the letters on the page into sounds, so that she might finish the chapter for herself.

"Isabel, dear, I've been thinking," Charlotte began, pacing as she spoke, flipping the phone cord behind her, as if it were a dress train, "and I have thought of the most cunning theme for Saturday night. Are you ready? It's 'The Last Time I Saw Paris.' You know, that perfectly wonderful Irving Berlin Song? Isn't that just an inspiration?"

As Charlotte knew she would, Isabel enthusiastically embraced the idea. "And so meaningful, too," she added. "Did you know that Jerome Kern wrote the lyrics for the song on the very day that Paris fell?"

"Why, no," Charlotte admitted, "I didn't. That's very touching, it truly is." Then she returned to what really interested her, the details of executing her theme. She described small round tables, reminiscent of Parisian cafes, edging the dance floor, a painted backdrop of the Eiffel Tower decorating the stage. She rambled on, unaware of how long the conversation had stretched—until she glanced at the Hamilton watch that John had given her, before he left, with the card "To Count the Hours Until I Return." It was after eleven.

"Forgive me, Isabel, dear," she said, "but I really must go now. Carrie is awake," she sighed. "Being a mother is a constant responsibility."

As soon as she hung up, she turned to Carrie, prepared to apologize graciously for the long delay. But the child had fallen asleep, the book still clutched in her arms. Charlotte picked her daughter up and carried her to bed. As she tucked her in, Carrie's eyes fluttered open. "We didn't finish the chapter, Mummy," she said sleepily.

"I'm sorry, sugar. I just got so busy again, didn't I?" She kissed the child's forehead. "I'll make it up tomorrow night. I promise."

THE officers' club was located on the north side of the harbor. Charlotte had been told that some of the wealthier townspeople had docked their boats here before the war. But now the water was crowded only with Naval tankers and carriers, so many that it was impossible to count.

Pulling on her white cotton gloves and adjusting her pill-box hat, she hurried up the stairs to the second floor, where the weekly ladies' luncheon was already in progress. Usually she made the drive with Isabel, so they could conserve their gasoline rations, but today Charlotte had decided to do a little shopping downtown before lunch. Though John's Navy pay was ridiculously meager, he had arranged for Charlotte to receive an additional monthly allowance from the First National Bank of Richmond. The May check had arrived this morning, and Charlotte had decided to treat herself to a new outfit for the dance—to keep her morale up.

It had been three weeks since she'd had a letter from John. Her fear had started to mount after the second week, but she had told no one. John's letters had calmed and soothed her so, reflecting as they did his good breeding and his years of education at fine private schools. He rarely troubled her with war news, choosing to write instead of the future they would share when he returned, or to quote passages from English literature that touched him, that made him think of her.

When John went away, Charlotte had tried to write every night, before she went to bed, but she soon found it hard to fill the pages. Now she wrote twice a week, on Wednesday and Sunday nights, anecdotes about the children and snatches of the base social news that John might find interesting. Last Wednesday, for the first time, she had failed to write. The silence had become too unnerving, and Charlotte had decided not to write anymore until she heard from him.

This morning she had found a lovely powder-blue crepe dress at Sharon's Treasure Chest, her favorite Pensacola shop. The alterations had taken longer than she'd expected, and now she was late. No one would mind, she knew, for the wives always enjoyed a leisurely cocktail hour before the weekly meal of chicken à la king and green peas. Charlotte was looking forward to her midday drink—a new custom for her since cocktails were never served at Richmond luncheons.

"My, my," she said, breezing towards her usual place at the table, "it certainly is quiet in here today. What's the matter? Cat got your tongues?"

As soon as the words were out of her mouth, she regretted them. Seeing the expressions on the women's faces, she asked quietly: "What's wrong?"

"Steve was shot down over the Philippines," said Jean Goodman, "Betty heard this morning."

"Shot down?" Charlotte repeated, disbelieving what she'd heard. John had often said that Steve was one of his best pilots. "That can't be true."

"It is," Isabel said, taking a sip of her martini. "He was reported missing in action, but he's probably dead."

"No!" Charlotte said vehemently. "John told me they all knew how to bail out if the planes got shot down. I'm sure Steve's on one of those little islands, waiting to be picked up."

"Grow up, Charlotte," said Vivien Leacock, a pretty dark-haired woman from Chicago. "He's dead, and there's no sense pretending he isn't."

"No," Charlotte protested, taking in Betty's empty chair. She turned to Thelma, their regular waitress. "Bring me a bourbon, please. On the rocks."

"He's the first one," Vivien said, voicing what they were all thinking. "Jesus, I hope Arnold's luck holds."

"We all have to pray," said Tillie Bisbee, who was a devoted churchgoer. "It's all in God's hands now."

"Don't say that!" Charlotte reacted passionately to the phrases she'd heard repeated over and over again when Howard had been killed. They had given Emily no comfort then and they frightened her now. Maybe John had been shot down, too. Maybe that was why there had been no letters all these weeks. Maybe the news was on its way, even now.

"God's hands, the War Department, the Japs, what does it matter?" Vivien said harshly. "We don't have much say in it. All we can do is wait and hope it doesn't happen to us."

"You're right," Isabel said, as she took out her compact and lipstick. "And we can help each other not to go crazy from the waiting. Now who wants to go over to Betty's?"

But Charlotte had stopped listening. They had to be wrong, all of them. Things like this happened to other people, not to Charlotte Lee Whittaker Randolph. She had suffered inconvenience and indignity in this war, but she would not believe that she was not safe from the misfortunes that life dealt other, ordinary people.

CHARLOTTE'S daughters loved to help her dress. Carrie usually sat on the sidelines, making editorial comments about Charlotte's outfit, while Nancy threw herself into the ritual, understudying Mommy, trying on shoes and jewelry, painting her face and preening in the mirror, alongside her mother.

But this Saturday evening, Charlotte was alone. She had taken the girls to Vivien's house, where they were being cared for, along with ten other children, by two secretaries from the base, while their mothers hostessed the cotillion.

Since this was the first time she'd been alone in weeks, she decided to indulge herself a bit. For atmosphere, she found some Benny Goodman music on the radio. She poured herself a short bourbon on the rocks and filled the bathtub with jasmine-scented bubbles. And though the reception was scratchy, the glass thick and indelicate, the tub discolored and peeling, the pampering revived her spirits.

Stepping from her bath, she wrapped herself in a mono-grammed towel of lemon yellow, patted herself dry and studied her naked body in the mirror. Her breasts were full and firm, her stomach flat and her thighs smooth. "Not bad for a woman of twenty-nine," she said smiling, striking a Betty Grable pinup pose, one arm behind her head, the other on her hip.

Still smiling, she put on her underwear and shimmied into her dress, a flame-colored taffeta that sculpted her breasts and hips with soft folds. The plunging neckline framed a deep expanse of creamy skin and accented her long slender neck. At the last minute she had changed her mind, deciding not to wear her new powder blue dress. Instead, she had chosen John's favorite, her gorgeous red taffeta.

She wished John were here, to see how lovely she looked, to tell her how beautiful and desirable she was. Unlike so many of her friends' husbands, John always noticed her clothes, appreciating the care she took to make herself attractive.

To finish off her ensemble, she swept her silky blond hair into twin pompadours, just as Joan Crawford had worn in *Mildred Pierce*. She added large gold earrings and applied makeup. But when she searched her dresser for the new fire-engine-red lipstick, she couldn't find it. Then she remembered that she had started to hide her good cosmetics in the top lefthand drawer of John's dresser, so the girls wouldn't find them.

She opened the drawer, and there it was, along with John's collection of cuff links and handkerchiefs, a toenail clipper and a 1943 pocket-sized legal diary. She took the lipstick and quickly shut the drawer, to seal off the rush of memories that the familiar objects had evoked. Memories of six married years of Saturday nights, when the two of them had dressed together, for cocktail parties or dinner dances at the club.

Always after those Saturday nights, their lovemaking had been best. Freed of the week's responsibilities, they had laughed and danced and rediscovered the pleasures of their courting days. Later, in bed, John was always especially gallant and attentive. As he murmured how lucky he was to be married to such a beautiful woman, he would stroke and touch her, in all the ways she liked, until she was ready for him. Unlike so many other men she'd heard about, John never took his own pleasure until she was satisfied and happy. And she always was, because John's lovemaking made her feel cherished and adored. Which was, she felt, no more or less than her due.

Only once had it been different. On the first night of their honeymoon in Paris. Perhaps it was because he had waited so long, so patiently, for the right to possess her; but that night, John had fallen upon her with a raw, physical hunger, fairly devouring her body with his passion. She had rather liked it, the sense of her own power to inflame her husband so. Later he had apologized for behaving "like an animal," and she had forgiven him prettily and graciously.

Remembering Paris brought her back to the evening ahead of her, and suddenly her body, the lovely body that had given her such pleasure in the mirror a few moments before, felt achingly lonely and unloved.

"Damn you, John," she hissed, "you had no right to leave me here. No right at all!"

THE dance was going very well, Charlotte thought, as she helped herself to another cup of fruit punch. She wandered towards the stage, so she could enjoy the swing band from Tallahassee close up. She closed her eyes and started to hum along with the music of "Bewitched, Bothered and Bewildered."

"Hey, ma'am," a man's voice interrupted her reverie.

"Are you speakin' to me?" Charlotte turned around slowly. She had never seen the dark, muscular petty officer before. He was good-looking, she noted, in a foreign sort of way.

"Yeah." He flashed an engaging grin. "Petty Officer Santini reporting for duty. Landon shipped out."

"Shipped out?" Landon had been such a nice boy, so polite when she worked with him and his crew of men on the cleanups after the dances. "I see," she said weakly, unable to take her eyes off the man.

"How about a dance?" Santini asked, moving closer.

"I . . . I don't think so," she replied politely. "But thank you for askin'." Charlotte rarely danced at these functions. She was, after all, a married woman, and the single men could get out of hand sometimes.

"Ah, come on," he coaxed seductively, his eyes bold and knowing as they held hers. "It's a terrific number."

The band was playing "The Last Time I Saw Paris," and the plaintively sentimental melody underlined the wistful longing she had been feeling, a longing that was now making her wonder how it would be to move around the dance floor in Santini's arms.

As if he were reading her thoughts, he moved in closer. "Follow me," he said huskily, slipping an arm around her waist, walking her onto the dance floor. His foxtrot was like a tango, sweeping and syncopated. He held her tightly against the lean hardness of his body, and although she knew there was nothing proper about the way he was holding her, she didn't pull away.

As the number came to an end, Santini maneuvered Charlotte into a deep dip, held her suspended for a moment too long and whispered: "Ooh, that's nice."

She blushed and pushed him away. No man had ever taken such liberties with her. "Petty Officer Santini," she said stiffly, trying to regain her composure, "please remember that I'm a lady."

"Yeah," he drawled, almost mockingly. "I can see that."

Still flustered, she hurried back to the punch table. He followed, but she tried to ignore him, pretending busyness, gathering up dirty punch cups, keeping her eyes away from his. He planted himself across the table, leaned towards her and asked: "So what are my orders, ma'am?"

"The chairs," she said hastily, anxious to be rid of him. "Fold up the chairs."

"Yes, ma'am," he saluted with an impertinent wink. He turned to a group of waiting midshipmen and gave orders for the gathering and stacking of chairs. Before he left, he came up behind her, brushing the red taffeta of her dress with his fingers. "That's a dynamite dress," he whispered— and walked away before she could put him in his place.

* * *

IT had been a hard week. Nancy had been sniffly and feverish for two days, keeping Charlotte from the Tuesday bridge club and the Wednesday wives' outing to a seashell museum down the coast. Carrie, too, had been particularly difficult, complaining every morning that she was bored with the base playschool because all they ever did was crayon and climb, when she wanted to read.

But worst of all, there was still no letter from John. Each morning, at eleven, she had stood by the living room window, watching for the postman to round the corner of Doral and 17th Street, waiting the five minutes it took him to reach their floor. Only after he was gone did she rush down the front stoop to the mailbox. She didn't want the man to know how desperately eager she was for a letter. It was none of his business. War or not, there were appearances to be maintained.

By Saturday night her mood was dark, her self-control frayed. She dressed for the cotillion mechanically, in a flared navy blue skirt and a white angora sweater. As she pulled up the zipper, she remembered that this was one of John's favorite outfits. "Smart and saucy," he had complimented, the first time she had worn it. "That's how I like my girl."

She had thought of staying home tonight, pleading fatigue and her daughter's illness. But with Betty Armstrong gone, the cotillion committee was already one member short. The volunteers rotated duties, and tonight was her turn to supervise the refreshment table, to see to it that there was enough to eat and drink for one hundred twenty-five sailors and girls. Because Nancy was still fussy with her cold, Charlotte had hired a babysitter for the evening. As she brushed her hair trying to decide how to wear it, she could hear the young woman reading the girls a bedtime story. Down, she decided, nothing fancy tonight. After giving herself a final check in the mirror, she ducked into the children's room for a quick goodnight.

As she drove along Route 5, she allowed herself to think about Petty Officer Santini, to consider how she would handle him tonight. But when she came into the lodge, she scanned the crowd—and felt something very close to disappointment when she failed to locate him. Later there was no more opportunity to think about Santini or to look for him. It was an unusually warm June night, and the dancers made frequent and regular trips to the refreshment table— keeping Charlotte busy running back and forth to the kitchen to get clean cups and to mix up fresh batches of punch.

She was relieved to hear the band strike up the finale, "I'll Be Seeing You." She kicked off her high heels for a moment, to rest her aching feet. She stared longingly at the crowded dance floor and hated being a woman alone. Blinking back tears of self-pity, she turned and began gathering up dirty cups, wanting to be out of the hall before the couples began their good-night embraces.

She was trying to figure out how to put the waiting sailors into action when Petty Officer Santini walked in. Tossing a breezy "Ma'am" in her direction, he quickly set the men in motion.

When the last chair had been folded, the tables cleared, the cups and tables put away, when the cleanup crew had been dismissed, leaving her free to go home, she slipped into the ladies' room to freshen up. No sense going home looking like a wreck, she told herself.

When she came out, Santini was waiting there, in the dark hallway outside the rest room, leaning against the wall, smoking a cigarette. "So, Miz Charlotte," he said, affecting a southern drawl, a tone of mocking intimacy, "how you all been?"

"Very well, thank you," she said icily, pretending a composure she did not feel. What she did feel, as she mentally measured the distance to the door, was the thrill of danger and the panic of a treed fox. She began to walk briskly, hearing the tap-tap of her high heels in the quiet stillness of the now-deserted lodge.

"What's your hurry?" he asked seductively, falling into step with her.

"I really must be getting home," she said in the same frosty voice, thinking as she spoke how ridiculous it was to be explaining herself to such a person.

"Yeah, you must," he smiled at her, slipping an arm

around her waist. Before she could protest, he had spun her around and pressed his lips into hers, his tongue snaking past her teeth, probing the soft wetness of her mouth.

Caught unaware, Charlotte's mind registered no outrage, yielding instead to the rush of feelings triggered by the pressure of flesh on flesh, intensified by the months of deprivation. But when a hand clamped itself on her breast, she snapped to attention. "How dare you?" she gasped, her indignation weakened by delay and by the pink flush of her cheeks. "I'm a married woman," she sputtered. "My husband's away at war. Don't you have any respect for that?"

Santini smiled lazily, his black eyes confident. "War times, lady," he answered. "You said it just now and I figure that changes the rules. If I'm going to get my butt shot at, I mean to do all the livin' I can. Right now."

"Goodness," Charlotte whispered, unpoised and unsettled by what Santini had said, by the conviction with which he had said it.

"Think about it, babe," he said, making no attempt to touch her again. "Think about it," he repeated, then turned and walked away.

ONCE again it was Saturday night. Charlotte and Isabel were on their way to the Lodge, traveling north on the winding sand-edged road from Pensacola. Isabel was driving, Charlotte fidgeting restlessly in the passenger seat. They had just deposited their children at Jean Goodman's house for another weekend slumber party, compensation for this night of freedom.

Nervously Charlotte tapped her red-enameled nails against her red leather clutch purse. She was worn thin from the strains of another letterless week, another seven days of makeshift life on a Naval base, in a town that had no heritage.

Despite herself, she had thought about Petty Officer Santini's words and found some truth in them. The rules she had learned and grown up with, the values that had cushioned her existence, they didn't seem to sustain her anymore. In place of certainties had come confusions, and without a man to direct her, to help order her choices, she felt lost.

Wednesday she had felt so blue that she had gone to the club for a cocktail before she picked the children up from playschool. She didn't know why, but late afternoon, just before sunset, she felt the loneliness most acutely. A bourbon on the rocks seemed to soften her misery, and so she had gone back to the club on Thursday and again on Friday. Late at night, as Vivien had once suggested, she had a snifter of brandy, to help her sleep.

That afternoon she had organized some of the girls into a movie party, in hopes of cheering herself up. But *Cry Havoc,* starring Joan Blondell and Ann Sothern, had only depressed her more. The story of American nurses sweating and dying in enemy-infested Philippine jungles had made the war seem even more immediate and awful, had made her realize how much John left out of his letters, the kind of horrors he faced, day after day. If he was still alive.

"I haven't heard from John in seven weeks," she said aloud, no longer able to contain her secret fear. "Five weeks and three days, actually."

"Oh, Charlotte, honey." Isabel was immediately sympathetic. "I had no idea. I wish you said something before, but listen to me now. Remember how scared I was right after Marshall left? Remember how I didn't hear anything for such a long time, and then I got four letters at once? I'm sure that's what's going to happen now. John's fine, I'm sure of it," she finished with the optimistic conviction with which the wives all attempted to sustain one another.

"I hope so," Charlotte said listlessly, picking at a cuticle. "I just don't know how much longer I can go on like this."

"You'll be fine, just fine," Isabel said reassuringly, flashing a supportive smile at Charlotte. Then, eyes back on the highway, she asked: "Have you checked with Headquarters to see if John's mailing address has been changed? Maybe they forgot to let you know. Those clerks—well you know, sometimes they're so swamped with paper work . . ."

Unconvinced, Charlotte promised to check with Headquarters, as Isabel slowed the car and made a left turn into the Lodge driveway. As usual the parking lot was full: there were four Naval Base buses and one battered vehicle that had transported women volunteers from the town.

It was another warm night, and the strains of "Swinging on a Star" drifted through the Lodge's open doors. The song was one of Charlotte's favorites, but the music failed to cheer her. Tonight she and Jean Goodman had drawn floorhostess duty. It was their job to police the dance floor, to make certain that none of the sailors behaved badly to the girls who danced with them. Charlotte did not enjoy this detail at all. Sometimes a polite reminder was enough to get a sailor to mind his manners, but sometimes the boys who had had too much alcohol to drink would become rude and difficult, and she would have to ask one of the MPs to help.

"I suppose I'd better get inside," Charlotte said after Isabel had parked the car. "Thanks for the pep talk."

Jean was waiting for her at the entrance, with the news that a large batch of shipping-out orders had been delivered the day before, and that there had already been some trouble on the dance floor.

"Wonderful," Charlotte said acidly. "I suppose this means we can look forward to a very long evening."

She hadn't even reached the edge of the dance floor when she felt a hand on her shoulder. She turned to face a smiling Tony Santini. "So how about a dance?" he invited, his eyes traveling her body.

"Well..." she hesitated, flushing with the remembered response of her body to his touch.

"You know you want to," he said, insinuating layers of meaning into his words, as he took her hand and led her to the music.

"You thought about what I said, didn't you?" he asked, rubbing his hand against the back of her neck. When she said nothing, he shortened his footwork and pressed her closer. "So?" he whispered against her ear.

"I... I don't know what you man," she stalled, confused and unbalanced by the directness of his question and the warm sensations that were radiating from the places he touched her.

"Sure you do." He took her earlobe between his teeth

and ran his tongue along the soft flesh. She gasped, her knees almost buckling. He laughed knowingly and steadied her, fanning one strong hand over her buttocks, spreading the other between her shoulders. His dance steps became smaller, closer, as he rubbed his legs against hers. "You're all alone, babe." He ran his fingers down her spine for emphasis, and I'm here. Just what you need." As the music ended, he dipped her, pressing his groin to hers, so she could feel his hardness through the layers of clothing. He released her and grinned. "Tonight," she said, as if there were no more questions to be asked and answered. "Villa Motel, up the road. Room 11. After midnight." He made his farewell gesture, smoothing back his shiny black hair with his palms. "See you."

FROM the moment that Santini left her on the dance floor, stranded in a fog of confusion and desire, until the dance was over, she couldn't stop thinking of him, imagining what it might be like to be with him. Her need shamed her. Tony Santini was coarse and common, the kind of man who had no place whatever in the kind of life she had designed for herself. A life that now seemed as distant and unreal as the man to whom she had pledged her fidelity.

To herself she recited a litany of reasons why she should go straight to the rented house on Doral Street and never speak to Tony Santini again. And when she was finished, she knew that she would go to the Villa Motel.

After Isabel dropped her off at home, she lingered long enough to have a stiff bourbon and to redo her hair and makeup. Then she was off again, in her own car, back on Route 5.

The Villa Motel was the kind of place Charlotte had never seen close up before. It was a rundown frame structure, rooms strung along a common porch. It reminded her of the clubhouse quarters of the Methodist Bible Camp she'd been sent to one summer, when Mama had decided the children needed more religious training.

She parked her car away from the rest of the automobiles

in the lot, away from the check-in cabin that flashed a "Vacancy" sign in red neon. Terrified that someone might see her, she tiptoed quickly across the gravel to room 11, which was, she gratefully noted, located at the end of the building. She tapped urgently on the door, and it swung open right away with a loud creak. Tony Santini was waiting, wearing a white sleeveless tee shirt and the trousers of his dress whites, holding a beer bottle in one hand, a lit cigarette in the other.

"Why, Miz Charlotte," he drawled, "so nice you came by . . ."

The room was small and musty-smelling, the walls paneled in rough pine. The double bed that crowded the room was covered with a worn peacock-patterned chenille bedspread, the kind that darkies and poor whites used, Charlotte noted with a shudder of distaste.

"Have a drink," he urged, handing her a beer from the six-pack that sat on the nightstand.

"A beer?" she repeated. It had been a long time since Charlotte had tasted a beer.

"Sure," he grinned. "Poor man's champagne."

She followed his lead, drinking quickly, seeking release from her own morality in the alcohol. As they sat down, the bed sagged and the springs squeaked. She winced and he caught the movement. "Bottoms up," he commanded, lifting the bottle to her lips for her.

"That's a good girl," he nodded when she had emptied its contents. He dropped the bottles on the floor near the bed. John would never do anything like that, she thought as Santini pushed her down. For a moment she was faintly repelled by the heavy smell of alcohol on his breath, as he buried his face inside the collar of her suit jacket, searching for her neck with his mouth. Impatiently he pulled open the four buttons, running his hands roughly along her satin-covered breasts. "Oh my," she moaned, dizzy with alcohol and desire as his fingers fired her skin.

Suddenly he stopped to peel off his undershirt. As he unzipped his trousers, she saw that he was naked underneath, long and thick and hard. He caught her stare and laughed out loud as he straddled her. "What's the matter, Miz Charlotte?" he teased. "Never seen a man before?"

Suddenly self-conscious, she whispered: "The light . . . please turn out the light."

He laughed again. "No way, babe. I wanna see what a lady looks like." He pushed up her skirt and slip, bunching the fabric around her, exposing her black garter belt, her new sheer stockings and the black panties she had bought on a recent shopping spree. "Oh, yeah," he muttered, as his fingers moved along the soft flesh of her thighs.

She heard her breath coming in quick short gasps, felt the blood pounding in her head as he pulled the silk of her panties aside and pushed himself into her. She moaned and dug her nails into his back, vaguely hearing him talk to her, saying words that no man had ever said in her presence, words that fired her excitement as he rode her for a long time, like a stallion, riding and riding her to a screaming climax.

Seconds later, he rolled over, sweating and panting—and passed out. She lay there, alone in the fading passion that had insulated her from the guilt and shame that was waiting to surface. "I have to go," she said to the snoring body, as she crawled from the bed and dressed quickly, without fixing her makeup or combing her hair.

It was three in the morning when Charlotte reached 29 Doral Avenue. The first thing she did was to strip off her clothes, which seemed to be reeking with evidence of what she had done. She stepped into a hot shower, scrubbing her skin with Ivory soap, letting the stinging stream of water sluice away the physical traces of her sin. Adultery, she thought. I have committed adultery.

Though the hour was late, she was restless and wide awake. She would write to John. That might help remind her of who she was and what she should do. She made herself some coffee and took several sheets of her favorite pink stationery to the little writing desk in the living room. *Dear John*, she wrote, trying to imagine her husband flying safely over a pretty Pacific island, but she kept remembering nightmare images from the film she'd seen that afternoon.

Making an effort to erase them, she wrote: *The weather is warm and almost summery. Soon it will be time for iced tea and day trips to the beach with the girls.*

Her pen froze, unwilling to go on with more of the easy chatter she had written. Charlotte had often prided herself on her ability to tell harmless white lies when they were needed, but now her skill to deceive offended, not pleased her. How could she sound so normal, so faithful when she had just betrayed her husband. Suddenly she was haunted by a line from her wedding vow: "I promise to be faithful, till death do us part." She began to cry.

NOT until next morning when they were all driving home from Vivien's, and the girls begged for ice cream cones, did Charlotte realize she didn't have her wallet. After she'd stopped the car and foraged through her purse, she realized she must have dropped it, in the motel, as she'd hurried to leave. If someone had found it, with all her identification, she would be ruined. But the idea of going back to reclaim it in broad daylight—no, she couldn't possibly do that.

"I'm sorry, girls," she said quickly to her daughters. "I don't seem to have any money. We'll have to go right home." She ran two red lights in her haste to get home and to the telephone.

As soon as she settled the girls, she dialed the base. "I want to speak to Petty Officer Santini," she said, trying to sound businesslike. "Crew 44. It's an emergency."

Finally, after what seemed like hours, she heard his voice, hoarse with sleep. "Santini . . . What's the goddamn emergency? I'm off duty."

"It's me," Charlotte whispered, intimidated by his tone.

"Speak up," he growled. "Who the hell is this?"

"It's Charlotte Randolph," she answered, struggling to keep her dignity.

"Why, Miz Charlotte," he said, suddenly awake. "What a surprise."

"I lost my wallet," she said quickly, anxious to get the call over with. "I must find it . . . Did you . . ."

"No sweat, babe," he replied smoothly. "I got it."

"Oh, thank God," she whispered, weak with relief.

"So when do you want it? How about Tuesday afternoon . . . same place?"

"I can't," she protested weakly. "I can't go there again . . ."

"Sure you can," he said. "If you want the goods, be there." She heard the phone click off.

She had no choice, and she felt anger at his oily self-assurance. From this she took some strength. Very well, she thought. She would go to the motel, collect her wallet because she must, but she would not let him touch her.

But despite her many rehearsals of what she would do and say Tuesday afternoon, nothing happened as planned. When Santini opened the door, he pulled her inside and held the wallet over his head, forcing her to reach for it, to chase him around the cramped room, as if they were children playing a game. Several times she almost touched it, but he was too quick for her. Finally she made a desperate lunge forward and tripped, falling head first into the mattress.

"Look at Miz Charlotte," he laughed. "She can't wait to get into bed."

"No, don't," she protested weakly, though his words, crude and mocking as they were, stirred her, reawakening the hunger that had brought her here the first time.

"Don't?" he teased, his voice husky, as he unbuttoned her blouse. "Really?" He was suddenly seductive.

She didn't answer. Just one more time, she said to herself, giving in to the pleasure of Santini's touch, and it was a pleasure.

He unzipped his pants, not bothering to undress before he pulled her skirt up. Then he was on her, inside her, hard and rough and demanding. And she was responding in kind, pushing to meet him, straining and reaching for the release that rolled through her body in great shuddering spasms.

It was over very quickly and Charlotte shut her eyes against the sight of him, wishing she could just be away from this awful place, away from Santini's mocking arrogance and her own humiliation.

But when she opened her eyes, she saw him looking at her, thoughtful and unsmiling, as if he sensed for the first time the reality of her misery. "Hey, Miz Charlotte," he said, slapping her rump in a gesture that was almost affectionate, "don't feel bad. You're just a lot of woman and you need a lotta man."

Then the moment passed, and the swagger was back, as he rearranged his clothing, slicked back his hair and tossed her the wallet, with a wave. "See ya, babe," he said, and then he was gone.

SICKENED even more by her second encounter with Santini, Charlotte swore to herself she would never see the man again, never put herself in a position where he could take advantage of her. Pleading illness, she begged off from her duties at the next Saturday night cotillion, and searched her imagination for a way to resign from that committee.

Another long week went by without word from John, shrouding Charlotte with loneliness and fear.

On a chilly, gray afternoon, as she nursed her second brandy, half listening to her favorite daytime drama, Tony phoned her.

"Miz Charlotte," he drawled, "I missed you at the dance Saturday night."

"I . . . I was sick," she stammered, wondering why she bothered to make an excuse to such a person.

"That's too bad," he said, "but I've got something guaranteed to make you feel better. Right now." His voice was husky, urgent. "Guaranteed to chase your blues away. Same place. Two o'clock . . . I'll be waiting." He hung up, without giving Charlotte an opportunity to answer.

In spite of her previous resolve, Charlotte weakened. There was so little that gave her pleasure these days, so little that made her feel alive . . .

Just once more, she vowed. And as she prepared to leave the house, she tucked the bottle of Courvoisier into a shopping bag. A touch of class . . . an antidote to the beer that Tony drank.

He smiled when he saw the brandy, but he accepted it with a sardonic bow. Together they consumed the amber liquid, with little attempt at small talk or conversation. Then, drunk and giddy, they fell on each other for a ferocious half hour before they passed out.

When she woke, it was almost dark. Tony was gone. Only the rumpled bed was evidence that he'd been there. Her watch read 4:30, more than a half hour past the time she usually picked up the girls. Feeling guilty and panicked, she dressed hurriedly and dashed from the motel room.

It was raining, torrential sheets that made driving difficult and slow, and she had a terrible headache. It was well past five o'clock when she reached the cement block playschool. The main door was locked and the grounds deserted.

Not knowing what else to do, she drove frantically across town to Doral Avenue, terrified that something awful had happened to her girls, as punishment for her sin and her negligence. As the car screeched to a stop in front of her house, she saw them, her two babies sitting on the stoop, being soaked by the downpour.

"Mummy!" Carrie shouted as she saw Charlotte running up the walk. "Oh, Mummy, you came home!"

She hugged the girls fiercely, sobbing her relief and her apologies. Once inside, she stripped off their clothes and gave them hot baths, hoping to take the chill from their little bodies. Then she buttoned them up in flannel pajamas and tucked them in bed, insisting that they stay there for the rest of the night.

The children loved the special attention, supper on trays, steaming cups of hot chocolate, and Charlotte reading, willingly, chapter after chapter from their new favorite book, *Mrs. Wiggs in the Cabbage Patch*.

It was quite late, almost ten, when Charlotte turned off the metal lamp between the two beds and tiptoed out of the room. Nancy had fallen asleep, but Carrie was still awake. "Where were you, Mummy?" she called out. "Why did we have to wait in the rain?"

"Hush," Charlotte commanded. "You'll wake your sister." Hastily she shut the door and escaped into the hallway.

Carrie's question echoed in her mind as she headed for the bourbon bottle in the living room. The alcohol did not stem the flood of self-recrimination that came upon her. Not only had she tarnished her marriage vows, but now she had recklessly endangered her children. She was behaving like a bad woman, and the only excuse she had was that she was lonely and miserable. Here in her own home, with her little girls nearby, that excuse seemed tattered and flimsy. She would have to get herself under control, and that meant not seeing Tony Santini again. Not ever.

She finished her drink and dozed off on the couch. She was wakened by Carrie, tugging at her skirt: "Mummy, mummy," the child pleaded, "wake up. Wake up, Nancy's sick."

Groggily, Charlotte pulled herself up and raced into the bedroom. Her daughter was tossing restlessly in bed, her little body flushed with fever and wracked with a croupy cough.

She did everything she knew to do: aspirin, cold compresses and a croup kettle draped with an umbrella and sheet. But she could not relieve either the cough or the fever. As the night gave way to early morning, Nancy's temperature climbed higher. She called the home of one of the base pediatricians, but no one answered. Panicked, she called her friend Isabel.

"I'll come right over," Isabel offered. "I'll look after Carrie. You bundle Nancy up and take her to the base hospital."

A half hour later, Charlotte laid her child, wrapped in blankets and now gasping for breath, on the front seat of her car, and sped through the deserted night streets of Pensacola.

Isabel had phoned ahead, and a doctor and nurse were waiting for her when she pulled around the circular driveway and screeched to a stop. Quickly the doctor lifted the child from the car and rushed inside, shouting instructions to the nurse who trailed behind him.

The nurse at the reception desk, a heavyset woman with bleached blond hair and an imperious manner, stopped

Charlotte from going past the swinging doors to the
emergency room, where the doctor and nurse had taken
Nancy. Not unkindly, she insisted Charlotte sit down and
have a cup of coffee while she waited.

Charlotte half-listened as the nurse launched into a monologue about all the people who arrived at the hospital in
the middle of the night in various stages of undress. It was
only then she realized that she was wearing a nightgown
and a robe, and that she must look a sight. And for the first
time in her life, she didn't care how she looked.

When the doctor finally appeared again, his face was
somber and unsmiling. "She has pneumonia," he said
gravely.

Charlotte's fears spiraled into terror. Pneumonia . . . a
cruel killer of children and adults alike. She hung on the
doctor's words as he explained that one lung had collapsed
and that Nancy's fever was dangerously high. "The next
twenty-four to thirty-six hours will be critical," he concluded, with no words of reassurance or encouragement.

"Critical?" she repeated blankly. "But she's going to be
all right, isn't she?" she pleaded desperately.

"We're doing all we can," he said evasively. "Now I
think you should go home and rest. I'm sorry, but I can't
allow you to see her."

"No," Charlotte protested stubbornly. "I'm going to stay
here with my baby. I want her to know her Mummy is
here."

"If you insist," the doctor agreed. "But there is really
nothing you can do for her."

She called Isabel from a pay phone in the hallway and
choked out the doctor's report over the wires. A short time
later, her friend arrived with clothing, a thermos of coffee
and the Bible that Charlotte had requested. "I took Carrie
to Jean Goodman's house," she explained, "so I can stay
with you."

"Thank you," she whispered, but for the next few hours,
Charlotte said very little to Isabel. Instead she paced back
and forth in the small waiting room, clutching the Randolph
family Bible to her chest, forming silent prayers to God.
Prayers for forgiveness. Spare my Nancy, she pleaded, and

I'll never do anything this bad again.

Towards the end of the afternoon, when there had been no change in Nancy's condition, Isabel suggested a call to alert the Whittakers of the child's serious condition.

"No!" Charlotte said vehemently, feeling that she could not ask for her family's solace without confessing her responsibility for Nancy's illness. "She's going to be all right," she insisted, resuming her pacing and her internal bargaining with God.

The hours crawled by on the clock over the Emergency Room doors, slowly depleting Charlotte's reservoir of stubborn hope. As fatigue, physical and mental, took her over, she began to feel that a penance was required of her, that she would have to confess her shame publicly before God would show her child some mercy.

But a few minutes past eleven, the doctor appeared in the waiting room. "She's going to make it," he said simply, smiling for the first time that day.

"Thank you, God," she sobbed, "Oh, dear God, thank you!" Then, to the doctor, she said: "May I see my baby now? Please?"

He nodded and held open the door, but Isabel squeezed her arm. "Wait a minute, honey. Comb your hair and fix your face. You'll give the child a fright if she sees you like this.

WHEN Charlotte returned to the house on Doral Avenue, it was well past midnight. Automatically she checked the metal post box before she unlocked the door. She found a tattered onion-skin envelope. It was from John. It was a sign from God. He was allowing John to speak to her, now that she had repented.

Rushing inside the house, she tore it open with shaking hands and began to read. It was only one sheet, penned in John's neat, precise handwriting.

"Dearest Charlotte," it began. The endearment brought fresh tears of remorse to her eyes, and she blinked them away as she read on:

I can't know if this letter or those of the past several weeks will have reached you. We are stationed on a small remote island, and there have been rumors that mail transport is not very reliable here.

The fighting has been heavy, but be assured that I am careful. I am as much at home in these Pacific skies as in the sunny ones of Florida or the cool clear ones of New England. I am weary from combat and a bit thinner, but no less steady and sure than I have been from the start.

Lately I have given some thought to your life on the base. I am proud of the adjustments you have made, but I cannot know how long it will be before we are all together again. It would give me comfort if you and the children would go to Breezy Hill, away from the long shadow of this war, to wait for me in the sheltering arms of your loving family. Will you do this for me?

Letter supplies and light are short here tonight, so I must close with hugs for my girls and a loving embrace for you, my dear wife. I long to hold you in my arms and to feel your heart beat against mine. The thought of you waiting for me is what sustains me. I love you, my beautiful Charlotte.

Yours,
John

She took the letter to bed and tucked it under her pillow, swearing that she would be a faithful wife until the day she died, and that John would never know of her betrayal. She fell asleep in a heavy haze of exhaustion and relief.

NANCY'S recovery and the packing took up almost three weeks, but by the middle of June, Charlotte was ready to leave Pensacola, grateful for the chance to put this sordid and troubled chapter of her life behind her. When she wrote to John, and she wrote every day now, she told him that she and the girls planned to be back in West Grove by the first of June, in time for Roland's eighteenth birthday and his graduation, which fell on the same day.

The base wives sent Charlotte off with a gala luncheon— salmon croquettes instead of chicken à la king, and a leather photo album filled with souvenir pictures of base life. Although Charlotte made her goodbyes with genuine tears, there was also relief in her leave-taking, for she was haunted by the gnawing fear that one of her girlfriends would somehow find out about her sordid affair. After the luncheon, and with the car fully packed, she picked up the girls from their last day at playschool and headed north.

As they passed out of the Pensacola city limits, Carrie asked: "Why are we leaving, Mummy?"

"Because your father wants us to," Charlotte snapped without meaning to, irritated by her elder child's uncanny knack for asking difficult questions.

"Why does he want us to?" Carrie persisted.

"Because of the war," Charlotte answered vehemently.

"I don't like this war," Carrie sulked, frowning and sinking down into the front seat.

"Neither do I." Charlotte was exasperated. "Now be quiet. You're making me nervous!"

She had intended to drive through the night, with a brief supper break, but after Nancy got carsick twice, she was forced to pull into a dreary roadside motel, ridiculously named The Blue Lagoon. An absence of hot water and the dingy gray color of the sheets put Charlotte into a further temper.

The rest of what was meant to be a three-day drive was punctuated with frustrations and delays, the worst being an oil leak on the second day in northern Georgia. Charlotte called West Grove that night to tell Clifton they probably couldn't arrive in time for Roland's birthday-graduation festivities. Clifton was concerned and sympathetic about her difficult journey. He tried to cheer her with the news that Bessie had prepared her old bedroom, that bunk beds had been set up for the girls so they all three could be together during their stay at Breezy.

"Be sure and congratulate Roland when you do get here," he said, his voice edged with pride. "That boy has surprised

us all. He's graduating with a B — average, so perhaps they
will take him at Washington and Lee after all."

Charlotte didn't care a bit about her brother's scholastic
achievement. What did register in her mind was the fact
that she and the girls were expected to share one bedroom
for God knows how long. Of course, she should have realized the house was full up, what with Meg and Emily and
their children already in residence. Damn, she swore to
herself, remembering the gracious, comfortable house she'd
left behind when this nightmare of a war had started.

It was mid-morning of the day following Roland's festivities when Charlotte drove up the lane, honking loudly and
expecting a hero's welcome. But only Bessie and Alexander
came out of the house to welcome her and the girls.

"Where's Papa?" she asked peevishly.

"Mistuh Clifton's on the telephone," Bessie answered,
wearing her time-of-trouble expression. "Po' man," she
added, so Charlotte would approach her father with the
proper deference and care.

"Oh, shoot," she muttered, too preoccupied with her own
fatigue and discomfort to ask about any problems Clifton
might be facing. "Where's Roland? We need some help
with these bags."

Bessie shook her head, but before she could answer,
Emily came out onto the porch. "Hi, Charlotte. Hi, Carrie,
Nancy. Come give Aunt Emily a big hug."

"What is going on here?" Charlotte demanded. "Where
is everyone?"

"Roland ran off to Bristol with Buddy Pruner last night.
They signed up with the Marines. Papa's on the phone with
the Pruners, trying to get some more information. He's very
upset."

"Oh, is that all? We always knew he was going to do
something like that. I don't see why Papa's so surprised . . ."

"Oh, hush, Charlotte," Emily interrupted. "That kind of
talk isn't going to do anyone any good. Here, let me help
you with your things."

With a final sniff of indignation, Charlotte went back to
the car to begin unloading her bags. This was some home-

coming, she thought. Here she had gone through hell back on the base (a hell she could never share with either of her sisters), endured a horrible trip to Breezy, and no one even cared. It was only Roland's leaving, not her arrival, that they cared about. It wasn't fair.

But as she carried one of the smaller bags up the front steps, a small smile came to her lips, and she said to no one in particular: "As far as I'm concerned, Roland's signing up will make life easier for us all. Now my girls can have his bedroom." It was the first pleasing thought she had had in days.

9

United We Stand
September 1944

September 7, 1944

My Dear Children,

How I wish you all could have been here last Saturday when the entire West Grove community convened in the town square for a War Bond Drive sale. Yours truly was the auctioneer, and in honor of the occasion I resurrected my wedding tuxedo (which I must admit still fits passably well).

The white pillars in front of the courthouse were decorated and a large American flag was swinging between the two pillars on either side of the main entrance. Underneath was a long table completely covered with donated goods for sale: flour, meal, hams, honey, cakes, cigars, blankets, petticoats and on and on. There were even several boxed pigs which my assistant, Alexander, tended until it was their time to be placed on the auction block.

Reverend Lowell initiated the proceedings by giving the auctioneer a twenty-dollar gold piece to sell to the highest bidder. It was sold at least six times, and each man bought

*it and gave it back to the preacher. In less than five minutes,
the Reverend's coin had brought a total price of $2,500.00,
launching our bond sale quite splendidly. . . .*

"Isn't it just like Roland," Charlotte complained, as she
fanned herself with her brother's brief letter which had arrived the day before. "Just a date . . . Not a word about what
time he's coming home or how he'll be traveling."

It was Sunday afternoon, the first week in September,
and a summer heat wave was still hanging over the valley.
The three Whittaker sisters sat on the front porch, sipping
lemonade and hoping for an occasional breeze.

"Wonder if we could get an advance on our meat rations
for October," Emily mused out loud, her mind already on
the practical aspects of Roland's coming leave. "We're more
than halfway through this month's book."

"Maybe I could talk to Bernard Pyle," Meg offered, as
she half-heartedly pumped the porch swing with her toes.
"He says it's a miracle I've managed to teach his Mary Sue
to play the piano. Maybe I can get him to show his appreciation with a roast . . ."

"Speaking of your piano lessons," Charlotte smoothed
down her skirt and recrossed her legs. "Do you think you
could rearrange your schedule Tuesday afternoon? It's my
turn to have the girls up here, and it would be so much
nicer if we didn't have to listen to all those scales . . ."

"That's just too bad." Meg reacted, stopping the swing
with her foot. "I don't think you should expect me to rearrange my work to fit your social calendar."

"Maybe you could play bridge on the back porch, instead
of in the parlor," Emily intervened diplomatically. "If the
door's closed, you can hardly hear the piano." She reached
for the new book she had ordered through the Literary Guild.
It was *Yankee From Olympus*, Catherine Drinker Bowen's
biography of Justice Oliver Wendell Holmes, and she had
been eagerly looking forward to reading it over the weekend.
Now that she was working full time at the *Gazette*, she had
very little free time.

"Isn't this a pretty picture?" Clifton said, pushing open

the screen door and coming out onto the porch. He was still dressed in his gray Sunday suit, his bowler in his hand. "My three lovely girls enjoying this beautiful afternoon together."

"Where are you going?" Charlotte asked, ignoring the flowery compliment. Her father had that slightly sheepish look that told his daughters he was up to something.

"Well," he said, a little too casually. "I thought I'd take a stroll into town. Walking's good for the digestion, especially after Bessie's popovers. I'll be back before dinner."

"It's Sunday, Papa," Meg teased to her father's retreating back. "None of the stores are open."

"I'm perfectly aware it's Sunday," he replied, as he continued to walk across the grassy hill. "There's nothing wrong with my memory," he muttered, almost to himself.

Clifton was barely out of earshot when Charlotte hissed: "He's going to see that woman. I just know it. He's getting more brazen about it all the time. What he sees in her I'll never understand."

"Whatever it is, he obviously enjoys her company," Emily said in her father's defense, "so let's respect that fact." She opened her book pointedly and started reading, not wanting to encourage Charlotte's ongoing sniping at Miss Jewel.

"Are you all rolling bandages on Tuesday? Or will it just be bridge all afternoon?" Meg baited Charlotte.

"We can't roll bandages all the time," Charlotte said defensively. "And for your information, we've done our quota this month!"

"Do you two think I could have some quiet before the children wake up from their naps?" Emily looked up from her book, irritated that her sisters were at each other again.

"I think you should forget the book," Meg said. "You've got a caller."

"A caller?"

"Why, it's Billy Gillespie," Charlotte announced, looking over the porch rail. "I guess I'll go inside and check on the girls."

"I'll go, too," Meg agreed, getting off the swing. "And I'll tell Bessie to bring out some more lemonade."

"You don't have to leave," Emily said, embarrassed that her sisters were behaving as they had years before, when young men came calling on Sunday afternoons. "He's my boss, for heaven's sake," she protested, though she had come to think of Billy as a friend.

The screen door slammed shut and her sisters were gone. Emily reached up and patted her hair, trying to remember if she had combed it after dinner.

As Billy approached the house, she was surprised to see that he was wearing a Sunday suit, not unlike her father's, and carrying an unfamiliar hat. He had once told her that he was a heathen like her Aunt Rose Mary, and that Sundays were for sleeping, not church, despite what the nuns at St. Luke's elementary school in Chicago had taught him.

"My goodness," she teased as he came up the porch stairs. "You're certainly looking like a church-going man, sir."

"Didn't dare walk down Main Street in the wrong costume," he said gruffly, his ruddy face flushing slightly. "I should have called. Am I interrupting anything?"

"Course not. Sit down. Bessie is bringing out some lemonade. Is anything wrong with the copy I did Friday? I was in a rush to get home..."

"Nope. Your copy was fine. You've got the makings of a crackerjack reporter. I've told you that a dozen times, Em. In fact, I think you're good enough to run the *Gazette* for a couple of days."

"Run the *Gazette*? But why..."

"Before you say anything, listen to this, Em. I'm on the trail of something, and I want to follow it through. I got a letter from Floyd McClintock, an old university buddy of mine. He's working for the Army, at the Clinton Engineer Works near Knoxville. He invited me to visit for a couple of days."

"Clinton Engineer Works, did you say?" Emily remembered something she'd read about the company located on the Clinch River in East Tennessee. Something about the government buying up great parcels of land there and constructing some kind of war plant. "Wasn't that the place they renamed Oak Ridge?"

"Good girl!" Billy grinned, his blue eyes shining with excitement. "I knew you didn't miss much. Neither do I, and I smell a story here, Em, a big one ... maybe the biggest one ever for me. What's going on at Oak Ridge could change everything. The Army hasn't released any figures to the press, but I hear tell that the government has bought up some 50,000 acres of farmland there. A firm called Skidmore, Merrill and Owens has designed an entire city, and get this, Em—Oak Ridge doesn't even appear on local maps, even though there's a rumored population of some 30,000."

"Really!" Emily leaned forward, sharing Billy's excitement now. "What does all this mean, Billy?"

"I have some suspicions, but I don't know for sure. Union Carbide and Monsanto built some mystery plants, and there's talk of some kind of death ray ... maybe something with uranium. Back a few years ago, my friend Floyd worked with Fermi on experiments with uranium at the university..."

"The University of Chicago?" Emily asked, remembering a diploma on the wall of Billy's office.

"Right again, kid." Billy smiled approvingly. "Anyway, I think a secret weapon of some kind is being built, and I mean to nose around ... see if I can dig up some stuff that isn't classified. That's why I need you to hold the fort for a couple of days. What do you say, Em? Do it ... for me?" He gripped her hands tightly, willing her to be a partner, an ally, and perhaps something more.

"I ..." she flushed, unsettled by the intensity of Billy's manner, by the warmth of his touch, his handsomeness and his physical closeness.

Then the mood was broken by the slamming of the screen door. "Hey, Mom ... Billy." Alexander appeared on the porch, rubbing his eyes, still sleepy from his afternoon nap.

"Hey, yourself," Billy greeted the youngster fondly. "Come on over here and help me persuade your mom to be boss at the *Gazette* for a couple of days."

"Boss ... Jeepers, creepers ... my mom?" Alexander squinted at Emily through his glasses, reappraising his mother on the basis of this new information.

"Take my word for it," Billy laughed, ruffling the boy's hair. "She's a smart one, your mom."

"You win." Emily joined the laughter. "And after all that flattery, I'll probably ask for a raise—how's that for confidence, Mr. Gillespie?"

"You'd be worth every penny," he said passionately, staring into her eyes. There was a moment of embarrassed silence. He loosened his tie and took off his jacket. Turning to Alexander, he said: "I have an invitation for you, too, young man."

"Me?" Alexander began to hop up and down excitedly. "What? Where?"

"I request the pleasure of your company in viewing the weekly basketball practice at the high school. Will you come?"

"Can I, Mom?" Alexander tugged at Emily's skirt. "Can I?"

"Yes, you *may* . . . thank you," she added softly, finding Billy's eyes again, touched by the big man's growing involvement with her son.

He nodded, slinging his jacket over his shoulder, and taking the child's small hand in his. "We're off, then. Don't wait for us, Em. If my friend here isn't too tired, we may sample the delicacies of Stoots' soda fountain later."

"I won't be tired, I won't!" Alexander fairly danced down the hill, his normally serious face glowing with pleasure as he tried to keep in step with Billy's giant strides.

As Emily waved goodbye, Carrie and Nancy skipped onto the porch. "Where's Alex going?" Carrie demanded.

"Billy's taking him to watch basketball practice at the high school."

"Why can't I go too?" Carrie asked petulantly.

"Basketball is for boys," Emily answered automatically. "You wouldn't enjoy it."

"I would too!" Carrie stamped her foot. "I like everything that boys do."

Emily smiled at her niece, sympathizing with her feeling of being left out. "All right, Carrie, perhaps another time. Why don't we make some pictures today. I have a brand new box of Crayola colors . . ."

"Birdie," Nancy piped up.

"She means she wants to make a picture of a bird," Carrie translated for her sister, as she always did.

"Grandpa's birdies," Nancy beamed, delighted at being included in the conversation.

"They're not Grandpa's birdies, silly," Carrie corrected. To Emily, she explained: "Just because Granddaddy has a bird feeder, she thinks all the birds are his."

"Isn't she lucky to have you to teach her, then."

"I suppose," Carrie said skeptically, with a heavy grown-up sigh, as if the weight of the world were hers.

IN anticipation of his visit, Roland's letter had been passed around the family many times:

> *Six more days of basic. Counting the hours till O'Hara stops yelling drills and we stop dragging around this stupid Carolina swamp. Got a two-week leave, so watch out, 'cause I'm coming home. Tell Bessie to start cooking—I'm starving! Got to go. See you all the 15th.*

So on Thursday the 14th, everyone took turns waiting at the drug store and station, meeting the buses and trains coming in from the south.

At 9:30, Charlotte and Clifton met the last train from Atlanta, certain that Roland would be on it. On the hill, Bessie was ready with all of his favorite dishes: fried chicken, cornbread and lemon meringue pie. His nieces and nephews had composed a welcome-home song, to be performed with a wash basin drum and darning-gourd rattles.

But Roland was not on the train.

"That does it," Charlotte snapped, as Mr. Sam waved the flag signalling the train's departure. "Roland will never change. You can't even depend on him to get here when he says he will."

Clifton said nothing. He refused to lose face and publicly vent his anger. In silent frustration, he clenched his hands into fists in his pockets. "I believe I'll stop at the office," he said stiffly as they approached his black Packard. "I'll be home later."

"But how will you get home if I take the car," Charlotte argued, knowing that her father was probably headed for Miss Jewel's. "It's dark. You shouldn't walk home in the dark."

"Nothing to worry about. I've done it many times," he said, handing her the car keys.

"What about supper? Bessie will be upset if you're not there, especially with Roland God knows where."

"She'll understand," Clifton said curtly, tipping his hat and walking away.

"So do I," Charlotte muttered, jerking open the car door and getting into the driver's seat. "I understand perfectly well," she said to herself, registering her disapproval of her father's behavior by speeding out of the parking lot, tires screeching, in a cloud of exhaust.

Normally such recklessness would have upset Clifton, but he was so preoccupied that he scarcely reacted to his daughter's irresponsible driving as he walked slowly up Station Avenue over to Main Street.

His unexpected visit found Miss Jewel in a flowered robe and floppy slippers, listening to the radio and doing a bit of crochet work.

"He didn't come yet, did he?" she asked, reading his face. "Never mind," she soothed. "Why, I'll bet that child plans to surprise you. Now you just sit down and I'll get a little something for you."

Her plump body moved with surprising grace as she crossed the room to the china closet that housed her thimble collection and her small liquor supply.

"That boy," Clifton sighed, sinking into the doily-covered armchair facing the sofa. "I had hoped he would acquire some sense of responsibility in the service. I'm afraid Elizabeth really spoiled him, and now, I don't know . . ."

Silently Jewel handed him a generous shot of Old Grand-Dad, his favorite whiskey, trying not to show her surprise. They had an unspoken understanding not to talk about Elizabeth, and it was rare that he even mentioned her name. As she always did, she dragged the tattered leather ottoman over from the sofa and lifted his feet onto it.

"You shouldn't do that," Clifton protested. "I've told you that before."

"Now you just make yourself comfortable," she said, tucking up a stray curl that had fallen across her cheek. "I'll get myself a nip of sherry. I'm sure Roland didn't mean to disappoint you. He just wants to surprise you . . . I'm sure of it." She held his hand, and once again Clifton felt very lucky to have Jewel's affection.

JEWEL'S prediction of a surprise arrival came true, but not in quite the way she had imagined. The following afternoon, an old Ford coupe honked noisily up the lane and braked to a stop behind the house. "Where is everybody?" Roland shouted, jumping from the car. "Come on, you all . . . Come on out here!"

The children were the first to burst out of the house. Though they were momentarily taken aback by how different their adored Uncle Ro looked in his Marine private's uniform, they kept to their carefully rehearsed plans, and chanted in unison, "We have a song for you."

Emily ran past the children to greet her brother, and after she hugged him, she whispered in his ear, "You should have called. Papa was worried sick."

"It's about time," Meg called as she pushed open the screen door. "Where have you been, you little devil?"

Ever curious, Carrie wandered over to look at the new car. "Who's that?" she asked, pointing to the woman sitting in the front seat.

"Who's with you?" Charlotte repeated as she came outside with Clifton, who was holding his lunch napkin in hand.

Roland swung open the passenger door and a blond, full-breasted woman in a tight blue dress stepped out of the Ford.

"Surprise!" Roland beamed, lifting up the woman's arm, as if she were a victorious prize fighter. "Meet Mrs. Roland J. Whittaker!"

There was a moment of stunned silence. "No." The word forced itself hoarsely from Clifton's throat.

"Easy, Papa," Meg cautioned, fearing not only for her father's health, but also for his relationship with Roland.

"We were married last night," Roland explained, not seeming to notice that no one was sharing his excitement. "It was kinda on the spur of the moment," he added sheepishly, "and that's why we didn't let you know." He waited expectantly, then he asked, "Isn't anyone going to congratulate us?"

Pained by her brother's plea, Emily forced herself to rise above her own shock and went to him, arms outstretched. "You certainly caught us by surprise, little brother . . ."

"Congratulations," Meg offered the word. Remembering her own painful experience with Clifton's disapproval, she nudged her father. "Say something," she whispered urgently. "It's you he wants to hear from."

"Well, son." Clifton cleared his throat several times. "This certainly is a surprise . . ."

"That's an understatement," Charlotte muttered.

"But, of course, we all wish you well," Emily finished.

Following her sister's lead, Charlotte tried to rise to the occasion. "Well, Roland," she said, using her "put on" sweet voice, "do introduce us to your . . . your bride. My goodness, she's going to think none of us have any manners."

Roland's face lit up at the word "bride." "Meet Clara," he said, draping his arm possessively around the woman's tiny waist. "Clara Polanski Whittaker. My wife."

WHILE his family tried to make conversation with Clara in the parlor, Roland crept into the kitchen where Bessie was preparing iced tea and cookies. He came up behind the big black woman who had always been his ally. "Boo!" he said in her ear, then laughed as she jumped.

"Git!" she commanded. "You git outta my way, chile. Bargin' in like this . . . Lawdy. Lawdy."

"Ah, come on, Bessie," he pleaded, drawing himself up to his full height, trying to impress her with his uniform, his newly developed physique. "I'm not a kid anymore. I'm a soldier and a married man. Give me a break."

"A break?" She repeated the unfamiliar expression. She put down the lemon she'd been slicing and planted her hands on her hips. "What you needs is a spankin'!" Her dark eyes were intense as she studied the boy she'd raised as her own. "You too young to be marryin'! You too young. You don't know nothin' yet."

Hurt, he hung his head, as he had done so many times before, in the face of disapproval. She softened, touching his face gently with her roughened hand. "Nevuh mind," she said. "What's done is done, and now you gots to be a man, if'n yo' likes it or not. Now git, and take these here cookies with yo'."

As she served the refreshments, Bessie informed Emily that she "done sent the younguns to the jelly cellar." "Lawd knows," she rolled her eyes meaningfully, "yo' done got plenty to worry 'bout without them bein' underfoot."

"The jelly cellar is down under the side of the back porch," Emily explained to the new Mrs. Whittaker, trying to make the young woman feel at home. "It's always been a favorite hideout on Breezy." She managed a small welcoming smile. "Though Roland always chose the barn for his headquarters."

"You got animals? Pigs and cows and stuff?" Clara looked puzzled. "Is this a farm?"

"We have a cow," Clifton answered stiffly, visibly pained by the young woman's bad grammar.

"Her name's Peaches 'n' Cream," Roland filled in. "I won her at the County Fair."

"Funny," Clara mused, "when you talked about the place, tellin' me the name and all, I kinda thought it would be like the movies. You know, like that place in *Gone with the Wind*."

"Tara," Charlotte supplied, with more than a hint of acid in her voice. Then, more sweetly, she explained patiently, as if to a child: "We live in the mountains of Virginia, dear, not on a Georgia plantation."

"Yeah, I see," the bride said, clearly disappointed as she surveyed the parlor furnishings.

"Tell us something about yourself," Emily invited. "How did you and Roland meet?"

"Oh, yes, do tell us that," Charlotte urged, as she offered a tray of cookies to her new sister-in-law, using the opportunity to get a close look at Clara's hair. Bleached blond, she noted with some satisfaction. The roots were definitely brown.

Clara took a large bite of a lemon wafer, chewed a bit, and shifted the cookie to the corner of her mouth as she spoke: "Well, I work at Al's Diner near the..."

"You're a waitress?" Charlotte almost dropped the tray she was offering.

"Yeah." Clara nodded, taking a big swallow of iced tea to wash down her cookie.

"She's the head waitress there," Roland explained. "She's really good." He smiled fondly at his bride, slipping his arm around her thin shoulders, which were nearly bared by the low cut of her dress. "And she's pretty, too. Isn't she the prettiest thing ever?"

Clara giggled, enjoying the hug and the compliment. "He says I look like Betty Grable." She fluttered her eyelids. "And he hasn't even seen me in a bathing suit yet. My mother named me after Clara Bow. That was her favorite movie star, but I don't think I much look like her..."

"Have you and Roland known each other long?" Emily questioned, trying to keep the conversation moving.

"Oh, a long time," Clara quickly answered. "Ever since his basic started. Right, Rolly?"

"Rolly?" Clifton repeated this strange new version of an old family name. "Is that what you call my son?"

"That's Clara's special nickname for me," Roland hastily explained. "She says Roland is too formal. You know."

"I see," Clifton said, though clearly he didn't. "Tell me," he asked, leaning forward in his chair, his legal mind now at work. "Where exactly were you married, and by whom?"

"Oxford, South Carolina. By a Justice of the Peace." Roland reached into the pocket of his uniform and pulled out a neatly folded piece of paper. "See, sir, I have the marriage certificate, right here."

Clifton studied it slowly, checking for proper documentation and a valid notary seal, and his slim hopes evaporated.

Everything was in order. His only son and this very common woman had been joined together for life, on May 14, 1944.

"Whoever would have thought I'd be a married man, hey, Pop?" Roland said proudly, as he reclaimed the document and replaced it carefully inside his jacket. His observation met with stony silence.

LATER that afternoon Roland decided to take Clara on a tour of West Grove. The minute the young couple walked out the front door, his sisters stared at one another, still shocked at what their baby brother had done.

Charlotte spoke first. "My, that's certainly not the sort of girl I expected Roland to marry. I can well imagine how that creature got him to propose," she added acidly.

Emily stood at the front door, watching through the beveled glass pane, as Clara walked, hips swaying seductively, across the porch, with her brother following behind. "Maybe she'll mature well," she offered. "Some people do. Obviously, she's never had many advantages."

Charlotte snorted. "Obviously . . . In fact, in Pensacola, a woman like that was called 'a dumb broad.'"

"Don't be such a snob," Meg said sharply. "If Roland loves her, we should make an effort, too."

Bessie walked into the foyer, her arms laden with sheets. "Mistuh Roland"—she said the "mister" in deference to Roland's new status as soldier and husband—"and his wife be sleepin' in your room, Miss Emily."

"Oh, Lord," Charlotte moaned. "That woman in Granny Sara Belle's old bed."

"It's my bed now," Emily reminded her sister. "Come on, Bessie, I'll give you a hand and get some of my things out of there."

"Perhaps I should plan a small gathering," Charlotte mused, apparently seeing no incongruity between her distaste for her new sister-in-law and the possible social aspects of this new development. "What do you all think?"

Before anyone else could answer, Clifton responded loudly and firmly: "No, Charlotte. This is a private family matter."

Charlotte dropped the subject, or rather shifted it to another angle. "Well, then," she asked, "will you be giving her . . . Clara, Mama's ring?"

Clifton looked insulted, as if he couldn't imagine why his daughter would ask such a question.

"But, Papa," she explained, "surely you noticed that Clara made a very pointed reference to that dime-store ring Roland bought for their wedding ceremony. I distinctly heard her say that Roland had promised her something better. Mama always said that her ring was for Roland's bride, though I'm sure she could never have imagined he'd marry such a person . . ."

"That's enough, Charlotte Lee." Clifton cut his daughter off from saying what they had all been thinking—because now it was not to be said, not when Clara Polanski was a member of the Whittaker family. "I'm going to retire now. It's been quite a day." And so saying, Clifton exited down the hall.

But the irrepressible Charlotte was already off on another tack, wondering how her new sister-in-law, since they were already stuck with her, might be better presented to the rest of the world. "I wonder," she mused, "if we took Clara to Gladys's Cut and Set, maybe if we had those roots of hers touched up, and a permanent, yes, I do think . . ."

"You're incredible," Emily marveled. "You think everything can be fixed at the beauty parlor. Even a marriage."

"I've had the strangest feeling all day," Meg said, almost to herself, as she sat curled up on the sofa, running her fingers through her long black hair.

"What kind of feeling?" Charlotte asked, immediately alert to the prospect of something else in the air.

"I just have this feeling that something's wrong . . ." Meg trailed off.

"Oh, well," Charlotte dismissed her sister's intuition, obviously disappointed. "I'll just bet it's that time of the month. You always get real funny a couple of days before."

"Still . . ." Meg said, her face haunted by something even she could not explain.

* * *

THE following morning, the children were up before the adults, eating their Rice Krispies in the kitchen and planning their day excitedly.

"Let's go wake up Uncle Ro," Carrie proposed.

"He's sleeping with that lady," Alexander announced solemnly.

"I hope he still likes us," Nancy pouted, worried about losing the attention she was accustomed to from her uncle.

"You will not disturb your uncle," Charlotte said sharply, as she swept into the kitchen, her peach dressing gown billowing about her. "Or his wife," she added.

"Why not?" Carrie persisted. "Why can't we wake Uncle Ro? He always lets us."

"Because," her mother explained impatiently, "he is married now, and he does not want to play with you anymore."

"What's that?" Roland questioned, bursting through the swinging door. "Who says I don't want to play? Who wants the first tickle today?" He reached for little Nancy, who was already giggling in pleasurable anticipation.

Behind him trailed Clara, who was considerably subdued this morning, in spite of the flamboyance of her clothes— a pink angora sweater and a pencil-slim black skirt, slit high on both sides. "Where's the coffee?" she moaned. "Me and Rolly sure tied one on last night."

"Clara!" Roland poked his wife, clearly embarrassed by her frank earthiness.

"What?" Then, realizing her husband was feeling self-conscious about her candor, she said petulantly: "Oh, for Pete's sake, we're newlyweds. Everybody knows about that."

"Good morning, all." Clifton entered the room, dressed for the office, his morning paper tucked under his arm.

Bessie followed, ready for action. "Y'all git now," she ordered, clearing the kitchen and shooing the family into the dining room.

As the morning meal of scrambled eggs and bacon was being served, Clara picked up a fork and examined Miss Elizabeth's silver. "This is nice stuff," she admired. "We don't have any stuff at all," she said plaintively. "I don't know how I'm gonna keep house."

"We'll manage," Roland said absently, his mouth filled with toast, for he had no interest whatever in keeping house. What had drawn him to Clara had nothing whatever to do with homemaking. It had been, in fact, the pressure of her voluptuous body against his, a whispered suggestion in his ear, and several Canadian Clubs with ginger ale. Now that the deed was done, the lark that had made them husband and wife, she was still a lot of fun at night. But in the daytime, well, in the daytime he didn't know quite what to do with her.

"Most brides have showers and things," she was going on, "but we just didn't have the time, did we, Rolly?" She stroked Roland's arm, a world of meaning in her attitude. He blushed, and everyone else looked away.

"Perhaps I should take Clara shopping in Abington," Emily volunteered. "We could buy them a few basics. What do you think, Papa?"

"My family can't do nothin' for us," Clara lamented, leaning into her husband's shoulder like a wilted vine. "My daddy hurt his back in the shipyard, and he can't work but part-time. But, Rolly told me not to worry about anything, didn't you, sweetie pie?"

"I suppose we should." Charlotte cast a "yes" vote because she felt a little sorry for the girl, starting out married life without any of the things she considered essential—a big wedding, an extravagant trousseau, and suitable furnishings of all kinds.

"Very well," Clifton agreed. He was a fair man, and if he was not tolerant enough to personally embrace the likes of Clara, he would nevertheless do his part in seeing that she was treated like a proper Whittaker. "You may take Clara to Abington. Buy whatever seems necessary. I'll go to the bank now, and you can stop at the office on your way."

"Oh, that's neat!" Clara exclaimed, delighted that, at last, something was going the way she imagined it would when she got Roland to propose. He was a swell kid, all right, but if she'd meant to stay poor, she could've stayed in Bayonne and taken up with one of the Albertalli boys, right next door.

As he prepared to leave, Clifton announced: "I'll be working late tonight. Don't count on me for dinner."

"Again?" Charlotte asked pointedly.

"Pop's head of the Draft Board," Roland boasted.

"Wow!" Clara said. "What a depressing job. I sure wouldn't want to do it."

"This war makes it necessary for all of us to do things we don't want to do," Clifton said sternly, annoyed by Clara's frivolous remark. "Now, if you'll excuse me."

THAT evening Clara was as excited as a child at Christmas, holding up towels, sheets, cookware and silverplated flatware, each and every item of her instant hope chest, to be admired. "I never got so many new things at once," she said ingenuously, "but I always thought it would be swell to get hitched and started with everything fresh. Nothing ripped or broken."

Charlotte smiled politely, her embryonic sympathy for her new sister-in-law threatening to evaporate on the spot.

Clifton, who had been uncomfortably enduring the extended display of domestic wares, rose and walked to the front window.

"Pop's like me," Roland hastened to explain, lest Clara feel hurt. "He isn't really interested in this kind of stuff."

"Walter Winchell says Patton continues to push across Brittany," Meg reported, from her chair beside the radio. "That's encouraging, Papa, don't you think?"

"I think so, Meg," Clifton nodded gravely. Though it was hard to keep a balanced optimism these days, when each allied victory seemed to be followed so swiftly with a defeat. "It does sound as if the tide could finally be turning."

"I'm so glad they're finally out of Paris," Charlotte said. "I can't bear to think of those horrible Nazis in the place where John and I spent our honeymoon." As always, Charlotte translated war news into personal terms.

"You had a honeymoon in Paris? Oh gosh!" Clara's pleasure in her new purchases was now somewhat diminished by this reminder that she and Roland had driven directly from their wedding in South Carolina to the family home in Virginia. "I guess we won't get a honeymoon, will we, Rolly?" She pouted again, in that way Roland had up until this moment found endearing.

"You're on it," he said, embarrassed to have his family hear yet another of Clara's plaints.

"David and I didn't have a real honeymoon either," Meg said. "We got married at City Hall—and then we spent two days at the Biltmore . . ." She dropped her eyes, a faint blush creeping along her cheeks, as she remembered exactly how those two days had been spent, a delicious excess of lovemaking and room service.

"The Biltmore!" Clara was enthralled. "Oh gosh! I never stayed at a hotel. Oh gosh, Rolly, do you suppose . . ."

"Sorry, babe." Roland nipped his wife's wish in midthought. "The car took all the pay I saved up. Maybe when I get back . . ."

Clifton looked up from his newspaper and cleared his throat. "Well, son," he said, "perhaps you and Clara might have a wedding trip in New York. As my gift to you."

"What in the world?" Charlotte questioned.

"Oh neat!" Clara squealed. "Oh, Rolly, this is a dream come true." She jumped up and leapt over to Clifton, delivering a heavily lipsticked kiss which he attempted unsuccessfully to evade.

"But we just got here," Roland said, a puzzled look on his face, "and I only have five days leave."

"Well," Clifton said, a shade too heartily, "when you reach New York, you will have two days at the Biltmore, just like your sister did."

Meg studied her father thoughtfully. She knew that Clifton had made the offer only to get Ro and Clara away from Breezy. She knew this side of her father because she had experienced it, and the knowledge saddened her because it diminished her father in the same way his rejection of David had done.

"Go on, sweetie pie," Clara urged. "Call up and reserve us a room. You have to do that, you know."

Roland stood, uncertain, not wanting to admit that he didn't know how to reserve a hotel room.

"Why don't I do it?" Emily offered, wanting to protect her brother from any more embarrassment.

While Clara chattered on about what a swell time they were going to have in New York, Emily and Roland went into the hall to make the reservation. But when they were alone, Roland turned to his sister, his expression young and vulnerable. "Why won't he look at me, Em? Why is it always the same with him?"

Emily knew what her brother meant, and her heart ached for him. While she didn't doubt that Clifton loved his only son, she had seen how often that love appeared distorted by his rigid and unforgiving expectations of what a male Whittaker should be. "He loves you, Ro," she said, "more than he can show you. He'll come around."

Conflicting emotions played across Roland's face. Then the muscle in his jaw tightened and his eyes grew hard. "That just isn't good enough, Em. Not anymore."

Just then the telephone rang. Emily picked up the receiver. "Oh, Mr. Steinmetz." She covered the mouthpiece and motioned to her brother. "It's Meg's father-in-law." Then she continued talking: "It's so nice to hear from you."

"Hey, Meg, it's for you, hurry," Roland called. "David's pop is on the phone."

Meg rushed to the phone. Emily took Roland aside, suggesting that while they were in New York they could take in a show at Radio City Music Hall. "I'm sure Clara would like that," she encouraged.

Meg reported proudly to her father-in-law that his grandson could now pick up a milk mug all by himself. Suddenly, she stopped in mid-sentence, her face crumpled, and she fell to the floor. Emily rushed to Meg's side, massaging her wrists and patting her face.

Roland picked up the dangling telephone receiver. "Sir," he said, his voice sounding very young, "this is Meg's brother. What the hell's going on?"

"What is it?" Clifton demanded, reaching for the phone.

"Cool it, Pop," Roland said heavily, as he hung up. "David's missing in action. They just got the telegram."

* * *

MEG lay very still on the sofa, her long black hair fanned around her, framing the ashen whiteness of her face. "There, there, honey chile," Bessie soothed, as she tucked a pillow under Meg's head.

Emily set a bowl of ice cubes on the floor, wrapped a few in a dish towel and gently stroked her sister's forehead. If anything could make Meg feel better now, it would be the sense of being loved and cared for, and Emily tried, with the quiet touch of her fingers, to give her sister that.

Off in the corner, Clifton, in subdued tones, discussed with Roland the pragmatic realities of the situation, David's last known position, with the troops that penetrated Europe from the north, moving past the Sorne River, the Marne, and across the Belgian border. David had been reported missing, just outside Luxembourg, near the Siegfried line. That was all the Army had said.

"How about some of this?" Clara offered the bottle of gin she'd packed in her suitcase.

"No, thank you," Clifton said coldly. "We do not serve liquor at Breezy."

"Oh gosh..." Clara shifted awkwardly, not knowing what to do with the offending bottle.

"It's okay, babe," Roland said protectively. Casting a direct, almost defiant look in his father's direction, he added: "I'll have some of that later."

"Sure." Not knowing what else she might contribute to this family crisis, Clara said in a funereal tone: "What a shame. With him being so young and a doctor and all."

Clifton stared disapprovingly. "My son-in-law is not dead," he said definitively. "He is simply missing. I am certain he will be found."

Roland stiffened, and Clara accepted the rebuke in silence, the now familiar pout beginning to play around her lips. This was not how she had pictured her new family at all.

Bessie had found some smelling salts and was passing them under Meg's nose, until she shook her head listlessly.

"It's all right," Emily said, as she continued her ministrations with the ice. "David's all right. I'm sure of it. You must believe that. You must."

"She's right, sugar," Charlotte added, with uncharacteristic fervor. "You must believe your man is comin' home to you. It's a lesson I learned . . ." She faltered and then trailed off. She had never admitted to learning a lesson in her life and it was hard to begin now, especially when the lesson came from a sordid episode she wanted to forget.

"Damn Nazis," Roland growled ferociously, as he hovered in the doorway, not knowing what to do or say to ease his sister's misery. In all his heroic visions of war, he had only imagined the ultimate contest of combat, of killing or being killed for a noble and just cause. He had not imagined the kind of suffering he had seen at home, first in Emily's bereavement and now in Meg's obvious pain. That kind of vision unsettled him, geared up as he was for combat, and he quickly shifted his imagination into easier, clearer channels, to thoughts of justice and vengeance. "Wait till I get them!" he said to no one in particular, as he clenched his fists and pounded on the door frame.

"You jes' listen to me, Missy," Bessie commanded, rearranging the pillows once again. "That boy jes' lost. You heah?"

Meg nodded tearfully and repeated mechanically: "He's just lost."

"Honey chile," Bessie went on, "y'all remember old Joe Pyle's daddy. He gots hisself lost over there in that other war, an' after a while, they done found him, safe and soun' over on some folks' farm."

Meg continued to nod, but her mind was elsewhere. "I have to go back to New York," she said, sitting up abruptly. "I have to wait for David there. I know that's what he'd want."

"You didn't want to stay with your in-laws before, you know," Charlotte reminded. "Their apartment is terribly cramped, you told me."

"Are you sure?" Emily asked softly, remembering her own confusion, her inability to think after the news of Howard's death. "Maybe you shouldn't do anything for a while . . ."

"No," Meg said decisively. "I'm going. I'll call David's parents back. We should be together."

"We'll drive you back, sis," Roland volunteered, glad of the opportunity to do something tangible for his sister. "We'll take you back with us tomorrow."

"Would you?" Meg's face lit up for a brief moment. "Oh, that would be so much easier than traveling with the baby on the train."

"But, Rolly," Clara stage-whispered to her husband. "This is supposed to be our honeymoon."

Roland shot his young wife a look redolent with disappointment and reproach. It was clear to the rest of the family that the newlyweds were having their first bit of marital discord. "She's my sister," he said fiercely, "and her husband is lost somewhere over there in the war. Don't you get it?" Clara crossed her legs prettily, smoothing her tight black skirt as she pouted, but no one paid any attention.

10

In Sickness and in Health
October 1944

October 25, 1944

My Dear Children,

Word has come from John who is fighting in the Pacific Theater. He has been promoted to Captain, if you please, and has been made commander of a fine squadron of men, Carrier Group 15, attached to Admiral Halsey's Third Fleet. He assures his wife that the promotion has not gone to his head, that his target hand continues to be sure and true, and that no Japs will ever take away our skies of freedom. So hurray for our Naval Officer with his new stripes out there in the "wide, blue yonder!"

I am also pleased to share the news that my youngest grandchild, Jacob James Steinmetz, age 16 months, has exhibited remarkable literary tastes. "Jake" has apparently inherited his grandfather's night-owl tendencies, much to his mother's chagrin. Last week I posted a copy of All's Well That Ends Well *to Meg in New York, suggesting she try reading the lad to sleep. She reports that the potion works and that in the Steinmetz household, Shakespeare is now a nightly lullaby....*

* * *

"ARE you sure you want to wear this old witch costume again this Halloween?" Charlotte asked Carrie. "Why on earth do you want to do that? I'm perfectly willing to make you a new costume..."

"No," Carrie insisted in that solemn knowing way that unsettled her mother. "I want to be a witch again. Witches cast spells. They make things happen."

"Oh, well, fine then," Charlotte conceded, losing interest in the subject. "You just go on and play with your sister while I fix it." She held the black dress up to her daughter for a last look. "I'll just put a ruffle on the bottom... Good gracious, child, you certainly have grown this year."

Later when the children were in bed, Charlotte returned to the parlor where Emily was working on Alexander's costume. "At least Nancy will be fun to dress up," she said. "I've been thinking she would look darling as Little Bo Peep. Don't you think so?"

"Absolutely. She'd look precious. But you'd have to do a lot of sewing. Only three more days till Halloween, you know."

"I'm perfectly capable of counting days off on a calendar," Charlotte said tartly. "It's all we seem to do around here these days. Actually I thought I might ask Miss Jewel to do it."

"Oh, I see." Emily nodded. She resisted the urge to advise her sister against employing their father's lady friend, knowing Charlotte never missed an opportunity to put the woman in her place. "Well," she said, "I'd better finish this thing for Alexander, or I'm going to start seeing feathers in my sleep."

"I can't believe your son actually wants to go as a turkey with a paper bag over his head."

"Oh, I can," Emily said, biting off a length of thread with her teeth, and adjusting another black crow's feather on the tan muslin leggings. "One of his last memories of his father was Thanksgiving at Fort Bragg. Alexander was a turkey in the pageant that day." She paused to settle the pain that always came with thoughts of Howard. "He figured the paper bag would hide his glasses."

"My, that is clever," Charlotte admitted, foraging in the scrap basket for another length of black material. "Just like Carrie. You know, that child can read just about anything. It's quite amazing."

"I know," Emily said fondly. Carrie was her favorite niece, and she often wondered how Charlotte had managed to produce such a thoughtful, serious child. "I saw her sitting up with Papa the other night. They were reading from *A Midsummer Night's Dream* and they looked so dear together."

"How she understands any of it, I'll never know." Charlotte shook her head. So much about her elder daughter was a mystery, which she attributed to some strange strains in the Randolph lineage.

"You should see what Alexander reads for fun." Emily stopped to count out the remaining feathers. "Can you imagine—he takes Ro's old algebra book to bed every night?"

The telephone rang. "That's probably Bea Watson from the Bridge Club," Charlotte said, getting up to answer it. "We're rolling bandages tomorrow morning."

But it wasn't Bea Watson's voice on the line. It was a man, a stranger, asking to speak to the wife of Captain Randolph.

"I'm Mrs. Randolph," she said. "May I ask who this is?"

"My name is Don Marcus. Lieutenant Marcus. Captain Randolph and I fly together." There was a disrupting crackle in the connection. "I have some bad news for you, ma'am," the voice resumed. "I wanted to talk to you before the Navy contacted you . . ."

"Bad news?" Charlotte whispered, feeling suddenly faint. "Is John . . . is he . . ."

"Oh, no, ma'am, Captain Randolph's alive. But he's wounded. Bad. Our plane was shot down over Leyte . . ."

"Leyte?" Charlotte repeated the foreign name that had no meaning for her at all. "Shot down? What . . ."

"It's his leg . . . the captain caught a lot of shrapnel. They did what they could in the field hospital and then they took him into Honolulu, but they couldn't save it. I'm sorry, ma'am . . . they had to amputate his left leg. As soon as he's strong enough, they're shipping him stateside, to San Diego."

"What?" Charlotte gasped, dropping the phone back into the receiver, before the man could say anything else. "No!" she said vehemently, staring with unseeing eyes at the instrument that had just mutilated her future.

"Charlotte? What's wrong?" Emily's face was pale with concern.

"It's too awful . . ." Charlotte whimpered.

"What's happened?" Emily asked, fearing that the worst possible misfortune had also struck her sister. "Are you all right?"

"No, I'm not all right!" Charlotte cried. "The most terrible thing has happened to John . . . the most terrible . . ."

"What? Tell me," Emily urged, bracing herself.

"They took his leg off," Charlotte wailed.

"He's alive . . . thank God." Emily put her arms around her sister and stroked her hair. "He's alive . . . He'll come home to you."

But Emily's words held no meaning, no comfort for Charlotte. As far as she was concerned, there was nothing to be thankful for. Nothing.

She had never, even in the dark dread of her most nightmarish imaginings, considered the possibility of a husband who was maimed. Now and then, when the fear insisted on a shape, Charlotte allowed one image to flicker across her consciousness—an image of herself in Richmond, stunningly tragic, holding court with sympathetic friends and relatives, dramatically swathed in well-cut widow's black. But a husband who was mangled or crippled in any way, a husband who was less than perfect. An object of pity rather than admiration. She had never considered that.

With that awful thought, Charlotte dissolved in a wash of self-pity and tears. She allowed Emily to lead her to bed, to bathe her face with cold compresses, to soothe her with murmured words of sympathy and support.

"I'm going to call Papa," she said, "then I'll come back and sit with you. Can I bring you anything?"

"No," Charlotte said dramatically through closed eyes. "Nothing." But as Emily started to leave the room, she reconsidered. "Wait. If you're going to call Papa, tell him to bring home some bourbon . . . I'm going to need a little something if I'm going to get any rest at all." Of all the things that could have happened to her, this had to be the worst.

WHEN Clifton received Emily's call, he and his colleagues were methodically working their way through a formidable stack of draft files. Less than two weeks before, the Russell County Draft Board had received a special directive from Lewis B. Hershey, Director of the National Draft Board, asking for a review of all registrants who had been deferred or who were currently under appeal.

"I'm sorry to interrupt your meeting," Emily apologized tersely, "but something's happened . . ."

"What is it, Emily?" Clifton asked with concern.

"It's John. Charlotte's had word that he's been wounded . . . he's lost a leg. Could you come home?"

"Poor Charlotte," he said heavily. "Poor child . . . I'll be right there."

"And Papa, could you bring some bourbon? Charlotte asked for it, and I think it might help calm her."

"I'll see what I can do. Tucker's is closed, but I'll find some . . . I'll be there as soon as I can."

Clifton explained to the other board members that there was a personal emergency on the Hill and left. Briskly, he walked across the street to the drugstore and up the side stairs to Miss Jewel's apartment.

She came to the door, dressed in a quilted green satin robe, her hair tied up, pickaninny-style, in white rag curls. "Cliff! Oh, my, this is a surprise!" she exclaimed, for he rarely came to call unannounced. "Oh, dearie," she touched her hair, "I must look a sight!"

He shook his head, finding in her homey appearance a kind of familiar comfort. "My apologies, Jewel, for disturbing you like this . . ." he sighed, and she saw that he seemed to be having trouble catching his breath after climbing the stairs, that his color was unnaturally pale.

"What is it, Cliff? Come in and sit down. Here, make yourself comfortable." She settled him in her best overstuffed easy chair, and slipped the ottoman under his legs.

"It's John," he said, closing his eyes and leaning his head against the chair. "He's lost a leg over there in the Pacific. I must get home to Charlotte..."

"Oh, the poor girl. I'm so sorry, Cliff." She covered his lean, tapering hand with her short plump fingers.

He opened his eyes and smiled at her. "I wonder if I might trouble you for a bottle of bourbon? Emily feels her sister might be helped if she had a little something. You know we don't keep liquor on the Hill..."

Jewel nodded knowingly. She had often felt Elizabeth's lingering presence at Breezy, particularly in the silent deference to her preferences, her straitlaced traditions. "It's no trouble at all, Cliff. I'm just glad I can help in some way." She went to the china closet and returned with the bourbon and a small tumbler of whiskey. "Here," she urged, "you take some of this now. You're looking kinda peaked, dearie."

Clifton took the drink without protest. "Thank you, Jewel. I believe I will and then I really must go.

"I don't know, Jewel," he sighed again and shook his head. "I just don't know how she's going to handle this. I know she appears confident, but underneath she's a great deal like her mother was... rather high-strung and delicate."

Jewel said nothing. Instead she patted his knee affectionately. It was not her place to differ with Cliff about his children, especially now, though she did not agree with his view of Charlotte as a delicate creature. High-strung, certainly, but not delicate. As far as she was concerned, his daughter had inherited some of Miss Elizabeth's traits, like her fondness for fancy things, without any of the qualities that had made her mother a real lady.

"I'll have to call the Randolphs," he said the dreaded thought out loud. Draining the last of the whiskey, he got up reluctantly. "I'd best leave now."

Silently she wrapped her plump arms around him and stroked his thinning silver hair. She drew his head down into the deep soft valley of her breasts and held him there for a moment, feeling the rhythm of his breathing, trying to give him shelter and strength.

"Ah, Jewel," he said huskily as he drew away from the flower-scented cushion of her bosom. "You are such a comfort to me . . . I wish . . . I wish you could be by my side tonight."

"Hush, now," she stopped his words with her fingertips, pleased and touched at hearing the expression of his need for her. "You're the strongest, finest man I've ever known, Cliff Whittaker, and you'll be just fine . . . And maybe someday . . ." she trailed off softly, knowing that this wasn't the time to speak of the "maybe" that neither of them had ever dared discuss or define.

"WE'LL never be able to go dancing again," Charlotte sobbed, adding yet another to her litany of laments. "Never, ever again."

"Close your eyes and try to get some rest," Emily urged. "You'll make yourself sick if you go on like this." Her sympathy for her sister had already been strained to its limit by listening for an hour to what seemed to be an outpouring of petty selfishness. She wanted to say: What is wrong with you? Why can't you thank God for sparing John's life? But she knew Charlotte well enough to know that her sister could not count her blessings, not when her personal private scheme of perfection had been so gravely altered.

"I don't care if I do get sick," Charlotte said vehemently, propping herself up against the pillows. "I wish I would get sick and die! Nothing's ever going to be the same again. Nothing!" Her eyes flickered over to the doorway where her father had appeared. "Oh, Papa, thank goodness you've come!" Then she began sobbing again.

"I'm here, Charlotte Lee. I'm here." He handed Emily the liquor bottle, which Miss Jewel had discreetly placed in a paper bag. She had a glass ready. He went to his daughter's bedside, handed her the bourbon and sat down.

"What ever am I going to do, Papa?" she wailed, turning red, swollen eyes on her father. "What's to become of me?"

"You must get hold of yourself, Charlotte Lee . . . You must . . ." he insisted, alarmed by her mounting hysteria. "This will do no good . . . no good at all . . ."

"Oh, go away," she wailed even louder. "I don't need any of your lectures now, for goodness sake!"

"You look exhausted, Papa," Emily said quietly, handing her father a cup of coffee.

He nodded and sat down at the kitchen table. "It's been a long day," he said, "and I'm worried about your sister..."

"She'll be all right... She'll come through in her own way... her own time."

Clifton looked thoughtfully at his firstborn, the young woman who had suffered the family's first and worst loss to the war. Emily had changed. She was no longer just "the plain Whittaker girl," bookish, thoughtful, reserved. Though still quiet by nature, there was now a sharp definition to her character that hadn't been there before, a force and clarity to her opinions and to her physical appearance. His eyes filmed over with pride. "You're a good girl, Emily," he said.

She smiled, understanding perfectly the layers of meaning in his simple statement. She reached across the table and touched his hand. "Why don't you wait until tomorrow to call the Randolphs? Or would you like me to..."

"No, Emily. It's my place to speak to John's parents... but I believe I will wait. We all need some sleep to absorb this latest blow..."

Both Clifton and Emily rose with the first light of dawn. As if she had been fine-tuned to the emotional wave-length of her family, Bessie, too, made her appearance extra early. And if she was surprised to see Clifton and Emily up and about, she did not show it, uttering no more than her usual "mornin'" as she went directly to her breakfast-making chores.

"Morning, Bessie," Clifton nodded gravely, and something in his manner made her stop. "We've had the bad news that John Randolph has been wounded. He's lost a leg. I know we can count on you to help us with Charlotte."

"Yes, suh," she agreed, making no comment on this fresh

tragedy. Bessie's affection for Charlotte was almost grudging, for although the second Whittaker was the prettiest, she did not live up to Bessie's standard of "pretty inside." In fact, there was a great deal about Charlotte that Bessie did not like at all. But she did feel sorry about Mr. Randolph, who was a fine gentleman, almost as fine as Mr. Clifton himself.

By 8:30, Clifton had gone to his office. Emily took the children into the barn to play so her sister could rest undisturbed.

Bessie was stationed outside Charlotte's door. She had a wicker basket full of mending, a task she always procrastinated, so the accumulation of odds and ends was sizable. She had darned several of Mr. Clifton's socks when she heard Charlotte's first stirrings in the bedroom.

Moments later, the door opened and Charlotte stuck her head out. She didn't seem surprised to see Bessie sitting there, nor did she behave as if anything was wrong. In her usual speaking-to-servants voice, she asked: "Bessie, go downstairs and find my peach negligee. It's not here. It's probably still with yesterday's laundry."

Bessie nodded her compliance, but when the door closed, she shook her head. "Lawdy, Lawdy," she muttered. "That one gotta be pretty all de time, even fo' her miseries." She sighed her way heavily down the stairs and delivered the requested nightgown to the bathroom, where Charlotte was running her bath.

Pushing her chair down the hall, Bessie continued her vigil and mending, absently working her needle around holes and tears in assorted pieces of household linen. Over an hour later, when the grandfather clock in the hall struck eleven, she decided that Charlotte had been bathing long enough. She rapped authoritatively on the bathroom door. "Miz Charlotte," she called, in her deep resonant voice. "Miz Charlotte, you comin' outta there?"

The door opened slowly. Charlotte was wrapped in the peach dressing gown. Wispy tendrils of hair framed her face, which was blurred with tears and touched with confusion.

Bessie's heart softened. "Heah, chile," she beckoned,

motioning for Charlotte to sit on the toilet seat. She took the brush and began working it gently through the silky blond hair, as she had done so many years before. "I hears 'bout Mistuh John," she said somberly, acknowledging the reason for Charlotte's tears.

"Oh, Bessie," Charlotte choked, grateful for a new and sympathetic audience for her unhappiness. "It's just so awful. My husband's going to be a cripple for the rest of his life."

"That's true, honey," Bessie agreed grimly, for her brand of Christian acceptance did not include false optimism or unwarranted cheer. "But he's comin' back," she added, seizing on the genuine article. "An' I bet yo' big sistuh, she be glad to change places with you fo' dat." This she concluded with some vehemence.

"But what am I going to do?" Charlotte asked rhetorically, though she didn't really expect more than kindness and sympathy from the family's devoted servant.

"You goes to him, honey," Bessie said firmly, as if there could be no doubt. "You gots yo' legs, yo' arms, all yo' pretty self. Mistuh John, he be in some hospital feelin' po'ly. He need you, Miz Charlotte, he sho'ly do."

Charlotte sat perfectly still through this narrative, listening, fascinated. It had not occurred to her to actually do anything—other than to be utterly miserable and accept the ministrations of her family. But as Bessie spoke, she had a new vision of herself—strong, heroic and noble, a little like Veronica Lake in *So Proudly We Hail*, but wearing something tailored and fashionable, inspiring John as he lay pale and wan in his hospital bed. She shut out any vision of his missing leg. Why not, she thought. It might be better than being stuck in this boring old house for God only knew how much longer.

"Mmm . . ." she said out loud.

A WEEK later, Charlotte was delivered by her family to the West Grove train station. Her girls waved animatedly as she boarded the train, excited by the idea of their mother's

journey and by the prospect of spending time on their own
with Grandpa and Bessie—free of Charlotte's admonitions
to be quiet and to act like ladies.

Clifton's Washington inquiries had produced limited but
fairly precise information about his son-in-law. The Navy
reported that on October 20th, his plane, the Southern Belle,
had been shot down in the South Pacific in the battle of
Leyte. Official notification had mistakenly gone to their
home in Richmond and was then forwarded to Pensacola,
which was why Charlotte did not receive the Navy Department telegram for four days after the call from John's
buddy.

Additional phone calls produced the news that John would
be evac-ed from Honolulu to San Diego Naval Hospital on
November 3rd. According to hospital records, his physical
condition was listed as "satisfactory," but his morale was
guardedly reported as "low."

When Charlotte had tentatively mentioned the idea of
going to John, Clifton had vigorously applauded it, frankly
astonished that his most self-centered child should have
arrived at such a selfless notion, that she was willing to
travel all the way across the continent to help her husband
through what he called "this difficult adjustment."

Now here she was, restless and impatient for the cross-
country journey to begin, dressed in a smart new navy suit
with darling peplum, and fortified with a large wicker basket
of provisions. As the West Grove station receded from her
line of vision, Charlotte flipped the basket open, pushed
aside the white linen napkin that had been folded neatly
across the top. She began to forage through the contents,
spreading them out in the privacy of the compartment that
Clifton had reluctantly secured through old contacts, after
Charlotte had kept up an unremitting stream of protests
against making a long-distance train ride in typical wartime
conditions.

Under the napkin, between the brown paper bag filled
with fried chicken and the mason jar of potato salad, was
a red velvet box. Inside was a small ruby brooch circled
with seed pearls, a piece her Mama used to wear with a

wine-colored suit and a white batiste blouse. It had been given to her by Grandma Whittaker. Under the pin was a note penned in her father's precise, elegant handwriting:

For Charlotte,

    Because you are so much your mother's daughter, this talisman of your heritage. Wear it with courage.

                                Your father,
                                J. C. Whittaker

Though she was not overly fond of antique jewelry, Charlotte was touched by her father's message and by the sentiments he expressed. *I must write him a nice thank-you letter when I get to California,* she resolved, as she refolded the note and tucked the pin back into its case.

From Emily, there were two books to read on the journey: Kathleen Windsor's scandalous *Forever Amber* and Betty Smith's sentimental *A Tree Grows in Brooklyn.* She looked them over and put them aside. When it came to reading, her attention span was short, her interest limited mainly to fashion and home-decorating magazines. But she was curious to see if *Forever Amber* was as shocking as everyone said it was.

Carrie had created a scrapbook composed of pictures cut from magazines and carefully printed messages. Nancy had made up a package for John—her play doctor's kit, with its toy stethoscope, gauze bandages and candy aspirin. "Get Well, Daddy," she had lettered across the top.

Finally there was the letter that had arrived that morning from Meg. Her younger sister had reminded Charlotte that Beethoven had composed a number of symphonies after he lost his hearing. She voiced her confidence that she and John would "weather this painful ordeal and survive with love stronger than ever." Unconsciously Charlotte made a face. She did not subscribe to any philosophy that attributed character-building qualities to misfortune.

For the next ten hours, Charlotte ate, napped, read a little and fixed her hair and makeup several times. Then she had to change trains in Washington, for the next lap of the journey, which would take her to Chicago. She gave up the solitary comfort of her compartment and found herself in a filthy passenger car, crowded mostly with servicemen, either on leave or on their way to camps in the Midwest. It was dark, and as the train sped through the night, the soldiers who were still awake seemed to be either drunk or noisily lonely or both. Several tried to start conversations, and one boy who looked scarcely older than Roland, insisted on sitting down beside her and having a smoke.

Though Charlotte liked to be noticed, she found their attentions abrasive and invasive—they seemed to require something of her when all she wanted was to be left alone. Yet although she was usually skillful at "putting people in their place," something in the youthful faces made her stop short of actual rudeness.

From Chicago, the train swung down across the Rockies to Salt Lake City and then into San Francisco. By this time, Charlotte had a headache from sitting in an upright position for three days and nights. But when they crossed the Rockies, she stared out the window at the majesty of the panorama and forgot for a while her discomfort and the reason for her trip.

It was late afternoon on Thursday when the train pulled into the San Diego station. Charlotte was so weary that she could scarcely cope with finding a porter and retrieving her luggage, one large trunk and one suitcase, from the baggage car. She decided to take Emily's suggestion that she check into a hotel and spend an evening resting before she made the trip to the hospital.

She asked the volunteer at the Traveler's Aid booth in the station for the name of a decent hotel. The Churchill Hotel on 3rd Street was recommended, and in spite of her weariness, she smiled at the name. Her father would sanction the choice for since the war had begun, Clifton had taken to quoting Churchill almost as often as he cited Shakespeare, saying that the British leader was "a giant presence in these tumultuous times."

With some difficulty, Charlotte found a vacant cab, chagrined that being an attractive woman certainly didn't warrant as many privileges here as it did in the South.

As the taxi sped through the streets, she marveled at the vast numbers of sailors who roamed the city. She noticed that the palm trees here were different from those that had lined the streets of Pensacola. They were taller, more gracefully fluted at the top. A profusion of flowers bloomed here which seemed all the more remarkable since scarcely twenty-four hours ago, she had traveled through a heavy snowstorm in the Rockies.

When the cab pulled up in front of the Churchill, a tall stone and cement building, the driver remarked that it was "just three blocks from the ocean." Remembering some of the holidays she and John had taken at Virginia Beach, she thought, maybe this won't be so bad after all.

But her optimism faded quickly when she stepped into the lobby and saw that the walls were lined with cots, some neatly made up, some occupied by sleeping sailors. Oh no, she thought, after all those long, cramped hours on the train, she had arrived at an encampment instead of a proper hotel. She was close to a burst of frustrated tears when she approached the desk clerk, a graying older man who reminded her a little of Dr. Giles. Charlotte threw herself on his mercy, pleading for a room, telling of her long trip, of the crippled husband who awaited her visit in a hospital bed.

"I'll find a room for you, ma'am," he promised "But it might take a while, so please have a seat and make yourself comfortable."

Making herself comfortable was not going to be easy, she thought grimly, as she scanned the lobby in vain, looking for a vacant chair or sofa. Finally she tipped over her trunk and dragged it towards a potted palm in a corner. She sat on it, kicking off the new slingback pumps that had pinched so during the last lap of the trip. She sat there stranded for an hour, massaging her swollen feet, fanning herself with a magazine and feeling that the entire scene was unreal.

When the gray-haired clerk finally tapped her gently on the shoulder, saying, "Miss, your room's ready," she stared at him blankly for a moment, as if she could not remember why she was here or what the man was talking about.

"Oh, yes," she recovered quickly. "Thank you very much." She followed the bellboy who took her up to room 603 and she tipped him fifty cents. She wondered if that was enough, and realized that this was the first time in her life that she'd had to handle details like this alone.

As soon as the boy left the room, she went into the bathroom and turned on the taps. Hot water. She smiled, grateful for small comforts in a way she never had been before. She rummaged inside the picnic basket until she found the Yardley Bath Salts that Meg had given her for Christmas. She threw a handful into the tub and inhaled the lavender fragrance released by the water.

She stripped off her clothes, not bothering to hang or fold anything, and lowered her body into the steaming scented water, feeling the travel weariness float away with the layers of grime. But along with the dust and fatigue also went the armor of bravado that had covered her all these days, all these miles away from Virginia. She felt alone, unsheltered and unprotected. And when she allowed herself to form the thought "tomorrow," to try to imagine what her reunion with John might be like, the fear rose, filling her with a panic that made her light-headed.

She tried to push unpleasant thoughts away as she washed herself purposefully. Next she tried to concentrate on physical tasks: drying her body, unpacking a few things, and setting her hair in wide curlers, so she could wear a pageboy, John's favorite style, the next day. And when she was finished, she turned down the bed, crawled in, and cried herself to sleep.

She didn't open her eyes until morning. Sunlight was streaming through the windows, and a cool breeze ruffled the gauzy white curtains. She yawned and stretched and swung her legs over the side of the bed.

She pushed the window up as far as it would go. The room faced the ocean, but the view was not a pretty one. Rolls of barbed wire curled along the beach, reminding her of the war footage she had seen on the Movietone News. She grimaced and closed the curtains.

She knew exactly what she would wear this morning. One of John's favorite outfits, a navy blue suit with a pleated skirt, a red crepe blouse and red pumps. She took the curlers from her hair and brushed it vigorously, then inspected the results critically. Not as good as a beauty-parlor set, but it would do.

The hotel dining room was crowded, so Charlotte decided to go out for breakfast. She strolled briskly until she found a drugstore with a soda fountain. Inside, all the booths were occupied. She took a seat at the counter and ordered coffee, waiting to see if any of the food being served looked edible. She decided to stick to coffee and toast.

As the waitress, a middle-aged woman with a ruddy complexion and a motherly air, refilled her cup, Charlotte plucked up her courage and asked for directions to the Naval Hospital.

"I thought you was one of them Navy wives," the woman smiled kindly. "They always dress up so nice to go up there. Was your man hurt bad?"

"Yes ... yes, he was," Charlotte faltered, feeling an intrusion in the woman's curiosity.

"Oh, you poor thing. Some of them come back a real mess." The waitress paused to refill her cup. "Why, last week a woman was in here from Milwaukee with a two-year-old in tow. Her husband got sent back with no arms."

"Oh, my God!" Charlotte gasped, spilling the full coffee cup on the counter. "Don't tell me things like that." Shaking, she stood up and fumbled in her purse. "How much do I owe you?"

"Forget it, lady. You didn't eat a thing." Leaning across the counter she pointed to the entrance. "Take the trolley out there to the end of the line. It goes straight up to the hospital. And good luck!"

The trolley was crowded with women of all ages—mothers, sisters, wives—a sprinkling of men, some sailors in white hospital uniforms, and a few children. As it moved away from the ocean, the trolley climbed up a steep hill for about six blocks, then turned a sharp corner. There, on a large bluff overlooking the city and the harbor, was the hospital, a mammoth three-story pink Spanish-style building.

Impulsively, she decided she didn't want to get off with

the rest of the passengers, and asked the conductor to let her off before the end of the line. She regretted the move immediately, when she found herself stranded outside a park area, fenced with barbed wire and marked with a sign that said "Military." There was nothing to do but march around the area and up the rest of the hill in her high heels.

Perspiring and breathless, she arrived at the twin Spanish towers that marked the entrance. She glanced at her watch, the one John had given her. A quarter of twelve. Maybe they would be serving lunch soon, she thought hopefully. Maybe her visit would have to wait until afternoon.

"The information desk is up there," said a uniformed nurse as she hurried past Charlotte. "Follow me."

"Thank you," Charlotte said politely, knowing now that there was no choice but to go inside.

A crowd of women, several from the trolley, stood in line, waiting for directions from a woman in Naval uniform. When it was her turn, she said, as confidently as she could, "Captain John Randolph, Seventh Fleet."

"Randolph," the woman repeated, running a finger down a dog-eared list that went on for pages. "How long have we had him, do you know? They keep coming in so fast, we can't keep our alphabeticals up-to-date . . . but if you know his admission date . . ."

"I don't know," Charlotte faltered.

The woman looked up, and her manner became less brusque. "Never mind," she said. "If he's here, we'll find him." She continued scanning her lists, and then the finger stopped. "Here we are," she smiled encouragingly. "Captain John Randolph. Orthopedics. Building Five."

Orthopedics. The medical word sounded ominous and ugly. Charlotte followed the directions she was given, walking first to the back of the building. There, a door opened onto a large courtyard. Gathered around a red-tiled pool were clusters of patients, on crutches and in wheelchairs, taking the midday sun, shepherded by attending nurses.

Charlotte averted her eyes, feeling a little queasy. She followed an arrow that took her along an indoor corridor, holding her head down and counting her footsteps. Once, when she was little, her mother had told her to count to a hundred when she was frightened. The fear would go away, Mama had promised, and although Charlotte didn't believe this anymore, she counted as she put one foot in front of the other, past the medical staff that rushed by her, past the benches where patients sat in their medical gowns, past the tall windows of the wards, trying to shut out the musty smells of illness, the muffled moans of the men who lay in the beds on the other side.

As she arrived at the staircase that would take her up to the second floor, she stopped to catch her breath and powder her nose. When she saw her pale face in the mirror, she snapped the compact shut, wishing she could be somewhere else, wishing it were someone else's husband up there on the second floor. As she leaned against the staircase, a nurse carrying a basin filled with dirty bandages knocked against her.

"Can't stand here," the nurse said briskly. "We all have to move fast these days."

"I'm terribly sorry," Charlotte apologized, as she grabbed the stair rail and climbed upwards.

A young officer who looked like a high school boy stood guard at the top of the stairs. He smiled encouragingly and pointed towards a door marked "Visitors." "This way, ma'am."

She nodded and took a deep breath.

"Chin up," he called after her. "You look mighty fine."

The sweet compliment propelled her across the threshold, into the province of yet another Navy nurse behind another desk.

"Good morning," she began. "I believe my husband is a patient on this floor. Captain John Randolph?"

"Could be," the plump woman said, in a voice syruped with the accent of Ireland. She consulted another list, and when she looked up, her face was sad.

Charlotte's breath caught in her throat as the young woman said: "I'm sorry, but . . ."

She gripped the desk until her knuckles showed white. "What's happened to him?" she whispered.

Seeing Charlotte's face, the nurse rushed to explain: "Oh no, dear, it's nothing like that." She stopped a passing orderly. "A glass of water, please. No," she went on, leading Charlotte to a bench in the waiting area. "It's just that Captain Randolph isn't quite . . . well, he's not quite ready to see anyone . . ."

"But I'm not 'anyone'," Charlotte argued, feeling relieved and annoyed at the same time. "I'm his wife, and I've come all the way from Virginia."

"I know," the nurse soothed. "But this often happens with the new amputees. Tell you what, dear. You come back tomorrow and I'll talk to Captain Randolph myself. I'll tell him you're here and that you're very eager to be with him."

Before Charlotte could say anything, she went on: "In the meantime, why don't you visit the Officers' Club here? It's in the park. I'll give you a pass and point you in the right direction."

"Thank you," Charlotte said uncertainly, feeling as if she had lost all control over her life. "Thank you, Miss . . ."

"O'Malley's the name." She grinned, flashing a crooked but thoroughly appealing smile at Charlotte.

Charlotte accepted the pass because she didn't want to hurt the nurse's feelings. But she didn't feel up to any more strangers, any more new experiences. She boarded the trolley and rode back into town. As she was walking back to the hotel, a liquor store sign caught her eye, and although she had never done that sort of thing at home, she went inside and bought a bottle of bourbon.

Alone in her room, she poured a stiff drink into the bathroom tumbler, settled herself in the upholstered chair near the window, staring out at the Pacific Ocean and remembering the times she and John had vacationed at the Randolphs' family cottage at Virginia Beach. Lovely warm days when she would sleep late, while John took his brisk early morning strolls along the beach. Later, the two of them would swim in the clear azure waters, and then . . .

"Damn," she muttered to no one in particular. "Hellfire and damnation." She cursed whatever fate it was that wreaked such random havoc on gracious, well-ordered lives.

* * *

DESPITE a dull, throbbing headache that she refused to acknowledge as a hangover—ladies did not get drunk, and they most certainly did not have hangovers—Charlotte made it to the hospital by eleven o'clock, dressed in the same outfit, carrying the girls' presents for John.

But when Nurse O'Malley told her that John would not see her, she reacted with irritation. This wasn't at all like John, she thought, to behave with such a lack of consideration. And after she had traveled all this way. She began to suspect that there might be more change in her husband than the loss of a limb.

As she watched the expression on Charlotte's face, Nurse O'Malley said softly: "I'm sorry, Mrs. Randolph. Try not to be discouraged. He's going through a bad time."

But what about me, Charlotte was going to ask and then thought better of it.

"Did you get to the Officers' Club?" the nurse asked brightly. "They serve such a nice lunch there."

"No, I didn't. I meant to, but I had so many things to do yesterday," Charlotte lied. "But I'll go today, right after I leave here."

THE Officers' Club, whimsically named The Captain's Shack, was located in Balboa Park, an enormous tract of land covering hundreds of acres. As Charlotte rode down the hill from the hospital, the trolley driver gave her a capsule history of the place.

"Goes back to Civil War days, this park," he said. "But nobody fixed up the place like it is now till 'bout 1900. Big doin's then, California International Exposition ... 'nother one in 1935, that's when they put up all the fancy buildin's—the museum and the Organ Pavilion and the theater, just like Shakespeare's place in England."

She half listened as he went on to explain how the military had taken over the park when the war broke out, using the large buildings to house hospital personnel and servicemen recuperating from the less serious wounds. "My," she said when she had reached her destination, "that's all very interesting, I'm sure."

The Pensacola Officers' Club had had a quiet country-club atmosphere, but this place was like a terminal teeming with activity. Men and women in uniform milled around the entrance. The officer on duty carefully examined her pass before he directed her towards the Ladies' Lounge on the first floor.

She had thought she might have a sandwich and a little "pick-me-up" drink, but the bar was jammed, and she didn't feel she could possibly sit at a table alone. As she hesitated in the doorway, she felt a tap on her shoulder.

"Hi," said a tall, dark woman in a tailored beige suit. "I'm Iris Rainer, and this is Eugenia Simpson," she added, introducing a sporty-looking blond in a green shantung dress. "Care to join us for lunch?"

"Why, yes, thank you very much," Charlotte said gratefully, though she did not usually take up with strangers.

"We have a standing reservation here every Tuesday," Iris said, pointing to a table near the window. "My husband's a doctor here on base, so I get some privileges. Eugenia's husband is a patient here."

"Mine, too," Charlotte said quietly. "He . . ." She took a sip of water before she could say the words that were so hard to speak. "He lost a leg . . ."

"That's rough," Iris said gently.

"Lord, yes," Eugenia agreed, refraining from saying anything about her husband's wounds, which were superficial and almost healed.

"I wish I could say something that would help you." Iris paused thoughtfully. "But all I can think of is what my husband says—that they're doing wonderful things with the prostheses—the artificial limbs—these days. He says they've learned so much since the last war, when they used to do very crude amputations in the field . . ."

Charlotte felt she was going to be sick to her stomach. She excused herself and rushed to the ladies' room. Standing over the sink, she splashed cold water on her face and braced herself against the porcelain until she felt steadier.

Now she understood why Emily hadn't wanted to talk to anyone during those first weeks after Howard's death. At the time Charlotte had thought her sister unreasonable and stubborn. She had been certain that some socializing would have helped her. But now all she wanted to do was get out of this place, to leave the other military wives and the talk about lost limbs and prostheses.

She returned to the table and excused herself, saying she had a terrible headache. The two women murmured sympathetically and suggested she return to her room for a nap.

But once she found herself back at the hotel entrance, she hesitated, remembering the afternoon of solitary drinking she'd spent the day before. She walked past the hotel, with nothing particular in mind, with only a need to use up some of the hours that stretched ahead.

She strolled the unfamiliar streets, taking occasional note of a face, a building, a shop. She kept walking until she saw the Paramount Theater, where the marquee advertised *Pin-Up Girl*, starring Betty Grable. The matinee had already started, but Charlotte bought a ticket and went inside.

In spite of her mood, she admired the movie house's baroque design and elaborate decorations, so elegant compared to the simple boxlike Roseland in West Grove. And in spite of her depression, she managed a few giggles at the story of a secretary who became a pinup girl. She took careful note of all the pretty outfits Betty Grable wore, thinking she might sketch some for Miss Jewel to copy. She watched the short subjects and shut her eyes when the war news came on. She stayed to see the beginning of the picture, and then decided to see the whole movie again. She was in no hurry to return to her solitary room.

When she left the theater, the afternoon light had faded. She walked some more, only half paying attention to the unfamiliar streets. Suddenly she noticed that the neighborhood had changed, giving way to bars and nightclubs with neon signs flashing and loud music spilling out into the street. Bands of sailors roamed the streets, their arms around women in cheap dresses and flashy makeup.

Hurriedly she turned around and tried to retrace her steps back. She bumped into a sailor who leered drunkenly at her. He was short and dark, and something in his manner reminded her of Tony Santini. She flushed with shame.

Against her will, she allowed a thought of John to creep into her mind, a picture of the two of them, back home in the lovely gold bedroom. She shook the picture away, refusing to imagine her husband's body, mutilated, disfigured, touching hers.

She fled back to the hotel room and the bottle of bourbon. Sleep that night was restless, troubled with horrible dreams. John's arms reaching for her, his mouth seeking hers. Her arms reaching back, clutching at empty spaces where his arms and legs should have been. She woke, shivering and crying.

The next morning, and the one after that, Charlotte made her pilgrimage to the hospital, only to be turned away by a regretful Nurse O'Malley. Mechanically, she fell into a routine—lunch at the drugstore, followed by a movie. She saw *Stage Door Canteen*, a light confection filled with more movie stars than she had ever seen in one picture. She smiled at the sweet little vignettes about wartime romance, where no one ever got killed or wounded.

She sat through *Since You Went Away*, thinking she might find some comfort in the story of a small-town American family trying to carry on while the men of the household were away at war. But Joseph Cotten in uniform reminded her of John. And Claudette Colbert, so brave and strong in the face of her tragedy, made Charlotte feel even less equal to her own future.

A week after she arrived, on a Sunday morning when she knew everyone would be back from church, Charlotte placed a long-distance call to West Grove.

It was Emily who answered. "Charlotte! We were just this minute talking about you! How's John?"

"Oh, Em," she complained. "It's awful. San Diego is horribly crowded, and there's hardly any service at the hotel, and John won't see me . . . ."

"Stop it." Emily's voice cut razor sharp across the miles. "What?"

"I said stop it, Charlotte. I don't want to hear any more of your complaining. If John won't see you, he must be feeling much worse than you could possibly imagine. And if you're any kind of a woman, any kind of a wife, you'd better find a way to help him. And dammit, Charlotte Lee, if you can't do anything else, just be grateful he's alive. Stop your whining." Before Charlotte could answer, Emily hung up.

She stared at the dead receiver. She had often caught the sharp edge of Emily's impatience before, but her sister had never talked to her like this, and certainly not at a time when she was expecting sympathy and support.

That afternoon she went to a double feature, wanting nothing more than escape. The first movie was *The Dough-girls,* a silly comedy about the shortage of living quarters in Washington, and the foolish carryings-on of a bunch of single girls. Charlotte didn't laugh once.

The second feature was *The Dragon Seed,* a Pearl Buck story set in China. Emily had liked the book. Funny, Charlotte thought, Katherine Hepburn looked more like Emily than the Chinese woman she was supposed to be. Although she didn't usually like serious pictures, she thought the story—about Chinese peasants who wouldn't give in to the Japanese—was rather touching. She cried when the farmers put their fields to the torch, rather than surrender their crops to the Japanese.

The following morning, she was filled with a sense of nobility of purpose and a determination not to make her daily pilgrimage in vain. When Nurse O'Malley began the familiar "I'm sorry but..." Charlotte broke in. "I'm sorry, too, Nurse O'Malley, but I want you to tell my husband that I am going to see him, one way or another. Please tell him that I didn't come all the way from Virginia just to stay in a miserable hotel room."

Nurse O'Malley took in Charlotte's tone, the set of her shoulders—and she smiled. "Maybe you're right, Mrs. Randolph. Maybe it's time we pulled a little rank on the captain. But not today. First I want you to understand what he's feeling, what he's going through. Come with me."

Charlotte gripped the other woman's outstretched hand and followed, out of the ward, onto the balcony that connected to the next building, which faced north into the open courtyard. O'Malley opened a door marked "Physical Therapy" and motioned Charlotte inside.

She winced when she saw so many young men, working on floor mats and dragging shattered bodies along parallel bars, struggling through simple exercises. As she watched, her first revulsion gave way to pain. She saw the enormity of the efforts being made here to perform the simple, everyday tasks she had always taken for granted.

A young blond boy, his cherub's face set in an expression of grim determination, fumbled one-handed with his shoelaces, while his left arm hung limply at his side. Another man, older, thinner, a blanket draped over his lower body, was practicing turns with his wheelchair.

In response to Charlotte's stare, O'Malley said quietly: "He's not an amputee. He's paralyzed from the waist down. He'll have to spend the rest of his life in a wheelchair. Captain Randolph won't."

"I think I've seen enough," Charlotte said faintly.

"Not yet." O'Malley gripped Charlotte's hand firmly and led her to the far corner of the room, where four wheelchairs were parked near a set of parallel bars. Two men pulled themselves along the rails, bracing their faltering footsteps. Another lay on his back, as a nurse demonstrated how to strap on a wooden leg and take it off. A fourth man sat in his chair, his eyes closed, in an attitude of desolation. One of his legs was missing.

"See that one?" O'Malley went on. "On the mat? His wife hasn't answered his letters. She's pretending it didn't happen. Yet there it is . . . a hard blow, but it's been dealt, hasn't it?"

"That's how it is for John," Charlotte whispered, almost to herself.

"That's right, dear," O'Malley said emphatically. "That's how it is."

Just then, one of the men at the bars stumbled and fell, cursing the pain as the artificial limb jarred out of place, grinding into his stump. O'Malley rushed forward to help while Charlotte quickly escaped from the room, blinking back her tears.

* * *

DREADING the inevitable, she returned the following morning, as ready as she would ever be to see her crippled husband. But O'Malley wasn't on duty, and when Charlotte asked for Captain Randolph, the strange nurse reported: "Sorry, but he already has a visitor."

Charlotte was stunned. "But that can't be! There must be some mistake."

The nurse consulted the Visitors Register. "Here it is, Private R. C. Whittaker."

"Roland?" Charlotte was thoroughly bewildered. She knew Roland had been transferred to Camp Pendleton somewhere in northern California, but what was he doing here? "I don't understand . . ."

"Why don't you wait outside?" the nurse suggested. "When Sergeant Whittaker comes out, we can see if Captain Randolph is up to another visitor."

Charlotte did as she was told. What on earth was Roland doing here? And why did John agree to see him and not her? She sat down on a stone bench in the open courtyard, watching the late afternoon shadows spread across the grass.

"Hey, Char!" she finally heard, her brother using the name he'd called her in childhood. His voice sounded deeper, and when she looked up, he seemed more substantial, more self-assured than he'd been one short month ago when he'd brought his dime-store bride to Breezy.

"Come on," he said, taking her elbow. "Let's go somewhere else."

She nodded, still staring into her brother's face, seeing the newness of his manhood in the fresh angles, the lost softness of childhood.

He smiled at her and it wasn't the goofy, lopsided grin he used to flash in an attempt to be engaging. "There's a park down the hill," he said.

As they walked, she asked politely, "How's Clara? How's your wife?"

"Not bad," he answered with a shrug. "But let's skip the small talk."

They passed the military guard, the Officers' Club and entered Balboa Park, walking until they came to a gravel path canopied with tall eucalyptus trees and bordered by ferns and birds of paradise. "Let's sit," he said when they came to an empty bench.

"How is he?" she asked, nervously tugging at her gloved fingers.

"He's skinny as a scarecrow," he answered tersely, "and his morale is lousy."

"He's lost a lot of weight?" she asked, avoiding the main issue.

"Yeah. He thinks you'll want to leave him, Char, so he's trying to make it easy for you."

She considered what Roland had said. Was there an escape from all this? Could she take it? Could she leave John? Did she still love him . . . as a wife should love a husband?

"Dammit, Char . . . say something!" He gripped her arms so fiercely that she cried out. "That's John up there. So he's lost a piece of his leg . . ."

"A piece of his leg?" she repeated the phrase, grasping at the hope it implied.

"Yeah. Didn't you know? From the knee down. The nurse said he'd be fine with one of those things, if only he'd try. I'll bet you'd hardly notice it when he's dressed."

"Really? Oh, Ro . . ."

"Listen, Char," he said, his voice softer, kinder now. "I know you're trying. But I want you to know that it's gonna be okay with you two before I go . . . and I'm shipping out tomorrow."

"Tomorrow? So soon?"

"Yeah . . . to the South Pacific."

She clung to her brother desperately, all their childhood differences forgotten. "Oh Ro," she said tearfully. "Don't let anything happen to you. Don't . . ."

"Hey," he said huskily, stroking her hair. "I'll be okay . . . and if I'm not," his voice cracked a little, boyish again for a moment, "if I'm not . . . it's like I said to John—a man has to be ready to fight for what's important . . . no matter what."

She hugged him closer. "What's going to happen to me?" she whispered. "What can I do?"

"Don't think about yourself," he said, decisively echoing Emily's sentiments. "Think about John. You'll figure out what he needs."

"I don't know if I can," she said in a small voice.

"Sure you can. Where there's a will, there's a way."

She pulled away and smiled at her brother through tear-stained eyes. "Now I know you've changed," she said. "You're quoting Papa."

"Yeah," he said sheepishly, "maybe he knows a thing or two, after all. Come on now—let's get something to eat. This is my last night to tank up on civilian food."

ROLAND shipped out early the following morning, from Dock 15, aboard a huge steel-gray Naval carrier. He had forbidden Charlotte a last farewell, saying he'd had enough tears back at Parris Island when he said goodbye to Clara.

But she wanted to hold on to him just a little longer, this baby brother turned warrior. So she sat in a taxi a half block away, watching as he swaggered up the gangplank, his duffel bag slung over his shoulder, straining for last glimpses until he disappeared into the hull of the ship.

"Please God," she whispered. "Please bring him back safe and whole."

The cab driver heard her prayer. He turned around. "I got a son in Italy," he said. "Army. Me and my wife, we're Catholics. She lights candles for him over at St. Christopher's on Third Street. I could stop there on the way back to the hotel..."

"Thank you," she said, not wanting to offend the man. "But there's something I have to do. My husband's in the Naval hospital. I...I want to take him something..."

He started the engine. "So what'll it be? You wanta get him some candy? Maybe some magazines...or a book?"

She shook her head. "No...no. It has to be more special."

He turned around again. "How about I take you to Marston's? That's the best department store in town. You could look around. That's what my wife does. Once she bought me a pair of silk pajamas when I was laid up with appendicitis. Course, you can't get nothin' silk these days, but it's a nice store."

"Yes," she agreed. "Let's go there."

NURSE O'Malley was on duty when Charlotte arrived at the hospital a few hours later.

"I'm sorry I left so quickly the other day," Charlotte apologized. "I looked for you yesterday, but..."

"I was on late shift...but you're back, and that's all that matters. I see you have a present for Captain Randolph."

Charlotte held out her gift almost shyly. It was a silver-tipped ebony cane wrapped in a fluffy red ribbon. "It's like the one Walter Pidgeon used in *Since You Went Away*. I thought..."

"It's lovely." O'Malley smiled encouragingly.

"I'm going to give it to him today. I'm going in there. Please don't try to stop me."

"I wouldn't dream of it. He's halfway down the hall. Ward three. Good luck to you both."

"Thank you." Charlotte took a deep breath and marched down the long corridor, her high heels clicking on the marble floor.

She paused. The door to Ward 3 was open. Then she saw him, sitting in a wheelchair, a blanket draped over his lap, staring out the window. In profile his face was gaunt. Her eyes dropped to the flatness on his lower right side.

She looked away, taking another deep breath. "John, honey," she called softly. "It's me, Charlotte."

His head jerked around, alarm spreading on his face. "Go away," he said hoarsely, trying to cover the empty space with his arms. "Go away," he repeated, and she could see the unshed tears in his sunken blue eyes. "I don't want you to see me like this."

His pain touched her in a way his love never had, with its intensity, its desperation. More than anything in the world, she wanted to make it better.

Awkwardly he tried to turn the chair in the narrow space between his bed and the window. He bumped against the bedside table, jarring the framed picture of herself and the girls that she'd sent the Christmas before. His clumsiness made him desperate. "For God's sake, go away!"

Suddenly she felt strong in the face of his weakness, strong enough to be more than she was, better, because John's future depended on it. She fixed her best smile on her face, the one that had made her Prom Queen and Miss Popularity. Confidently, in her best "belle" voice, she said sweetly: "Why, John, I do believe you have forgotten your manners, to be speakin' to a lady in that way. But I forgive you because I know you have been to war and you have suffered. I have somethin' here—for you, Captain Randolph, suh." She presented the cane with a sweeping curtsy.

His face was a kaleidoscope of emotions. Pain, fear, hope. His eyes flicked over her face, searching for the lie— and then they went to the gift in her hands.

Finally, after what seemed like an eternity, he took the cane. Then he grasped her hand and brought it to his lips. Trying to answer her gesture, he managed a ghost of a smile. "Thank you, ma'am," he said hoarsely. "I hope you will forgive me for not standin' in the presence of a lady."

11

Hail to the Chief
April 1945

April 10, 1945

My Dear Children,

The constant presence of grandchildren on Breezy is both a constant joy and an ongoing education. There are days when I think of Methuselah, hoary with age and riddled with exasperations, and then I must remind myself of our Savior's admonition: "Forbid them not!" Yet there are days when I cannot begin to number the delights that their innocence and curiosity give me.

It was raining the other day, and Carrie wanted to go outside, weather notwithstanding. Charlotte said: "No, it's raw out there." But still the child persisted, and her mother said: "Don't you understand what 'raw' means?" "Certainly," Carrie replied, "that's what celery and carrots are."

Later that day when the skies cleared, Nancy went outside and pulled the concrete bird bath off the pedestal. Hearing her wails and fearing the worst, we rushed her to the hos-

pital. A thorough examination by Dr. Giles assured us that Nancy was fine except for a Band-Aid treated scratch on her left leg. Needless to say, we were all so relieved that the scolding which was administered was merely pro forma.

A postscript to the incident: when Bessie examined the broken bird bath, she invoked "Jesus, sweet Jesus." Carrie solemnly informed her, "He's not here, today, Bessie—it's only Friday."

As the Seventh Avenue subway roared uptown, Meg read the April 10th edition of the Breezy Hill Bulletin. Her father's chronicles continued to keep the family connected, as he had hoped they would. She smiled as she reread the account of her nieces and their latest escapades.

The Bulletins always restored her equilibrium. For her, life in West Grove had been boring and maddeningly slow of pace compared with New York, yet Clifton's prosaic renderings made everything back there seem so delightfully mundane, so refreshingly manageable. As Aunt Rose Mary had once said: "A dying rose blooms with Clifton's pen behind it."

Even the way he described little Jake's asthma made it sound like a perfectly normal part of childhood, instead of the constant fear it was.

Meg writes that her father-in-law, the restaurateur Maurice Steinmetz, has purchased a large rocker for the Steinmetz kitchen. Now when young Jake has the need to commune with the tea kettle at night, he and his mother can do so in comfort.

Clifton had gone on to explain that the doctors at Columbia Presbyterian were "optimistic" that Jake would outgrow his "malady."

Meg shook her head in wonder. If only she could share her father's perceptions, she would simply be a young mother who had a child with a chronic cough. Instead, her son's frequent attacks of wheezing left her anxious and worried.

She held her own breath each time he struggled for air and suffered pangs of guilt because the only relief she could offer came from the steam kettle and the lullabies she sang to soothe him.

David didn't know about the baby's asthma because it had developed soon after she and Jake had returned to the city. For the first two months after he had been reported missing she had continued writing letters, putting them in a box, to chronicle the gap in their lives after he was found. But after Christmas, she had stopped the one-way correspondence because the writing upset her too much.

It was now six months and six days since he had been reported a prisoner of war. She kept count on the Firestone calendar Bessie had given her for Christmas. It hung on the back of her closet door for she didn't want anyone to see that she was crossing off the days, or to know that each time she made another "x" her faith weakened a little bit more.

The subway slowed down as it approached the 72nd Street station, so she tucked the Bulletin into her purse. It was a lovely spring day, and she usually enjoyed the walk across 72nd Street to the Claessens' Central Park West apartment, but today she dreaded each step of the way.

Usually Mrs. Claessen opened the door and ushered Meg into the music room, but this morning it was the professor himself who answered her timid knock. "Rebecca has gone out for yarn," he explained, "for one of her pieces."

Meg nodded. To supplement her husband's teaching income, Mrs. Claessen copied still-life masterpieces in crewel and sold her work to decorating shops on Madison Avenue. "Is it the bouquet of violets by Durer?" she asked. Rebecca had shown her the beautiful pattern she'd made the week before.

The professor smiled and patted her arm. "So you remember, Liebchen, yes? Do you remember the Chopin Nocturne also?"

All week long she had debated about what to say, when to speak to the professor. Should she do it before or after she played the Nocturne in B flat minor—the piece he wanted her to play for his old friend Nathan Ulrich, the man he wanted to manage her career? Finally she had decided to play first—her last concert for the professor. For any audience.

She sat down, flexed her fingers and began to play, reverently bringing the sounds from the big Steinway. The melody was a haunting one, filled with expressions of mysterious longing. Something about the lovely melancholy of the composition reminded Meg of her mother's playing of Vivaldi and Scarlatti, sounds that in childhood had made her think of raindrops, of wind blowing through a crystal chandelier. At the Nocturne's end, her hands lingered reluctantly on the keyboard, as the last poignant notes faded into memory.

"Bravo!" The professor tapped his baton enthusiastically against the piano. "The Nocturne is yours. You are indeed ready for Ulrich."

"No," she said quietly. "I can't see Nathan Ulrich."

"Cannot? I do not understand." The professor was perplexed.

She took a breath and looked her beloved teacher in the eye. "I can't go on as we planned. Everything has changed for me. The war . . ."

"But music does not change, Liebchen. It is the same in war and in peace."

"Not for me," she said. "I have a husband who is a prisoner of war. A child who's ill . . ."

"But your talent?" The professor gripped the baton with both hands, as if he might snap it in two. "Your dream? The dreams we have?"

She took a deep breath and tried to explain how much she had changed, how the realities of her life had pushed the dream further and further away, until she could no longer feel it anymore. "I'm so sorry to disappoint you . . ." Her voice trailed off, entreating him to understand, though she feared he could not. Just as she suspected, her mother would not have understood. She had not dared to give form and substance to her fantasies, so she had passed them on to her daughter. She would have been heartbroken, Meg knew, if the dream were to end, stillborn with her. "I'm sorry," she repeated.

"There are always choices, Liebchen," he began sadly, obviously struggling with his own disappointment and his affection for his favorite pupil. "To give up the music will diminish your life. This I know. And I regret that one day you will know it, too." Then he left abruptly, overcome by his emotions.

Quickly she gathered up her things and let herself out of the spacious high-ceilinged apartment that had always felt like a sacred cathedral to her.

As she waited for the elevator, she wondered if she should have tried harder to explain. If she should have mentioned that most of the music lesson money Clifton gave her at Christmas had gone for Jake's medical expenses. That she had questioned her right to such a privileged pursuit when she had the responsibility of a child, a child she might have to raise alone. That now she had come to wonder whether the dream of a musical career had been simply that—a dream.

The elevator doors opened, and Rebecca Claessen stepped out, handsome in a tailored suit and felt hat, carrying a string bag filled with yarn and a bunch of daffodils. "Good day, Meg dear," she said affectionately.

"I'm sorry," Meg blurted out, fleeing into the elevator. "I'm so very sorry..."

THE weather had turned warmer these past few weeks, and the Vienna Cafe was busier than usual, especially on weekends, its white-covered tables constantly occupied. Most of the cafe's regulars were Jews from Eastern Europe, immigrants or the children of immigrants. They congregated there to exchange reminiscences about the "old country" and "the old days," to enjoy a bottle of wine or a fine Sacher torte. But now that Meg was providing music at lunch and dinner, there were more "street" customers than ever before.

It had all started six weeks ago, before Christmas, when two slightly tipsy men had driven up in a van and wheeled

an upright piano into the cafe. Moments later, Uncle Max's
cab had pulled up. The big, bearish, boisterous man had
swung Meg around, laughing and enjoying her confusion.
"So how can a piano player play without a piano?" he
demanded, insisting that she play something at once. And
though she was accustomed to fine grand pianos, the moment she touched the keyboard, she fell in love with the
old upright.

"I love it!" she exclaimed. "How can I thank you?"

"Make much music! Play!"

At first, Eva had been a little skeptical about her brother's
largesse, suspecting the piano had been won in one of Max's
infamous poker games. But after a few of Meg's impromptu
concerts, after the customers' obvious appreciation, Eva's
speculations were forgotten.

It had been Eva who had the idea that Meg should play
for the customers in the restaurant. At first, Meg had used
the piano only to practice during off-hours. But after Maurice and Max had tried unsuccessfully to get the upright up
the narrow staircase to the apartment, Eva's practical mind
had gone to work.

One day, she had brought home a bag full of sheet music,
arranged the folders on the piano bench and invited Meg to
inspect her selection. "A nice young man helps me with
these," she said. "The latest songs, he tells me. If you play,
the customers will be happy, no?"

Meg had looked over the titles her mother-in-law had
chosen: "Bewitched, Bothered and Bewildered," "Rum and
Coca-Cola," "Sentimental Journey," "Accentuate the Positive," and "Paper Doll."

Although Meg had always prided herself in being classical in her musical tastes, she could not say "no" to her
mother-in-law.

Now as Meg hurried towards Thompson Street, she was
relieved to see the "Closed" sign still hanging in the cafe
door. She still had a few minutes to change her clothes and
to check on Jake, before she took her post at the piano.

Upstairs, the baby was happily handing blocks to Hilda
Meyerson, the spinster who lived down the hall. Weekdays,
Hilda worked as a sales clerk at Macy's; on weekends she

was Jake's self-appointed babysitter and playmate. "He takes a nap this morning," Hilda reported, "and," she added triumphantly, "he makes a number two."

Meg ruffled her child's hair and rushed into her room, to slip into her good black dress, ironically the same one she had worn for the competition, three years ago.

Downstairs, her in-laws would be setting up for lunch. She was glad that the cafe would open soon, that they would be too busy to notice that she was so upset. They would only hover over her, smother her with attention if they suspected anything were wrong. "Chicken soup for everything," David had joked once. "Enjoy it, but don't drown in it."

The radio would be on, tuned to the station that carried Gabriel Heatter's broadcasts. The family listened, every day. The week David had been reported missing, Maurice had bought an RCA Victor table model and set it above the cash register. "We listen for news of our boy," he might inform a customer, as he paused to hear a bulletin about the latest Allied advances in Eastern Europe. "Soon now, they will find our David."

Maurice never doubted that his only son would be found. Whatever had happened to David was temporary, like the time his friend Gunter had been cut off by an avalanche in the Pyrenees. As he told the story, Gunter had been reported missing for two months, before rescuers had found him, alive and well and demanding to know what had taken them so long.

While Eva professed the same unwavering faith, Meg knew that she had doubts. Recently, when she had been up with Jake one night, she had seen her mother-in-law sitting in the darkened living room, holding David's Bar Mitzvah picture and crying softly.

Now as Meg sat down to play, she was surprised, as always, at how the simple tunes with their contemporary lyrics affected her, how well they reflected the feeling of the time. It gave her pleasure to see how these songs touched the customers at the Vienna Cafe. "It is not Chopin, but it makes people happy, yes?" Eva said one night, and Meg had to agree. It wasn't like performing in a concert hall, but it was satisfying to employ her talent in an everyday way, and perhaps even to make some tiny contribution to the war effort.

When it had become obvious that Meg's playing attracted a new, younger clientele, couples who would come in as much for the music as for the food, Eva had insisted that Maurice pay Meg a small salary. At first she protested, arguing that the restaurant was a family business, and that she made no other contribution to the family's expenses. But Eva refused to listen. "You work, you make business better, you get paid. Fifteen dollars a week. You will need the money when David comes home."

Meg had started to save the money in a Chinese music box Aunt Rose Mary had given her on her twelfth birthday. So far she had put away almost $85 toward furnishing an apartment, towards the day that David came home . . . if he came home.

The luncheon crowd had almost disappeared when a thunderstorm broke, bringing with it a driving rain. Instinctively Meg responded with the opening bars of the light and happy "April Showers." The few remaining customers applauded, and she smiled, humming to herself as she played.

But as her fingers moved across the keyboard to the melody of "It isn't raining rain, you know, it's raining violets," she felt the warm salty wetness of tears on her cheeks. There didn't seem to be any violets in her life. Everything wasn't coming up roses. There weren't any silver linings in the clouds. How could she believe any of it anymore? She had a baby who might choke to death any minute, a husband she feared was already dead.

Her mood took her into a tumultuous Peer Gynt Suite, and she wasn't even aware when the last customer departed, leaving her alone in the restaurant. As she went into the last movement with its dominant bass beat, her ear picked up a pounding that wasn't coming from the piano. She stopped and listened. The pounding continued, from the direction of the door.

A young boy in a yellow slicker, a bicycle by his side,

was standing outside. She opened the door to let him in. "Western Union, ma'am," he said, just as a clap of thunder drowned out his words.

"What did you say?"

"Western Union. I have a telegram." He held out an envelope, and she recoiled in horror.

"Oh, no," she whispered. "Please, no."

The boy shifted uncomfortably, knowing why the woman was frightened, not knowing what he might say. Finally he asked timidly: "Do you want me to read it, ma'am?"

She nodded, leaning against the front counter for support, closing her eyes as he broke the seal.

"The War Department informs you that Lieutenant David Steinmetz, of the Medical Corps, U.S. Army, has been liberated. He is in satisfactory condition in London, England. More details will follow. Signed, Secretary J.A. Ulio, Major General."

"Oh, thank God," she sobbed, her knees nearly buckling with relief. "Oh, thank God." She rushed forward to embrace the boy. "Oh, thank you! Thank you so much. Don't go away, I want to give you something. My husband's alive! Oh, my husband's alive!"

"That's nice, ma'am. I'm glad for you," the boy smiled, relieved that this was not one of those other telegrams.

Meg ran to the back of the restaurant and yelled into the kitchen: "Eva! Maurice! He's alive! David's alive!"

In his unwavering faith, Maurice had hidden away several bottles of champagne in a corner of the basement cellar, for the day that his son would be found. They were all brought out, to drink now with the Western Union boy and to share with all the customers that would come in later, that evening.

Meg thought of calling Breezy at once, but instead she hugged the news to herself. She was so afraid it might disappear. After several triumphant toasts, she slipped upstairs to feed her baby, and as she held him close, she crooned, "Your daddy's coming home, Jake. Your daddy's coming home."

"Dada," he laughed and clapped his hands, delighted

with the sound of the word, his dark eyes lighting up, just
the way David's did.

"Meg . . ." It was Eva, standing in the doorway, her face
still damp with tears of joy. "Meg, will you come with us
now to the synagogue, you and the baby?"

"To the synagogue? Now?"

"To pray and give thanks. Uncle Max waits with the taxi.
The services begin soon. Will you come?"

Meg had never been in a synagogue. Since the one attempt to persuade her to convert, there had been an understanding. And after her refusal to have Jake circumcised,
there had been no further attempt to include her in any
religious activities. But today was different. It was right
that they should all be together in a holy place, giving thanks
to their God, to her God, that David was coming home.
"Yes," she said. "Yes, I'll come."

As the family returned to Thompson Street in Uncle Max's
taxi, Maurice pressed some crumpled bills into Meg's hand.
"For you," he said. "You go to Virginia and tell your family."

"Maurice—no," she protested. "It's too much . . ." She
knew how limited the Steinmetz funds were, for whatever
extra they had went to help relatives and friends trying to
escape from the Nazis.

"Do not argue," Maurice said firmly. "David would want
it so."

"But don't stay too long, hah?" Eva cautioned affectionately. "We get ready for David, yes?"

"Yes," Meg nodded, "don't worry . . . I know where I
belong now." She placed the baby in Eva's arms. "And so
does your grandson."

ALMOST a day later, at 6:30 in the morning, the Greyhound
bus pulled into West Grove. Main Street was deserted,
except for Bernard Pyle, who sat on the front steps of his
store with his morning cup of coffee and the colored boy
at Ralph's Garage pumping gas into an old pickup.

Carrying her baby in one arm, her suitcase in the other,

Meg tried to kick open the screen door of Stoots' Pharmacy. "Wait now," a familiar voice called out. "Let me help you."

Miss Jewel rushed out from behind the cosmetic counter. "Why, honey, where'd you all come from?"

"From New York," Meg answered laughing. "And it's been quite a trip, let me tell you. I'm about to collapse."

"Here, honey, let me take the baby. Oh, Cliff is going to be so pleased. He doesn't know you're coming, does he?"

"No." Meg smiled. "We're a surprise. A tired, hungry surprise."

"You poor dear. Tell you what, I'll close up and take you to my place. You can freshen up there and I'll make a nice pot of coffee. Gladys is in Garden City today, visiting her mother—she's in the hospital. I said I'd help her out," she explained, hanging the "Closed" sign on the door. She giggled. "We won't tell her I played hookey for a while.

"Guess you know Charlotte and John are comin' home today," she chattered as she led Meg up the wooden stairs to her apartment. "Cliff fixed up the downstairs bedroom for him, so he won't have to struggle with the stairs. Everyone's all excited . . . and kinda nervous but don't let on I said anything."

Meg hadn't been in Jewel's apartment since childhood, when she and her sisters would come for fittings. Everything was as she remembered it: the china closet full of thimbles and miniature doodads, the faded satin souvenir pillows and the chalet cuckoo clock near the kitchen doorway. After her time with her in-laws, Meg found a certain helter-skelter charm in the place.

"You little sweetheart," Jewel crooned, settling the baby onto the couch. "You must be such a comfort to your mama."

"He is." Meg nodded. "I wouldn't have gotten through this without him."

"Your daddy's been so worried about you," Jewel said, in deference to Meg's near-bereaved condition.

"I know, but everything's all right now. David's been found! He's alive! That's why I came back . . ."

"Heavenly Father, thank you." Jewel turned her eyes heavenward, pure joy on her face.

The baby began to cry. "Let me take the little angel," Jewel offered. "I'll give him a bath and warm up a little milk. And why don't you stretch out on my bed and take a teeny nap. Go on, dearie. It's not as if they're expecting you..."

Meg surrendered to her fatigue and gratefully curled up on Jewel's frilly pink bed. Before she closed her eyes, she saw a photo of her father, the one taken several years back for the Virginia Bar Association listing, in a handsome silver frame on the night table. Strange, she thought, as she drifted off to sleep, that he could have chosen Miss Jewel, yet had had so much difficulty in accepting her David.

THREE hours later, Meg arrived on Breezy Hill in Ed McBain's cab, just as the family was sitting down to lunch on the back porch.

"It's Miss Meg!" Bessie shouted as Ed tooted the horn and pulled into the driveway.

"Thank the Lord!" Clifton gasped hoarsely when she had shared her good news, embracing her fervently, with none of his usual formality.

"Are you all right, Papa?" Emily asked, alarmed that the color had drained from her father's face.

"I'm fine," he said, sinking down on the porch steps, "though all this excitement has taken my breath away."

"Why don't you lie down a bit?" Emily persisted. "We can all catch up later."

"No... no... I just need a moment or two, and then I must call Giles and Walter and Annie... I should call the War Department too. Perhaps they can provide us with more information on David's whereabouts."

Emily shrugged and shared a rueful smile with her sister, a silent comment on their father's continued stubbornness, his refusal to acknowledge that his blood pressure was high.

Jake started to cry, and Bessie immediately mobilized. "Heah, give me dat baby, honey chile. Mistuh Clifton, we needs de crib from de attic."

"I'll help," Alexander volunteered. "I'm good at putting things together, you know."

"Thank you, Alex, I'll take you up on that offer." Clifton got up and walked slowly into the house.

Meg watched him thoughtfully, struck by how much her father seemed to have aged since she'd been gone.

"DADDY won't play horsey on the knee anymore," Carrie said to her sister, as they sat in the porch swing waiting to be taken to the train station. The two sisters were dressed in matching dresses appliqued with red cherries, sent by their mother from Washington, especially for this day.

"No more horsey," Nancy pouted, picking at the red bow on her collar.

"Alex says Daddy's going to look like Long John Silver," Carrie said, pumping with her patent-leather Mary Janes.

"Who's that?" Nancy asked, annoyed at her sister's superior body of information.

"The pirate in *Kidnapped*. He had a wooden leg, too."

"I want my daddy!" Nancy complained.

"Stop being a baby," Carrie scolded. "We have to be very good today."

"I don't want to," Nancy argued.

"What's going on out here?" Emily opened the porch door. "Come on now. It's time for a trip to the bathroom before we leave."

"I don't have to go," Carrie declined, "but she better." After Nancy went dutifully into the house, she told her aunt, "I don't want my daddy to have a wooden leg," she confessed, her face clouded with uncertainties.

"I know, honey," Emily said sympathetically, sitting down beside the child and slipping a protective arm around her shoulders. "He doesn't want to have it either."

"Then why does he have to?" Carrie asked.

"It was the war," Emily explained, stroking her niece's fine brown hair. "It was an accident."

"I hate this stupid old war," the child said passionately. "I hate it."

"So do I, honey," Emily said softly. "But we have to be brave and help each other. Today we all have to welcome your daddy home. All right?" She held the child close, but Carrie made no response.

As the train pulled into the West Grove station, the family scanned the debarking passengers. Although Charlotte had phoned and written any number of times, reassuring them that John's recuperation was "just amazing," their mood was one of subdued thanksgiving.

"There they are." Meg shifted the baby in her arms to point out two figures at the end of the platform.

"Mummy! Daddy!" Carrie and Nancy broke away from their Aunt Emily and raced towards their parents.

From a distance, Charlotte and John still made a strikingly handsome couple, she in a red linen suit with black patent-leather accessories, he in his dress whites, decorated with his service ribbons and a Purple Heart. The silver-tipped black cane, the slow and deliberate steps were the only visible signs of John's "injury."

"My, don't the girls look darling!" Charlotte remarked as their daughters approached.

Suddenly Carrie stopped short a few feet from her parents, searching her father for signs of change. Nancy followed suit, positioning herself behind her sister. "He doesn't look like a pirate," she whispered.

"Girls, come give your daddy a hug," Charlotte said impatiently, but the children didn't move.

"They've grown so much," John said quietly, his voice filled with wonder at the sight of his children after fifteen long months.

"Yes, of course they have," Charlotte agreed. "That's what children do."

"John . . . welcome home." Clifton removed his bowler hat and offered his hand to his son-in-law. "You're looking fit."

"I'm feeling fine, sir." John returned the handshake. "Just fine."

"Well," Clifton said heartily as he observed his grand-daughters huddling together. "We have two young ladies here who have been waiting patiently for you to return. Isn't that right, girls?"

"I think the cat has their tongues, sir." John stepped forward, tapping his cane lightly, taking command of the situation. "But I wonder if some ice cream cones from the drugstore might not do the trick."

"Yes! Yes!" Nancy responded immediately, for there could never be enough ice cream in her life. But Carrie, ever the skeptic, hung back.

"Carrie, honey," Charlotte pleaded, her voice edged with anxiety, "say something to your daddy."

"Do you really have a wooden leg?" Carrie demanded.

"Oh, Carrie, no!" Charlotte gasped.

"Welcome back, John," Emily intervened, hugging her brother-in-law. "I think ice cream sounds like a fine idea," she added.

"Do you?" Carrie persisted stubbornly.

"Yes, I do." John smiled at his daughter's candor. "And when we get home, I'll show you. But first, ice cream all around. All right?"

"John Randolph, you haven't changed a bit!" Meg laughed as she finally caught up with the others, her squirming son in tow. "You're still the handsomest man in uniform I've ever seen . . . Except for David, of course."

"What in the world are you doing here?" Charlotte asked. "And look at Jake. He's walking!"

"Sorry to steal some of your thunder," Meg apologized, a hint of mischief in her smile. "But this is kind of a double homecoming. David's been found! He's alive!"

"That's wonderful news, Meg! The very best kind of news." John clasped his cane and embraced his sister-in-law clumsily. "All the more reason to celebrate now."

As she watched her sisters walk away, Emily felt a twinge of the now-familiar sadness. She thought of the little banner that Miss Jewel had embroidered for the front parlor window—three white stars and one gold. Four of their men had gone to war; one returning a cripple, another was a

POW, one was still fighting and one had died.

"Hey, Mom." Alexander put his hand in hers. "Ice cream at the drugstore. Come on."

"You run along, honey." She smiled at her son's solemn bespectacled face and the sadness was gone. "I have to go somewhere for a little while. I'll see you back on Breezy."

SLOWLY Emily walked up the hill to the West Grove Cemetery. The graveyard was bordered with a white picket fence and scattered with cedar trees. In the late afternoon sun, it possessed a serene pastoral atmosphere.

Emily had not made this trip in years, not since the first anniversary of her mother's death, when she'd brought a bouquet of magnolia blossoms, Elizabeth's favorite, and laid them on her grave.

Howard's funeral had been a simple memorial service at the Methodist church. When the Army had shipped his body back several months later, the train had been met by Clifton, Easterly Boyd of Boyd's Funeral Home and Reverend Lowell. Together they had attended to the burial, with no ceremony save her requested reading of the Twenty-third Psalm. She had called herself a coward for not being there, yet she had been relieved to be spared the experience of watching Howard's coffin lowered into the ground.

Now she was finally here, almost two years later, to see the place where he rested, to say her final goodbye. The Whittaker plot was neat and well tended, shrubbed with blooming azaleas and forsythia. A few feet from her mother's grave was the newest marker, of dark gray granite, bearing the simple inscription:

HOWARD CHARLES EMMETT
October 12, 1912—May 7, 1943

She touched the stone lightly, kneeled and kissed the smooth, cool surface and left the cemetery. As she walked down the hill, she thought: it was true, what everyone had told her so many months ago—Time heals.

*   *   *

THAT night Charlotte lingered longer than usual over her evening toilette. Closeted in her father's bedroom, she put on the new red satin nightgown she'd bought in Washington, smoothed her pageboy and freshened her scarlet lipstick. She looked quite lovely, but tonight her concern was not for her appearance.

This would be the first time she and John had shared a bed since the "injury" that had changed their lives. She wished she had a little something to ease the moment, a small bourbon or a bit of brandy. Taking a deep breath, she left the safety of the bathroom.

The bedroom was lit by the green ginger jar lamp on the night table. John was already in bed, under the covers. The wooden prosthesis, its leather straps dangling off to one side, leaned against the chair by the window. She shuddered, feeling cold and exposed, wishing she'd bought a matching negligee to cover the gown.

"You look beautiful," John said, his voice low and thick with longing.

"Thank you," she said politely. "Would you mind turning out the light?"

Wordlessly he complied and the room became mercifully dark. She made her way to the bed and arranged herself under the covers, her body parallel with her husband's. She lay very still, listening to the sound of his breathing, which seemed unnaturally loud in the quiet of the room.

"I want to hold you," he said finally, almost in a whisper. "It's been so long." Taking her silence for acquiescence, he leaned over and kissed her, tentatively at first and then with all the hunger and need he had not shared with her for so very long.

He slipped the gown from her shoulders and kissed her breasts. And then his body was on hers, his maleness hard against her, his strong upper thighs holding her. She closed her eyes and then she felt it, the mangled remnant of his left leg, pressed against her perfect body. She stiffened, recoiled from his touch and shuddered with revulsion.

He pulled away instantly, as if he had been struck, and
retreated without a word to his side of the bed. "I'm so
sorry," she whispered. "I can't. I just can't!" When there
was no answer, she ran back into the bathroom.

She sat down on the toilet seat and began to cry, half
expecting John to come after her, the way he always had
when she was upset, to say something sweet that would
make her feel better. But he didn't come and she didn't
know what he could say that would make this better. She
knew she had failed him, but she couldn't help it. She had
married a man who was handsome and whole. How could
she know that he would not always be that way?

THE next morning Clifton's reverence for routine took him
to the office at nine o'clock as usual, but after checking the
morning mail and determining there were no pressing matters of business, he sent Tillie home and declared the day
a holiday.

When he returned to the house, he found his daughters
in the parlor, lingering over coffee, sharing in detail their
experiences since they were last all together. Meg was sitting
on the carpet, encouraging her son as he tottered between
the piano bench and her outstretched arms.

"That boy looks more like his father every day," Clifton
said, smiling fondly at his grandson. "Look at that fine head
of hair."

"He does look like David, doesn't he," Meg agreed
proudly. "Oh, Papa, do you think David will be all right
when he comes home? Those prison camps are so awful . . .
and it's been so long . . ."

"Don't borrow against adversity," Clifton counselled. "If
there were something wrong with David's health, the Army
would have informed us." Changing the subject, he turned
to Charlotte, and asked: "Where is John this morning?"

"He's . . . he's out in the barn," she replied. "He's been
showing the children his . . . his leg. Though why they find
it so fascinatin' is beyond me."

"The worst is behind you, Charlotte Lee," he reassured,

"and you are to be congratulated for your part in your husband's recovery."

"I suppose," she said listlessly, picking at a chip of nail polish on her ring finger. "Oh, Lord, I'm just going to have to do this over again."

THAT afternoon, the Randolphs went for a drive. "I need to get behind the wheel of a car again," John insisted, overruling Charlotte's protests that it was "too soon."

The children disappeared into the barn to play hospital with Alexander as doctor. Carrie and Nancy were the nurses. Baby Jake, the docile patient, gurgled cooperatively while his older cousins wrapped and rewrapped him in bandages made out of strips of old sheets.

Emily and Meg settled into the parlor with their father. As each of them had done so often these past months, they paged through the latest newspapers and magazines, scanning the war news, searching through the reports of territories gained and enemy losses for signs that it would be over soon.

"Billy told me that the biggest turning point in Europe came last month, when Eisenhower crossed the Rhine at Regamen," Emily said, looking up from her *Time* magazine.

Meg smiled fondly at her sister. "Working at the *Gazette* really suits you, Em. So does Billy."

Emily blushed and pretended not to understand her sister's meaning. "Billy is a remarkable man. West Grove is lucky to have such a fine journalist and historian."

"Did your sister tell you that she has ventured into the field of literary criticism?" Clifton asked Meg. "Billy has syndicated her book reviews in the Russell County papers."

"That's wonderful, Em. I can't wait to read them. I'll bet they're really good. You always were such a bookworm. And now you've made something of your talent . . ." Meg trailed off, a little wistfully.

"It's not so grand as Papa makes it sound," Emily said, "and I've had a great deal of help."

"Any news from Roland?" Meg asked. "It's been weeks

since you've mentioned him in your Bulletins."

"Nothing," Clifton replied, shaking his head.

"So the last news we had was after Iwo Jima?" Meg asked. "God, I can't believe he was there. It must have been horrible."

"From the letter we got, you'd have thought it was a church picnic," Emily commented, quoting from his letter.

The Marines really had to show their stuff on this Jap-infested island, but old Roland slid through un-scratched again. Please send chocolates and Betty Grable.

"That was more than six weeks ago," Clifton said, his voice heavy with concern.

"Six weeks isn't so long between letters," Emily said reassuringly. "We learned that, didn't we, Meg?"

"That's true, and let's face it, Ro was never the letter-writing type. Neither is Clara, apparently. Have you heard from her lately, Papa?"

Clifton shook his head. "Not since the Christmas card she wrote, declining our invitation to spend the holiday here. I continue to send her copies of the Bulletin, of course, in care of Ray's Bar and Grill in Norfolk, but there have been no replies."

"Isn't that odd?" Meg nodded, thinking that it might be for the best that they didn't know what Roland's wife was up to. Ray's Bar and Grill in the navy port of Norfolk certainly sounded suspicious to her.

"Here," Clifton said, returning to the *Life* magazine article on the Marine landing on Okinawa. "This is interesting. Apparently Okinawa gives our forces an air base only 350 miles from Japan."

"That's right," Emily said. "Billy showed me the ticker tape when that hit the wires. About the same time, the carrier *Yamato* went down, marking the end of the Japanese fleet . . . so they shouldn't be able to last long."

Suddenly there was the sound of heavy footsteps hurrying up the hallway. "Lawd have mercy," Bessie wailed. "Oh, sweet Jesus, he's daid . . . daid and gone."

"What's that?" Clifton asked, his voice unsteady. "Did the telephone ring?"

"No, Papa." Emily moved quickly to her father's side, noting that the color had again left his face. "Do you have those pills that Dr. Giles gave you?"

"Oh Lawdy." Bessie burst into the room, tears as big as raindrops streaming down her cheeks. "De President done died, down dere in Georgia . . . it come on de radio . . . Mistuh Roosevelt, he daid."

"Thank God it's not Roland," Emily whispered, as she slipped a protective arm around Clifton's shoulders.

"Thank God," Meg echoed fervently.

But their father did not seem to hear, as he stared into space. "President Roosevelt," he said hoarsely. "FDR . . ." His voice broke. "To lose him now . . . Oh, God, to lose him now . . ." Clifton covered his face with his hands and began to cry.

WEST GROVE GAZETTE BULLETIN

DATELINE April 13, 1945

PRESIDENT ROOSEVELT DEAD, NATION GRIEVES

On the afternoon of April 12, 1945, Franklin Delano Roosevelt, thirty-second president of the United States, died of a cerebral hemorrhage at Warm Springs, Georgia. Not since the death of Abraham Lincoln have Americans been so united in a national expression of grief. The late president has been described in the *New York Times* as "a man of the world and the world's man." We echo the sentiments of the *Omaha World-Herald:* "There are no Republicans in America today, no Democrats, no New Dealers or anti-New Dealers. There are only Americans, united in a sense of national bereavement."

12

The Homecoming
September 1945

September 19, 1945

My Dear Children,

As we all know, our Roland, now Lieutenant Sergeant R.J. Whittaker, was part of the difficult conquest of the Japanese island of Iwo Jima. Accounts record this battle as the costliest in 168 years of Marine Corps history. Six thousand eight hundred lives were lost; 18,200 were wounded. In fact, only one other U.S. offensive action in our military history, Pickett's Civil War charge at Gettysburg, had so great a percentage of casualties. We are grateful that our Roland came through this bloody skirmish unscathed, and that he will be returning to us soon.

With her usual flair, my sister Rose Mary joins us (in absentia) in welcoming Roland home, with her gift of a ceremonial spear. "For the returning warrior, the full-blooded Whittaker brave," she wrote—and I could not have phrased the sentiment better myself....

*   *   *

CLIFTON stopped typing the Bulletin and picked up the Marine Corps press release stating that Lieutenant Sergeant R.C. Whittaker was the recipient of both the Purple Heart and the Congressional Medal of Honor, "for courage under fire and valor at Iwo Jima, above and beyond the call of duty." He shook his head in disbelief as he refolded the notification and tucked it into his vest pocket. His son, his irresponsible, undirected teenage son was returning to West Grove a hero.

Outside his windows, down in the town square, the high school band was preparing to greet Roland at the train station, to escort him back to the courthouse steps for a welcoming ceremony, and then to the fairgrounds for a gala picnic. Despite Roland's apparent desire for a quiet homecoming, West Grove had decided to roll out its red carpet for the young hero whose picture had actually appeared in *Life* magazine the week before.

Clifton's dictionary defined a hero as "any man noted for feats of courage or nobility of purpose," words he had never expected to apply to his son. It was not that he had ever thought of Roland as a coward; it was simply that he had seen him as a child who lacked strength of character and who had never demonstrated any hint of a "nobility of purpose."

Now Roland was coming home, wreathed with military laurels. Clifton was proud of him, of course, but Roland's unforeseen military achievements made him question his small-mindedness and lack of vision, not only where his son was concerned, but also in his relationship with Miss Jewel.

He stared out the window, contemplating the bustle of activity on "the Rialto." Soon it would be over, and the parades and the celebrations of the war's end would be over. All the children would go their separate ways once again. Roland would not linger long in West Grove, and Emily, he suspected, would soon announce her plans for marriage to Billy Gillespie. Meg's future was in New York, Charlotte's in Richmond. So it wouldn't be long before they would all be gone from Breezy Hill. And he would be left alone in the big, old empty house.

But Jewel would still be here for him, as she had been during these four hard and painful years. "Coward," he muttered to himself. "Coward," he repeated, damning himself for his reluctance to share his name with her.

Though she must have been disappointed by his inability to publicly acknowledge their relationship, she had never wavered in her devotion, not only to him, but to those he cared about. It was Jewel who urged him to help Roland with his divorce from Clara. Clifton had shown her Roland's letter, stating that he'd received a "Dear John" from his wife, and asking his father to do "whatever has to be done." "Poor boy," she had murmured. "But it is for the best, Clifton. We should settle this as quickly as possible." As always, Miss Jewel had been right.

Although no member of the Whittaker family had ever been divorced, Clifton was relieved, not shamed to lose Clara as a relation by marriage. He assumed, from his brief acquaintance with her, that she would be as interested in a money settlement as she ever had been in Roland and he had acted accordingly.

Preparing himself for a return onslaught of additional demands, he had mailed some preliminary papers to Clara, care of Rex's Bar in Norfolk, along with an offer of $1,500 as a lump sum settlement. To his relief, the offer was accepted without comment. The divorce was filed, and it was uncontested.

Now Roland was a free man, a seasoned veteran. Perhaps now he would make something substantial of himself. "Time will tell," Clifton murmured, as he reached for his bowler hat and prepared to leave the office.

"WE'RE about to hang the banner, Mr. Clifton," Denny May Field explained, her squeaky voice reminding him, as always, of a fingernail scraping a blackboard.

"That's very nice, Denny May," he said politely, tipping his bowler as he hurried up the courthouse steps. A sudden knot in his chest stopped him for a moment. Too much cornbread, eaten too quickly, he thought, as he walked towards the portico, where Giles and Walter hovered around

the flag-draped lectern. Around the pillars, several high
school girls, under Annie Burns' direction, were filling tall
vases, with bouquets of fall chrysanthemums.

"Goodness, Clifton," Annie chirped, her freshly bobbed
hair bouncing as she rushed towards him, "you look like
you're going to court. Smile, for heaven's sake. Your son
is coming home today!"

Realizing that his physical discomfort had registered on
his face, Clifton attempted to produce the requested smile.
Then suddenly the pounding in his chest exploded through
his body, filling his eyes with blinding light. As he fell
forward onto the cement in agonizing pain, the last thing
he heard was Annie screaming his name.

Within seconds, Giles was at his friend's side, loosening
his bow tie and unbuttoning his vest. Clifton was having a
heart attack, Giles was sure of that. "Damn!" he cursed as
he realized his black bag had been left behind at the office.
There was nothing to do but get him to the hospital as quickly
as possible, pray that there wouldn't be a second attack and
that the damage hadn't been too extensive.

Standing, he commandeered a plank to serve as a makeshift stretcher, the dusty gray Dodge from the lumberyard
as an ambulance. As Giles and Walter carefully carried an
unconscious Clifton onto the waiting truckbed, a small crowd
gathered, whispering concern and speculations among one
another. "Dear God," Annie Burns prayed aloud from the
sidewalk, "not today, not like this." Clifton's face was a
deathly white.

As the Randolphs' green Studebaker sped along the highway, Charlotte fidgeted impatiently in the front seat. They
were late. She was sure they were going to miss Roland's
parade and all the speeches at the courthouse. It was all
John's fault. She had asked him not to go to the office
today, but he had explained, ever so patiently, that he had
to at least check the mail. Ever since he'd come back, he
had become much more serious about his law practice. It
was necessary, he'd said, after a two-year absence, to re-
establish his place in the business community. And he wasn't
nearly as social as he used to be. His "war injury," as she

called it, had made him much less eager to accept party invitations or to entertain people.

It was 12:15 when the car pulled into the driveway at Breezy. "We're here!" the girls shouted, bursting out of the car after hours of quiet good behavior.

Alexander, resplendent in his brown Sunday School suit and a striped tie, a gift from Billy, ran to greet them. "Hurry," he urged, "Granddaddy's in the hospital. He fell at the courthouse."

"Easy, son," John said, as he swung his legs from the car onto the ground. "Let's go through that again. Slowly."

Alexander repeated the message, which was all he knew about Clifton's illness. Ever since Annie Burns had called, he and Bessie had waited by the telephone for more information, but none had come.

"Oh, Lord!" Charlotte flung her arms heavenward. "Hasn't this family suffered enough?"

Carrie quickly went to her mother's side, patting her arm, trying to calm her, as she so often did.

"Come on," John said, rapping his cane against the front fender. "Let's go inside and see what's to be done." He was less tolerant of his wife's histrionics since his return.

Bessie sat on the ornate gilt chair near the telephone, her hands clutching on her apron. "Oh Lawd be good to yo' chillen," she chanted. "Lawd have mercy."

"What's going on, Bessie? What's happened to Clifton?" John's question prompted a wave of tears and "Lawd, Lawds" from the black woman. "His heart done give way."

"Oh, no! Papa's had a heart attack!" Charlotte gasped.

Manfully Alexander stepped forward and tried to amplify what had been said. "Auntie Annie called us," he said. "My mama is at the hospital and so is Billy. Uncle Ro's train is late. Sam at the station told us."

"What about the parade?" Carrie asked, trying to imitate her cousin's crisp adult tone. She looked up at her father for some confirmation that she was behaving correctly under the circumstances. He patted her head.

"Bessie, talk to me," he said firmly. "Have you notified the rest of the family?"

"Yessuh." She wiped away the tears that were running

down the broad planes of her cheeks. "I done tole Lucy Mae at the switchboard to call Miss Meg up in New York. She's acomin' too."

"Meg's coming?" Charlotte asked. "I didn't think David could travel yet. Are you sure?"

Meg had written an uncharacteristically short note to Charlotte explaining that they could not be at Roland's homecoming because David was not strong enough.

"Mr. David sez they comin'," Bessie replied. "Po' Miss Meg, she jest cries when she hears."

"Then I assume they're en route," John said, knowing that he would have made the same decision for his wife's sake. He hoped the long train trip would not be too much for David. In San Diego he had seen how ravaged and weak the returning POWs could be. "Has anyone contacted Rose Mary?"

"You know it's impossible to reach her by telephone."

"Charlotte," he said softly, seeing how frightened his wife's beautiful face had become. "Darling," he said, using an endearment that had been all but forgotten between them, "we'll send a telegram to her school . . . Now I think we should go to the hospital as soon as possible. You go powder your nose. Carrie and Nancy can stay here . . ."

"I'm in charge here," Alexander said, repeating what Billy had said to him when he had called from the hospital.

"That's right, son," John smiled fondly at the boy who so resembled his dead father. "And you're doing a fine job, too. Carrie and Nancy will help you. Right, girls?"

"Right, Daddy." Carrie draped an arm around her cousin's shoulder, reestablishing the camaraderie between them. "We'll be good. You go and help Granddaddy get better."

THE West Grove Hospital stood near the site of the town's first well, marked now with a bronze plaque and bordered with English boxwood and flame flowers. Clifton's father had supervised the drilling of the well back in the 1870s with a crew brought all the way up from Knoxville.

The hospital was a dome-shaped building with large white pillars, inspired by the Rotunda at the University of Virginia, which had been designed by Thomas Jefferson. Judge Gilmer had broken ground for the building in 1936, after the whooping cough epidemic, which had claimed so many lives in Russell County because the nearest medical facility was on the other side of the mountains.

A cluster of townspeople had made their way up the hill out of concern for Mr. Clifton. They stood around the well, facing the hospital entrance. Those who recognized the Randolph car waved respectfully as John and Charlotte arrived.

The two hurried across the front lobby, floored with pink marble from distant Georgia quarries. Regina Houston, head nurse for fourteen years, sat at the front desk.

"I'm so sorry," she murmured when she saw them. "We're all praying for Mr. Clifton."

"How is he?" John asked.

"There's been no change in his condition," she answered, her tone formal and starched now. "Dr. Giles is with him in the emergency room."

"What is his condition?" John pressed.

Nurse Houston hesitated. "Mr. Clifton suffered a massive coronary a few hours ago," she said reluctantly. "His condition is critical."

"I see." John slipped a protective arm around his wife's waist, anticipating one of her usual reactions to emergencies.

But instead she shifted her clutch bag from one arm to the other. Squaring her shoulders, she asked: "Where are Emily and Billy? Are they with Papa?"

"No one is with him but Dr. Giles and Nurse Henderson. Your sister and Mr. Gillespie just left for the train station. Sam called to say your brother's train was arriving."

"Then we'd best go inside," she replied, pushing through the double doors marked "Emergency". A few steps into the small waiting area, Charlotte stiffened. A plump woman in a flowered pink dress and a straw picture hat sat on the one bench, her face drawn, her hands fumbling nervously in her lap.

"It's her," Charlotte hissed. "Of all the audacity . . ."

"Charlotte . . ." John warned. "Not now!"

Awkwardly Jewel stood up, clutching a straw bag which

matched her hat. "Charlotte . . . John . . ." she acknowledged the couple's presence in a voice that was ragged with strain. "He's still with us." She seemed close to tears.

"Us?" Charlotte repeated, her face dark with anger. "Us? You don't belong here, Miss Jewel McInnes. That's my father in there and he needs his family now."

Conflicting emotions played on Jewel's face. She straightened her dress, drew herself up and looked Charlotte in the eye. "I'm sorry you don't like me, Charlotte, I truly am. But I love your father, and he's been asking for me. Dr. Giles says I can see Cliff in a little while and I mean to do that, and no one will stop me."

"Well, I never," Charlotte sputtered, and then found that for once in her life, she had nothing to say.

SITTING in the crowded club car, Roland finished the last of his vodka on the rocks. Clara had introduced him to vodka early in their relationship, saying, "This is the only stuff you can drink that doesn't show on your breath."

Clara had taught him a lot, things a boy from West Grove might never have known had he married a girl from home. Most of all he remembered the early thrill of their love-making, the long nights of drinking and dancing in bars.

Yet even before he'd shipped out, the excitement had started to fade, the relationship had begun to tarnish. So he hadn't been surprised when Clara's letter had arrived, telling him that she'd met a forty-year-old insurance salesman who could give her everything she wanted, a big house in Birmingham and lots of nice furniture. She wrote that she was returning Mama's ring to Clifton, which did surprise him. Clara was like a kid when it came to jewelry and pretty things.

He was lucky to be quit of her, he told himself. It never would have lasted in peace time. He suspected, though, that his perfect father would throw up his marriage as just another of the ways he'd "messed up," just as he'd always found fault when he was still living at home.

Despite the medals and service ribbons in his pocket, there were still moments when he felt like the same mixed-up kid he'd been two years ago when he signed up, the Whittaker family's ne'er-do-well boy. His father's personal disappointment. But he wasn't that boy anymore, and he didn't know if any of them would understand—his father, his sisters, and all those people who'd be at the station, waiting to see him and hear his war stories. Most of them hadn't ever left the state of Virginia, so how could they know what he had been through, living in those mosquito-ridden trenches, crawling over those volcanic ledges, killing other men and waiting to be killed.

Out of a corner of his eye he caught his reflection in the train window as it sped past a dark mountainside, his jaw set, his expression tense and brooding. R.C. Whittaker— R.C., that was what his buddies had called him, not Roland, Ro or Rolly. R.C. Whittaker, Lieutenant Sergeant, Marine Corps. War hero. That's who was coming back to Breezy. But would his father recognize him, let him be the man he'd become? Time will tell, he thought, and then he smiled as he realized he was using one of his father's ponderous adages.

"West Grove," the conductor called from the front of the car. "West Grove, Virginia," came the call as the train braked. With one swift clean motion, he reached up and grabbed his duffel bag from the baggage rack. Jauntily he swung it over his shoulder and made his way towards the door.

As the train drew into the station, he leaned out. Although he had modestly told his father he didn't want any kind of celebration, he fully expected one, and felt let down as he surveyed the station and saw nothing out of the ordinary was happening.

"Roland! Roland!" He heard a woman call as he jumped off the train. Down the platform he saw a tall slender stranger waving at him. As she came closer he saw that the stranger was Emily—a new Emily sporting a short hairdo that brushed her cheeks and wearing tailored slacks, sharper and slimmer than he ever remembered her.

"Hey, look at you," he said approvingly, as he dropped his bag and picked her up. He swung her around, showing off his muscular strength.

"Put me down, silly." She was crying and laughing at the same time.

With an expression of mock contriteness, he deposited her on the platform. "Yes, ma'am," he said. "Anything you say."

"Roland . . . oh, Ro, you've changed so much," she said fondly as she stared at the tall, husky man who had replaced her teenage brother.

"So have you, Em. Real sharp," he said shyly. "So? Where's Pop?" He peered over his sister's head, expecting a surprise welcoming crowd to appear at any moment.

"Oh, Ro . . ." Emily's voice shook and her eyes turned dark. "I have some bad news."

"Oh, yeah sure." It was a joke they were playing on him, with Emily as the decoy.

"It's Papa, Ro . . . he's had a heart attack."

He felt as if he'd been hit in the stomach. "No," he said fiercely, his eyes welling with tears. "He can't do that. He can't!"

"AIN'T no funeral yet," Bessie snapped at Bernard Pyle when he brought up one of his special salt-cured hams.

"I know that, Bessie," he said softly. "It's just that folks in town are worried about Mr. Clifton, and I wanted to do a little something for the family. After all," he added, "I had three hams ready to take to the fairgrounds for Roland's celebration. Now what with that being canceled, well, you just take this and put it away."

Bernard's ham was followed by two potato casseroles, a chocolate cake and a tray of gingerbread. After she'd given the children their supper and put them to bed, Bessie started to clear the kitchen for the offerings that would surely come tomorrow.

She heard the sound of a car in the driveway, then Meg's voice calling from the back porch. "Bessie? Bessie, where are you? I need some help."

"Comin', honey, I'se comin'," Bessie called back as she dropped her dish towel on the counter.

Meg was standing inside the door, her baby tucked inside her billowing black cape, her husband holding on to her with both hands. His haunted eyes stared out from a gaunt, white face. Later Bessie would say that she hardly recognized Mister David as the man in those nice wedding pictures, so thin and emaciated was his body, so blank and empty were the eyes that had once held so much laughter.

"Sam brought us up from the station," Meg explained, as Bessie picked up the large battered suitcase and headed for the kitchen. "How's Papa?"

"Don't know nothin'," Bessie reported, shaking her head. "Been waitin' and waitin' fo' news. Come on, honey chile . . . you all looks plum' wore out."

"It was a hard trip," Meg admitted. "The trains were very crowded and noisy." She paused and stroked her husband's head as he sank into one of the kitchen chairs. "We're not used to that kind of thing anymore. We . . . we've just been resting since David came back . . ."

"Resting," David repeated in a voice that was devoid of expression. "I'm not able to work yet . . ."

"You needs fattenin' up, that's what you needs," Bessie said emphatically, heading for the pantry.

"Let me put the baby down first," Meg said. "It will be easier on all of us if he sleeps through the night. Is my old room ready?"

"Yes, honey . . . all ready." Bessie returned with a plate of ham and biscuits and set it down on the table. "Heah, give me that youngun."

Meg tucked Jake into Bessie's arms. Then she went to the swinging door and beckoned to her husband. "Follow me, David."

"Yes," he answered leadenly, standing and struggling to orient himself to his surroundings. "I'm all right . . . I'm just tired . . ."

Poor man, Bessie thought as she watched David walking through the house like a blind man. He had been spooked real bad. Spooked and starved.

As they entered the front hall, a low-flying mail plane passed over the house, momentarily shaking the pictures on the wall, jarring the china knickknacks on the table tops.

David screamed, breaking away from Meg and covering his head with his arms. He ran back into the dining room, looked around frantically, and then crawled under the dining room table. Within seconds, Meg was down on the carpet with him, too. "It's not a bomb, David," she reassured. "It's not a bomb. Take my hand," she coaxed.

But David backed away, whimpering. Meg waited a moment, careful not to move too quickly or too suddenly. Slowly she extended her hand again. "It's all right, sweetheart. There's no bomb here. You're home, David, home with me."

Still he didn't seem to hear her. His eyes were unfocused, his face tight with fear.

Meg turned to Bessie and motioned her to bring the baby. "Wake up, Jake," she coaxed as she took her son. "Wake up for daddy."

The child opened his eyes and smiled angelically at his mother. "Jake wakes," he chanted in a two-year-old's singsong. "Jake wakes."

"Jake," Meg said gently but urgently as she set the baby on the floor. "I need you to find your daddy. Find Daddy. That's a good boy. Over there."

Delighted with the new game, Jake crawled towards his father. "Dada. Dada." He went under the table, giggling.

As the child's small hand touched his, David's nightmare ended. He hugged Jake close and turned pain-filled eyes on his wife. "I'm sorry, Princess . . . I'm sorry."

"It's all right, David," she said, weary and relieved at the same time. "It's over now. It's all over."

"Come on, chile," Bessie commanded, helping her up. "You all is plumb wore out for sure. No hospital for youse. You all needs sleep."

"All right, Bessie," Meg agreed, leaning her head onto the colored woman's shoulder, "but first let me call and find out if Papa's better now. He has to get better, Bessie, he just has to . . ."

IT was around midnight when Dr. Giles told everybody to leave, promising he would call if Clifton's condition took

a turn for the worse. Roland had been up for days and knew
he had to hit the hay for a while, but Emily insisted on
staying. Charlotte made no protest. Sitting in the corridor
hour after hour, doing nothing but waiting for bad news
was hard enough, but knowing that Miss Jewel was in her
father's room, by his side, made the situation intolerable.

As soon as they returned to their bedroom, Charlotte
blurted out what she'd been thinking for hours. "He's going
to die, John. I know Papa is going to die."

"Now, Charlotte, that is only speculation on your part."
He stood by the window, staring out at the darkened valley,
his fine profile silhouetted by the lamp on the nightstand:
"Your father's condition is critical, but Giles is still hope-
ful . . ."

"I know it's going to happen, I just know it," she confessed, wringing her hands. "And what will I do if Papa
dies, John? What will I do?"

"Charlotte Lee, get ready for bed. You must rest now."
Years of marriage had taught John that it was useless to try
to reason with his wife when she was distraught. "I'll spend
the night in Clifton's room."

"Don't leave me," Charlotte pleaded. "I don't want to
be alone tonight."

John stopped for a moment, gripping his cane tighter.
Ever since their disastrous attempt at sexual reunion four
months earlier, John had occupied the guest room at home.
On the surface their marriage seemed to be satisfactory, but
there had been no physical contact other than the polite
kisses he gave Charlotte each morning and every evening.
"All right," he said with careful control. "I'll stay until
you've fallen asleep."

Grateful for the offer, she opened her suitcase, took out
her nightgown and her cosmetic case, and went into the
bathroom to change. As she brushed her long blond hair,
she examined her image in the medicine cabinet mirror.
Tension lines marred the beauty of her face. With her fingers
she tried to massage them away. She closed her eyes, relaxed her face and then looked again. Better . . . but some
of the lines were still there. And soon there would be more.
The horrible thought came with the suddenness of a thun-

derbolt, as if she had never before considered the inevitability of her own physical decline, never before believed in the ultimate reality of death.

She tried to push the thought away and began to shiver uncontrollably. She hugged herself, willing it to stop, the fear, the awful feeling of aloneness.

John. His image flashed on her mind like a beacon. He could make it go away with his love, his certainty that she would always be beautiful. As she summoned up the memory of their lovemaking, a wave of longing passed through her. So many months since she had felt warm and safe and adored. She needed that now—the reflection of love in her husband's eyes, the feeling of being cherished and protected.

She straightened up and smoothed the nightgown over her body. With trembling hands she dabbed perfume on her earlobes, between her breasts. She was losing her father and had never needed her husband more. But even in her desperation she knew instinctively she could not go to him naked in her need. Too much time, too much distance yawned between them.

No, she would have to go to him like a thoroughbred. She smiled at her recollection of a time when things had been easier, though they certainly hadn't seemed so then. She took a last look in the mirror, coaxed a lock of her shoulder-length hair across her forehead, Veronica Lake style. There. She conjured a seductive smile.

She left the bathroom and walked down the hallway. Opening the bedroom door wide, she paused for a moment, lingering in the dramatic backlighting from the hallway, inviting John to take in the full impact of her beauty.

"Charlotte..." His voice was unsteady. "Charlotte..." He reached reflexively for his cane in a gesture of self-protection.

Deliberately she closed the door and locked it behind her, closing the distance between them with a few provocative swaying steps. "Captain Randolph, sir," she said huskily. "I do believe you have shirked your conjugal duties long enough...I am telling you that I mean to have satisfaction tonight, one way or another."

John searched his wife's eyes for signs of pity or revulsion. Finding none, he simply stared at her for a moment and then burst out laughing as he reached out and brought her tumbling down on the bed beside him. She laughed, too, as his strong arms drew her close, sheltering her, loving her, driving away the fears she had borne alone so long. "Oh, John," she sighed, "I've missed you so much. Welcome home, darling . . . welcome home."

"I'm running out of cigarettes," Emily announced, as she put out a Camel in the overflowing ashtray Nurse Houston had given her. Smoking was prohibited in the waiting area, but the nurse had winked conspiratorially and said she would make an exception, "Seeing as how it's you, Miss Emily."

"Ration yourself, kid," Billy suggested. He checked the nearly empty package on the bench. "Four left. It's 3:10 now. If you can make them last till 8:30, Pyle's Store will be open and I'll drive down and get you some."

She jammed her hands into her trouser pockets and started pacing the corridor outside her father's room. She stopped suddenly and smiled down at Billy, who was sprawled on the bench, his long legs stretched straight out. "Everyone else criticizes my smoking," she said. "But you even buy cigarettes for me. Why is that?"

He smiled back lazily. "Because you're a grown woman. A darn pretty one. And I'm a sucker for a pretty face."

"You're not a sucker," she said heatedly, blushing at Billy's compliment. "You're . . . you're a flirt, but you are a nice man."

"Ah, go on," he teased, "all that smoking has addled your brain, Emily. No one has ever before accused Billy Gillespie of being nice. No," he went on, his face clouding with remembrance, "if you had known me back in Chicago, you'd have a very different opinion of me. Very different . . ."

She knew that he was referring to a time he had described to her in harsh, unsparing detail, without excuse or justification. A time spent in cheap hotels on the South Side. "One long hangover," he'd said, until finally his editor at

the *Herald* had fired him. With the help of his old friend
Floyd McClintock, he'd gone "cold turkey" and stayed sober
ever since. He had told her how he'd seen the *Gazette*'s
bankruptcy notice in a trade paper—"a sign from the gods,"
he'd called it—and decided to come to West Grove for a
fresh start. "The rest is history," he'd said, with that self-
deprecating smile she found so endearing.

She looked at him thoughtfully, forgetting for a moment
the reason they were both in this hospital corridor. "It was
hard for you to beat the whiskey, wasn't it?" she asked
gently.

"Hell. Just plain hell to let go of it." He ran his fingers
through his thick wavy hair. "Hardest thing I ever did,
except for teaching you to run a linotype machine," he said
lightly.

She smiled, appreciating the way he'd been trying to
keep her mind diverted, her spirits up. She glanced at the
door to her father's room. Miss Jewel was still inside, no
longer able to hide from the world her feelings for her
"Cliff." It didn't surprise Emily that her father had called
for Jewel during his few seconds of consciousness. And it
hadn't bothered her when Giles had decided that Jewel should
be the one to hold his hand while he struggled for his life.
It was right, she thought, and it was time.

"So how about it?" Billy interrupted her reverie. "Are
you going to write that editorial for me or not? The idea's
swell, tying in a Victory Day roundup with Roosevelt's last
penned words. Are you ready to spread your wings and fly
with it?"

Emily had offered the idea to Billy, for him to execute.
She had read somewhere that the afternoon before Roosevelt
died, he'd been working on a speech, which would have
been delivered on Jefferson Day, April 13th. It had closed
with: *"The only limit to our realization of tomorrow will
be our doubts of today."* In pencil, the President had added
another line: *"Let us move forward with strong and active
faith."* A perfect ending, she had thought. A perfect statement for peace times, she had said to Billy. And he, as he
had done so often before, had pushed her to take yet another
step forward, to move beyond feature writing into the for-

mulation and expression of opinion. An editorial.

"I dare you," he prodded. "I double-dare you, Miz Emmet."

"You're on," she flashed back, taking the challenge. "Just watch me, Mr. Editor, just watch me."

"Atta girl! That's what I like to see, all that spunk and fire you've been saving up. Now come sit over here. You're wearing me out with all that pacing."

"Okay." She arranged herself, cross-legged on the bench, her head leaning against his shoulder. "Papa wouldn't approve of this," she mused. "He'd say it wasn't a proper way for a lady to sit."

"You're a grown woman," he said, stroking her hair, "and you can sit any way you damn please. Your Papa doesn't approve of your smoking or wearing pants, but you do that. As a matter of fact, I'll bet he doesn't approve of me," he teased. "I'll bet he thinks I'm one of those left-wing radicals out to corrupt his daughter."

"Stop that, Billy Gillespie, just stop it." She reached up and touched his cheek. "He does too approve of you, and your politics don't bother him at all. He thinks you're hard-working and intellectual and decent. I wished we could have told him at the picnic. Papa would have been so pleased that we wanted to be married Christmas Eve . . . on Breezy."

"What's this past tense nonsense?" he growled. "He's in there putting up one hell of a fight and you're out here writing his obituary? Stop that right now, do you hear?"

"I'm sorry. I didn't mean to. It's just that he looks so bad."

"Nobody looks good after a heart attack," he reminded her gruffly. "Come on, buck up. *'Strong and active faith,'* remember?"

"You're right," she agreed quickly, covering her face with her hands to hide the tears that were about to come.

"Emily, sit up. Dr. Giles is coming out of your father's room."

"What's happening?" She was upright in an instant, her eyes wide with fear.

"He's slipping," Giles said tersely, his face etched with strain. "Better call Breezy and get everyone up here."

* * *

BY the time the family arrived at the hospital, Jewel had persuaded the night nurse to bring up some chairs from the staff cafeteria, so that all the Whittakers might be seated around Clifton's bed.

"How is he?" Roland demanded as he came into the room.

"Having a hard time," Jewel whispered, weary from the long vigil, her flowered parade dress rumpled and wilted.

"He's got to fight harder," Roland said vehemently. "He's got to, dammit!"

"Easy, son," Giles cautioned. "Easy now."

"John," Charlotte whispered, plucking nervously at her husband's sleeve, "David looks awfully peculiar. Do you think we should ask him to wait outside. If he does something odd, it might make Papa worse."

"Charlotte," he said softly, so no one else would hear, "I share your concern for David, but I don't think we should interfere."

"You're right, darling," she agreed readily, grateful that her husband had relieved her of any difficult decision making. "You're absolutely right." She fluffed up the ruffles of her white crepe blouse, wanting to look as pretty as she could for her father in what might be the last moments of his life. She glanced over at Meg and David who were holding hands at the bedside. Both of them were disheveled; Meg hadn't combed her hair and David had simply put his jacket on over his pajama top.

"His breathing is irregular," David noted automatically, his medically trained mind indexing his father-in-law's symptoms. "His expression is comatose. Not good signs."

"David," Meg pleaded, "please don't frighten me anymore."

"I'm sorry," he apologized tenderly. "I didn't mean to frighten you." Then his eyes shifted to some distant place outside the darkened window. "I used to talk to the badly injured in the camp. There was nothing else I could do . . . Sometimes it seemed to help."

He turned back to his wife and with an animation that hadn't been there before, he urged, "Talk to your father,

Meg. Your voice will soothe him and give him something to hold on to..."

"I don't know what to say," Meg whispered, close to tears. She laid her head down on the bed. Clinging to the hope her husband had offered, she pleaded: "Papa...don't leave us..." she pleaded. "Please don't leave us."

Emily stepped forward, full of resolution. Gently, she stroked her father's forehead. "You've pulled us through these four long years, Papa. Stay with us now."

"Maybe a few words from the Bible," Jewel offered, beginning to recite in a tremulous voice: "The Lord is my Shepherd, I shall not want..."

"No!" Roland reacted explosively to the same psalm he had heard prayed over his mother's casket. "No! He's not dead yet!" Turning to his father he raged, "You can't do this to me! I went through living hell out there and came back."

"Easy, Roland." Billy stepped forward. "Your father's too weak for a frontal assault."

Roland swallowed hard, accepting the restraint with a nod. He reached into his pocket and pulled out the Congressional Medal of Honor, the five-pointed star suspended from a pale blue ribbon, and laid it carefully on his father's chest.

Clifton's eyes fluttered weakly. "I'm proud, Roland." The words came breathlessly from his parched lips. "Proud."

"Sweet Jesus." Miss Jewel began to cry.

"The heartbeat's a little stronger," Giles pronounced as he listened with his stethoscope to Clifton's heart. "Good work, J.C. Keep it up."

Clifton's lips moved as he struggled to speak again.

"That's enough, sir," Roland commanded. "Now don't you die...Pull yourself together and fight...Dammit!"

IT was about six-thirty in the morning when Giles announced that Clifton was "out of the woods." "It's too soon to say exactly how much damage has been done to the heart, but it's my educated guess that he's going to be with us for quite a while."

"Thank God." Jewel collapsed into her chair, finally

allowing the fatigue and tension of her vigil to take over.

"Time for you folks to get home," Giles suggested.
"You're all looking kinda peaked yourselves."

Charlotte's hand automatically reached for her pageboy,
searching for stray hairs.

"Let me drive you back to Breezy, Em," Billy offered.
"You too, Roland, if you want a ride."

"Yeah," Roland said. "I guess it's time to give the old
man a rest." He leaned over his father's bed and pinned the
Medal of Honor onto his sheet, so Clifton could see it when
he woke up.

"You, too, Jewel," Giles insisted. "Git."

"But if we all go, he'll be all alone. If Cliff wakes up
and needs something . . ."

"Are you telling me my job?" he teased. "Why, here's
Nurse Houston, fresh as a daisy and ready to go on duty.
If J.C. wakes up and starts asking for his Shakespeare or
his legal briefs, she'll call me, and I'll be back up here
lickety-split."

"Oh, Giles," Jewel giggled. "You and Cliff are two of
a kind."

"Yep. We're both tough old birds. You're not. And that's
why I'm going to escort you home. J.C. would want me
to." He offered his arm with a formal gesture. "Now pick
up that pretty hat and all your whatchamacallits and let's
git."

WHEN the adults returned to Breezy, they found Bessie and
the children up and in the midst of a pancake breakfast.
"Praise de Lawd," she rejoiced, when she heard that Clifton
was out of danger, and the children echoed her relief with
a chorus of "hurrays."

"Gots to git de younguns outta heah," she muttered.
"You'all needs sleep, an' so does I." It was true the adults
in the family were exhausted.

"Why don't I drive the kids to Annie and Walter's?"
Billy suggested. "Give you all a chance to catch up on your
sleep."

"Good idea," Emily agreed. "I'll call Annie and get things organized."

A half hour later, with the children gone and the family upstairs sleeping, Bessie sank into a kitchen chair, her brows knitted in concentration. She was bone-tired and needed a nap as much as anyone, but she knew folks would be coming by soon, with food and questions about Mr. Clifton. Suddenly she grinned, as the solution to the problem came to her.

She hurried to the pantry, where she found two pieces of cardboard saved from cracker boxes. With one of Alexander's old crayons, she began printing, just like Miss Emily had been learning her, the word S-L-E-E-P-I-N-G on each of the cardboards. Then, she poked some twine through the homemade signs, hung them proudly on the front and back doors, and locked the locks. Praising the Lord again, she kicked off her shoes, arranged herself comfortably on the back porch sofa, and fell straight to sleep.

"I'M warning you, J.C., fifteen minutes and not a second longer." Dr. Giles' voice boomed out into the hospital corridor. "You need your rest. How I ever allowed you to convene another gathering of Whittakers in less than twenty-four hours . . . well, never mind. In fifteen minutes I aim to scatter the lot right out of here. Understand?"

The gathered clan outside Room 14 couldn't hear Clifton's muffled response, but Giles' message wasn't lost on them. John consulted his wristwatch. "That gives us until 7:30," he said.

"Right." Roland knelt down and circled the children around him. "Now, listen, troops," he said, "Granddad's too tired for a long visit, so when I give the order to scram, out you march, got it?"

"Yes, sir," Alexander said, saluting solemnly.

Tugging on her uncle's pants' leg, Nancy asked: "Can I give him a big hug now?"

"No hugs and no noise," Charlotte intervened. "Your grandfather is still a very sick man."

"Ain't never been to no hospital befo'," Bessie fussed, shifting her weight in her tight catalogue shoes. "Don't know why Mistuh Clifton sez I should come heah."

It was obvious that little Jake shared her sentiments, as he strained against the harness Meg had slipped over him so he wouldn't wander off. "Jake go," the child insisted, waving his arms as he tried to break his mother's hold.

"Can't you do something with that child?" Charlotte asked irritably.

"I'm doing the best I can," Meg answered defensively, looking around for David. He had stopped to examine a piece of hospital equipment in the corridor, and she was thankful for this small step toward recovery.

"How about this?" Billy offered, reaching into the pocket of his tweed jacket and pulling out a piece of licorice. "May I bribe this young man?"

"Jake wants. Jake wants." The baby reached out for the treat.

"Sure," Meg agreed gratefully. "Thanks."

Just then the door swung open and Giles strode briskly into the corridor. "Fifteen minutes," he repeated the warning. "I mean to get J.C. out of here, alive and kicking, with his cooperation or without."

Miss Jewel was already in the room, at Clifton's side, wearing a white summer dress and a corsage of tea roses. "Hello, everybody," she said cheerily, waving her white lace hankerchief. "Come on in."

"Hi, Miss Jewel," Carrie greeted. "Do you have any new thimbles?"

"I do, dearie, one all the way from China," Jewel smiled. "You come by to see it, you hear?"

"That's enough, Carrie," Charlotte hushed her ever curious elder child, annoyed at discovering that she had once again been up to something on her own.

"Does your heart still hurt, Granddad?" Alexander asked.

"Good question," Clifton laughed. "And the answer is no, it simply feels rather bruised."

"You sho' you ain't jest playin' possum?" Bessie teased, wagging her finger at her boss and old friend, after she had satisfied herself that he seemed to be mending.

"Not possum," Clifton teased back, patting her black hand affectionately. "But I am up to some mischief."

"Cliff, dearie." Jewel leaned over and stroked his brow tenderly. "Remember what you promised Dr. Giles."

"Yes. Yes, I suppose we should begin." He reached under his pillow and took out a folded page. He cleared his throat and settled himself comfortably, enjoying the undivided attention of his family. "First," he said, "I want to share with you something I wrote before my heart attacked me." He smiled at his little pun and continued. "I ask your indulgence for yet another of my infamous epistles." Then he read:

My Dear Children,

At last, the war is over and peace has come to our great land. We are all now reunited. Our struggles on the battlefields and on the home front are ended. And so the Breezy Hill Bulletin ends, for its task is done.

These past four years have demanded hardship and sacrifice. But we have survived our hard times and our heartbreaks, sustained and nurtured by the love we share for one another.

In this time of peace and new beginnings, may we continue to draw strength and purpose from our family, for it is our finest heritage, our rock and our everlasting joy.

The room was quiet, except for Bessie's furtive snuffling. Finally Roland spoke: "Well, Pop," he said with a grin, "You sure do have a way with words, don't you?"

"Thank you, son," he said with more affection than Roland had ever heard addressed to him. "Well," he continued briskly, "I didn't summon you here simply to listen to my eloquent prose. I have an announcement to make." He reached for Jewel's hand. "This fine woman has accepted my proposal of marriage, and so we're going to have a wedding here today."

"Weddin'? Lawdy, if dat don't beat all!" Bessie chuckled. "A weddin' in bed. Mistuh Clifton, yo' is somethin', yo' surely is."

"Indeed I am, Bessie." Clifton chuckled. "A fortunate

man who was too foolish to appreciate the blessings the Lord sent me." He squeezed Jewel's hand. "So the Lord took me to death's door to show me what a jackass I've been."

Everyone laughed, except for Charlotte, who leaned against her husband, too stunned and unbalanced to make even a token protest.

"Well, sir," Roland spoke up, exercising his new status as war hero and beloved son. "If that's what you want . . . it's fine with me." He shook his father's hand and pecked Jewel's cheek with a kiss.

"But this isn't a church," Carrie pointed out, not at all convinced of the propriety of the situation.

"And," Alexander added soberly, "you don't have a minister."

As if on cue, the door opened. "Did I hear someone ask for a minister?" It was Reverend Lowell, resplendent in the long black robe and white cassock he wore when he officiated at weddings. With him was Giles, still in his white jacket, but with a pink carnation in his lapel. He carried a small corsage of pink roses, like the one Miss Jewel was wearing, which he pinned with a flourish onto Bessie's brown housedress.

"Bessie," he said solemnly. "You and I have been drafted for this occasion. "Can I count on you?"

"What y'all talkin' bout?" she fussed.

"Bessie," Jewel explained, "this all happened so quickly, I didn't have time to ask you properly, but Cliff and I both agreed that you should be my maid-of-honor."

"Me? Lawdy, Lawdy me!" She shook her head in disbelief.

"Come on," Carrie stepped in, taking Bessie's hand, "you have to go and stand by Miss Jewel." Weddings were one of her favorite games, and she assumed the role of wedding director with confidence. "Dr. Giles, you have to move up there next to Granddaddy, 'cause you're the best man."

"I don't believe this is happening," Charlotte whispered to John. "What are we to do?"

In response, John turned to his father-in-law. "Sir, on

behalf of the Randolph contingent, I want to wish you all the best." He held his wife's hand in his, squeezing it tightly when she started to protest.

"We second that." Billy laughed, hugging Emily close, "even if you have beaten us to the altar!"

"I think it's wonderful!" Meg said, her eyes shining as she slipped an arm around her husband's waist. He kissed her then, with a kiss that reminded her of their first days. Their child stood between them, sucking contentedly on his candy. "We hope you'll be so happy!" she said, flushed with hope and joy.

"Agreed," Giles said, looking fondly at his old friend. "And now that we have the blessings out of the way, let's get this knot tied. Pronto."

Reverend Lowell opened his Bible to the passage he'd designated with a red silk marker. "Your father has asked me to begin this ceremony by reading from Ecclesiastes, Chapter Three, verses one through eight:

> *To every thing there is a season,*
> *and a time to every purpose under heaven...*

The minister's voice rose and fell in the gentle quiet of the hospital room. Three generations of Whittakers stood together, filling their hearts with the words of acceptance and hope, with the promise of joys and sadness yet to come. The seasons of war had yielded their harvest of pain and separation, but this was a time for renewal and love, a time for coming home.

Bestselling Books
from Berkley

Turn back the pages of history...
and discover

Romance

as it once was!